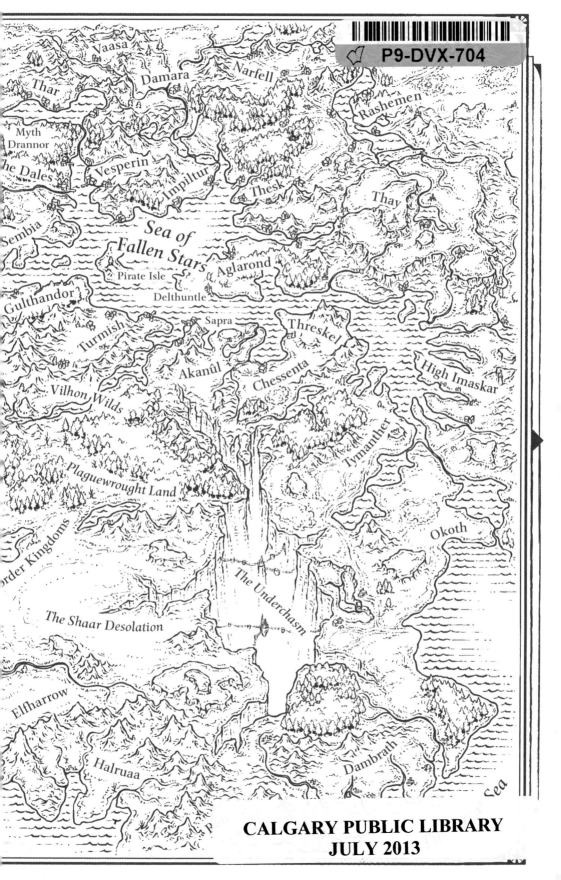

When the trials begin,
in soul-torn solitude despairing,
the hunter waits alone.
The companions emerge
from fast-bound ties of fate
uniting against a common foe.

When the shadows descend,
in Hell-sworn covenant unswerving
the blighted brothers hunt,
and the godborn appears,
in rose-blessed abbey reared,
arising to loose the godly spark.

When the harvest time comes,
in hate-fueled mission grim unbending,
the shadowed reapers search.
The adversary vies
with fiend-wrought enemies,
opposing the twisting schemes of Hell.

When the tempest is born,
as storm-tossed waters rise uncaring,
the promised hope still shines.
And the reaver beholds
the dawn-born chosen's gaze,
transforming the darkness into light.

When the battle is lost,
through quake-tossed battlefields unwitting
the seasoned legions march,
but the sentinel flees
with once-proud royalty,
protecting devotion's fragile heart.

When the ending draws near,
with ice-locked stars unmoving,
the threefold threats await,
and the herald proclaims,
in war-wrecked misery,
announcing the dying of an age.

—As written by Elliandreth of Orishaar, c. −17,600 DR

FORGOTTEN REALMS®
THE SUNDERING

FORGOTTEN REALMS

R.A. SALVATORE
THE COMPANIONS

FORGOTTEN REALMS

THE
SUNDERING

Book

I

THE COMPANIONS

©2013 Wizards of the Coast LLC.

Published by Wizards of the Coast LLC. Manufactured by: Hasbro SA, Rue Emile-Boéchat 31, 2800 Delémont, CH. Represented by Hasbro Europe, 2 Roundwood Ave, Stockley Park, Uxbridge, Middlesex, UB11 1AZ, UK.

Printed in the U.S.A.

Prophecy by: James Wyatt
Cartography by: Mike Schley
Cover art by: Tyler Jacobson
First Printing: August 2013

9 8 7 6 5 4 3 2 1

ISBN: 978-0-7869-6371-3
ISBN: 978-0-7869-6435-2 (ebook)
620A2242000001 EN

Cataloging-in-Publication data is on file with the Library of Congress

Contact Us at Wizards.com/CustomerService
Wizards of the Coast LLC, PO Box 707, Renton, WA 98057-0707, USA
USA & Canada: (800) 324-6496 or (425) 204-8069
Europe: +32(0) 70 233 277

Visit our web site at **www.dungeonsanddragons.com**

This book is dedicated to anyone who believes that the hero isn't the one
with the biggest sword,
but the one with the biggest heart,

Who believes that doing the right thing is its own reward,
simply because it's the right thing to do,

Who believes in karma, or divine justice,
or simply that the greatest reward of all is being able to go to sleep with a
clear conscience.

This book is for Drizzt Do'Urden.

This book is dedicated to anyone who believes that the hero isn't the one
with the biggest sword,
but the one with the biggest heart,

Who believes that doing the right thing is its own reward,
simply because it's the right thing to do,

Who believes in karma, or divine justice,
or simply that the greatest reward of all is being able to go to sleep with a
clear conscience.

This book is for Drizzt Do'Urden.

PROLOGUE

The Year of the Awakened Sleepers (1484 DR)
Kelvin's Cairn

THE STARS REACHED DOWN TO HIM, LIKE SO MANY TIMES BEFORE IN THIS enchanted place.

He was on Bruenor's Climb, though he didn't know how he had arrived there. Guenhwyvar was beside him, leaning against him, supporting his shattered leg, but he didn't remember calling to her.

Of all the places Drizzt had ever traveled, none had felt more comforting than here. Perhaps it had been the company he had so often found up here, but even without Bruenor beside him, this place, this lone peak rising above the flat, dark tundra, had ever brought a spiritual sustenance to Drizzt Do'Urden. Up here, he felt small and mortal, but at the same time, confident that he was part of something much larger, of something eternal.

On Bruenor's Climb, the stars reached down to him, or he lifted up among them, floating free of his physical restraints, his spirit rising and soaring among the celestial spheres. He could hear the sound of the great clockwork up here, could feel the celestial winds in his face and could melt into the ether.

It was a place of the deepest meditation for Drizzt, a place where he understood the great cycle of life and death.

A place that seemed fitting now, as the blood continued to flow from the wound in his forehead.

The Year of the First Circle (1468 DR)
Netheril

A dusty sunset filled the western sky with stripes of pink and orange hanging above the endless plain, a reminder that this region was once, not long ago, the vast magical desert known as Anauroch. The advent of Shadow, then the trauma of the great Spellplague, had transformed this region of Toril somewhat, but the stubborn nature of Anauroch's enchantment of barrenness had not allowed all that had been to be so easily washed away. There was more rain here now, perhaps, and more vegetation, and the drifting white sands had settled to a dirtier hue of earthen brown, as renewed flora grasped and held.

The dusty sunset, however common, served as a warning to the newcomers to the region, particularly the Netherese of Shade Enclave, that what once was might some day be again. To the nomadic Bedine, such sights rekindled their ancestral tales, a reminder of the life their predecessors had known before the transformation of their ancient homeland.

The two Shadovar agents making their way west across the plain hardly gave the sunset a thought, though, and certainly didn't dwell on any deeper implications as to the sky's coloring, for their months of intensive investigation seemed at last to be coming to fruition, and so their eyes were firmly rooted on the road ahead.

"Why would anyone live out here?" asked Untaris, the larger of the pair, the brawn to Alpirs's brain, so it was said. "Grass and wind, sandstorms, phaerimm and asabi, and other such monsters." The muscular shade warrior shook his head and spat down from his pinto horse to the ground.

Alpirs De'Noutess laughed at the remark, but wasn't about to disagree. "The Bedine are ever blinded by their pride in their traditions."

"They do not understand that the world has changed," Untaris said.

"Oh, but they do, my friend," Alpirs replied. "What they do not understand is that there is nothing they can do about it. To serve Netheril is their only course, but some, like the Desai who camp before us, think that if they just remain far enough out from the civilized cities of Netheril, among the lions and the phaerimm, we will not bother too greatly with them." He gave a little laugh at his own words. "Usually, they are right."

"But no more," Untaris declared.

"Not for the Desai," Alpirs agreed. "Not if what we have come to believe about the child is true."

As he finished, Alpirs nodded to the south, where a lone tent shuddered against the unrelenting wind. He kicked his chestnut mare into a trot and made a straight line for it, Untaris close behind. A solitary figure clad in an ankle-length robe of white cotton emerged from the tent at the sound of their approach. The collar of the Bedine man's garment was round in design and set with a large button and tassel, signifying the Desai tribe, and like most of the Bedine in this region, the man wore a sleeveless coat, called an aba, striped in brown and red.

"Long have I waited," the man said as the two riders approached, his leathery, windblown and sun-drenched face peeking out at them from inside the frame of his white kufiya head scarf. "Pay well, you will!"

"Sounds angry, as usual, the Bedine dog," Untaris whispered, but Alpirs had a remedy already in hand.

"Well enough?" Alpirs asked the Bedine informant and he reached out with his hand, holding a crown of camel hair and woven gold, an igal fit for a chieftain. Despite the legendary bargaining prowess of the Bedine, the older man's eyes betrayed him, sparkling at the sight.

Alpirs dismounted, Untaris close behind, and walked his horse over to the robed figure.

"Well met, Jhinjab," he said with a bow, presenting the precious igal—which he pulled back immediately as the Bedine reached for it.

"You approve of the payment, I take it?" Alpirs said with a wry grin.

In response, Jhinjab reached up and touched his own igal, which secured the kufiya upon his head. It was a weathered, black affair, once woven with precious metals, but now little more than fraying camel hair. To the Bedine, the igal spoke of stature, of pride.

"De girl is in de camp," he said in his heavy Bedine accent. Every word was spoken crisply, distinctly, and efficiently—to keep the blowing sand out of their mouths, Alpirs had once explained to Untaris. "De camp is over de ridge in de east," Jhinjab explained. "My work be done." He reached for the igal once more, but Alpirs kept it just out of his grasp.

"And how old is this girl?"

"She is de little thing," Jhinjab replied, holding his hand out just below waist level.

"How old?"

3

The Bedine stared at him hard. "Four? Five?"

"Think, my friend, it is important," said Alpirs.

Jhinjab closed his eyes, his lips moving, and a few words, a reference to an event or a hot summer, occasionally slipped forth. "Five, den," he said. "Just five, in de spring."

Alpirs couldn't contain his grin, and he looked to the similarly smiling Untaris.

"Sixty-three," Untaris said, counting back the years.

The two Shadovar nodded and exchanged smiles.

"My igal," Jhinjab said, reaching for the item. But again, Alpirs pulled it back from him.

"You are certain of this?"

"Five, yes, five," the Bedine informant replied.

"No," Alpirs clarified. "Of all of it. You are certain that this child is . . . special?"

"She is de one," the Bedine replied. "She singing, all de time singing. Singing words dat make no words, you know?"

"Sounds like any other child," Untaris said skeptically. "Making up words and singing nonsensically."

"No, no, no, not like dat," Jhinjab replied, frantically waving his skinny arms around from out of his triangular sleeves. "Singing de spells."

"A wizard, you claim," said Alpirs.

"She make de garden grow."

"Her garden. Her shrine?"

Jhinjab nodded enthusiastically.

"So you have told us," said Untaris, "and yet, we have not seen this shrine."

The old Bedine informant squinted and looked around, shading his eyes and obviously trying to get his bearings. He pointed to the southeast, to a high sand dune with a white alabaster pillar showing among the blowing sand. "Beyond dat dune, to de south, hidden among de rocks where de wind has blown de sand away."

"How far to the south?" Alpirs asked, holding up his hand to prevent Untaris from speaking.

Jhinjab shrugged. "Long walk, short ride."

"Across the open, hot sands?" Alpirs asked, not hiding his own skepticism now.

Jhinjab nodded.

4

"You said the camp was to the west," Untaris said before Alpirs could stop him.

Again, the Bedine informant offered a nod.

"A new camp, then," said Alpirs.

"No," said Jhinjab. "Been dere since de spring."

"But the girl's shrine is the other way, a long walk."

"We are to believe that a child crosses the desert alone? A long walk, you said, and across dangerous ground," Untaris reasoned.

Jhinjab shrugged, letting his answers stand.

Alpirs hooked the igal over a loop on his belt, and held up his hand when Jhinjab started to protest.

"We will go and see this shrine," he explained. "And then we will return to you."

"It is hidden," Jhinjab protested.

"Of course it is." Untaris snorted, and he climbed up on his pinto. "Could it be any other way?"

"No, unacceptable!" Jhinjab protested. "I have done as you asked, and will be paid. De girl is in de camp!"

"You will remain here, and perhaps you will be paid," Alpirs replied.

"Oh, there will be some reward, indeed," Untaris added ominously.

Jhinjab swallowed hard.

"If you are confident in your information, you will remain here."

"You will pay!" the Bedine insisted.

"Or?" asked Alpirs.

"Or he will go and tell the Desai," Untaris added, and when both Shadovar turned to regard the old Bedine threateningly, the blood drained from Jhinjab's face.

"No," he started to protest, but the word was cut short as a long dagger appeared in Alpirs's hand, its tip coming to rest against the poor Bedine's throat in the blink of an eye.

"Ride with my friend," Alpirs instructed, and Untaris reached a hand down to Jhinjab.

"I cannot go . . . ," the Bedine stammered. "I am . . . de Desai do not know I am out . . . dey will miss Jhinjab. Dey will look for . . ."

Alpirs retracted the knife and kicked the old Bedine hard in the groin. He bent low as Jhinjab doubled over, and whispered into the man's ear, "The Desai can do nothing to you that I won't do if you don't get up on that horse right now."

Without even waiting for an answer, Alpirs moved to his own horse and mounted, and indeed, Jhinjab took Untaris's hand and settled in as the two mounts charged off toward the high dune in the southeast.

Five-year-old Ruqiah scrambled around the side of the tent and crouched low against the fabric, trying to control her breathing.

"Over here!" she heard Tahnood call out, but fortunately, her tormentor was moving in the wrong direction, between a different pair of tents.

Ruqiah dropped to her belly and crept forward, smiling as the gaggle of older children followed Tahnood further astray. She had avoided them, for now, but it was only a temporary reprieve, she knew from long experience, for Tahnood was a relentless adversary and took great pleasure in showing his dominance.

The girl sat back and considered her next move. The sun sank low into the western sky, but the tribe had found a new wellspring and the celebration would continue long after dark, she knew. The children would not be told to go to sleep, and the mud fight would continue, encouraged by the adults.

The mud pit caused by the wellspring symbolized that there was enough water to waste, after all, and for the desert-dwelling, nomadic Bedine, that was surely cause for celebration.

Ruqiah just wished that the joyous games didn't hurt so much.

"Sitting alone, always alone," came a voice, her father's voice, and he grabbed her by the ear and ushered her to her feet.

Ruqiah turned to regard the brilliant smile of Niraj, a smile full of life and mirth and love. He was short by Bedine standards, but stout and strong and quite respected. He rarely wore his kufiya, letting his bald brown head shine gloriously in the desert sun.

"Where are the other children?" he asked his precious daughter.

"Looking for me," Ruqiah admitted. "To make me darker."

"Ah," Niraj replied. Ruqiah was lighter-skinned than most Bedine, lighter even than her mother, Kavita. Ruqiah's thick wavy hair, too, was a lighter hue, with many red highlights showing among her light brown locks, instead of the normal Bedine darker brown or even raven black.

"They tease me because I am different," she said.

Niraj winked at her and rubbed his hand over his bald pate. "Not so different," he explained.

Ruqiah smiled. Her father had told her that her lighter hair had been inherited from his side of the family, although she hopefully wouldn't lose hers as he had shed his own. The young girl didn't completely believe the tale, for others had told her that Niraj's hair had been as black as a starless night, but that only made her appreciate her father's gesture all the more.

"They will hit me with their mud balls and throw me in the pit," she said.

"The mud is cool and soft to the touch," Niraj replied.

Ruqiah put her head down. "They shame me."

She felt her father's hand under her chin, lifting her face up to look into his dark eyes, eyes very unlike her own deep blue orbs. "You are never shamed, my Ruqiah," he said. "You will be like your mother, the most beautiful woman of the Desai. Tahnood is older than you. He already sees this truth of Ruqiah, and it stirs him in ways he does not understand. He does not seek to shame you, but to keep your attention, fully, until you are old enough to marry."

"Marry?" Ruqiah replied, and she almost burst out laughing, before realizing that such a reaction wouldn't be seen as appropriate from a child her age. As she suppressed her reaction, she realized that among the tribal Bedine, Niraj was probably correct. Her parents were not among the leaders of the tribe, but they were well-respected, after all, and had a well-appointed tent and enough animals to provide a proper dowry, even to Tahnood, whose family was in high standing among the Desai, and who was regarded as a potential chieftain. He was barely ten years old, but he commanded the children, even those about to be formally deemed adults, two years his senior.

Tahnood Dubujeb was the ringleader of the Desai's child gang, Ruqiah thought, but did not say. He used victims like her to strengthen his standing—and no doubt with the great encouragement of his proud father and overbearing mother.

It crossed Ruqiah's mind to pay the Dubujeb tent a visit when the tribe had at last settled in for the night. Perhaps she would bring some stinging scorpions along . . .

She couldn't contain a little chuckle at that, conjuring images of Tahnood running naked and screaming from his tent, a scorpion stinger firmly embedded in his buttocks.

"That's better, my little Zibrija," Niraj said, patting her head and using his pet name for her, which was also the name of a particularly beautiful flower found among the windblown rocks in the shadows of the dunes. He had misconstrued her sudden gaiety, obviously, and Ruqiah wondered—and not

7

for the first time—how Niraj and Kavita might react if they ever discovered what was really going on behind her five-year-old eyes.

"This way!" It was Tahnood's voice, closing in, and it seemed as if he had figured out Ruqiah's ruse at last.

"Run! Run!" Niraj said to her playfully, pushing her away. "And if they get you muddy, smile all the while and know that there is plenty of water to wash you clean!"

Ruqiah sighed, but did indeed start away, and she realized that she had run off not a moment too soon when she heard her father laughing as Tahnood and the others came rambling by. She thought of a dozen ways she might avoid them, and perhaps even make them all look foolish in the process, but her father's laughter made her put those dark thoughts out of her mind.

She would let them catch her, and pelt her, and throw her in the mud.

For the traditions of the Bedine, the playful bonding the Desai tribe demanded of its children.

For Niraj.

Untaris couldn't contain his gap-toothed smile as he kneeled before the small break in the windblown rocks, a narrow channel leading to a wider area that was protected from the wind and sand by the rock walls. They had passed by this spot several times already without even noticing the break, so completely did the rock shading camouflage the narrow entrance.

"It could be left over from the days of Rasilith," Alpirs reasoned, speaking of the ancient city which had once dominated this region. "Some perennials are stubborn."

Untaris shook his head and crawled through, coming into a small secret garden, hidden by the stones. It was too clever, he thought. This area was tended—well tended—and many of the flowers, vibrant and fragrant, seemed to have been recently transplanted.

"You see?" Jhinjab asked. "Like Jhinjab told you, eh?"

"Not enough water here to sustain these plants," Untaris told his partner. He reached out and touched a large red rose, slowly wrapping his fingers around the plant and rubbing the petals into pieces.

"So someone is bringing water out here," said Alpirs.

"Not 'someone,'" Jhinjab insisted. "De girl."

"So you claim," Alpirs said skeptically. He turned to his partner, who was much more acquainted with gardening than he, and inquired as to how much water would be needed by these particular plants in any given day.

"In the heat of the desert sun?" Untaris shrugged. He looked around at the area, some ten strides across and half that deep, and all of it filled with vibrant plants, flowers, vines, and even a small cypress tree, flat-topped and shading the southern half of the secret garden.

"More than a child could carry," Untaris decided, and both the Shadovar turned to regard Jhinjab.

"She does not bring out de water!" the Bedine informant insisted. "Never have I seen her. Never has Jhinjab said dat!"

"But you claim it's her garden," said Alpirs.

"Yes, yes."

"Then how does she sustain it without water?"

"M-many is de water near Rasilith," the Bedine stammered, and he looked around as if expecting to see a river flowing through the garden under the flora.

"The ground is moist," Untaris reported, rubbing some dirt between his fingers. "But there's no water source here."

"Nearby, den," said Jhinjab.

"Or the girl creates it," said Alpirs, and he and Untaris shrugged. She was, after all, a mortal Chosen of a god, so they believed.

"However it is done, it is clearly maintained," Untaris pointed out. "The plants are neatly trimmed, and I see no weeds, and no desert plants at all in here. And they would be in here if there really was a water source nearby."

"So someone tends it, and well," Alpirs agreed.

"De girl!" Jhinjab insisted. "It is like Jhinjab told you. All of it." He eyed the precious igal looped on Alpirs's belt as he spoke.

"Do we lay in wait for her to return?" Untaris asked.

Alpirs shook his head. "I have seen enough of Rasilith and smelled enough of these Bedine dogs already." He turned to Jhinjab. "Her name is Ruqiah?"

"Yes, yes, Ruqiah. Daughter of Niraj and Kavita."

"She comes out here? Just her?"

"Yes, yes. Just her."

"Day or night?"

"In de day. Maybe in de night, but Jhinjab only see her in de day."

Alpirs and Untaris looked to each other. "Miles to the Desai camp," Untaris said. "Long walk for a little girl."

At that moment, a lion called out in the darkness, its mournful cry echoing off the stones.

"Long walk through dangerous lands," said Alpirs.

"De lions, dey don't bother her," Jhinjab interrupted, seeming a bit frantic once more, and reverting more fully to his thick Bedine accent. "I have seen her walk right past dem as dey sleep in de grass."

Alpirs motioned for Untaris to follow and started out of the secret garden. He paused to glower at Jhinjab, and told the man, "Wait here."

"Quite a tale," Untaris said when the two were back out among the windswept rocks, near to a large dune with an alabaster spire protruding at a strange angle.

"Too much so to be a lie, perhaps."

Untaris shrugged, seeming unconvinced.

"Someone is tending the garden," Alpirs reminded him.

"We can make Shade Enclave by midday," said Untaris. "Let Lord Ulfbinder unravel this mystery."

Alpirs nodded his agreement, then motioned with his chin back toward the secret garden. While he went to retrieve the horses, Untaris crept back in to offer Jhinjab his reward.

They left the old Bedine face down under the cypress tree, his blood pouring from his opened throat and wetting the ground around the roots and flowers.

The indignity assaulted Ruqiah's sensibilities. Thrown over Tahnood's shoulder like a sack of feed for the camels, the poor girl kept reaching back to pull her sarong down over her bare legs. There was no use in resisting. Tahnood's friends were all around, escorting the pair between the many Desai tents, and out of the village to the wellspring just to the south.

The parade collected many happy elders, chanting and singing—many others, nearly the whole of the tribe, were already down at the growing mud pit. Barefoot women danced without inhibition in the slop, kicking their feet up high and often sliding and slipping down into the mud, to the happy howls of the onlookers.

Several hollow poles were driven down into the ground around the area, the water bubbling up over their hollow tops, catching the fiery reflection of the many fires that burned around the edges of the pit. The Desai would celebrate through the night, as tradition demanded whenever a wellspring was discovered.

Ruqiah tried not to be distracted by the cheering and the singing and the tumult all around her. She focused on her own song now, hoping to heighten the celebration even more. She whispered to the winds, calling upon the clouds to gather.

Then she was pitched through the air, her song turning into a shriek. She twisted around and even managed to get her feet under her as she landed, but it did her little good as the mud slipped out from under her and she unceremoniously flopped down on her back, legs and arms splayed wide.

The women laughed, the men cheered, and Tahnood stared down at her superiorly. He crossed his arms over his slender chest, the supreme conqueror.

Ruqiah didn't react, just fell back into her quiet song, calling to the clouds. Strong hands grabbed her by the ankles and began swirling her around, then rolling her onto her stomach and swirling her some more. Her brown hair matted against her head, and she couldn't see where her sarong ended and her bare legs began, for they were all the same color then, a mat of muddy clay. She smelled it in her nostrils and tasted it in her mouth.

The torment continued for some time, but Ruqiah didn't notice, for she had her song, and it was a safe place for her. Up above, the clouds gathered, answering her call.

Finally the older boys let her go, and a chant went up for Tahnood the Conqueror, and the older women sang a song to him, and of him. Ruqiah noted his father, beaming with pride, and noticed her own parents, Niraj standing with a wide and warm smile for her, nodding his gratitude to her for accepting the game with dignity and restraint. Beside him stood Kavita, with her silken black hair. She wore an uncomfortable smile, and tried to nod, but Ruqiah could tell that she was filled with sympathy for her daughter, or perhaps it was simply a silent lament that Ruqiah had been so chosen.

There were implications to this "game," after all. Tahnood had singled her out, above all others. He had signaled to the Desai that pretty Ruqiah, with her lighter hair and startling blue eyes, would be his choice.

Ruqiah noted that many of the tribe's girls, some her own age or just a bit older, looked upon her with open hostility now.

"Clean her!" Tahnood's mother called out, and several other women joined in the call. "The water! The water!"

11

Ruqiah looked to Niraj, and again he nodded, and offered her a warm smile. She felt Tahnood's hand grasp her by the wrist, strong but gentle. He pulled her up to her feet and began leading the mud-covered girl to the nearest spigot. They had just arrived, the cold water splashing over her, when a streak of lightning split the sky above, and the accompanying boom of thunder brought with it a sudden and heavy downpour.

Cries of surprise became shouts of joy as all the tribe began to dance and sing, and surely this was a good sign that promising young Tahnood had chosen wisely this wellspring night!

Ruqiah lifted her face to the sky and let the rain wash the mud away.

"You cannot escape me," Tahnood whispered at her side. "You can never escape me."

Ruqiah looked at him, almost with pity, and certainly with enough clear amusement to unnerve the boy. So suddenly, in that simple exchanged glance, Ruqiah had gained the upper hand. Tahnood licked his lips nervously and sulked off to dance with the others.

Ruqiah watched him go. Despite his puffery and his near-constant picking on her, she liked the boy. He was playing against high expectations, she knew. Many of the Desai had placed their future hopes upon his slender, boyish shoulders. He had been born of good blood, born to lead, and any failure would crash down around Tahnood many times more heavily than the foibles of other children. Ruqiah could not but sympathize with him.

The rain settled into a steady rhythm, shots of lightning occasionally lighting up the clouds above. Ruqiah moved to the spigot and let the cold water pour over her, invigorating her as she rubbed the last of the mud away. She found as she did, though, that she had torn her sarong. With a heavy sigh, she slid across the mud over to her parents.

"Zibrija!" Niraj greeted her. He tousled her wet hair with his thick hand, then pulled her against him for a hug.

"Are you all right, my love?" Kavita asked, bending low to look into Ruqiah's eyes.

Ruqiah smiled and nodded. "Tahnood would not hurt me," she assured the woman.

"If ever he did, I would stake him to an anthill!" Niraj proclaimed.

"I may help you, Father," Ruqiah said, and she showed her parents the tear in her sarong.

"It is nothing," Kavita assured her, inspecting the rip. "Come, let us fetch another and hang that over the chair to dry. I will sew it in the morning."

"In the afternoon, you mean!" Niraj said heartily, and he grabbed Kavita by the hands and began to twirl her in a dance. "For tonight is the wellspring and the rain! Oh, the rain! Tonight we dance and we drink, and tomorrow, we sleep through the morn!"

The woman, laughing, spun away from her husband, took her daughter's hand and started from the celebration. Together they moved down the empty lanes between the many tents. The drumbeat of rain on the tents accompanied them, like the background music of the celebration at the mud pit. Every so often another boom of thunder shook the ground.

"You make your father so proud, Zibrija," Kavita said to Ruqiah. "The elders watch you closely. They believe that you will be among the leaders of your age. They will train you as such."

"Yes," Ruqiah said obediently, though she didn't think Kavita's prediction likely—in fact, it seemed impossible to her.

They came around the corner of their tent, and Kavita reached for the flap. She didn't pull it open, though, and noting that hesitation, Ruqiah looked up to her, then followed Kavita's frozen expression across the way, to the form of a large man, a man who was not Desai, coming toward them, torch in hand.

"What do you—?" the woman started to say, and she grunted and stepped forward.

She looked down at Ruqiah and pushed her away, whispering, "Run, run!" and there was such pain in Kavita's voice that Ruqiah knew even before her mother stumbled past her that Kavita had been stabbed.

The swordsman behind Kavita grabbed the woman and threw her in through the tent flap. The other shade—for these were indeed Netherese shades—circled fast to cut off Ruqiah's escape.

But Ruqiah wasn't running away. No, she rushed into the tent after her stumbling, falling mother, her little feet splashing in the mud and the blood. She yelped as she crossed in front of the smaller shade, feeling the bite of his blade.

She didn't care as she desperately scrambled to keep up with her wounded mother. She fell over Kavita as the older woman tumbled in the tent, her lifeblood pouring from a deep wound in her lower back, already too far from consciousness, too near to death, to even respond to Ruqiah's frantic calls.

"You stabbed the little one, fool!" the larger Shadovar said to his companion as they came into the tent.

"Bah, but shut your mouth," the other said. "Ruqiah, girl, come along now, or your father will be the next to find death at the end of my sword!"

Ruqiah kept calling, but her words were not aimed at Kavita. She had fallen into a special place now, singing the sweet refrains. A scar on her right forearm began to glow as blue as her eyes, the light wafting out of her long sleeve in curious, magical tendrils, as if it were smoke. She felt her hands growing warm as that soft glow enveloped them and she pressed them against the hole in her mother's back. The blood washed over her, for just a bit, before subsiding.

She could clearly sense her dying mother's spirit trying to leave the body, then, but she held it in place, her song pleading with Kavita, begging her that it was not time to pass on. Ruqiah put her other hand over her own wound then, feeling her lifeblood dripping from her side, just under her ribs.

"Ruqiah, girl!" the Shadovar said from behind her.

Ruqiah sat back on her heels, moving away from her mother a bit, and slowly rose up from the floor. "My name is not Ruqiah," she said quietly.

"Just get her," the other Shadovar said, and she heard the first step coming toward her.

She spun around, blue eyes flashing, now with both sleeves glowing and wafting blue magical energies, like trained serpents of drifting light, reaching forth and twirling around her.

"No!" she cried, and she waved her hand, and a burst of smoke issued forth, right in the smaller man's face.

"No!" Ruqiah repeated, and the smoke became a hundred bats, a thousand bats, swarming around the intruders, slapping against them.

"My . . . ," Ruqiah said, and bat's wings became like scythe blades, slashing at the two Shadovar, who began to thrash and call out in surprise. Spinning and cutting, the bats swarmed in focused rage, taking fingers and digging long lines of blood.

". . . name . . . ," Ruqiah said, and a ball of flame appeared in the air between the two men, then shot down in an explosive line. The shades thrashed and spun and slapped at the flames and slapped at the barrier of blade-winged bats.

". . . is . . . ," Ruqiah said, and seven separate missiles of arcane energy flew from the fingers of her left hand to blast at the attackers.

". . . Catti-brie!" she finished, reaching high and calling to the storm she had brought in celebration, and it answered, a great bolt of lightning reaching down from on high to obliterate the two Shadovar where they stood.

A blinding flash, a thunderous, reverberating boom, and it was over. The attackers lay dead, their bodies crackling and burning. The larger had been blown right out of his boots, which stood upright, with wisps of smoke wafting forth.

And Catti-brie, the little girl who was not a child, turned back to her mother, imparting more waves of healing and whispering words of comfort in Kavita's ear.

PART ONE

THE REBORN HERO

So many times have I pondered the long road I have led, and likely will still walk. I hear Innovindil's words often, her warning that a long-lived elf must learn to live her life to accommodate the mortality of those she may come to know and love. And so, when a human passes on, but the elf lover remains, it is time to move on, time to break emotionally and completely and begin anew.

I have found this a difficult proposition, indeed, and something I cannot easily resolve. In my head, Innovindil's words ring with truth. In my heart . . .

I do not know.

As unconvinced as I am about this unending cycle, it occurs to me that measuring the lifespan of a human as a guideline is also a fool's errand, for indeed, don't these shorter-lived races live their lives in bursts, in fits and starts, abrupt endings and moments of renewal? Childhood friends, parted for mere months, may reunite only to discover that their bonds have frayed. Perhaps one has entered young adulthood, while the other remains in the thrall of childhood joys. I witnessed this many times in Ten-Towns (though it was less frequent among the more regimented kin of Bruenor in Mithral Hall), where a pair of boys, the best of friends, would turn corners away from each other, one pursuing a young lady who intrigued him in ways he could not have previously imagined, the other holding fast to childish games and less complicated joys.

On many occasions, this parting proved more than a temporary split, for never again would the two see each other in the previous light of friendship. Never again.

Nor is this limited to the transition of childhood to young adulthood. Far from it! It is a reality we all rarely seem to anticipate. Friends find different roads, vowing to meet again, and many times—nay, most times!—is that vow unrealized. When Wulfgar left us in Mithral Hall, Bruenor swore to visit him in Icewind Dale, and yet, alas, such a reunion never came to pass.

And when Regis and I ventured north of the Spine of the World to visit Wulfgar, we found for our efforts a night, a single night, of reminiscing. One night where we three sat around a fire in a cave Wulfgar had taken as his home, speaking of our respective roads and recalling adventures we had long ago shared.

I have heard that such reunions can prove quite unpleasant and full of awkward silence, and fortunately, that was not the case that night in Icewind Dale. We laughed and resolved that our friendship would never end. We prodded Wulfgar to open his heart to us, and he did, recounting the tale of his journey back to the north from Mithral Hall, when he had returned his adopted daughter to her true mother. Indeed, in that case, the years we had spent apart seemed to melt away, and we were three friends uninterrupted, breaking bread and sharing tales of great adventure.

And still, it was but one single night, and when I awoke in the morn, to find that Wulfgar prepared a breakfast, we two knew that our time together had come to an end. There was no more to say, no stories left that hadn't been told. He had his life now, in Icewind Dale, while the road for Regis and I led back to Luskan, and to Mithral Hall beyond that. For all the love between us, for all the shared experiences, for all the vows that we would meet again, we had reached the end of our lives together. And so we parted, and in that last embrace. Wulfgar had promised Regis that he would find him on the banks of Maer Dualdon one day, and would even sneak up and bait the hook of his fishing pole!

But of course, that never happened, because while Innovindil advised me, as a long-lived elf, to break my life into the shorter life spans of those humans I would know, so too do humans live their lives in segments. Best friends today vow to be best friends when they meet again in five years, but alas, in five years, they are often strangers. In a few years, which seems not a long stretch of time, they have often made for themselves new lives with new friends, and perhaps even new families.

This is the way of things, though few can accurately anticipate it and fewer still will admit it.

The Companions of the Hall, the four dear friends I came to know in Icewind Dale, sometimes told me of their lives before we'd met. Wulfgar and Catti-brie were barely adults when I came into their lives, but Bruenor was an old dwarf even then, with adventures that had spanned centuries and half the world, and Regis had lived for decades in exotic southern cities, with as many wild adventures behind him as those yet to come.

Bruenor spoke to me often about his clan and Mithral Hall, as dwarves are wont to do, while Regis, with more to hide, likely, remained cryptic about his earlier days (days that had set Artemis Entreri on his trail, after all). But even with the exhaustive stories Bruenor told me, of his father and grandfather, of the adventures he had known in the tunnels around Mithral Hall, of the founding of Clan Battlehammer in Icewind Dale, it rarely occurred to me that he had once known friends as important to him as I had become.

Or had he? Isn't that the mystery and the crux of Innovindil's claims, when all is stripped bare? Can I know another friend to match the bond I shared with Bruenor? Can I know another love to match that which I found in Catti-brie's arms?

What of Catti-brie's life before I met her on the windswept slope on Kelvin's Cairn, or before she had come to be adopted by Bruenor? How well had she known her parents, truly? How deeply had she loved them? She spoke of them only rarely, but that was because she simply could not remember. She had been but a child, after all . . .

And so I find myself in another of the side valleys running alongside Innovindil's proposed road: that of memory. A child's feelings for her mother or father cannot be questioned. To look at the child's eyes as she stares at one of her parents is to see true and deep love. Catti-brie's eyes shone like that for her parents, no doubt.

Yet she could not tell me of her birth parents, for she could not remember!

She and I spoke of having children of our own, and oh, how I wish that had come to pass! For Catti-brie, though, there hovered around her the black wings of a great fear, that she would die before her child, our child, was old enough to remember her, that her child's life would parallel her own in that one, terrible way. For though she rarely spoke of it, and though she had known a good life under the watchful gaze of benevolent and beneficent Bruenor, the loss of her parents—even parents she could not remember—forever weighed heavily upon Catti-brie. She felt as if a part of her life had been stolen from her, and cursed her inability to remember in greater detail more profoundly than the joy she found in recalling the smallest bits of that life lost.

Deep are those valleys beside Innovindil's road.

Given these truths, given that Catti-brie could not even remember two she had loved so instinctively and wholly, given the satisfied face of Wulfgar when Regis and I found him upon the tundra of Icewind Dale, given the broken promises of finding old friends once more or the awkward conversations that typically rule such reunions, why, then, am I so resistant to the advice of my lost elf friend?

I do not know.

Perhaps it is because I found something so far beyond the normal joining one might know, a true love, a partner in heart and soul, in thought and desire.

Perhaps I have not yet found another to meet that standard, and so I fear it cannot ever be so again.

Perhaps I am simply fooling myself—whether wrought of guilt or sadness or frustrated rage, I amplify and elevate in my memory that which I had to a pedestal that no other can begin to scale.

It is the last of these possibilities that terrifies me, for such a deception would unravel the very truths upon which I stand. I have felt this sensation of love so keenly—to learn that there were no gods or goddesses, no greater design to all that is beyond what I already know, no life after death, even, would pain me less, I believe, than to learn that there is no lasting love.

And thus I deny the clear truth of Innovindil's advice, because in this one instance, I choose to let that which is in my heart overrule that which is in my head.

I have come to know that to do otherwise, for Drizzt Do'Urden, would be to walk a barren road.

—Drizzt Do'Urden

CHAPTER 1

THE CIRCLE OF LIFE

The Year of the Elves' Weeping (1462 DR)
Iruladoon

Eh?" THE RED-BEARDED DWARF ASKED. WHAT WIZARD, WHAT MAGIC, WHAT force, had done this to him, he wondered? He had been in a cavern, deep in the ancient homeland of Gauntlgrym, struggling to pull a lever and enact an ancient magic that would harness once more the volcanic primordial that had so ravaged the region.

Had his effort caused the volcano to erupt? Had that surge of power thrown him far from the mountain? Surely it seemed so, for here he was, out of the cavern, out of the Underdark, and lying in a forest of flowers and buzzing bees, with a still pond nearby . . .

It could not be.

He hopped to his feet, surprisingly easily, surprisingly smoothly for a dwarf of his advanced age.

"Pwent?" he called, and his tone reflected more confusion than anything else. For how could he have been so thrown across the lands? The last voice he remembered was that of Thibbledorf Pwent, imploring him to pull that lever to close the magical cage around the primordial.

A wizard had intervened, then? Bruenor's mind swirled in confused circles, overlapping, finding no logic. Had some mage teleported him from the cavern? Or concocted a magical gate, through which he had inadvertently fallen? Yes, surely that must be it!

Or had it been a dream? Or was this a dream now before him?

"Drizzt?"

"Well met," said a voice behind him, and Bruenor nearly jumped out of his boots. He spun around, to see a plump halfling with a cherubic face and a smile that promised trouble stretching from ear to ear.

"Rumblebelly . . . ," Bruenor managed to gasp, using his nickname for his old friend. No, not old, he realized. Regis stood before him, but he was younger by decades than he had been when first he had met Bruenor in Lonelywood in Icewind Dale.

For an instant, Bruenor wondered if the volcano had somehow thrown him back in time.

He stuttered as he tried to continue. He couldn't find any sensible words to unravel his incoherent, spinning thoughts.

And then he nearly fell over, as out of the front door of the small house behind Regis stepped a man, a giant in comparison to the diminutive halfling.

Bruenor's jaw fell limp and he didn't even try to speak, his eyes welling with tears, for there stood his boy, Wulfgar, a young man once more, tall and strong.

"You mentioned Pwent," Regis said to Bruenor. "Were you with him when you fell?"

Bruenor reeled. The great battle on the ledge of the primordial pit in Gauntlgrym replayed in his thoughts. He felt the strength of Clangeddin, the wisdom of Moradin, the cleverness of Dumathoin . . . They had come to him on that ledge, in his final effort, in his victory in the ancient land of Gauntlgrym.

That victory had come with a grave cost, however, Bruenor now knew without doubt. He had been with Pwent—

Regis's words hit him right in the gut and took the wind out of his lungs. Were you with him when you fell?

Rumblebelly was right, Bruenor knew. When he fell. He was dead. He swallowed hard and looked around at this place that was surely not Dwarfhome, the Halls of Moradin!

But he was dead, and so were these two. He had buried Regis a century before in a rocky cairn in Mithral Hall. And Wulfgar, his boy—age had taken Wulfgar, no doubt. He appeared to be barely past his twentieth birthday, but he would be halfway through his second century of life by now, if humans could live so long.

They were dead, all three, and surely Pwent, too, had fallen in Gauntlgrym. "He's with Moradin," Bruenor said, more to himself than to the others. "In Dwarfhome. Got to be."

He looked up at the two. "Why ain't meself?"

Regis smiled, comfortingly, almost sympathetically, confirming Bruenor's fears. Wulfgar, though, wasn't looking back at him, but rather past him. The expression on Wulfgar's face caught Bruenor's eye anyway, for it was filled with warmth and enchantment, and when Bruenor glanced back at Regis, he saw that the halfling's smile had shifted from sympathy to joy, as Regis, too, looked past Bruenor, and nodded with his chin.

Only then did the dwarf even hear the music, so quietly, so seamlessly, so fittingly had it grown around them.

Slowly, Bruenor turned, his gaze drifting out over the still pond and across the small lea to the tree line opposite.

There she danced, his beloved daughter, dressed in a layered white gown of many folds and pretty lace, and with a black cape trailing her every twist and turn like some living shadow, a dark extension of her lighter steps.

"By the gods," the dwarf muttered, overwhelmed for the first time in his long life. Now that his long life was no more, Bruenor Battlehammer fell to his knees, put his face in his hands, and began to sob.

And they were tears of joy, of just rewards.

Catti-brie wasn't singing.

Not consciously.

The words were not of her own making. The melody of the song flowed through her, but was not controlled by her, and the harmony of the forest music, which permeated the air and added to the song, was not her doing.

Because Catti-brie wasn't singing.

She was learning.

For the words were Mielikki's song, giving voice to the harmony of this place, Iruladoon, this gift of Mielikki. Though Catti-brie, Regis, Wulfgar, and now Bruenor had come into this strange paradise, the gift of Iruladoon was a gift, most of all, to Drizzt Do'Urden.

Catti-brie understood that now. Like the Weave of magic she had studied as a budding mage, the patterns of Mielikki's domain were becoming ever clearer to her. Mielikki was of the cycle, of life and death, of the autumn withering and the spring renewal.

Iruladoon was the spring.

Through the words of the song, Catti-brie cast a spell without realizing it. She walked toward her three friends, stepping upon the waters of the pond. As she gracefully drifted over the water to stand before the others, her song became clear to them, not just in the music of the forest, but in specific words, spoken in many languages, new and old:

> What is old is new again,
> When Magic is re-woven,
> And the Shadows diminish,
> And the heroes of the gods awaken
> To walk Faerûn again.
> What is built can be destroyed,
> But what is destroyed can be built anew.
> That is the secret,
> That is the hope,
> That is the promise.

The woman closed her eyes and took a deep breath, steadying herself, silent for the first time since she and Regis had come into this place—a span of many tendays for them, but of nearly a century in the world of Toril outside of Iruladoon, where the magical forest occasionally anchored.

"Me girl," Bruenor breathed when she opened her eyes once more, to look upon the forest's newest visitor.

Catti-brie smiled at him, then fell over him in a great hug. Regis leaped over and joined in, for many of his days here had been spent in chasing the singing woman, always unsuccessfully. The three broke and looked back at Wulfgar, whose expression reflected the turmoil within.

The barbarian had only been here for three days in Iruladoon's time, and had no more understanding of the place than Bruenor—or than Regis, even, who had wiled away his many hours here sitting by the pond, tending his small garden, and fashioning pieces of scrimshaw out of the knucklehead trout bone that always seemed to be readily available.

"You finally stopped that singing . . . ," the halfling started to say, but Bruenor cut him short.

"Ah, me girl," he said, running his strong hand—his strong young hand, he noted—across Catti-brie's pretty face. "So many's the years gone by. Ye've ne'er left me heart, and every road I been walking's been an emptier way without ye."

24

Catti-brie put her hand atop his. "I am sorry for the pain," she whispered.

"Surely I have gone mad!' Wulfgar roared suddenly, and all turned back to consider him once more.

"I was on the hunt," he whispered, speaking more to himself than to the others, and he began to pace, his long strides propelling him back and forth before the others. "An old man . . ." He paused and turned to the other three, holding his arms out wide.

"An old man!" he insisted. "A man with children older than I now appear, with grandchildren older than I now appear! What healing I have been given, I do not know. Am I cursed or am I blessed?"

"Blessed," Catti-brie answered.

"By your god?"

"Goddess," the woman corrected.

"Goddess, then," said Wulfgar. "I am blessed by your goddess? Then I am damned by Tempus!"

"No," Catti-brie started to answer, and she broke free of Bruenor and stepped toward Wulfgar, who visibly winced and backed from her, step for step.

"This is madness!" Wulfgar cried. "I am Wulfgar, son of Beornegar, who serves Tempus! I am slain. I accept my defeat and my mortality, but this is no hall of my warrior god! Nay, this is no blessing!" He spat the last sentence at Catti-brie as if casting his own curse.

"Youth?" he asked with a derisive snort. "Healing? Are those the blessings? At what cost?"

"It is not like that," Catti-brie assured him.

Bruenor touched her on the cheek and she turned around.

"You died in Gauntlgrym," Catti-brie told him. "Beside Thibbledorf Pwent, yes, but know that you won the day and were buried with honor beside your shield dwarf and beside the gods' throne in the entry chamber."

Bruenor started to reply, but the words caught in his throat. "How could ye know?" he asked instead.

Catti-brie merely smiled contentedly, erasing all doubt anyone might have had of her claims.

"I'd be a lyin' old dwarf if I said that me heart's not full in seein' ye, all three of ye!" Bruenor whispered. "But I'd be a liar, too, if I told ye that any halls but Moradin's are me place and reward for the life I knowed."

Catti-brie nodded and started to reply, but a rustle turned her back again, just in time to see Wulfgar disappearing into the brush, moving from them at great speed.

"Me boy!" Bruenor yelled after him, but Catti-brie put her hand on the dwarf's pointing arm to quiet him, then took him by the hand, bade Regis to take her other hand, and led them off in pursuit.

"Wulfgar, do not!" she called after the man. "You cannot leave. You are not prepared!"

They caught sight of Wulfgar again a few moments later, crossing a small clearing and running toward a lighter area that seemed to mark the forest's edge. Bruenor and Regis tried to speed up and heighten their pursuit, but now Catti-brie held them back, and the very grass around their feet seemed to agree with the woman, or answered the woman's call, the blades rolling up over Bruenor's boots and Regis's furry toes to hold them fast in place.

"Do not!" she warned Wulfgar one last time, but the stubborn barbarian didn't slow at all and charged to the forest's edge.

"Ye stopped us, so stop him!" Bruenor told her, tugging at the unyielding roots, but Catti-brie continued to stare after Wulfgar and shook her head.

The trees hung thick and dark around him, but Wulfgar saw the light and made for it, hardly aware of his movements. He felt more like he was swimming than running, felt moist and warm, though it was not raining and the forest had seemed dry enough.

But he was not in the forest, he realized, and the light became a pinpoint and nothing more, and his movements were jumbled and uncoordinated. He felt as if he had been wrapped in thick cloth and thrown into a pond.

He felt . . . he didn't know what he felt as his thoughts jumbled incoherently. He saw the light, though just a speck now, and he made for it, his body twisted and turning, arms trapped, legs moving weirdly, uncontrollably.

The light grew and he couldn't breathe. Frantic, Wulfgar pushed on more forcefully, and the wrappings around him seemed to flex and writhe—he could only think of a giant constrictor snake or a purple worm! Yes, it was as if he had leaped into the maw of a purple worm, but its convulsions, whether inadvertent or not, served him in his current course, as the light grew before him.

He pushed his head through and tried to reach his arm above him, when he was grabbed, suddenly, rudely, powerfully! Oh, so powerfully!

Yanked forth, he felt as if he was flying, rising up high into the air, one titanic hand wrapping around his head fully, the other grabbing at his body and hoisting him with such ease. For a moment, he feared that he had been thrown among a horde of giants, for they were all around him, but then he realized that they were too large even for giants! He could feel them, he could hear the reverberations of their thunderous voices.

Not giants! Too large! Titans, the forest had thrown him into a lair of titans!

Or gods, even, for these creatures were so far beyond him, so much more powerful than he. His hand hooked on one giant finger and he pushed with all his strength, but he might as well have tried to move a boulder the size of a mountain!

Gurgling through gobs of spittle and some slime he did not understand, he fought and he coughed and finally, finally, Wulfgar cried out for his god, "Tempus!" His voice sounded so thin and indistinct. He struggled, and the titan-beast holding him cried out. Wulfgar cursed it, evoking Tempus's wrath.

And then he was flying—nay, not flying.

He was falling.

Standing at the edge of the lea in the magical forest, Catti-brie began to sing once more.

"Girl, go get me boy!" Bruenor cried, but his voice sounded distorted.

"What are you doing?" Regis asked, his words slowing and speeding strangely as the magic of Catti-brie's song warped time and space itself. Then they three, too, found themselves in a strange tunnel, winding their way quickly along. This wasn't the same as Wulfgar's experience, however, for no sooner had Bruenor or Regis even registered the strange effect than they came out of it, rushing out from the root of a willow tree to suddenly find themselves standing with Catti-brie beside the small forest pond once more.

And there lay Wulfgar, gasping and trying to rise, propping himself up on his elbows and muttering, only to fall back to the grass.

He managed to turn to face his friends at Bruenor's call, his face ashen, his arms trembling.

"Titans," he rasped. "Gods. The altar of the gods!"

"What do ye know?" Bruenor demanded, speaking to Wulfgar, but turning as he ended to encompass Catti-brie with the question.

"Not titans." Catti-brie walked over to Wulfgar and helped him to his feet. "Nor gods." She waited until she had the complete attention of all three.

"Reghed barbarians," she explained. "Your own people."

Wulfgar's expression denied her claim. "Huge!" he protested.

"Or you were tiny." She paused to let that perspective sink in. "A babe. A newborn babe."

CHAPTER 2

THE REBORN HERO

The Year of the Reborn Hero (1463 DR)
Netheril

Lord Parise Ulfbinder of the Empire of Netheril shifted uncomfortably in his seat, poring over each of a hundred parchments again and again. He kept glancing to the side, to his crystal ball, almost expecting another magical intrusion from his peer and friend, Lord Draygo Quick, who resided outside the city of Gloomwrought in the Shadowfell, the dark sister of the Prime Material Plane.

Everything Draygo Quick had just told him had only reinforced that which Parise feared. The gates between the Shadowfell and Toril were growing weaker, and the pockets of shadow on Toril seemed to be diminishing.

Most of Netheril's scholars, and there were many among the learned Netherese, had viewed the stronger bonds between the worlds as a great change in the multiverse, a new and permanent paradigm, in the lifespan of a shade, at least.

Parise Ulfbinder was beginning to grow uncertain of that, and the pile of parchments, ancient writings of long dead scholars, Netherese and otherwise, whispered to him of things that seemed to be coming true all around him.

The gates were . . . thinning.

The vibrant young lord shifted the parchments before him, drawing forth his copy of the cornerstone of his theory, an ancient sonnet known as "Cherlrigo's Darkness."

> Enjoy the play when shadows steal the day . . .
> All the world is half the world for those who learn to walk.

To feast on fungus soft and peel the sunlit stalk;
Tarry not in place, for in their sleep the gods do stay.
But care be known, be light of foot and soft of voice.
Dare not stir divine to hasten Sunder's day!
A loss profound but a short ways away;
The inevitable tear shall't be of, or not of, choice.
Oh, aye, again the time wandering of lonely world!
With kingdoms lost and treasures past the finger's tip,
And enemies that stink of their god's particular flavor.
Sundered and whole, across the celestial spheres are hurled,
Beyond the reach of dweomer and the wind-walker's ship;
With baubles left for the ones the gods do favor.

Parise and Lord Draygo had discussed this sonnet extensively and repeatedly, particularly the poem's volte, the ninth line: Oh, aye, again the time wandering of lonely world!

" 'Of lonely world,' " Parise read aloud. "Of."

To him, this resolution seemed a clear enough statement, more than a hint, that the magical proximity of Abeir and Toril was not likely as permanent as many believed.

"How long?" he wondered aloud and his eyes drifted up to the dual globe and calendar he had placed on the far edge of his desk.

Parise read the header of the calendar. " 'Dalereckoning, 1463.' "

He knew the current year as measured on Toril, of course. He was a mathematician, a scholar, and one quite interested in the movements of the heavenly spheres, which had played no small role in his current investigation regarding the fate of Abeir-Toril. So naming the year should not have come as a revelation to the learned Netherese Lord . . . and yet, it had.

"1463?" he muttered, and suddenly, he sucked in his breath.

He rushed from his chair so quickly that he sent it spinning and tumbling out behind him, and just as quickly, he flopped into the chair set before his crystal ball and frantically began reestablishing the connection to the Shadowfell, to Lord Draygo Quick.

He was greatly relieved to find that his friend was still in his study, and so heard his call.

"Well met again," greeted Lord Draygo, a withered old warlock of great influence and magical power.

"You know a favored hero," Parise said, "a chosen of one of the old gods, so you believe."

"Yes," Draygo Quick replied, for they had just been over this.

"Perhaps you err."

Inside the crystal ball, the somewhat distorted image of Parise's counterpart seemed taken aback. "I have never spoken with certainty—"

"Perhaps we err," Parise Ulfbinder corrected, "in believing that the heroes of the old gods are out there, preparing."

Now Draygo Quick looked simply perplexed.

"What year is it?" Parise asked.

"Year?"

"Yes, what year, in Toril's calendar? In Dalereckoning?"

Draygo Quick's face scrunched up as he considered the question, which Parise expected would take him a few moments to unravel, given that Lord Draygo lived in the Shadowfell, where time itself was measured differently.

"Too long are you upon the land of light, that you even care," Draygo Quick remarked, before properly answering, "1463, I believe."

"Not the date, the name."

"1463 . . . ," Parise Ulfbinder replied, "the Year of the Reborn Hero."

"What is the significance of this?" Draygo Quick asked.

Parise could only shrug. "Perhaps none," he admitted. "It is a lead, not a clue. Potentially a lead, I should say. We should not alter our respective courses or investigations."

"Regarding Drizzt Do'Urden?"

"Him or any others who catch our attention," said Parise. "We will build our network to find and scout these favored mortals, these heroes. But as we go forth, perhaps we should tell our spies to pay particular attention to any seeming as Chosen who happened to be born this very year."

"It is a remarkable coincidence," Draygo Quick admitted, and he began poring through the listings of previous years. "But they may hold clues," Draygo Quick pointed out.

Now it was time for Parise to sigh, for he had feared that he would open this very box of troubles. Scholars had spent their entire careers trying to make sense or order of the Roll of Years, the prophecies of Auguthra the Mad.

"It is work for acolytes," Lord Parise suggested. "Take a cursory glance and nothing more, I pray you."

"The Year of the Singing Skull," Draygo Quick said, seeming to ignore Parise.

"What?"

"1297," the older lord answered. "The year of Drizzt's birth, I believe. The Year of the Singing Skull."

"Do you see significance in that?"

"No."

"Then why interrupt . . . ?"

"Why would there be significance?" Draygo Quick asked. "He was just a drow, among tens of thousands."

"Then why . . . ?" Parise Ulfbinder let his voice trail off and let the thought dissipate. Indeed this had been his fear when first he had learned of the current year's formal name. Perhaps it was coincidence—likely it was coincidence, and likely, too, that investigating the name would garner no information worthy of his time and energy.

"Let our work continue as it was," he suggested to Draygo Quick. "We have networks to build and spies to recruit."

"Like Bregan D'aerthe."

Parise nodded. "Like Bregan D'aerthe, practical and helpful in ways they will not even understand."

"So you reopened our discussion here for nothing more than a curiosity," Draygo Quick stated.

Parise considered the words carefully, then finally nodded. "Indeed," he agreed, "a curiosity."

Draygo Quick replied with a smile, showing his friend that he understood completely. With a corresponding nod, he draped a cloth over his crystal ball, ending the connection.

Parise Ulfbinder rested back in his chair and touched the tips of his index fingers together against his lips.

The year's name could mean many things, of course, and perhaps it was nothing more than a curiosity, a coincidence.

But Parise Ulfbinder wasn't one to count something with such cataclysmic potential as a coincidence.

"The Year of the Reborn Hero . . . ," he whispered.

CHAPTER 3

MIELIKKI'S IRULADOON

The Year of the Reborn Hero (1463 DR)
Iruladoon

WULFGAR KNEELED BY THE POND, TRYING TO ABSORB WHAT CATTI-BRIE had just told him, trying to get past the shock of his rebirth experience. It could not be—somewhere deep in his heart, he simply could not grasp the truth of the woman's statement.

"But I knew," he whispered, and though he spoke quietly, his words abruptly silenced the conversation behind him, where Bruenor and Regis babbled about this same mystery, seeking some explanation.

"You remembered everything," Catti-brie said to Wulfgar, and he turned to regard the three.

"I knew," he replied. "I knew who I had been, who I was, and where I had come from. Not a newborn . . . ,"

"Not a newborn in heart, nor in mind," she explained. "In body alone."

"Girl, what do ye know?" Bruenor asked.

"Regis and I have been in this place, Iruladoon, for several tendays," she started.

"For a hunnerd years, ye mean," Bruenor interrupted, but Catti-brie shook her head immediately, as if anticipating that exact response.

"A century in the lands beyond Iruladoon, but only a matter of tendays within," she replied. "This is the gift of Mielikki."

"Or the curse," muttered Wulfgar.

"Nay, the gift," Catti-brie said. "And not a gift to us, but to Drizzt. The goddess has done this for our friend."

"Eh?" Bruenor and Regis asked together.

"The old gods knew," Catti-brie said. "With the advent of Shadow, the connection to the Shadowfell, this collision with this other world known as Abeir and our world of Toril . . . the old gods anticipated the chaos. Not all of it, to be sure, like the falling of the Weave and the Spellplague, but they understood indeed the greater truth of the worlds coming together."

"Might be why they're gods," Bruenor muttered.

"And they know, too, that it is a temporary arrangement of the spheres," said Catti-brie. "The advent will meet its sundering, and that time, the Sundering, is soon upon us."

"And here I be, thinking we were dead," Bruenor muttered sarcastically, mostly to Regis, but Catti-brie wasn't listening, and didn't slow in her story. She took on the role of a skald then, even beginning a bit of a dance as she continued, much like the dancing she had done around the flowery boughs of Iruladoon through the hours of the previous tendays.

"It will be a time of great despair and tumult, of chaos and realignment, both worldly and among the pantheon," she proclaimed. "The gods will claim their realms and their followers—they will seek their champions among some, and make champions of others. They will find prizes among the mortal leaders of Faerûn, among the Lords of Waterdeep and the Archwizards of Thay, among the chieftains of the great tribes and the heroes of the North, among the kings, dwarf and orc alike.

"Most will be as it ever has been," she explained. "Moradin and Gruumsh will hold their tribes fast, but around the edges, there will be chaos. Who will lead the thieves, and to whom will the wizards credit their arcane blasts? And who will mortals, grieving and lost, choose to serve as the roadways of their journey winding ever wider?"

"What?" Regis asked in obvious exasperation.

"More riddles?" Wulfgar grumbled.

But Bruenor caught a bit of her meaning more clearly. "Drizzt," he whispered. "Grieving and lost, ye say? Aye, but I left him with that Dahlia girl, and trouble's sure to be brewin' with that fiery child!"

"Grieving, and so, perhaps, easy prey," said Catti-brie.

"He loves ye," Bruenor was quick to answer, comfortingly. "He still loves ye, girl! Always has!"

Catti-brie's laugh almost mocked the notion of carnal jealousy. "I speak of his heart, of his soul, and not of his physical desires."

"In that, Drizzt is for Mielikki," said Regis, but Catti-brie merely shrugged to dispel his certainty.

"He will choose, in the end," she said. "And I hold faith in him that he will choose wisely. But more likely, his choice will cost him—everything. That is the warning of Mielikki, and so this is her gift."

"Bah, but it's not for her to be giving!" Bruenor said.

"My place is in the Halls of Tempus," Wulfgar insisted, catching on to the dwarf's meaning and rising to his feet imperiously and defiantly.

"And so the choice is yours to make," Catti-brie agreed, "for never would the goddess demand such service from the follower of another. Mielikki demands of you no fealty, but offers you, then, this choice."

"I am here!" Wulfgar argued. "There is no choice!"

"Aye," agreed Bruenor.

"There is," Catti-brie replied with a smile that surely disarmed both. "For this place is not permanent and everlasting—indeed, its time of end is nearly upon us. The enchantment of Mielikki, Iruladoon, will soon be no more. Forever gone, not to return. And so we must choose and we must leave."

"As I tried," Wulfgar reminded.

"Indeed," Catti-brie replied with a nod. "But you did so blindly, without preparation, without bargain, and so you were doomed. Better for you that your experience ended as soon as it began. Better for you that the midwife dashed you down upon the stones!"

"Without bargain?" Regis echoed under his breath, the halfling catching the curious phrase buried within Catti-brie's explanation.

The blood drained from Wulfgar at Catti-brie's remark, as memories of his brief experience outside of Iruladoon came flooding back to him— magically, he knew, through the words of Catti-brie. He had come forth into the arms of a giantess, so he thought, but in truth, into the arms of a midwife. And when he had protested, when he had called out in the voice of a babe, but in the words of one much older, the horrified midwife had done her duty and had thrown him down, dashing him on the warm stones heating the hut.

The memory of the weight of that terror, of the explosion as his soft head struck the unyielding rock, stunned him once more. He stumbled back into the pond a couple of steps and sat there in the shallow water for many heartbeats before dragging himself back to the bank.

"Aye," Catti-brie explained to Bruenor and Regis as Wulfgar floundered, "the goddess revealed it all to me. Indeed, she likely incited the midwife to destroy the haunted child."

"Not much of a merciful goddess!" Bruenor argued.

"The cycle of life and death is neither merciful nor merciless," Catti-brie explained. "It is. It has ever been and will ever be. Wulfgar could not leave Iruladoon as he attempted—none of us can. That is not the pact or the choice Mielikki offers to us four. We are afforded two paths from this forest before the magic fades. The first is as Wulfgar chose, but on condition." She looked directly at Wulfgar. "One you had not met, and so you were doomed to fail."

Wulfgar stared back at her, his expression rife with suspicion.

"The second route from here is through that very pond," Catti-brie finished.

"On condition?" Regis asked.

"To leave the forest, to return to Faerûn, requires an oath to Mielikki."

"You would proselytize?" Wulfgar protested.

"By Moradin's hairy arse!" Bruenor similarly protested. "I love ye girl, and love Drizzt as me brother, but I ain't for chasing flowers in a glade of Mielikki's choosing!"

"An oath, a quest, not everlasting fealty," Catti-brie explained. "To accept the blessing of Mielikki and depart Iruladoon to be born again upon the lands of Faerûn, you must accept one condition alone: that you will act on the side of Mielikki in the darkest hour."

"To be sure, I'm not knowin' what that's to mean, girl," said Bruenor.

"In Drizzt's darkest hour she means," said Regis. When the others all looked to him he added, "A gift to Drizzt most of all, you said."

"Are ye sayin' that Drizzt will be needing our help?" asked Bruenor.

Catti-brie shrugged, appearing sincerely at a loss. "It seems likely."

"So we can return to the aid of Drizzt, whatever that might mean, but we are free to honor and serve a god of our choosing?" Regis asked, and it was obvious from his tone that he was only asking the question to help clarify things for Bruenor and Wulfgar, whose faces continued to express grave doubts.

"When the cycle turns once more, when you die again, as you surely will," Catti-brie replied, "you will find your way to the altar of the god of your choosing, at that god's suffrage." She whirled around to face Wulfgar and the pond, and added, "Indeed, that choice is the second option before you now." She pointed into the pond. "For beneath the waters of this pond is a cave, a tunnel winding through the multiverse to the promised rewards of devoted followers. That path is open to you now, should you so choose. For you, Wulfgar, the road to Warrior's Rest, and the children and friends you knew among your tribe who had predeceased you, or have died in the years since you entered Iruladoon. A place of honor is there for you, I am sure. For you, my father, Dwarfhome and your seat beside Moradin, and a grand seat it will be, for you have sat upon the throne of Gauntlgrym and have been touched by his favor and power. For you, Regis, the Green Fields, and more to roam in the ways of Brandobaris, and know that I will find you there when I am no more of this world, and Drizzt will find us both, for the Deep Wilds of Mielikki touch the Green Fields."

"What're ye sayin', girl?" Bruenor asked. "Are we dead or ain't we?"

"We are," Regis answered. "But we don't have to be."

"Or we can be," Wulfgar stated coldly, almost angrily. "As is the way of the world, natural and right." He met Catti-brie's stare without blinking, without bending. "I lived a good life, a long life. I have known children—I have buried children!"

"No doubt they are all dead now," Catti-brie admitted. "Even had they been blessed with your longevity, for many decades have passed on Toril since you entered Iruladoon."

Wulfgar winced at that, and seemed near panic, or rage, at that moment, digesting the almost incomprehensible truth.

"Nothing is demanded of you, of us, any of us," Catti-brie said to them all. "The goddess intervened, for the sake of her favored Drizzt, but will not take from us our choice. I am her messenger here, nothing more."

"But yerself's going back," Bruenor said.

Catti-brie smiled and nodded.

"Well, if ye're going back to be born as a baby, then ye ain't to be much help to Drizzt, I'm thinking," said Bruenor. "Not for many the year!"

Again she nodded. "The Sundering is not yet upon the world of Toril. I expect then, that the time of Drizzt's peril is not yet upon him."

"So ye're to go back and grow up all over again?" Bruenor asked incredulously. "And where might ye be?"

Catti-brie shrugged. "Anywhere," she admitted. "I will be born of human parents, though in Waterdeep or Calimport, Thay or Sembia, Icewind Dale or the Moonshaes, I cannot say, for it is yet to be known. To be reborn into the great cycle is to fly free in spirit until you are found and bound within a suitable womb."

"When druids reincarnate, they can come back as different races, as animals, even," Regis remarked. "Am I to leave the forest to become a little rabbit, scampering away from wolves and hawks?"

"You will be a halfling, born of halfling parents," Catti-brie promised. "That would surely be more in the way of Mielikki, and more in accordance with Mielikki's demands."

"What good might ye be to Drizzt as a rabbit, ye dolt?" Bruenor asked.

"Maybe he's hungry," Regis replied with a shrug.

Bruenor sighed against the halfling's sly grin, but the dwarf turned more serious again, obviously so, as he spun back on his beloved daughter. He breathed hard and tried to speak, but shook his head, defeated by emotion.

"I can'no do it," he said suddenly, and he choked upon the words. "I had me day and found me rest!" He seemed almost frantic, and looked at Catti-brie with eyes rimmed with moistness. "I earned me way to Moradin's seat, and so Dwarfhome's waitin'."

Catti-brie stepped aside and motioned to the pond. "The road is there."

"And what'll me girl think o' me, then? Bruenor the coward?"

Catti-brie laughed, but sobered quickly and rushed to throw a great hug upon Bruenor. "There is no judgment in this choice," she whispered into his ear, and she let herself then slip into the Dwarvish accent she used to carry when she was very young and living in the Battlehammer tunnels beneath Kelvin's Cairn. "Me Da, yer girl'll e'er love ye, and not e'er forget ye."

She hugged him tighter, and Bruenor returned the grip tenfold, crushing Catti-brie against him. Then, abruptly, he pushed her back to arms' length, the tears now rolling down his hairy cheeks. "Ye're going back to Faerûn?"

"I am indeed."

"To help Drizzt?"

"To help him, so I pray. To love him once more, so I pray. To live beside him until I am no more, so I pray. The Deep Wild awaits, eternally so, and Mielikki is a patient hostess."

"I'm going back," Regis stated flatly, surprising them all and turning every eye toward him.

The halfling didn't melt under those curious looks.

"Drizzt would go back for me," he explained, and he said no more, and crossed his arms over his small chest and set his jaw firmly.

Catti-brie offered him a warm smile. "Then we will meet again, alive, so I hope."

"Oh, by the iron balls o' Clangeddin !" Bruenor huffed. He hopped back from Catti-brie and put his hands on his hips. "Beardless?" he asked.

Catti-brie smiled, seeing all too clearly where this was heading.

"Bah!" the dwarf grumbled and spun away. "Let's be goin' then, and if we're to be landin' all around Faerûn, then where're we to meet and how're we to know, and what . . . ?"

"In the night of the spring equinox in your twenty-first year," Catti-brie answered. "The Night of Mielikki, in a place we all know well."

Bruenor stared at her. Regis stared at her. Wulfgar stared at her. The gaze of all three burned into her, so many questions spinning, so much left to ask, and yet none of it, they all knew, possible to answer.

"Bruenor's Climb," she said. "Kelvin's Cairn in Icewind Dale, on the night of the spring equinox. There we will join anew, if we have not found each other previously."

"No!" Wulfgar stated flatly behind her, and she turned around to see the big man step farther into the pond. His stern visage softened under the gazes of his three friends. "I cannot," he said quietly.

He lowered his eyes and shook his head. "My days beside you, I treasure," he told them. "And know that I did love you once," he said to Catti-brie directly. "But I gained a life beyond our time, back in my homeland with my people, and there I found love and family anew. They are gone now, all of them . . . ," His voice trailed off and he pointed to the pond, and he was pointing toward Warrior's Rest, they all knew, the promised heaven of his god, Tempus. "They await. My wife. My children. Forgive me."

"There is nothing to forgive," Catti-brie said, and both Bruenor and Regis echoed the sentiment. "There is no debt to be repaid here. Mielikki would offer the choice to Drizzt's dearest friends, to the Companions of the Hall, and you are among that group. Farewell, my friend, and know that I once and ever loved you and will never forget you."

She walked to the pond, right into the water, and embraced Wulfgar warmly and lovingly and kissed him on the cheek. "Warrior's Rest will be greater with Wulfgar, son of Beornegar, who too awaits your arrival."

She walked out as Bruenor and Regis moved to similarly embrace the barbarian. Regis came back from the pond eagerly, Catti-brie noted, but Bruenor glanced back many times as he moved to join the other two.

With a final wave to Wulfgar, the three friends moved off into the forest, traveling a path that would take them to where, they could not know.

Up to his knees in the water, Wulfgar watched them go. He allowed himself to reminisce about those years he had spent beside Bruenor and the others, the three decades, the prime of his life.

Good years, he decided, among good friends.

He turned back to the water and noted his own reflection in the pool, dancing over the ripples his movement had caused. He looked like a young man once more, the way he had looked when he had walked the road of wild adventures beside Drizzt and the others.

He wondered if he would keep this appearance in Warrior's Rest, and if his family would appear in their finest hour. And what of his father, Beornegar, whom he had never known as a young man?

Wulfgar stepped deeper, slipping under the waves.

CHAPTER 4

SON O' THE LINE

The Year of the Reborn Hero (1463 DR)
Citadel Felbarr

"SUREN THAT THE WINTER'S IN ME OLD BONES," KING EMERUS WARCROWN said to Parson Glaive, his friend and advisor. King Emerus stretched his arms wide, his muscular shoulders flexing and bulging. He was past his two-hundredth birthday by many years, but still possessed a physique that would make a fifty-year-old jealous, and few of any age would wish to engage in combat with this proud old shield dwarf! He walked to the side of the room and grasped a large log in just one hand, easily hoisting it in his powerful grip and tossing it onto the flames.

"Aye, but she's a rough one," agreed Parson Glaive, the principle cleric in Citadel Felbarr, leader of the church, and the dwarf Emerus had recently appointed as Steward-in-Waiting should anything ill befall the king. "Snow's piled high around the west Runegate. I've set a horde o' shov'lers to work cleaning it afore the next caravan rolls through."

"Won't be rolling anytime soon!" Emerus said with a belly laugh. "Sledding, maybe, but not rollin'!"

"Aye," said his black-bearded, bald-headed friend, and he joined in the laughter. For the dwarves of Citadel Felbarr, the turn of 1463 had brought with it a welcomed respite from the constant conflicts—orcs and highwaymen and other such annoyances—that had plagued the area throughout the previous year. Hammer, the first month, had been quite frigid, allowing little melt from the ending snows of 1462, and the second month, aptly nicknamed the Claw of Winter, had come in with a roar, dumping heavy snowfalls across the Silver Marches. Parson Glaive's description of the situation at the Runegate was not an exaggeration, not in the least.

Emerus Warcrown clapped his hands together to get the wood chips and dirt from them, then ran them through his great beard, more gray than yellow now, but still as thick as any beard any dwarf had ever worn. "Can't seem to get the chill from me old bones this day," he said, and he tossed his friend an exaggerated wink. "Bit o' brandy might be needed."

"Aye, a good bit," Parson Glaive happily replied.

Emerus went for his private stock, set in a sturdy decorated cabinet to the side of the comfortable room. He had just grasped the most decorated bottle of all, a thin-necked but wide-bodied flask of Mirabar's best brandy, when the door of his private chamber burst open with a loud bang. Emerus Warcrown dropped the bottle and cried out, "What!" and only caught the bottle again as it crashed against the cabinet's shelf, fortunately without breaking.

"What?" the dwarf king cried again, turning to the door to see a muscular, wild-eyed warrior dwarf jumping around and waving his arms, his face as red as his fiery beard. A myriad of terrible scenarios rushed through the king's thoughts as he considered the newcomer, Reginald Roundshield, or "Arr Arr" as he was more commonly known, Citadel Felbarr's Captain of the Guard.

But those imagined catastrophes faded away as Emerus calmed and considered Arr Arr more carefully, particularly the red-bearded dwarf's supreme grin.

"What'd'ye know?" Emerus demanded.

"A son, me king!" Reginald answered.

"What ho!" cried Parson Glaive. "What ho! But I'll be blessin' that lad in the name o' Clangeddin, or Arr Arr's sure to be whining!"

"Clangeddin's the choice," Reginald confirmed. "Son o' the captain."

"Son o' the line," Emerus Warcrown agreed, and he set three large cups out and began pouring the celebratory brandy, liberally so!

"Me Da was the captain, me Grand Da was the captain, and his Da afore him," Reginald said proudly. "And so's me son to be!"

"Son o' the son o' the son o' the son of a captain, then!" Parson Glaive congratulated, taking his cup from Emerus and hosting it immediately in toast.

"A strappin' big one," Reginald told the others, tapping their glasses hard. "And 'e's full o' fight already, I tell ye!"

"Could'no be any other way," Emerus Warcrown agreed. "Could'no be any other way!"

"And what's his name to be? Same as yer own, then?"

"Aye, both halves, as me Da and his Da and his Da and his Da."

"A little Arr Arr, then!" the king of Felbarr proclaimed, lifting his brandy for another toast, but then he reconsidered and pulled it back down.

Reginald Roundshield and Parson Glaive looked at him curiously.

"Gutbuster?" Emerus Warcrown asked slyly, referring to that most brutal and potent of dwarven beverages.

"What else'd be fittin' for the birth of a Roundshield?" Parson Glaive replied.

The king nodded and looked at his guard commander somberly. "Ye just make sure that meself's about when ye're for givin' little Arr Arr his first sip o' the Gutbuster," he said. "Ah, but I'm wantin' to see the look on the tyke's face!"

"It'll be a look wantin' more," Reginald boasted, and the three laughed again as King Emerus went for his private stash of the potent liquid.

He wasn't prepared for this. How could anyone be properly prepared for this?

Bruenor Battlehammer, twice King of Mithral Hall, lay in a cradle in a dark room in Citadel Felbarr, his baby arms waving, his baby legs kicking, and little of that in his control. It was all too strange, all too weird. He could feel his limbs, was aware of his body, but only vaguely, distantly, as if it was not really his own, but a borrowed thing.

And was it, he wondered, in the few clips of time when he could keep his thoughts straight, for even his brain seemed only partially his to control!

Was this the way it was for babies, then? Were they all like this, strangers in their own forms, lacking more than simple coordination, but an actual path to find that dexterity, as if their little brains had not yet found a way to speak to their own limbs?

Or was it something more, the old baby dwarf feared. Was this a perversion, a theft of another's body, and as such, might the act have damaged the corporeal coil? Would he be ever doomed to flail and gurgle?

A helpless stooge and a fool for leaving the forest as he had, for not continuing on to his just rewards at the side of Moradin!

Bruenor tried to focus, tried to concentrate deeply, calling to his arms to stop their incessant flailing. But he could not, and he knew that something was wrong.

Mielikki's gift was a curse, then, he realized to his horror. This was no blessing, and now he'd suffer out his days—how many years? Two hundred? Three hundred?—as a bumbling fool, a curiosity.

He fought for control.

He failed.

He battled with all of his strength, the willpower of a dwarf king.

He failed.

He felt the frustration bubbling up inside of him, a primal terror that pushed forth a primal scream, and even in that shriek, Bruenor could not control his inflection or timber.

"Ah, me little Reggie," he heard a comforting female voice, and a cherubic dwarf face peered over the edge of his cradle, her smile bright, her expression tired.

Giant hands reached in and so easily lifted Bruenor, guiding him toward a monstrous, huge breast . . .

"Ah, ye brought yer brat," Emerus Warcrown said to his captain of the guard when Reginald Roundshield arrived in the war room, his child strapped into a dwarfling holster on his back.

Reginald grinned at his king. "Can't be havin' me boy layin' about all day. He's much to learn."

"The boy's been breathing for a month," Parson Glaive remarked.

"Aye, should have a sword in his hand by now, I'm thinkin'," said Reginald, and they all laughed some more.

Bouncing around on his father's back, Bruenor was glad to be out of the nursery and the cradle, and his happiness at being brought along only increased when the three dwarves began discussing the political and security situation of the Runegates of Citadel Felbarr.

Bruenor listened intently—for a few moments. But then he thought of eating, because his stomach growled. Then he thought of the itchiness around his backside.

Then he looked at his hand, his chubby little dwarfling hand . . . and a "goo" sound came forth from his saliva-dripping lips.

He tried to remind himself to focus, to listen to this conversation, for it would take him from the immediate needs that seemed so ever-pressing to him. But he found himself lamenting the indignities of his station. He, King Bruenor Battlehammer, was bouncing around helplessly on the back of a guard captain. He, the king of Mithral Hall, had to be fed and changed and bathed and . . .

The baby let out a shriek, one that came from somewhere deep inside and simply bubbled out before Bruenor could even consider it. How he hated this!

" 'Ere now, ye keep yer brat quiet or drop him back on his Ma," Parson Glaive said.

"Bah, not for worryin'," King Emerus said. "Them shrieks'll be battle cries soon enough, and little Arr Arr's got some orc heads to squish."

So they went on with their meeting, and Bruenor tried to listen, hoping to catch up on the events here in the Silver Marches.

But he was hungry, and he was itchy, and his hand was so enticing . . .

"And how long?" Uween Roundshield asked Parson Glaive when he arrived at her house one morning a couple of months later. The Roundshield home was a neat stone affair in the upper level of the Citadel Felbarr complex.

Bruenor perked up his ears and tried to turn around on the blanket his mother Uween had set out on the floor for him. He wanted to get a better look at the speaker, but alas, his little body would barely move to his call and he had to settle for turning his too-big head hard to the side and staring at the cleric out of the very corner of his eye.

"Hard to say," Parson Glaive replied. "The passes're open again, and the orcs been fast to fill 'em."

"Orcs, always orcs!" Uween grumbled. "Many-Arrows, many orcs!"

Those words caused the child on the blanket to wince, and brought great discomfort to the confused sensibilities of Bruenor Battlehammer. Many-Arrows . . . the kingdom of orcs . . . set up by the beast Obould, its existence ratified in a treaty signed by Bruenor himself a century before. Bruenor had spent the rest of his life—his first life at least—wondering if he had erred in signing the peace with Obould. He had never been content with his decision, even though he had been given little choice in the matter. His forces of Mithral Hall could not have defeated Obould's thousands, could not have begun to drive them from the land, and the other kingdoms of the Silver Marches, notably Sundabar and Silverymoon, and even the dwarven citadels of Felbarr and Adbar, had deferred from entering such a war. The price would have been too high, so they all had determined.

And so the Kingdom of Many-Arrows had come to be, and peace had ensued . . . such as it was.

For these were orcs, after all, and the constant incursions of rogue bands had plagued the land throughout the rest of Bruenor's (first) life, and apparently, given the conversation before him now, continued to this day.

"Arr Arr'll put 'em back in their holes," Parson Glaive assured Uween.

"We should be marchin' across the Surbrin, and put 'em down for the dogs they are," Uween replied.

"I'm not for arguin'," said Parson Glaive. "And know that many're grumbling that same song o' late. Too many fights, too many raids. King Obould the Whatever's been telled to put a rein on his underlings, and even Mithral Hall's been sounding that warning."

"Good on Mithral Hall, then, that they might be fixin' the mistake o' their old king . . . ,"

Bruenor's eyes grew moist at that, even when Parson Glaive cut Uween short. "Don't ye be speakin' such things," he said. "A different time, a different world, and King Bruenor signed with the blessing o' Emerus Warcrown himself. Might be that we were all wrong, then. Be sure that our king's never been happy with that long-ago choice."

"Might be," Uween agreed.

Parson Glaive took his leave then, and Uween went about her chores (which included a fair amount of sword play as she put herself back into fighting condition), leaving Bruenor, Little Arr Arr, to his own amusement on the blanketed floor. Soon after, the baby fell asleep.

Images of Garumn's Gorge filled Bruenor's dreams, a quill floating in the air before him, scratching his name on the treaty that bore the place's name.

A gnarled and wart-covered orc hand pulled the quill from the air and Obould—and how clearly Bruenor still pictured that ugly beast!—nearly broke the writing instrument's tip when he dug his own name into the document. The great orc was clearly no more satisfied than Bruenor by this "peace" even though it had been his demand.

Bruenor's thoughts flew away from that place, to his old chambers in Mithral Hall, with Drizzt sitting beside him, assuring him that he had done right by his people and for his legacy.

But had he? Even now, it seemed, a century removed, the doubts remained. Had he done anything more than give the filthy orcs a foothold from which thousands of rogue bands could launch their incessant ambushes?

He tried to think it through, but he could not, for though he was nearly three months old, the pestering demands of a body he could hardly control gnawed at his sensibilities, pulling him from his dreams and then his con-templations to more immediate needs.

"No!" the baby growled, and another memory came to him, washing through him as poignantly as the moment of the experience. He sat on the throne of Gauntlgrym, and the wisdom of Moradin, the strength of Clangeddin, and the mysteries of Dumathoin all were revealed to him and imparted to him.

He was up on his hands and knees then. He tried to curl his toes under to put his feet flat on the floor, but he toppled to the side.

"Ah, but ye finally rolled, did ye?" he heard his mother say, and then she gasped as Bruenor stubbornly forced himself back to his hands and knees.

"Oh, well done!" Uween congratulated. "Ain't yerself the smart . . ."

Her voice fell away, for this time, Bruenor did get his toes properly curled. He felt the power of the Throne coursing through his veins and he pulled himself upright, standing firmly on two feet.

"But how'd ye do that?" Uween cried, and she seemed distressed, and only then did Bruenor realize that he was pushing it too far and too fast. He looked at her, and took care to paint a look of astonishment, even fear, upon his cherubic, beardless face, before falling over to the floor.

Uween was there to grab him up, holding him before her and telling him what a smart and mighty little one he was.

Bruenor almost formed a word then, to tell her that he was hungry, but he wisely remembered his place.

Now he had his focus like never before. Now when he lay in the dark for a nap or the nighttime sleep, Bruenor narrowed his always-jumbled thoughts more keenly, remembering the Throne of the Gods, feeling again the blessing of the mighty three. He should have been lying still, perhaps twitching and half-rolling to get more comfortable, but instead, Bruenor worked his little fingers and his toes, bent his legs and straightened them repeatedly, and worked his jaw, forming words, remembering words, teaching this new body the patterns of speech.

He tried to keep the lingering doubts regarding his previous choices far away, and tried not to even think about the responsibility and oath he had accepted in coming back to this place anew. There would be time for that, years hence. For now, he had to try to simply learn to control this strange body.

Still, he was thrown back into those old doubts and the political morass of who he had once been one afternoon only a tenday later, when King Emerus Warcrown and Parson Glaive arrived at the Roundshield house, their expressions grave.

Bruenor couldn't hear the conversation, for they spoke low to Uween over by the door, but her sudden cry of denial said it all.

King Emerus and Parson Glaive each grabbed her under an arm and helped her in to the table and to a seat.

"He fought as a Roundshield ought," King Emerus assured her. "The orcs were piled around him, breaked to bits."

"Aye, a great warrior was Arr Arr," said Parson Glaive.

"Reginald," a now-composed Uween corrected. "Reginald Roundshield, o' the Felbarr Roundshields, the son of a son of a son of a captain."

"Aye," the other two agreed in unison, and all three turned to regard the baby on the floor, and Bruenor felt their sympathy keenly.

"To Little Arr Arr, then," he heard the king of Felbarr say, but distantly, for Bruenor's thoughts were spinning back to Garumn's Gorge, to his choice, to his doubts.

"Son of a son of a son of a son of a captain," Emerus Warcrown decreed. "For one day he'll be leadin' the guard o' Felbarr, don't ye doubt!"

With the spinning jumble of unformed sensibilities, the overwhelming nature of everything in his newborn life, Bruenor felt the overwhelming urge to cry roaring up inside of him.

But he went into his past, to the Throne of the Gods, and he denied that.

He remembered then that he was the king.

CHAPTER 5

PLANETOUCHED

The Year of the Reborn Hero (1463 DR)
Delthuntle

Regis walked out of Iruladoon and into the blinding light with sure and determined strides. His resolve was no less than that of Catti-brie, who took this journey as a matter of faith and devotion to her goddess, Mielikki.

For Regis, it was the second chance that he dearly, desperately wanted. For so long had he been the tag-along, the one to be rescued instead of the heroic rescuer. He couldn't help but believe that he had ever been the weak link in the chain that formed the Companions of the Hall.

No more, he decided.

Not this time around.

He was holding Catti-brie's hand, and then he was not. He was in the springtime forest, and then he was not.

He was walking, and then he was floating.

He was up among the stars, it seemed, with the world, all white and brown and so much blue turning below him, and he felt free, freer than he had ever been in his corporeal days, freer than anything he had ever known. At that moment, swallowed by the celestial spheres, Regis felt as if he could float and swim forevermore and be perfectly content.

The world grew larger—that was how he perceived it until he realized that he was falling, diving back into the sphere of Toril, and he was not afraid. He saw the outlines of the great land of Faerûn, of the Sword Coast that he had sailed many times and knew well, of the lands of the Silver Marches and then an inland sea, a vast great lake, with jagged coastlines of jutting peninsulas and long harbors.

Into the water he went, and it did not feel to him as if he was swimming, or submerged, but rather as if he had joined with the substance, had become as liquid himself, flowing breezily through the wash with barely an effort.

He reveled in the journey, excited by the elemental domain. He guessed this to be another gift of Mielikki, because he was unaware of his genetic heritage, unaware that he was venturing the long roots of his rebirth. He expected that his two companions were similarly soaring, but he was wrong, for this was his journey alone, a particular added touch to the halfling he would become.

Darkness enveloped him, dark and soft walls pressing against him tightly, holding his arms close to his chest. Still he felt as if he was deep within the liquid of the Inner Sea, and his own heartbeat reverberated in his ears.

Ka-thump.

No, not his own heartbeat, he realized to his horror and his comfort, all at once.

He was in the womb.

The heart was his mother's heart—or would this female be considered his surrogate mother? He could not be sure, could not sort it out. Not then, not there, for there was only the impulse, the urge to struggle and twist until he was free. The walls worked around him, nudging him, twisting him, pushing him, bidding him to find his escape.

The heartbeat grew more intense, louder and faster, louder and faster.

He heard the calls of the outside world, a cry of pain, a plea from a deeper voice.

"Don't you go!"

The flesh walls pressed in on him, squeezing him, urging him. He flailed and worked furiously, recognizing this as the moment of his birth, and knowing, instinctively and reflexively, that he had to get out.

The heartbeat intensified. Another scream sounded from afar, followed by more frantic pleas and cries.

Ka-thump. Ka-thump.

The muscles pressed, squeezing him more tightly.

Ka-thump. Ka-thump.

He could sense that it was too tight, too intense, the cries too desperate.

Ka-thump. Ka-thump.

Another cry. Something was amiss, he sensed.

Silence.

Darkness.

The flesh walls did not contort around him.

He reached and clawed, unable to draw breath. He tried to squirm and fight, but he could not. He got one arm up high, over his head.

He felt the bite of a blade, but he could not cry out, and his arm slid back before him, a coppery taste filling the watery tomb around him.

But then it was opened, peeling apart before him at the edge of a sliding knife, and he was pulled free, hoisted from his womb, his tomb, and roughly spun around and thumped hard upon his back. He sputtered and gagged, then coughed and cried. He could not help but cry, terrified, confused.

In that jumbled moment, he didn't know, didn't understand, that his new mother was dead.

He felt the bugs crawling over him, but could not coordinate his little arms enough to swat at them.

An annoyance, he told himself repeatedly though the days and dark nights, for these were merely bedbugs and cockroaches and the like, the same insects he had suffered in Calimport. In truth, the insects were the least troubling of the surroundings the baby Regis found. He couldn't move much—even his head was too heavy for him to swivel it around while laying on his back—but he had noted enough of the ramshackle abode to realize that his new family, which seemed to be comprised of only himself and his father, was perfectly destitute.

This wasn't even a house, not even a shack, but merely a piling of sticks, a lean-to in a decrepit part of some dirty city. A wet nurse tended to his needs, but only arrived sparingly, twice a day by his count, leaving him to lie in his own waste, leaving his belly to growl with hunger, leaving the bugs to crawl around him.

He could see the sky above through the openings in the hastily piled boards, and noted that it was almost always gray. Or perhaps that was a trick of his young eyes, still trying to find some focus and clarity.

But it did rain quite often, he knew, the water dripping in upon him.

If he had been wearing clothes, they would always have been wet.

He lay there one morning, drizzle coating him so that his skin glistened in the diffused daylight, trying hard to get his hand to slap a particularly annoying gnat aside, when a loud crash alerted him that he was not alone.

His father came up beside him, towering over him as he lay in his makeshift crib, which was no more than a piece of old wood with beams piled along its sides to prevent him from rolling off.

Regis studied the man carefully, his dirty face, his missing teeth, his glassy eyes and scraggly hair. The years had broken this one, though he was not very old, the baby who was not a baby realized. He had seen this before, so many times, on the streets of Calimport in his first youth, some century-and-a-half removed. The constant struggle for basic needs, the helplessness, with no way to escape and no place to escape to; it was all there, etched indelibly on the face of this halfling standing over him, in lines of sadness and helpless frustration.

Surprisingly strong hands reached down to grab Regis and he was easily hoisted from his bed.

"Here's to hoping you're your mother's son," the halfling said, bringing Regis against his shoulder and moving swiftly out of the house.

Regis got his first view of the city then, and it was a large place, with rows of shacks and shanties stacked before the high-walled lines of more respectable houses. One hill, far off, sported a castle. His father turned onto a board-walk, leading downward from their position, and rambled along for many, many steps, through turns and down stairs, along some more declines. Few buildings were to be seen around the raised planks, and those were merely ramshackle and simple things.

Soon there were birds all around them, everywhere, flying and diving and squawking noisily, and it took Regis some time to recognize that these were water birds, mostly, and indeed, it wasn't until this halfling he presumed to be his father turned down yet another long and declining way that Regis came to understand this boardwalk as a long wharf, and this city a port—though, strangely, a port built far from the water's edge.

And what a grand ocean it was, he noted at one turn, catching a glimpse of seemingly endless waves. He thought of Luskan or Baldur's Gate, Waterdeep or Calimport, but this city wasn't any of those. Still, they were traveling west, he knew from the sun in the sky, and so he figured this must be the Sword Coast.

He didn't smell any salt in the air, though.

They moved down to the shore, a small beach tucked between a variety of smaller wharves and boardwalks. Many boats bobbed in the waters around them. A human couple threw an oft-repaired net out into the surf. Another halfling dug for shellfish in the sand at water's edge.

His father splashed into the water, up to his waist.

"Breathe deep, runt," he said, and to Regis's shock, he flipped Regis around from his shoulder and plunged him under the water!

The baby squirmed and thrashed for all he was worth, for his very life!

Futilely, of course, for this tiny, uncoordinated, little-muscled form could not begin to counter the strength in the elder halfling's hands. Reflexively, Regis held his breath, but he could not for long, and the bubbles came forth from his lips. He tried to hold out, fought to keep his mouth shut.

His father was drowning him!

All of the dreams that had carried him out of Iruladoon flashed through his thoughts then. He had imagined the Companions of the Hall rejoined, and this time, he had sworn, he would not be the tag-along, the helpless soul hiding in the back of the battle. No, he would become an equal in the coming trials, and would fight bravely to save Drizzt from the darkness Catti-brie had hinted of, from the clutches of Lady Lolth, perhaps!

But now he wouldn't.

His little mouth opened and the sea rushed in. He tried not to swallow, not to gasp, but alas, he could not resist.

As he could not break free of his father's iron grip.

So he would find his final reward, as surely as if he had gone with Wulfgar into the pond. Before he had even been given a chance to prove his worth, it would all be over.

And he would not see his friends again, unless it was in the Green Fields . . .

"Is that Eiverbreen?" asked a halfling working on the dock not far away.

"Aye," answered his dwarf companion. "Eiverbreen and his new runt. Pity that Jolee passed in birthing him."

"Aye."

"So, eh, what's that then? Eiverbreen's set on killin' the waif? Ah, but who could blame him, and the little one's better off anyway."

"Nay, not that," the halfling answered, and he paused in his work and moved to the near edge of the dock, watching the scene more closely. His dwarf friend followed, hands on hips, neither harboring any intent to interfere, whether this was indeed infanticide or something else.

Regis came out of the water as abruptly as he had been thrust in, his father twirling him up and spinning him around to look him in the eye. The little one sputtered and spat, water flowing out of him as easily as it had gone in.

His father, who had just tried to kill him, smiled.

"Not blue," he said with a hoarse laugh. "Aye, so you're your mother's son. By the gods, but luck's with you, ain't it? It's our secret, you know, and you're to make a fine wage!"

With that, he tucked Regis under his arm and headed back up the long, long boardwalk, back to the lean-to.

The baby's thoughts spun in confusion. What had that been about? To torture him? To terrify him? To make him think he was being drowned, being murdered? But to what end? What possible gain . . . ?

Regis forced himself to calm down, forced the pulsing questions aside.

He hadn't drowned—in truth, he hadn't come close to drowning and had felt no physical discomfort at all beyond the strong and tight grip of his father's hands.

But he had been under the water for a long time. He couldn't keep holding his breath. He couldn't keep his mouth closed, couldn't keep the water away.

But he wasn't blue, his father had just told him, and indeed, when he had come up from the water, he hadn't even been gasping for air.

Was this all the result of his young age, as if, perhaps, his mind couldn't yet even acknowledge such discomfort? That seemed a possibility, but Regis didn't think it likely. No, more likely, it seemed to him that he hadn't registered any discomfort because there hadn't been any discomfort.

How was that possible?

He clutched tightly at his father's raggedy shirt as he considered the mystery. He felt something round and hard in his little hand, and gripped it instinctively, and only as they neared their home did he even realize it to be a button.

A button held by a single thread, he realized as he worked it around, and as his father moved to set him back down in his crib, he tightened his grip and pulled with all his strength.

The button came free, and Regis took care to keep his hand closed over it.

"So you've got the genasi blood," his father said, though Regis had no idea of what that might even mean. "That'll make you worth keeping, lucky runt. Like your Ma. Aye, but we'll put that gift to work!"

54

He walked away then, out of the lean-to.

Regis didn't understand any of this, of course, but he told himself to be patient. The one thing he had now, Mielikki willing, for all of his plans, was time. Lots of time, but not time enough to be wasted.

Twenty-one years of time, and he would put them to good use. As he had determined when he had walked out of Iruladoon, he would waste not a day.

He managed to lift his little hand up before his eyes, and opened his fingers just enough to see the button. He thought to roll it around his fingers, but an involuntary twitch jerked his arm then, and he nearly lost the item.

If it fell free, he would have no way to collect it . . . likely a rat would pick it up and scurry off with it.

So he squeezed it instead, repeatedly, training his fingers, training his muscles, and slowly maneuvering one finger or another around it a bit, gaining strength, gaining dexterity. He held it tightly when the wet nurse came to feed him, then he brought his arm down to his side and leaned upon it to secure the button as he slept.

Days later, he managed to shift it to his other hand, his left hand. Again, he brought it up before his eyes, and then he paused and stared.

He noted his thumb and the three fingers beside it, and the stump where his pinky should be.

The image jolted the halfling back in time, to the captivity he had endured under Artemis Entreri, where Entreri had cut off his finger as a warning to Drizzt . . .

Had that physical wound carried over to this new body? How could that be?

He stared at the stump, and noted then the jagged line of skin and the scab, not yet fully healed. No, this was not a carryover of Entreri's cruelty, he realized, but an ironic twist of fate. He recalled the moment of his rebirth, when his mother had died, he now understood, and so the midwife had used a knife to slice her open and get him out. He remembered the sharp and burning pain, and now he understood the source.

For a long, long while, the halfling baby lay there, staring at the wound, lost in memories more than in his current hopes and aspirations.

He pressed beyond the shock, though, and repeated the exercises, exactly as he had done with the other hand, squeezing and holding, building his strength and his muscle memory.

Tendays later, he began to roll the button around his fingers, one hand and then the other, feeling the play as it rolled over one knuckle to be caught between that finger and the next and rolled again. Back and forth, pinky-to-thumb, thumb-to-pinky, on his right hand, thumb-to-ring finger, ring finger-to-thumb on the left.

Hand-to-hand.

He could almost feel the connections forming in his little brain and muscles, as indeed they were, so that he became attuned to his fingers and to the subtle muscle movements controlling each.

Some time later, he could not guess how many days or even tendays had passed, his father came for him and took him again to the small beach between the docks.

Under the waves he went, until the bubbles came forth and the water rushed in. He tried to mentally count the passage of time until he was hoisted out and shaken, only to be thrust back in soon after.

"You'll find the deeps," his father said on one lift, then thrust him back under.

"Where the oysters rest," his father added on the next lift.

"A master diver, as your Ma!" the dirty and bedraggled halfling declared, and under the waves Regis went once more.

This time for longer, much longer. He lost count of his heartbeats, lost all sense of time around him. Only gradually did he feel the need for air, and it was not an urgent sensation, as if he were drowning, but more a desire.

Many more heartbeats passed before his father lifted him once more. The elder halfling inspected him carefully, then issued a belly laugh, clearly pleased as he declared, "Not blue in the face!"

CHAPTER 6

THE CHOSEN

The Year of the Reborn Hero (1463 DR)
Netheril

No moment of fear, not an instant of doubt, followed Catti-brie out of Iruladoon. In the days she had spent there—the century on Toril— she had danced the movements of Mielikki and sung the song of Mielikki, and so it was with great understanding of the goddess and great confidence in the eternal circle of life itself, that Catti-brie had stepped from the forest to begin her floating journey, to find the womb, to gasp her first breath in her new body, reincarnated, reborn. It happened on the night of the spring equinox.

The holy night of Mielikki, the night of the birth of the goddess's Chosen.

Wrapped in swaddling clothes, the infant seemed fully helpless before the adult humans milling around in the tent. But even though she could not move her arms under the tight wrappings, Catti-brie instinctively understood that there remained at her disposal several potent spells she could utilize to defend herself, dweomers that needed no movements to enact.

Unlike her friends who had similarly journeyed from Iruladoon, Catti-brie had taken no infantile confusion with her. The instincts of childhood gnawed at her, of course, but because of her communing with the goddess, she was better prepared for this journey by far, and more knowledgeable and thus able to keep those penetrating pangs and desires in their proper place.

Good fortune had followed her, as well, for her mother—she heard the name Kavita spoken tenderly by her father and others—doted on her, lifting her often and holding her close. That is, when Kavita wasn't passing the baby around to the other women who flocked to the Bedine tent, all wanting to cuddle with the newborn. To the Bedine tribe of the Desai, the birth of a child was a grand celebration indeed, and Catti-brie—Ruqiah, they called her—was the center of that play.

She wisely held silent throughout the pawing and the cooing and the continual conversations directed at her, just inches from her face, for she understood well what had happened to Wulfgar when he had been reborn, and feared that she, too, could forget herself and spout some actual words.

And so, like her journey in the first phases of her departure from Iruladoon, the baby who was really a woman lay back and observed, and let the beauty of the experience grant her insight and more knowledge. Many times in those first days, did Catti-brie silently give extra thanks to Mielikki.

Only a few days later, the tribe was on the move again, Catti-brie, swaddled tightly as always, strapped to her walking mother's back. She strained her eyes, focusing on the land as the miles rolled by, trying to get a feel for where she might be.

Patient and observant, the baby learned and watched, and when she was alone in the dark of night, she prayed and she practiced, perfecting her little voice so that she could again sing the notes of Mielikki. She regretted the tight binding of the cloth wrapped around her, though, and feared that it would take her some time to properly perfect control of her arms and legs.

But she had time, she reminded herself.

◖◗

"She's beautiful," Kavita said to Niraj as she stood by Ruqiah's cradle. The night outside was dark and quiet—even the wind seemed to have drifted off to sleep. "But her eyes are so blue! How can that be?"

"They will darken with age," Niraj assured her. "As did mine."

"And so her hair will fall out?" Kavita asked, teasing her bald-headed husband.

"No," he said, moving near and placing his hand gently on Kavita's bare shoulder, and feeling, as he did, the raised skin of her long scar. He bent in and kissed her there, on the shoulder blade, where she had been marked so dramatically by the whip of a Netherese enforcer who had heard a whispered rumor that Kavita was practicing magic.

That one had learned the hard way that Kavita was indeed a wizard, and so was her husband, Niraj, who had laid the man low with a bolt of lightning.

58

How pathetic the brutal enforcer had seemed then, trying to work his arm and snap his whip from his back in the sand—Sand Kavita's spell had then dug out from under him, and which had been abruptly put back, only now atop him, burying him alive, by the subsequent enchantment of Niraj and Kavita.

"She will have the thick tresses of her mother, I am sure," Niraj added, running his hand through Kavita's hair. He could feel the tension within his wife. "What troubles you, my love?"

"The Netherese are everywhere," Kavita said. "With every pilgrimage, there are more to be seen, shadowing us from the hills, stopping and inspecting and questioning, always questioning."

"They are sand crabs," Niraj agreed, "who came uninvited to our land. Our land I say, and we will be here long after they are gone, when the winds of Anauroch return and the land of Netheril is long forgotten!"

"By then, we'll be long forgotten," Kavita replied.

"But our descendants . . . ," Niraj replied, nodding his chin toward their baby girl.

"We must take care, special care," Kavita said. "For Ruqiah, more than for ourselves."

Niraj didn't disagree. They were wizards, but secretly so, for the Netherese rulers of this land had forbidden the Bedine to practice the Art.

Kavita looked around, left and right, then focused her gaze on the tent flap for a few moments, holding silent and craning her neck, listening for any intruders. With a glance at her husband, she bent over the cradle and unfastened the ties, loosening the swaddling cloth. She pushed the fabric aside and pulled forth Ruqiah's bare left arm, lifting it a bit and turning it so that the meager candlelight would reflect off the inside of her forearm.

Niraj sucked in his breath. He had seen the birthmark before—or at least, had seen what he hoped was a birthmark.

But now there could be no doubt, for this was no ordinary birthmark. A distinct figure, resembling a seven-pointed star, was set in a circular field of red.

"Spellscar?" Niraj asked, seeming confused, for he had not heard of one quite this distinct before.

Kavita pulled out the baby's other arm and turned it to reveal the inside of the forearm, where a second marking loomed.

"A curved blade?" Niraj asked, and peered closer. "Nay, a horn, a unicorn's head! She is twice-marked?"

"And her scars will be harder to conceal."

"She should wear them with pride!" Niraj insisted.

"The Netherese would not agree."

"Damn them! We are Bedine, not chattel!"

Kavita put her finger over her husband's lips to silence him. "Be at ease, my husband," she quietly coaxed. "We are free upon our land. Let us not be bound by our hatred for those who claim dominance. Claim, but do not truly hold us in chains."

Niraj nodded and kissed his wife, and pulled her across the room to their bed.

Little Ruqiah opened her eyes, having heard every word. They had not rewound the cloth around her and so for one of the rare times in her young life, her arms were free. She took the opportunity to flex them and move them, and felt indeed as if a great weight had at last been lifted from her. She managed to get both of her little arms into view long enough to study that which her parents had discussed.

The images, the scars, brought her back to a morning long ago, when she had awakened in her tent beside her husband Drizzt. They were on their way back to Mithral Hall, unaware of the great changes that were even then beginning to befall their world.

On that fateful day, Catti-brie had been struck by a falling strand of Mystra's magical Weave, the Weave of Magic itself, and the blinding power of magical energy bared had overwhelmed her and driven her mad.

The Weave of Mystra, the Lady of Magic, who carried as her symbol the seven-pointed star.

She had not recovered from that interaction, and indeed, had inadvertently afflicted Regis with the insanity as well. In that confused state, Catti-brie had passed away, and Mielikki had taken her spirit from Mithral Hall.

She looked at her right forearm, at the horn, the unicorn horn symbol of Mielikki, and gave thanks and praise, her blue eyes filling with tears of joy.

The Year of the Six-Armed Elf (1464 DR)
Netheril

Ruqiah sat in the corner, pretending to play with the polished stones Niraj had given to her. It had been a long first year of life anew, full of deception that had greatly wearied this imposter child. She had crawled early, the Bedine believed, at only five months, and had walked before her tenth month, and quite capably, it seemed. In truth, the baby could have climbed from her crib a month after her birth, stood up and paced around the house with little trouble. In fact, she had done just that one quiet night, and had spent every moment she was not wrapped in swaddling cloth testing and strengthening her infant limbs.

She hadn't talked yet, though she had much to say, and she wasn't even sure of when such conversation might be appropriate, for in her previous life, Catti-brie hadn't had much contact with children.

She knew it was important to seem somewhat appropriate to her age, both for her own sake and for that of her parents, whom she had already come to love as if they were actually her family.

Catti-brie had learned much in the year she had spent as Ruqiah. The Bedine were prisoners in their own land, this land that had been Anauroch, but was now known as Netheril, the heart of Netherese power. These conquering Netherese would not suffer Bedine to be more than simple tribesmen and nomads, wandering the wasted ways of the still barren and windblown lands that had once been the great magical desert of northern Faerûn.

Her outward appearances aside, Catti-brie was not a simple one-year-old child, and could not be. She had been studying the ways of arcane magic when the falling strands of Mystra's Weave had assailed her in her previous life, and her time in Iruladoon, dancing and singing to the song of Mielikki, had given her greater insights into the magic she had previously known, and had also, of course, taught her how to call for the divine magic of the goddess who had come to hold her so close. Such skills required practice and repetition, as surely as the movements a warrior might make to defend and thrust forth his weapon.

The little girl watched her parents carefully. Niraj left the tent, and Kavita was busy repairing some weapons—how ironic it was for Catti-brie to see the woman glancing around nervously, then calling upon some magic of her own to help her in mending the blade of a curving sword.

Ironic, because her child was doing the same thing in the corner of the same room. Catti-brie held each of the polished stones close to her breast and whispered into them, imbuing them with symbols that only she could see with an enchantment she had cast upon herself. These invisible markings turned the stones into a sort of oracle, and the child began casting them forth, silently asking questions.

With the stones providing guidance.

She studied one answer for a long while, not really trusting what her magically enhanced eyes were telling her. It seemed too dangerous.

She collected the stones and asked again, then tossed them out before her. The same response was given.

Catti-brie nodded. She would find a way.

That very night, her parents asleep across the room, Catti-brie cast an enchantment around the room, one designed to compel sleep. A bluish mist curled around her left arm with the magical enactment, but while it startled Catti-brie, she did not fear it. She slipped from the crib and quietly padded out of the tent on little bare feet.

The camp was asleep. Somewhere out on the dusty plain, a wolf howled and was answered.

The little girl was not afraid—certainly she did not feel threatened by any of Mielikki's animal children. She moved past the tents and out into the wastes, following the path the oracle stones had shown to her.

That night, in a secret and sheltered clearing, she planted her first garden shrine to the goddess. She returned to the place often, always at night, and when the tribe moved on, as was their way, the girl created another garden shrine, and another after that. In these sanctified places, hidden amongst the rocks, Catti-brie found Mielikki more keenly, and was taught about the land, this land.

A land that had been, not so long ago, a great desert.

A land that would be, not so long hence, a desert once more.

The Year of the First Circle (1468 DR)
Netheril

Soaking wet from the downpour, her hair still muddy from being thrown by Tahnood into the mud pit, five-year-old Catti-brie stood defensively in front of her fallen mother, her eyes glowing fiercely, the blue strands of magic wafting out of the sleeves of her torn sarong like living serpents.

She noted the boots of the Netherese assassin, smoke wafting from them. Her lightning bolt had jolted the man violently into the air, so abruptly and powerfully that he had left his shoes behind!

She shivered, humbled and overwhelmed by the power she had

created—nay, not created, she realized, but by the power she had been allowed to access through the magic of her spellscar.

She wanted to turn back and enact more healing magic on Kavita, but she didn't dare. Not yet. The immediate threat was no more, obviously, for the two Netherese assassins were surely dead, their smoking, lifeless husks lying motionless, the entire front section of the tent torn away behind them.

She prepared another spell, reaching up once more to the thunderstorm she had earlier conjured, ready to pull more lightning from it to vanquish any new enemies that might appear. The view of the encampment lay open before her now, the flashes of lightning above showing the tents and baskets and piled supplies in stark detail.

"Ruqiah!" Niraj cried, sliding into view and skidding to a stop in the mud just outside the opening. He danced around, turning circles, clearly overwhelmed as he surveyed the scene. "Kavita!"

Catti-brie waved her arms, dissipating the streams of magical blue energy, as Niraj stumbled in, scrambling past the Netherese bodies, half-running, half-diving to get to his daughter and wife.

Other Desai appeared outside, rushing around the corners of nearby tents.

Catti-brie wasn't sure what to do. How could she begin to explain this scene before her? What might the tribal elders think, and what danger would she be creating for them all, given her secret identity?

All of those questions swirled around in her thoughts, slamming at her sensibilities, demanding immediate action. The woman kept her wits and used her decades of experience, forcing herself to remember the primary question: what would a five-year-old girl do?

She began to wail.

Niraj wrapped her in a hug, but pulled her down with him as he fell over Kavita. The woman stirred as he touched her.

"Assassins," she whispered.

"What happened? My Kavita!"

Other members of the tribe milled around the destroyed entryway, shaking their heads and mumbling.

"Girl, what is this?" one man called to Ruqiah. He picked up a smoking boot, staring incredulously.

"They hurt Ma," the child blurted. Between sniffles she continued, "They wanted gold. They said they would hurt me if I didn't get it."

"What gold?" Niraj asked, and he helped Kavita turn over, the woman groaning and dropping a hand over her bloody wound—bloody, Niraj noted, but not bleeding.

Ruqiah shrugged and began to cry again. "The thunder hit them," she said innocently, pointing to the sky and wearing an expression to show that she did not understand.

"The blessing of the storm is twofold this night," remarked one of the women outside.

"Netherese," a man inspecting the smaller body said. "Netherese thieves."

"N'asr take them, then," declared another, referring to the merciless god of the dead.

"He laughs with At'ar in their coupling," a woman said. "Or perhaps he was sated enough for this one moment to take the time to kill these dogs!"

Kavita sat up then, although Niraj tried to keep her still. The gentle Bedine woman stared at her daughter intently.

"What is it?" Niraj whispered to her, but she hushed him and shook her head. She brought her hand down her back to the wound, and continued to simply stare at Ruqiah.

And more particularly, at her little hands, Catti-brie realized, for they were covered in Kavita's blood from when she had healed the wound. She brought them down to her sides sheepishly and cried all the louder.

"Search the camp!" one large man ordered. "There may be other assassins about."

Catti-brie had to sort it all out quickly, she knew, for the questions would only grow about what had actually happened, particularly when Kavita's wound was more carefully inspected. The little girl put her head against Niraj's shoulder, and very close to Kavita's face.

"I will explain everything when we are alone," she said, in a somber tone no girl her age would ever use, and her parents stared at her all the more incredulously and wide-eyed then.

Niraj grabbed her hard at the elbow. "Ruqiah? What do you know?"

Catti-brie looked at him with sympathy, fully aware that she was about to shatter his conceptions of the world around him, and worse, those conceptions that he held for his beloved family.

"Good fortune saved us," she whispered to Niraj, and motioned behind him, for the chieftain of the Desai was approaching. She repeated more loudly and with great emphasis, "Good fortune."

She went back to her mother's embrace, as Niraj turned to talk to the man. Niraj was truly shaken, but he relayed Ruqiah's explanation, offered with the weight of a magical suggestion behind it, that good fortune alone had saved his wife and child.

The chieftain looked around, shaking his head. "Are you well, Kavita?" he asked, and the woman nodded and climbed shakily to her feet.

"A twice-blessed storm, then," the chieftain said, and he went outside to join in the scouring of the encampment.

In the ensuing hours, many came to help Niraj repair and clean the tent. Many more came with salves and herbs to the aid of Kavita, and to Ruqiah, offering calming words and assurances. The storm—magically conjured, though only Ruqiah knew that—had long blown away, and the night had passed its midpoint before the family was at last left alone.

Niraj and Kavita stared at their little girl.

"Ruqiah?" Niraj asked her repeatedly.

Catti-brie considered whether she should dispel him of that moniker, but decided against it. Not now. She had her own nagging questions to deal with, after all, concerning the unexpected arrival of these Netherese. The assassins had come looking for her in particular, so it seemed obvious that they had learned at least part of the truth of her. But how? And why would they care?

"She healed me," Kavita said. "My wound . . . it was mortal."

"No, you were lucky," Niraj replied. "The sword did not bite deeply."

"It did," Kavita insisted, and she looked at Ruqiah, directing Niraj to do likewise. "From back to belly, and I felt my spirit departing. The wound was mortal, but then I felt the healing warmth."

"The gift of Mielikki," their child told them.

"You healed her?" Niraj asked, and Catti-brie nodded.

"The lightning strike was no accident," the child admitted.

Niraj and Kavita sat across from her, staring, unblinking.

The young girl pulled up her sleeves. "The stars of Mystra, the horn of Mielikki," she explained. "I am twice-scarred, but this you knew."

Niraj swallowed hard, Kavita began to cry. "Who are you?" her father asked, and surely those words, that desperate tone, stabbed at Catti-brie's heart.

"I am Ruqiah, your daughter," she answered.

"Mielikki?" the tribesman asked, shaking his head helplessly. The Bedine did not worship Mielikki. Their goddess was At'ar the Merciless, the Yellow Goddess of the scorching desert sun. "I do not understand."

"I was born on the spring equinox, Mielikki's most holy day," the child explained. "The goddess blesses me, and teaches me—"

"At'ar," Kavita corrected.

Catti-brie shook her head. "Come with me," she bade them, starting for the makeshift tent flap. "I will show you."

Her parents hesitated.

"There is a place, not too far from the camp—"

"It is high night," Niraj replied. "The time of N'asr. The lions are out and hunting."

The child laughed. "They will not bother us. Come."

When her parents still hesitated, she added, pleaded, "Please, do this for me. I must show you."

Niraj and Kavita looked to each other, then rose and followed their little girl out of the tent, out of the encampment, and onto the open plain. Catti-brie led them at a great pace, but they hadn't gone far before Kavita rushed up and grabbed her child by the arm to stop her.

"It's too dangerous," she said. "We will come back when the sun goddess has returned."

"Trust me," Catti-brie said. Again there was magic behind her words. And on they went.

They came to the high dune before sunrise, though the sky was beginning to lighten with its approach. Through a narrow entrance between wind-blown rocks, they came into Catti-brie's secret garden, only to find one of their tribesmen lying dead beneath the lone tree, face down in a pool of his own blood.

"Jhinjab," Niraj said, turning the dead man over.

Catti-brie kneeled beside Niraj.

"No, child," Kavita said. "This is not a sight for young girl."

But Catti-brie was not a young girl, nor was she listening. She had already fallen into spellcasting, blue tendrils of magic beginning to creep from her right sleeve as she called upon the power of Mielikki. She put her head close to Jhinjab's chest and whispered something her parents could not hear, then nodded as if receiving an answer.

Niraj stepped back, and Kavita took his arm, standing very close to him, both watching their little daughter with confusion and more than a little bit of horror.

A few moments later, Catti-brie stood up and turned to face them.

"Jhinjab betrayed me to the Netherese," she explained. "They came for me."

"No!" Kavita cried.

"How? Why?" Niraj said at the same time, both moving forward to embrace their daughter, who managed to stay away from them.

"They learned that I am different, spellscarred, perhaps, but certainly . . . unusual," she explained. "Jhinjab told them this. He just admitted as much to me, though the words of the dead are ever cryptic and not easily deciphered."

"This is madness," Niraj wailed.

"You spoke with the dead?" Kavita asked at the same time.

"I am a disciple of Mielikki," Catti-brie explained. "I am blessed with powers divine and arcane—not unlike either of you in the latter, though my spells date to a time long lost and to a goddess who is no more, I fear."

Both of her parents were shaking their heads in confusion. They looked to each other helplessly.

"I am your daughter," Catti-brie said to try to calm them. "I am Ruqiah, but I am more than that. I am not cursed—quite the opposite!"

"The way you speak . . . ," Kavita said, shaking her head.

"I am a child in body only," Catti-brie replied. She considered going further with her explanation, but changed her mind, thinking that she would be bringing pain to these two, who certainly did not deserve it. Nor did she wish to endanger them, and it seemed obvious that knowledge could bring great peril.

As could simple association she realized. She didn't know why the Netherese were after her, of course, but they were, as the assassin had claimed and as the spirit of Jhinjab had just confirmed. Perhaps it was simply a matter of their ban on the Bedine using magic, and Jhinjab had betrayed her in that regard alone. But even then, attention to her would bring attention of Niraj and Kavita.

Unwanted attention.

Dangerous attention.

Catti-brie wanted to go to her altar and pray to Mielikki. She looked to the tree and winced. No, she realized, not to pray. She wanted to go there and have Mielikki tell her that she was wrong in what her instincts were telling her.

But she was not wrong.

"I must leave you," she heard herself saying.

Kavita wailed.

"You cannot!" Niraj cried at her. "You are just a baby—"

"I will find you again, I promise," Catti-brie said. "But I'm in danger here."

"You cannot know that!" Kavita insisted.

"But I do, and so do you. And I put you in danger—all of the Desai in danger. And so I must go, and if the Netherese come looking for me, tell them the truth—it matters not. For they will not find me."

"No, my Zibrija!" Niraj cried, coming forward.

Catti-brie held up her hand, and enacted a simple spell, one that stopped Niraj in his tracks as surely as if he had walked into a mountainside.

"I leave you with this," said the child who was not a child. "Take heart, for you and all the Bedine. The old ways will return to Anauroch. The Yellow Goddess, who is Amaunator, who is Lathander, will return in all her glory, and desert sands will devour Netheril. This I foresee, and the Bedine will live once more as they had for centuries before the return of the archwizards.

"Fear not for me, my parents," she went on. "I go with the goddess, and my road is well-known to me. We will meet again."

The two continued to plead with her, and tried to come forward, but this time, Catti-brie used another spell to hold them at bay. She spun and she sang, and her waving arms became wings and her form became that of an owl.

And away she flew, silently into the desert night.

PART TWO

THE CHILDHOOD PURPOSE

The world moves along outside the purview or influence of my personal experience. To return to Icewind Dale is to learn that the place has continued, with new people replacing those who are gone, through immigration and emigration, birth and death. Some are descendants of those who lived here before, but in this transient place of those who flee the boundaries of polite society, many, many more are those who have come here anew from other lands.

Similarly, new buildings have arisen, while others have fallen. New boats replace those which have been surrendered to the three great lakes of the area.

There is a reason and logic to the place and a wondrous harmony. In Icewind Dale, it all makes sense. The population of Ten-Towns grows and shrinks, but mostly remains stable to that which the region can support.

This is an important concept in the valuation of the self, for far too many people seem oblivious to the implications of this most basic truth: The world continues outside of their personal experience. Oh, perhaps they do not consciously express such a doubt of this obvious truth, but I have met more than one who has postulated that this existence is a dream—his dream—and the rest of us, therefore, are mere components within the reality of his creation. Indeed, I have met many who act that way, whether they have thought it out to that level of detail or not.

I speak, of course, of empathy, or in the cases stated, of the lack thereof. We are in constant struggle, the self and the community, where in our hearts we need to decide where one line ends and another begins. For some, this is a matter of religion, the unquestioned edicts of a professed god or gods, but for most, I would hope, it is a realization of the basic truth that the community, the society, is a needed component in the preservation of the self, both materially and spiritually.

I have considered this many times before and professed my belief in community. Indeed, it was just that belief that stood me up again when I was beaten down with grief, when I led my newfound companions out of Neverwinter to serve the greater good of a worthy place called Port Llast. This, to me, is not a difficult choice; to serve the community is to serve the self. Even Artemis Entreri, that most cynical of creatures, could hardly disguise the sense of satisfaction he felt when we pushed the sea devils back under the surf for the good of the goodly folk of Port Llast.

As I consider my own roots and the various cultures through which I have passed, however, there is a more complicated question: What is the role of the community to the self? And what of the smaller communities within the larger? What are their roles or their responsibilities?

Surely common defense is paramount to the whole, but the very idea of community needs to go deeper than that. What farming community would survive if the children were not taught the ways of the fields and cattle? What dwarf homeland would thrive through the centuries if the dwarflings were not tutored in the ways of stone and metal? What band of elves could dance in the forest for centuries untold if not for the training given the children, the ways of the stars and the winds?

And there remain many tasks too large for any one man, or woman, or family, critical to the prosperity and security of any town or city. No one man could build the wall around Luskan, or the docks of Baldur's Gate, or the great archways and wide boulevards of Waterdeep, or the soaring cathedrals of Silverymoon. No one church, either, and so these smaller groupings within the larger societies need to contribute, for the good of all, whether citizens of their particular flock or group, or not.

But what then of the concentration of power that might accompany the improvements and the hierarchical regimentation that may result within any given community? In societies such as a dwarf clan, this is settled through the bloodlines and proper heirs, but in a great city of mixed heritage and various cultures, the allocation of power is certainly less definitive. I have witnessed lords willing to allow their peasants to starve, while food rots in their own larders, piled deep and far too plentiful for one house to possibly consume. I have seen, as with Prisoner's

Carnival in Luskan, magistrates who use the law as a weapon for their own ends. And even in Waterdeep, whose lords are considered among the most beneficent in all the world, lavish palaces look down upon hovels and shanties, or orphaned children shivering in the street.

Once again, and to my surprise, I look to Ten-Towns as my example, for in this place, where the population remains fairly steady, if the individuals constantly change, there is logical and reasoned continuity. Here the ten communities remain distinct and choose among them their respective leaders through various means, and those leaders have a voice at the common council.

The irony of Icewind Dale is that these communities, full of solitary folk (often numbering among their citizens many who fled the law or some gang, using Ten-Towns as a last refuge), full of those who could not, supposedly, live among the civilized societies, are in truth among the most cooperative places I have ever known. The individual fishing boats on Maer Dualdon might vie fiercely for favored spots, but when the winter sets in, none in Ten-Towns starve while others feast heartily. None in Ten-Towns freeze in the empty street when there is room near a hearth—and there is always such room to be found. Likely it is the ferocity of the land, where all understand that numbers alone keep them safe from the yetis and the goblinkin and giantkind.

And that is the point of community: common need and common good, the strength of numbers, the tenderness of a helping hand, the ability to work as one to attain greater heights for all, the widening of horizons beyond one's own perspective and one's own family, the enrichment of life itself.

Oh, but there are many who would not agree with me, who view the responsibilities to the community, be it in tithe of food, wealth, or time, as too cumbersome or infringing upon their personal liberties ... which I find too oft defined as personal desires and greed buried in the disguise of prettier words.

To them I can only insist that the ultimate loss exceeds the perceived gain. What good is your gold if your friends will not lift you when you have fallen?

How long lived our memory of you when you are gone?

Because in the end, that is the only measure. In the end, when life's last flickers fade, all that remains is memory. Richness, in the final measure, is not weighed in gold coins, but in the number of people you have touched, the tears of those who mourn your passing, and the fond remembrances of those who continue to celebrate your life.

—Drizzt Do'Urden

CHAPTER 7

ARR ARR'S BOY

The Year of the Third Circle (1472 DR)
Citadel Felbarr

MURGATROID "MUTTONCHOPS" STONEHAMMER SIGHED AND PULLED AT his thick black beard, tugging hard enough to flex the muscles in his large arm. He gritted his teeth and pulled his beard back the other way.

It was not an uncommon gesture from the old fighter, who was indeed very old, the oldest dwarf in Citadel Felbarr as far as anyone could tell. Muttonchops had lived an adventurous life, had fought with King Emerus against Obould and the orcs, and had even been in Mithral Hall when King Bruenor had made his legendary return to the battlefield to meet the charge of Obould's thousands in the valley known as Keeper's Dale, beyond the complex's western gate. For all his battles, though, the Stonehammer patriarch had never truly distinguished himself, and his greatest accomplishment, so it now seemed, was his longevity.

Certainly he was respected among the denizens of Citadel Felbarr, as none would dispute, but this new job he had been given . . .

Muttonchops served as a trainer now, typically considered a position of high respect and regard, except that his trainees included dwarflings, the oldest of this particular group being twelve. These elders in his charge invariably ended up the worst fighters of that age group.

"Arr Arr's boy's not showin' much," remarked Rocky Warcrown, third cousin to the king, twice-removed.

The old Stonehammer wanted to argue the point, but he could only sigh and tug his beard again, for across the room, little Arr Arr, who was just past his ninth birthday, engaged in battle with a lad from the Argut clan, a promising and powerful ten-year-old.

73

Bryunn Argut swept his shield out far before him and off to the left, driving young Arr Arr back a step. Without missing a step, without the slightest hesitation, Bryunn leaped forward as he twisted around, sweeping his weapon, a wooden axe, across ferociously.

Arr Arr ducked—just barely!—and stumbled backward a few steps. Bryunn Argut pursued with a series of chops and swipes that kept the younger dwarfling off-balance all the way.

"He's a head taller than Little Arr Arr," Muttonchops remarked, but Rocky's snort made his excuse seem quite ridiculous.

"A year older, too, then," said Rocky. "Ye think that's for makin' any difference?"

The concern in his tone struck Muttonchops profoundly, for many eyes were upon this dwarfling known to everyone in Felbarr as Little Arr Arr. For as long as anyone could remember, the Roundshields had served as captains of Citadel Felbarr's garrison, a proud tradition of fearsome warriors and grand and loyal subjects to the Warcrowns. Reginald Roundshield, Arr Arr's father, had been among the most popular and respected dwarves in all of Felbarr until his death at the hands of rogue orcs when Little Arr Arr was but a toddler.

Everyone in Felbarr wanted Little Arr Arr to succeed, to step up in the tradition of his father and those grandfathers before him. This was the security of the clan, after all, the solid dependability of generational continuity, the son of a son of a son of a son of a captain.

But Little Arr Arr wasn't showing that kind of promise, and even King Emerus himself had noted as much on his last visit to Muttonchops's training grounds.

Rocky Warcrown sucked in his breath as a last-heartbeat twist brought Little Arr Arr's shield up just in time to deflect an axe swipe that would surely have knocked the child silly.

Muttonchops, too, winced, but he came out of it more quickly, his veteran eyes noting something here that he hadn't before, and with a hunch in his gut speaking a different story to him than what his eyes were telling him.

Young Reginald fought the urge to jab the tip of his own wooden axe into the exposed armpit of Bryunn Argut.

How would a nine-year-old dwarfling respond? Bruenor kept asking himself, kept reminding himself. The awkwardness of the attacks—and not just those of Bryunn, who was quite formidable compared to most of the others in this class—constantly caught the old dwarf king in a young body off his guard.

But they were only at the training grounds once a tenday, after all, and this was but rudimentary training. Muttonchops Stonehammer's job was merely to acquaint the dwarflings with the sensation of giving and taking a hit, and to allow them their first opportunities of the rolling spin and slash, or the shield rush, or any of the other building blocks of straightforward, basic dwarf fighting.

For Bruenor, though, as many times as he might remind himself of this, the whole experience proved mind-numbingly simple. He was well-acquainted with this new body he had been given, and had been for years.

Bryunn Argut came forward with a powerful downward chop, but one that could only fall short, Bruenor recognized, and as he did, he knew the movement to be quite obviously a diversion for the coming shield rush.

He was moving at the same time as Bryunn, cleverly disguising his dodge as a slip and stumble. As Bryunn came charging forward, Little Arr Arr "fell" forward and to the side, tucking his head under his lifting shield and rolling behind the approaching opponent.

He resisted the urge to kick out Bryunn's trailing foot and send the lad sprawling to the floor. He liked Bryunn, after all, thought him a promising dwarfling fighter, and didn't want to embarrass him!

"Bah, but good thing he tripped o'er his own feet, eh?" Rocky Warcrown remarked. "Or to be sure that th'Argut kid would've flap-jacked him!" Rocky laughed, obviously picturing the event, for the term "flap-jack" referred to pancakes, and a flap-jacked fighter was one laid out flat, sprawled under the crush of a shield rush, truly among the most comical outcomes to be found on the training grounds.

"Aye," Muttonchops replied, but without conviction, and he was nodding as he spoke, though surely not in agreement with his companion's assessment.

"Ah, but Uween's to be heartbroken to learn that her one son, the heir to the Roundshield legacy, is just a flat-footed oaf," Rocky said. "Poor old Arr Arr's turnin' in his grave, don't ye doubt."

But the wily old veteran Muttonchops did doubt.

"He's bored," he muttered.

"Eh?" asked Rocky Warcrown, and he followed Muttonchops's stare across the grounds just in time to see Bryunn Argut launch an endgame assault, what Muttonchops had taught the dwarflings to think of as "the killing frenzy."

Bryunn's wooden axe swooped in with abandon, from the left, then right, overhead and stabbing straight forward, over and over again. He continually pressed and bulled ahead, purely offensive in design, keeping Arr Arr on his heels the whole time and almost hitting him—almost!—with every devastating strike.

Almost . . . but never quite.

Rocky sucked in his breath repeatedly, obviously expecting Little Arr Arr to take one on the chin in short order.

Muttonchops suppressed a knowing laugh and nod and wasn't the least bit surprised when Bryunn Argut finally relented and Arr Arr, still back on his heels, hadn't actually been touched. The teacher slapped his fingers against the chimes hanging beside him, signaling the end of the matches, and soon after dismissed his twenty trainees.

"He did well to keep his beardless head on his shoulders," Rocky admitted. "But ne'er got close to hitting the Argut lad."

"Aye, Bryunn Argut's a promisin' one. He'll find hisself in with the stubble group soon enough," Muttonchops agreed, "the stubble group" referring to the dwarf teenagers, their little beards just beginning to sprout. The old veteran looked around, then settled his gaze on Rocky Warcrown. "Be a good friend, then," he asked, "and see to getting them off to their homes. I got something what's needin' to be done."

"Stubble group's coming in next, ain't they?" Rocky asked. "Was hoping to see the Fellhammer sisters. Word's that them two might be joining a battlerager brigade."

"Aye, and aye again, that they might," Muttonchops replied. "Fist'n'Fury, I call 'em. Fist'n'Fury, and any I'm puttin' against them ain't the happiest o' me students! Be a good friend then for me and send the little ones on their way. And might that ye start the next group to their strengthening exercises. I'll not be gone long."

Rocky nodded and Muttonchops left in a hurry, the cagey old dwarf realizing that he'd have to be quick now.

Bruenor walked along the quiet tunnels of Citadel Felbarr soon after, his practice axe swinging at the end of his right arm, shield still strapped on his left.

Another day.

Another wasted day.

That was how he saw it, at least, for he had long ago acclimated to this new body—it was fully his own now, as surely as had been the muscled and scarred one his spirit had departed in the depths of Gauntlgrym. He even looked like himself, his old self, like Bruenor Battlehammer at the age of nine! That notion had surprised him when first he had realized the resemblance. He had wondered about it, of course, unsure of how Mielikki's "gift" might affect such things. Might he have been a blue-bearded dwarf? Or even a female? Catti-brie hadn't said, after all, explaining only that they would be reborn somewhere in Faerûn to parents of their own race. She hadn't mentioned gender, or their expected appearance, at all.

Wouldn't Drizzt be in for a surprise if he met Catti-brie again, only to find her not a "her" at all, but a strapping young lad!

Bruenor shook that discomforting thought out of his head. He felt like himself now—there was no other way to describe it. His reflection looked familiar to him; his hands were the young hands he had known as a Battlehammer dwarfling. And he was fully in control of this young body, more so even than he had been the first time around at a similar age. His private practice sessions showed him the truth: he could execute moves that a nine-year-old Bruenor had never imagined. His understanding of battle remained and all the centuries of training had followed him through the spirit world to this new physical form.

He had to attend the classes of Murgatroid Stonehammer, of course, for they were not optional in Citadel Felbarr, but he feared that these sessions were actually dulling his senses and unlearning the great lessons repetition and action had so deeply imbued within him.

And of course, there was always the possibility that he would forget himself in one of these ridiculous training fights and accidentally humiliate, or even lay low, a fine young dwarf.

The dwarf sighed and turned down a lonely lane in the quarter of the underground complex that housed the city soldiers. He brought his wooden axe up onto his shoulder and thought of another weapon, one many-notched . . .

The attack came from the side, a heavy and squat form charging out at him, shield-rushing behind a thick oaken buckler. Hardly even thinking of the movement, indeed thinking of nothing but getting out of the way, the surprised Bruenor threw himself forward and down to the side, exactly as he had done with the Argut boy earlier. Up came his shield to cover his head and facilitate the roll, and he came around in perfect balance as the highwaydwarf, or whomever or whatever it might be, sped past.

Unlike in the practice fight, however, Bruenor wasn't about to let this one get past him so easily. He flung himself around, his wooden axe reaching out fast at the attacker's trailing ankle. With a proper weapon, he might have severed the fool's foot, but with the practice axe, he took a different tact, hooking the axe head around his attacker's ankle and tugging hard. When that proved futile, given the difference in size, where Bruenor could not hope to pull this one's feet out from under him, Bruenor instead scrabbled forward with all speed.

He unhooked the axe as he crashed against the attacker's leg and again, could barely budge the assailant, who had recovered his balance by then. Up went the practice axe's tip, right between the attacker's legs, prodding at his groin, and when Bruenor's opponent predictably hopped up on his toes and rushed forward, Bruenor swatted the trailing foot so that it tripped up on the back of the suddenly retreating attacker's forward ankle.

Now the assailant staggered, and when he tried to put his feet back under him and swing around, he found a dwarfling flying upon him, crashing against him ferociously, climbing up him and rolling right over him, and so perfectly setting the wooden axe handle across the assailant's throat as he did.

Bruenor threw himself over the shoulder, twisting as he went, gripping the handle down low with one hand, up high with the other, as if his very life depended upon it. For indeed, such seemed to be the case!

The assailant gasped something indecipherable as he fell back with Bruenor tumbling atop him as they went down in a heap.

Bruenor knew that he couldn't hope to choke the life out of this one, or even to extract himself and get away. For all his skill, he couldn't outfight an attacker so much heavier and stronger, and certainly not with a practice axe. So he bit the assailant's ear instead, his jaw clamping down through the thick fabric of a veil or mask of some sort, and with a growl, he stubbornly took hold.

His victim issued a stream of invectives, along with a long, grunt, "Arr!" And he pushed back against the chokehold and Bruenor couldn't hope to counter the strength of this adult.

Or could he?

His thoughts swirled back to the throne of Gauntlgrym and he felt the power of Clangeddin coursing through his veins, tightening his muscles. He let go of the ear then and focused on the axe handle, bringing it in tight against his victim's throat, pressing the assailant's windpipe despite the desperate counter-push.

But then from the memory of the throne came the wisdom of Moradin, reminding him that no dwarfling his age could possibly win out in a contest like this. He was revealing a great secret in holding fast against the stubborn pull of his frantic victim.

Better that, he realized, than being murdered in an empty lane.

The attacker growled again, so Bruenor thought, but then he realized that the "arr" was really "Arr Arr!" and in a voice that the old dwarf in a dwarfling's body surely recognized.

With a squeal, Bruenor gave up the fight and let the assailant, Muttonchops Stonehammer, wrest the wooden practice axe from his grasp. As Muttonchops came forward with the sudden release, Bruenor rolled out to the side, put his feet under him and scrambled away.

"By the gods, ye little rat!" Muttonchops said, gasping and choking through each word. He rolled up to a sitting position and stared back at the young dwarfling, who was on his feet again, set in a defensive posture and ready to throw himself into the fray or to run away in the span of an eye-blink.

"Ye near broke me neck," the old dwarf said, rubbing his throat, his other hand going to his bleeding ear.

"Why?" Bruenor demanded. "Master, why? Was I angerin' ye, then?"

Muttonchops began to laugh, though he found himself coughing repeatedly as he did.

Bruenor didn't know what to make of any of this.

"I knew ye was cheatin' in the fights!" Muttonchops declared as if in victory. "And cheatin' against yerself, ye durned fool!"

Bruenor shrugged, still not catching on.

Muttonchops stood up and Bruenor inched aside, ready to flee, but the old dwarf tossed him his practice axe and seemed to relax then.

"Ye ain't for doin' yer father proud in the fightin' classes," Muttonchops explained. "Yer father, ye know? Arr Arr, Captain o' the Guard. As fierce a fighter as Felbarr's e'er known."

Again Bruenor merely shrugged and held his hands up helplessly, at a loss.

"And ye ain't losing in yer fights because yer fightin' yer betters, oh no," Muttonchops accused. "Ye're losin' because ye ain't tryin' to win! I seen it and I knowed it!" He rubbed his bloody ear again and spat onto the cobblestones— and there was a bit of blood in his spittle, too, from his bruised throat. "And ye just proved it."

"B-Bryunn's a tough one, then," Bruenor stuttered, trying to find some out.

"Bah! Ye could've put him down. Ye just put meself down!"

Bruenor stammered over that dilemma. "Fighting for me, uh . . . life," he tried to explain. "Ye scared me crazy."

"Ye're always fightin' for yer life, ye little fool!" Muttonchops scolded, coming forward and poking a twisted old finger Bruenor's way. "Always! Ye win a hunnerd and lose but one, and ye're dead, like yer Da."

Bruenor started to respond but thought better of it.

"Ye're only losin' in the class because ye don't care for winning—and what's Uween to say, then? How's she to tell Arr Arr to rest easy under the stone o' his cairn when his only child's a coward, then?"

Bruenor's eyes narrowed at that remark, and he had to call upon the wisdom and temperance of Moradin once more to stop from launching himself at the irreverent old warrior yet again. He didn't know where to go with this. He couldn't deny Muttonchops's observations, though surely the old veteran couldn't have been farther off regarding the motivation behind Bruenor's half-hearted efforts. He held back not out of boredom, and surely not out of cowardice, but because he was hiding something, something he could not reveal. Not yet.

"I seen ye now, Little Arr Arr," Muttonchops said. "I seen what ye can do, and I'm not for lettin' ye spend yer fights running away and pretendin' with yer trips and yer stumbles. Ye do yer Da proud, I tell ye, or ye're to feel the broad side o' that axe o' yers slapping about yer rump! Ye hear me, then?"

Bruenor stared at him, not sure how to respond.

"Ye hear me, then?" Muttonchops repeated emphatically. "Do ye, Little Arr Arr?"

"Reginald," Bruenor corrected. Yes, it was time to make a stand.

"Eh?"

"Reginald is me name. Reginald Roundshield."

"Little Arr Arr . . ."

"Reginald," Bruenor insisted.

"Yer Da was Arr Arr . . . ," Muttonchops started to say, but Bruenor interrupted him.

"Me Da's dead and cold under the stones."

That stole Muttonchops's voice, and the old dwarf stood staring blankly at the impudent whelp.

"But meself's here, and don't ye ne'er think again that I ain't to do him proud. Me name's Reginald. Reginald Roundshield, o' the Felbarr Roundshields. Ye wanted me to own it—that's why ye jumped me in the dark—and so I'll be ownin' it, but on me own terms and with me own name!"

"Ye little rat," Muttonchops replied, but he seemed more surprised—and pleased—than angered.

"So ye send 'em at me next tenday," Bruenor insisted. "Start with Bryunn Argut and send 'em all, one after another, or two together if that's yer choice, or three, or all together! And when I put 'em all down, one after another, then know that yer class ain't teaching the son o' Arr Arr nothing. Then ye move me along to the next class."

Muttonchops paused for a long while, staring at him, trying to gain a measure of him. "Young dwarf warriors, next class, and not dwarflings," he warned.

Bruenor didn't blink, and matched Muttonchops's stare with equal intensity and more. He was surprised by his own anger, deep and profound, and his discomfort and anger were about more than the boredom of basic martial training, or the indignity of being attacked in the dark by this old codger. On one level, Bruenor felt foolish for the path he had just taken, and yet he had no thought of turning back. Not in the least.

"Ye got nothin' to teach me with them dwarflings," he said.

Muttonchops assumed a less aggressive posture. "So ye think ye can put 'em all down, eh?"

"All o' them together, if that's yer choice," Bruenor replied.

"Might be."

Bruenor didn't flinch. Indeed, he merely shrugged, already growing bored with this conversation.

"Ye best put a priest in the room," he said in all sincerity. "Know that them others're sure to need a bit of Dumathoin's dweomers o' healing."

Muttonchops started to respond, but instead reached up and touched his bleeding ear once more, and then with a grunt that was half growl and half snort, he turned and walked out of the lane.

Bruenor Battlehammer stood there alone in the dim light for a long, long while, considering the encounter, and the one sure to come. Most of all, though, he considered his anger, swirling within him. He was distinctly uneasy, and had been for as long as he could remember. This whole experience of his second chance at life hadn't been as he had expected—the years moved more slowly than he could have imagined when he had walked out of Iruladoon.

On that remote day, he had stepped from the forest to go to the aid of his old friend, Drizzt, a friend he had left, by his reckoning, only a couple of days before, though it had been years in the time as measured by the living. But now Bruenor had been away from Drizzt for nearly a decade by his own reckoning as well, and the energy and enthusiasm that had overcome him and allowed him to choose the return above a deserved rest in Dwarfhome had long faded.

He was out of his time and out of his place, and terribly lonely and terribly agitated, and with more than a decade to go.

He picked up his practice axe and set it over his shoulder, then headed for home. Muttonchops was going to try to punish him, he knew, and probably would send the whole class charging at him in one wild frenzy the next tenday.

Should he back down, he wondered? Should he apologize to the old dwarf and explain his bluster away as a reaction to his lingering excitement and fear because of the ambush?

The dwarfling let a wad of spit fly to the stone and stamped his booted foot on it as he stormed past. "Send 'em all together," he muttered under his breath, and in that instant, Bruenor could well imagine a dozen dwarflings flying around like straws in a hurricane.

No, he wasn't about to back down, and maybe when he finished with his peers, he'd give Muttonchops a swat or ten just to make a point.

He shouldered through the door of his house, startling Uween, who turned on him with a scowl.

"So I be hearin' that ye ain't much for fightin', are ye?" she scolded. "Ye thinkin' to make yer Da hang his bearded head in shame at Moradin's side, are ye?"

"I'm thinkin' I'd rather be killing orcs than playing tap-battle with a bunch o' whinin' brats!" Bruenor roared back and stormed past her, leaving her so flustered that she couldn't even remember to swat him on the backside for his tone and back-talk.

CHAPTER 8

SPIDER

The Year of the Third Circle (1472 DR)
Delthuntle

WHERE'D HE GO?" THE TEENAGER YELLED, SKIDDING TO A STOP. HE HAD come around the corner of the building in close pursuit, expecting to snare the child thief in a couple of strides. But the sneaky halfling had simply vanished.

"Get him!" cried the teenager's friend as he hustled past.

Across the street, a group sitting at a table in front of a fishmonger's mercantile laughed at the two, and at the others who came bobbing up behind them . . . and laughed all the louder at the other group of teens that came around the other side of the building, apparently to head off the little halfling.

The first teenager, the leader of the gang, scowled at the group of diners, which only made them laugh all the louder, of course. One of them pointed upward. The leader of the teens leaped away from the building and looked up, and sure enough, there went his prey, moving easily and swiftly from ledge to ledge, already nearing the roof.

"You rat!" the teenager yelled. He leaped to grab the ledge atop a window and began to hoist himself up.

But this was no easy climb, and indeed, within a few heartbeats, he had reached an apparent dead end, as had his companion who was similarly trying to scale the wall.

"How?" asked a third of the group, for the fleeing halfling was easily going over the roof's edge, while the two older, taller, and stronger human boys—and even an elf girl at the other end—couldn't begin to scale the tall building.

The leader of the gang dropped back down to the ground and shouted up "You rat!" at the disappearing form.

"More like a spider," one of the men across the street called, and that group laughed all the harder at the foiled teenagers' expense.

"Spider," agreed the lithe and pretty elf lass, who had also surrendered the seemingly impossible climb and moved back toward her friends. "That little one can climb anything."

"He'll be climbing through the mud trying to get out from under my boot when I catch him," the gang leader promised.

"Ah, but let it be gone from your mind," said the elf girl. She looked up toward the roof line, admiration clear on her face. "He's just a child. Cannot be more than eight or nine years alive, and he's a clever one." She ended with a giggle.

The boy stared at her, his lips moving this way and that, but no words coming forth.

"I like him," the elf stated flatly. "He makes it fun. And all he took was your whistle."

"The whistle my Da gave me!" the gang leader protested.

On cue, that whistle sounded from up above, and all eyes turned that way just in time to see the stolen item fly over the edge of the roof, back down to the teenager's waiting hands.

"He only did it to prove he could, and only because you were mean to him," said the elf girl, and she giggled again and walked off with her friends, pausing only to say again, "Let it be gone from your mind. You'll not lessen your embarrassment by beating up a halfling child."

"Spider," said the man at the table across the street. "An apt name for that one, I think."

"Aye, don't think I've seen anyone climb the face of a building as capably," another replied.

"Or near as fast," said another. "Course, he was running for his little life!"

That brought some laughter and the conversation continued about this mysterious little Spider character. Delthuntle was a fair-sized city, though, and none knew the identity of the halfling, or where he might have come from or where he might be going. Throughout their talk, the four discussing the matter kept glancing toward the fifth of the group, one who had not spoken at all since the shouts had begun from the distant lane and the little halfling, Spider, had bounded into view.

This fifth, unlike the other four at the table, was also a halfling. Dressed in the finest silks, with a fashionable golden sash belt and a fancy blue beret, its front edge tacked down with a large golden pin, Pericolo Topolino rested back in his seat with the easy confidence of competence and experience, and the wisdom of age.

That confidence, of course, was boosted more than a little by a well-earned reputation, for few in Delthuntle would deign to cross Pericolo Topolino.

He feigned indifference, but in truth keenly registered every word spoken by his companions. He never returned their looks, however, focusing instead across the street to the teenage ruffians.

"Who is that one?" he asked at length, and the other four fell to abrupt silence, eagerly following his gesture to indicate the leader of the teenage gang.

"Bregnan Prus," two answered in unison, the other two quickly agreeing.

"Aye, and his Ma serves at a lord's palace as a handmaid and he lives on the grounds," one added.

Pericolo tapped his stubby fingertips together before his chin, unblinking as he considered this arrogant young ruffian who was still shouting curses up at the empty roof line.

A young ruffian, he figured, who might be in need of a proper . . . education.

"We're not to catch him that way," complained Pater, one of the other boys.

Bregnan Prus turned a hateful glare his way, backing him down.

"Are we to stand here all day and yell at a wall?" another asked, coming to Pater's defense, for without that show of solidarity, the infuriated Bregnan might have begun throwing his fists, as was often the case.

"I want that one," Bregnan Prus said in a low, threatening tone.

"He's just a child!" protested the elf lass, standing with her friends not far away.

"Let's get out of here," offered another of the boys.

Bregnan Prus took a moment to glower at the elf, but nodded his agreement and brought his returned whistle to his lips, blowing a sharp note to collect the members of his gang.

He cut that note short, however, and a curious expression came over his face, first a sour look, then one of confusion, and finally with his eyes widening in horror. His face contorted weirdly, and it took the others, both his immediate companions and the group of girls, a few moments to realize that no matter how hard Bregnan twisted his features, his lips would not come free of the whistle!

"Oyster glue!" Pater shouted in shock, and all around gasped, and gasped again, then began to titter, then began to laugh.

For it was true enough. Spider, or whatever the little thief's name might be, had sneakily coated the whistle with the substance found in a particular breed of Sea of Fallen Stars shellfish, a sticky and stubborn sealant known as oyster glue, an innocuous enough substance until it met with water, or in this case, with the moisture of Bregnan's lips.

Bregnan Prus grunted repeatedly, issuing little toots from the stuck whistle in the process—and to the great amusement of all onlookers.

"So let's get him," Pater offered, though he couldn't stop himself from giggling between words. "We're not to do that standing here."

Bregnan Prus punched him in the mouth, and tooted at him as he did, though whether for good measure or inadvertently, none around could tell.

A few days later, Regis put his back against the wall and took a deep breath. He had brought the conflict to this point on purpose, he reminded himself. This was a test he would not fail. In the days and nights that had passed since the theft and sabotage of the whistle, he had led Bregnan Prus's band on a merry chase indeed, all around the shadows of Delthuntle's streets.

But now that the moment of truth closed, dark wings of doubt fluttered up all around him. He was too young and too frail for this, perhaps. For all his training, his incessant exercise and practice, his body remained that of a child, and a halfling one at that!

He heard the approaching shouts; they had cornered him and there were no high rooftops in this poor district beside the great lake. Instinctively he looked around for an escape, and though he noted one distinct possibility, he shook the notion away.

He had purposely baited Bregnan Prus and the others and had led them to this point.

But he was merely a child, barely nine years old. Bregnan stood almost twice his height and easily carried twice his weight.

"You can do this," Regis whispered and he thought of Drizzt and Catti-brie, of Wulfgar and Bruenor, and of the role he had ever played in that band. True, he had found moments of usefulness, usually by accident, but mostly he had been the tag-along, hiding in the shadows while his heroic friends had protected him.

It could not be like that again. He wouldn't allow it.

A shout from beside the very warehouse where the young halfling sat, told him that his pursuers were close, so he stood up, dusted himself off, and stepped out around the corner to meet them.

Bregnan Prus, in the lead, skidded to a stop.

Regis didn't blink.

"No walls to climb, Spider?" the boy asked, a bit of a lisp to his voice since he had torn his lips extracting the whistle.

Regis glanced left, then right, then shrugged as if it didn't matter.

"You think I'm to be easy on you, then, because you're just a child?"

"Ah, but just punch him hard," another of the group said. "Let's all punch him hard!"

That brought a few nods and cheers from the group of five.

Regis held his nerve and wouldn't let them see him shift nervously, or even let them hear him clear his throat.

Behind him, the halfling heard the other group rushing in, this one led by the elf girl.

Bregnan Prus stepped up to him, towering over him.

"Beg me not to kill you," he said.

But Regis stared up at him, locking his gaze, unblinking, and the halfling even managed a bit of a wry smile.

"Last chance!" Bregnan Prus said, and grabbed Regis by the collar—or tried to, for the halfling's hand flashed across, slapping Bregnan's fingers aside.

"Little rat!" the boy cried, and he launched a wild left hook aimed for Regis's head.

But the halfling, surely not caught by surprise, ducked and backed up a step. He knew the counter move he should then execute, had practiced it a thousand times before, but he found that he could not.

Bregnan Prus pursued, launching a barrage of punches, though clumsy hooks one and all, and Regis rolled away time and again.

"He's just a boy!" he heard behind him, the elf girl.

Regis liked that one, and for some reason, the sound of her voice emboldened him.

"One last warning," Regis said loudly, suddenly, and all the chatter stopped, and Bregnan Prus stopped as well and stared at him incredulously.

"It was all just a game until now," Regis warned. "Walk away."

"What?"

"You are a clumsy ogre," Regis said. "I have embarrassed you once before your friends. Would you have me do so again?"

Bregnan Prus let out a strange garbled sound and leaped at Regis, fists flailing. But Regis moved, too, the maneuver he had practiced repeatedly, day and night. He dived at the teenager's feet, curled and rolled, and the older boy, coming forward, tried to straddle him so that he did not get tripped up.

But that was the whole point, and as Bregnan Prus awkwardly slithered past the ball of halfling, one leg on either side, Regis rolled so that the back of his head and the back of his shoulders were planted squarely against the ground. With that brace, he kicked straight up with both feet, connecting solidly with the teenager's groin.

Bregnan Prus gave a cry and a grunt, and tried to press past, but Regis began a furious pumping of his feet, left and right alternately, smashing one heel after the other into the older boy's tender loins.

Bregnan Prus hopped weirdly and kept trying to sidle past. He brought his hands down for cover, yelping all the while. Too late, though, both he and his assailant realized, as Regis's foot connected perfectly, driving the older boy to his tip-toes and even lifting him off the ground.

Regis tucked and rolled through, spinning around as he did to catch Bregnan Prus's trailing foot as the gasping young man tried to stagger away. The sneaky little halfling had all the leverage here, and he drove in hard, pushing up and over Bregnan Prus's other leg.

The teenager crashed to the ground.

Regis untangled himself and ran right up the back of the fallen lad's thighs, leaping onto his back with a stunning knee drop.

He went for the lad's hairy head and almost got there before being swept aside by a flying tackle. Now he rolled and punched, bit and scratched, but the boy atop him was too strong and too heavy for that. A balled fist came in at him and he got his hand up to block—but the power of the punch drove right through and crushed Regis's nose and sent him sprawling.

"He's just a boy!" the elf girl yelled.

But in reply, Bregnan Prus ordered in a gasping and pained voice, "Kill him!"

Suddenly it wasn't just a game, or a youthful play of dominance, for in that tone, Regis heard, unmistakably, a serious death sentence.

He had underestimated this group; he hadn't realized just how tough the streets of Delthuntle might be.

He tried to get up and run, but got tackled again, and the next punch sent him spinning—or more accurately, the world around him spinning.

He felt himself lifted to his feet, then into the air, and a heavy slug, a punch by Bregnan Prus, took his breath away.

Pericolo Topolino tapped his ivory-tipped cane against the counter, drawing the fishmonger's attention. She stood straight indeed when she recognized the halfling.

"Grandfather," she said, dipping into an awkward bow.

"You have quite the assortment of deepwater oysters," the cultured halfling remarked.

"Y-yes, Grandfather," she stammered. "Fresh, too. They were brought in just today."

"The boats are out at the Sandy Banks, chasing the bass," Pericolo said. He wasn't surprised by the oysters, of course, nor did he doubt that they were fresh as stated. His informants had led him here, after all, and for precisely this reason.

The fishmonger stammered as if cornered.

"An independent diver, then," Pericolo reasoned. "A good one, it would seem."

"Yes, Grandfather."

"You were here the other day, when there was such a commotion across the street?" Pericolo graciously asked. "The *toot-tooting* of the whistle?"

"Aye, yes," she answered, and she nodded and managed a smile. "Was myself that extracted the instrument from Prus's glued lips. Poor boy."

"And the one he pursued?" Pericolo asked. "The one called Spider?"

The fishmonger looked at him curiously.

"Ah, yes, of course," the halfling clarified. "It was myself who gave him that name, so you would not know him by it."

"The halfling?"

"Yes, the halfling. The one who went up to the roof. You know him, I believe."

The woman seemed very concerned suddenly, and she inadvertently glanced at the oysters, tipping her hand. Indeed, this little halfling, this Spider creature, was a valuable commodity to her, the astute Pericolo recognized.

"Tell me his name."

"Spider, you said."

"His real name," Pericolo said, shifting his tone just enough to carry an undercurrent of a threat.

"I'm not for knowing," she said with a gulp. "Don't know that he's even got one, for his Da's not a man to be bothering with such things."

Pericolo narrowed his eyes.

"He's Eiverbreen's boy!" she blurted.

"Eiverbreen?"

"Eiverbreen Parrafin. His boy and Jolee's, though she went and died when the little one was born."

"Spider?"

"Aye."

"And he is a deep diver, this one?"

"Aye, so it'd seem, and so was his mum."

Pericolo Topolino nodded at her and looked away, considering the information, and though he wasn't paying the fishmonger any heed, he heard her profound sigh of relief. He liked that he could do that to people.

Barely four feet tall and he could elicit such a response from almost everyone in Delthuntle, and in many other places in greater Aglarond, as well.

"Fill a basket with some oysters, then," the halfling said cheerily, reaching for his pouch of coins. He paid the fishmonger well for the shellfish. That was Pericolo Topolino's way, of course, eliciting a mixture of fear and gratitude, for he was a person to be feared and to be loved.

That was his way.

This wasn't working out as he had planned. His maneuver with Bregnan Prus had been executed perfectly, and the older boy was still reeling, walking tentatively, as much on his toes as on the balls of his feet, and wincing with every step, barely able to keep from cupping his bruised groin.

But the boy hadn't come alone, of course, and despite the protests of the elf girl, Regis found himself sorely overmatched. Worse, while he could accept the beating, this had progressed beyond that.

They weren't trying to humiliate him.

They weren't trying to hurt him.

Nay, they were trying to kill him.

Two boys held him up by the ankles, and despite his twisting and turning, they managed to get his legs apart just wide enough for Bregnan Prus to chop his hand down into Regis's groin, taking the halfling's breath away.

"That hurt, did it, little Spider?" the older boy taunted, and he hit the halfling child again.

Indeed, it had hurt, but not as badly as Regis had anticipated. He was still a child after all, and that particular area of vulnerability wasn't yet as tender as it would become in future years.

That seemed of small comfort, though, given that the beating had only just begun.

Regis began to cry and just hung there limply, arms hanging low.

There would be no pity forthcoming, however, and Bregnan Prus stepped back and wound up for a great kick into the halfling's face.

Regis waited and slyly watched, and as the older boy's foot began to move, he threw his head backward, arching his back as far as he could.

Bregnan Prus missed, and Regis snapped himself back the other way, curling up at his waist, bringing his head up to look alternately into the faces of the two boys holding him by the ankles. Out went Regis's hands, to either side, where he flicked the middle finger of each hard under the nose of his respective captors. One cried out and let go, cupping his stung proboscis.

Regis threw himself down the other way, and turned violently as he went, and the second boy, caught off guard, overbalanced and with a stung nose of his own, couldn't hold on.

The halfling executed a perfect flip, landing in a run and sprinting for all his life toward the nearby shoreline.

Bregnan Prus yelled from behind, and Regis soon heard the footsteps as the older boy and his friends closed upon him. He splashed into the water and dived forward, and almost got out of reach, but alas, a strong hand closed on the back of his collar.

He was pulled from the water, to stare into the hateful eyes of the teenager he had humiliated. With a little evil laugh, Bregnan Prus thrust him back under the water, and held him there.

Regis struggled mightily. At one point, he broke from the water enough to hear the elf girl screaming, and prayed that she might prove to be his salvation. Even in that instance, though, he never quite managed to get his mouth or nose out of the water, to draw breath.

Bregnan Prus wasn't letting go.

Regis struggled some more, for many, many heartbeats. He went into one last, great fit of scrabbling, in complete desperation, it seemed.

Then he went limp, and let the older boy and the waves determine his movements fully. Still Bregnan Prus pressed down on him; there could be no doubt of the boy's murderous intent.

Regis didn't fight it. He knew that he could remain there for a long, long while. He could dive fifty feet, a hundred feet, and remain on the bottom for long periods of time as he gathered up oysters for his father. He was a deep diver, indeed, though he knew not how or why. Surely in his past life, he could never have dived so deep, and indeed, in his past life, he would be dead right now, as he was feigning.

Finally the older boy let him go, shoving him off toward deeper water. Regis turned his head as he went, just slightly, so that he could hear the screams of the elf girl, the protests against the apparent murder, and Bregnan Prus's abrasive dismissal of the whole affair. He heard the teenagers splashing out of the surf and felt himself drifting, for the tide was going out.

So he just floated, face down, relaxing in the gentle ebbs and flows of the inviting liquid around him.

He smiled widely, though none on the shore could see it, of course, for he had exacted his revenge, and more than that, he had fought past his fears. He replayed the drumbeat of his heels into Bregnan Prus's groin.

He had stared into uncertainty and had stood tall against fear. True, he had almost died for his "courage," and indeed, only luck—this uncanny ability to survive underwater—had saved him, but it didn't matter to Regis at that time.

He had faced his fears and had defeated them. He had willingly walked into battle, indeed had goaded that fight, against seemingly impossible odds. He hadn't defeated his external enemies, perhaps, but he had surely beaten back his own fear, and that, of course, had been the entire point.

He thought of Drizzt and the other Companions of the Hall. He remembered the role he had too often played among that group, that of tag-along, or of the helpless little halfling needing to be protected.

"Not this time," he mouthed, tickling bubbles bouncing up all around him. "Not this time!"

CHAPTER 9

ZIBRIJA

The Year of the First Circle (1468 DR)
Netheril

SILENT AS SHADOWS, THE OWL DRIFTED ALONG, WATCHING THE TWO DESAI, Niraj and Kavita, shuffling across the dark plain through the desert night. The couple held each other close for support, clearly rattled by the startling revelations of the evening. They swayed and walked a swerving line.

But they held each other, and that was good, Catti-brie knew. Their family had been torn asunder and they would need each other in the coming days. The shapeshifting child set down upon the ground and reformed yet again, now taking the host body of a wolf.

The wolf loped along in the darkness, paralleling the couple, then moving ahead of them, making sure that the way was clear, that no animals or monsters would threaten these two, distracted as they were.

She noted that they were soon walking straighter and leaning less upon each other; there seemed to be a determination growing within them.

She broke off her shadowing when her parents, oblivious to her presence, came in sight of the Desai encampment, home again and safe—for now.

But what might happen when the Netherese came calling once more, looking for Ruqiah?

Catti-brie moved back out into the empty night, a child now, a girl, little Ruqiah. She, too, was reeling, she only then realized. For her home had been torn asunder. The security of her parents, even though they might be new parents and only through extraordinary circumstances, was gone now.

And the love was distant.

Yes, love, the girl realized. She had come to truly love Niraj and Kavita. Though she needed them far less than a true child of theirs might, she loved them both as dearly as any child could. She hadn't planned on leaving them this early. Indeed, she had hoped to remain in their home until she set out for Icewind Dale, some fifteen years hence.

But now what could she do? She turned around and considered the imposing wasteland around her, this Empire of Netheril, formerly the great desert of Anauroch.

"Fear not for me, my parents," she said again, replaying her parting words to the couple, but this time to bolster her own confidence. "I go with the goddess, and my road is well-known to me. We will meet again."

Her voice sounded tiny in the empty plain, the whisper of a child. For Catti-brie understood that she was in trouble, out alone in the wilds of Netheril and with dangerous hunters of Shade Enclave eagerly pursuing her. She'd killed the two assassins at the tent. It was good fortune alone that had saved her at the tent. Before they'd arrived, she'd summoned the storm—a time-consuming spellcasting, indeed—to bring the washing rains. Had she not previously thought to bring the storm clouds, she would never have had the devastating magic of the lightning at her fingertips.

Her other spells—the bat swarm and the magic missiles, even the pillar of fire—would not have defeated those two, and those spells represented the most powerful magic she had.

The girl pulled up her sleeves and looked down at her arms. The symbol of Mielikki gave her the power to summon the storms and to assume the animal forms. Perhaps she could have become a bear and battled the assassins.

It was not a comforting thought, for the animal forms were limited, Catti-brie had come to understand, both in duration and effectiveness. No, without the storm already in place above the encampment, the best she might have done was distract and wound the killers with her bats, sting them with her missiles and fiery tricks, then become an owl to soar away, leaving her mother to die and her father to the mercy of the murderers.

The thought of her dying mother reminded her of her other powers, the healing warmth of Mielikki. Indeed, in this regard Catti-brie recognized that she was powerful, as much so as an acolyte of many years, perhaps, or even on par with a priestess. Her days of close communion with the goddess in Iruladoon had given her that much.

She looked at her other arm, at the spellscar that resembled the symbol of Mystra. She had been training exhaustively in her past life, until the falling Weave had damaged her, but she had been fairly new to the Art before being taken, and she remained a minor trickster at best. She could sting with magic missiles, or throw a patch of grease upon the ground at the feet of a charging enemy, but her repertoire remained severely limited, and worse, she could not improve in the ways of arcane magic without a teacher, a mentor.

She looked around at the empty plain once more and sighed deeply. In her past life, she had been a formidable warrior, but even if she could recall those fighting skills and train her body to move as she had before, what strength and speed might a child know? Surely not enough to match blades with a skilled assassin, or even a novice warrior!

Catti-brie nodded, understanding the message Mielikki imparted to her through the coalescing lines of her own reasoning. She needed to hide. The goddess would protect her from the animals of Netheril's dark night, but she could do little against the determined killers of Shade Enclave.

The thought had Catti-brie sitting upon the ground, staring up at the stars, her little mouth moving through various curses. She had left Iruladoon full of hope and determination, certain that she would find her friends and Drizzt, and that they together would triumph. Not a doubt had tugged at her as she had jumped into the light of reincarnation.

But now she understood the truth of it all. Would she even get back to Icewind Dale? Would she survive another fifteen years, and even if she did, would she find her way though this confusing and dangerous world?

And would Bruenor and Regis?

Suddenly the plan on which the three had embarked seemed a desperate ploy, a dive from a high cliff into shallow water.

"Mielikki guide me," she whispered into the empty night.

Somewhere far off, a wolf howled.

But not for her, she understood. The world was wide, too wide, and she was but a tiny child in the midst of a vast and dangerous plain.

A tenday later, Catti-brie flew through the night in the form of an owl once more. She drifted on unseen currents, soaring around the Desai encampment.

Many milled around among the tents; there was a palpable tension in the air and an occasional shout of protest lifted above the din.

She flew up high, above the torchlight, and listened carefully, finally picking out the accents that were not Desai. Along with them, she heard Niraj.

Catti-brie swooped down toward the group in question, alighting on the peak of a nearby tent in full view of the gathered Desai leaders, her parents, and a small group of shades.

Shades!

In short order, she realized that they were speaking about her, about the incident that had left two of the Netherese agents dead at the entryway of a blasted tent.

"Ruqiah!" one of the Netherese agents demanded.

If any had been close enough, they might have been startled to hear an owl gasp.

Catti-brie scolded herself, reminding herself that if she was discovered, she would be doing no good for any of those Desai before her.

Kavita began to cry.

"She is dead," Niraj wailed. "My beautiful little girl is dead! Struck by the rage of N'asr!" He spun away and grabbed his wife, hugging her close.

"You will come!" one of the shades said, and the burly tiefling took a step toward Niraj. Perched on the tent, Catti-brie had to fight the urge to revert to her human form and throw some magic—anything!—at the tiefling to back him away, but before she even had begun to wage that internal battle, a trio of Desai leaders, three proud warriors including the tribe's sultan, intercepted the tiefling.

"His child is dead, Master Tremaine," the sultan said. "Killed by the same stroke of lightning that slew your agents. What more would you ask of this man?"

"So you say," the tiefling shade replied.

The sultan stepped back and swept his hand out to the side. "I will show you."

The group of several Desai and the Netherese contingent moved away. Catti-brie waited a few moments to watch her parents, who remained behind and stood hugging and sobbing.

Or were they?

Catti-brie's keen ears caught a whisper from Niraj to Kavita, telling her that she had played the ruse well.

The girl didn't know what to make of this, of any of it. She set off into the night, fast catching up to the Netherese and the sultan, who were now out of the camp and moving to a small cemetery just off to the side.

The owl landed in a tree overlooking the group. Weariness seeped into Catti-brie's frame. She could feel the magic of the spellscar growing thin, warning her to fly away. But she could not. Not then, for the Desai had begun exhuming one of the graves. In short order, they pulled out a small body, wrapped in swaddling clothes, tightly bound.

"Ruqiah," the ruler explained, and he gently unwrapped the head scarf of the burial shroud, revealing a small girl, recently deceased.

Again the owl gasped; Catti-brie knew this girl, older than her by a couple of years. She had died several tendays before her battle with the Netherese.

"The grave was newly dug," one of the Netherese shades confirmed for the others.

"Why did you seek this one?" the sultan of the Desai asked. "What purpose might a little girl—"

"Silence!" Tremaine, the burly tiefling shade, demanded. He turned to his associates and they moved off and began whispering secretly—but not so, since Catti-brie's owl hearing penetrated their circle.

She heard the name "Ulfbinder" and an agreement among them that whatever importance Ruqiah might have held was lost now, and the girl irrelevant.

Only then did Catti-brie come to fully appreciate what her people had just done for her. They had colluded to deceive the Netherese overlords, at great risk. They had come together as a tribe to protect her, and to protect Niraj and Kavita.

Overwhelmed by gratitude, by the love this act had shown to her and her family, Catti-brie could hardly find the strength to fly away. But she had to, she knew, for the magic of her shapeshifting dweomer was fast diminishing.

As she flew out of the camp, she entertained the thought of resuming her life with her parents—the Netherese thought that Ruqiah was dead, after all—but she knew that she would be putting all of the Desai into grave danger by doing so. If they came for Catti-brie and found her, they would destroy her—and everyone she loved.

Some distance away, she became a little girl once more. And she cried.

"They buried her," Tremaine told Parise Ulfbinder when his scouting party returned to Shade Enclave.

"Along with Alpirs De'Noutess and Untaris?"

"They did not bury our dead. They wrapped them in cloth and put them out in the desert sun. They said they knew we would come for them." The tiefling's anger mounted with each word. "They should have brought them to us! Nay, they should not have dared to strike at them!"

"You said Alpirs and Untaris were killed by a lightning strike," Lord Ulfbinder said calmly. "A burst of lightning from a storm that raged in the area."

"We should punish them. We must punish them," said Tremaine, running on as if his master had not spoken a word. "Grant me a force and I will lay waste to the tribe of Desai. Speak the word and I will kill them all!"

Parise Ulfbinder looked at the burly warrior incredulously, and shook his head slowly and deliberately.

"Get out of here," he said quietly.

The tiefling smiled broadly.

"Not like that!" Lord Ulfbinder insisted. "Not to your coveted revenge! Remain in the city. Trouble yourself no more with the Desai. They are not your concern."

"But lord—"

"Not your concern!" Ulfbinder said with a low growl. He shook his head in disgust and waved the feebleminded warrior away. The Desai were no minor tribe and it would take a sizable force to attack them. And to what end? Such an act would likely inspire a larger uprising, and that, in turn, would force Parise before the Netherese rulers to explain himself.

He could well imagine that meeting, and a shudder coursed down his spine. Simply having to mention "Cherlrigo's Darkness" and his various theories regarding Abeir-Toril would bring him great humiliation.

Still, the story his scouts had returned to tell seemed far too convenient to him. By coincidence a bolt of lightning from a natural storm had slain Alpirs De'Noutess and Untaris just as they closed in on this Ruqiah child? And it had killed her, as well? That was the tale the Desai were telling.

Too convenient.

"Tremaine!" he called to the tiefling, who was just exiting the room. The warrior looked back over his shoulder and Lord Ulfbinder instructed, "Fetch the Lady Avelyere at once."

The tiefling stared at him for a moment, as if confused, then hustled away.

Parise nodded to himself as he considered his impulsive decision. Avelyere was the proper choice now. She was a skilled diviner and could speak with the dead. And she could detect magic as well as any in Shade Enclave. If, as Parise suspected, the curious little girl was still out there, Avelyere would find her.

"Ruqiah!" Kavita gasped, the word blurting out as if she had been kicked in the gut. She scrambled from her chair, nearly tumbling over, and started for the tent flap, where her daughter stood staring back at her.

Catti-brie eagerly leaped up into her mother's arms, accepting the crushing hug.

"We thought we would never see you again!"

"I thought so too," the girl admitted. "But I missed you terribly."

Kavita kissed her and crushed her close and swung her around in a great dance that went on and on until they both grew dizzy.

"I saw what you did, what the whole tribe did, when the Netherese came looking for me."

Kavita looked at her curiously.

"I have been around—as the owl who left you in the secret garden," Catti-brie explained.

"My Zibrija," Kavita said, tears streaming down her face, and she wrapped Catti-brie in another crushing hug, and Catti-brie did not begin to protest.

"Zibrija!" sounded the nickname again, spoken in a plaintive gasp, as Niraj entered the tent. The man jumped over to his wife and child and propelled them both onto the bed with a great flying tackle. "Zibrija, you have come home!"

Catti-brie's weak smile showed the limitations of that happy event, something neither of her parents missed.

"Not for long," she said. "It is not safe for you . . . or for me," she added quickly as stubborn Niraj began to protest.

"But you will return?" Kavita asked.

The question burned at Catti-brie. She knew that she shouldn't be doing this, that she shouldn't be here. Not now. She had returned to Faerûn for one purpose, and it had nothing to do with the Desai tribe, or with these parents who were not really her parents. She could not afford such distractions and risks. But she loved these two, dearly so, as much as she had loved . . .

Catti-brie swallowed hard and blew a determined sigh, reminding herself of who she was and how and why she had returned.

"I am well," she assured her parents. "And I'm grateful for what you and the Desai have done for me in deceiving the Netherese."

"Zibrija!" Niraj cried. Catti-brie understood the sad look on his face. She was his child, and what parent would not take such action in defense of his child?

"My name is Catti-brie," she corrected, because she had to, because if she did not keep these emotions at arms' length, she would never find the courage to leave this camp again, which she knew she must do.

Kavita threw her hands up over her mouth.

"Ruqiah," Niraj insisted.

The little girl squared her shoulders, but in looking at Kavita, she had to relent. What harm, after all?

"Ruqiah," she said. "But I still like Zibrija."

That brought back Niraj's smile, and again he tackled her in a great fatherly hug. Catti-brie didn't fight it, and indeed, she felt warm and safe in his strong embrace.

She did not want to leave, but she had to. She wanted to return, but how could she justify it?

"You're wizards," she said suddenly.

Niraj pulled her back to arms' length and looked to his wife.

"Both of you," Catti-brie continued. "I have seen it. I have seen you," she said to Kavita, "using spells to aid in your daily chores."

"Kavita!" Niraj scolded, but his anger was surely feigned.

"You inherited our skill, perhaps, and that skill led to your curious scars," Kavita replied, and Catti-brie nodded, though she didn't agree. Her scars, she knew, had come from a different place and a different time, scars rightly earned, scars paid for dearly.

"So you admit that you're wizards," she stated more than asked. "You practice the Art?"

The two looked at each other, then Niraj stared hard at her. "You must never tell anyone," he said quietly. "The Netherese do not allow the Bedine such powers."

Catti-brie nodded and smiled. "I'm a wizard," she said.

"A priestess, you mean," said Niraj.

"A druid, more like it," Kavita said.

"A bit of both," she replied. "And a wizard. I was studying the ways of magic in the time of the Spellplague, when the Weave fell."

Both of them swallowed hard.

"I had only just begun my studies," she explained, "and my repertoire was, and is, meager indeed—a few minor spells, a few cantrips. Less now than when I was afflicted, even, for I cannot remember all that I knew of my studies."

"A lightning bolt to burn an assassin out of his boots," Niraj dryly remarked.

"A gift of the spellscar, and no wizard's bolt," she assured him. "I had lived most of my life with the sword and the bow, until I was injured in a battle. And so I turned to magic."

She paused, realizing that she was overwhelming both of them. First she had demonstrated magical powers beyond her years. Then she had flown off from them in the form of an owl. And now she had just strongly implied to them that not only was she not their child, not only was she not a child at all, but that she was a century older than either of them! She questioned the wisdom of telling them any of the truth of herself then, for what unwanted curiosity might that long tale bring?

But then she looked into the dark eyes of Kavita and her doubts melted away. This was her mother, whatever bizarre circumstances surrounded the event of her rebirth. There was nothing but love for her in those dark eyes.

Nothing other than tears, of course, and Catti-brie did not wish to see those tears. Not ever.

"I had only just begun my formal training when the Spellplague struck me, and alas . . ." Her voice drifted off. "But I was under fine tutelage," she said almost immediately, pushing forward with her impulsive decision to help these two, her beloved parents, sort through the pain of confusion and the grief of losing their only child. "Perhaps you have heard of Lady Alustriel of Silverymoon?"

Niraj and Kavita again exchanged looks, their expressions revealing a great confusion.

"I'm a wizard, but merely a novice. You're both skilled at magic. Will you train me further in the Art?" Catti-brie asked, bringing them back to the moment at hand.

"Then you will not leave us?" Niraj asked.

"I will return as often as I can," Catti-brie heard herself saying, and she could hardly believe the words as they came out of her mouth.

But she meant them.

103

"The child is a clever one," the young sorceress, Eerika, said to Lady Avelyere, her more accomplished mentor.

Avelyere was in her early forties but still strikingly youthful and beautiful in appearance, with light gray eyes and rich brown hair bouncing below her shoulders. She and her companions had little trouble in locating this mysterious Desai child named Ruqiah. First they had gone to the grave, supposedly of Ruqiah, and a simple spell to speak with the dead had told them the truth: that the corpse within was not the body of the girl they sought.

The spirits of dead Untaris and Alpirs had filled them in on the general details of the fight at the Desai encampment—and it had indeed been a fight, one that this child, this little girl named Ruqiah, had clearly dominated.

Soon after, Lady Avelyere and her charges had witnessed a taste of that same magic that had destroyed the two Netherese agents, when first they had managed to actually locate Ruqiah in a scrying pool. That image, and the sky to the east of their position, had flashed brilliantly in the discharge of a summoned burst of lightning.

"She does not fear the lightning," Eerika had noted, "because she summons it to her bidding!"

"Druidic magic," agreed a third woman, Rhyalle, like Eerika barely more than a teenager. "Like her shapechanging."

Lady Avelyere, meticulous as ever, had absorbed it all, trying to make some sense of this unusual child. Lord Ulfbinder, her dear friend Parise, had not exaggerated, she knew in that moment, and she could certainly understand his interest! She was a teacher most of all, and her students exclusively female, like Eerika and Rhyalle and the other three she had brought to the plains of Netheril. She wondered what Lord Parise's intentions for this one might be; wouldn't it be grand for her to add this marvelous little Ruqiah to her house of magic?

Another lightning bolt flashed, and a growling rumble of thunder shook the ground beneath their feet.

"When this child waters her garden, beware!" the lighthearted Rhyalle remarked with a laugh, and the others joined in—all except for Lady Avelyere, who intently watched the girl and her dance through the magic of the scrying pool, wondering what she could teach her, and wondering even more so what she might learn from the child.

But first, of course, she would have to catch her.

THE COMPANIONS

The Year of Splendors Burning (1469 DR)
Netheril

Some months later, Catti-brie drifted on the hot updrafts in the guise of a great hawk, far above the dark brown sands of Netheril. The day was bright and clear and the world spread wide below her. She saw the snake of a river, glistening silvery in the sunlight as it wound its way to a small lake far in the northwest.

Straighter north, she saw the distant outline of Shade Enclave, with its dark towers and high walls, an entire city hovering above the plain on an inverted floating mountain of rock. Of all the sights Catti-brie had ever known, from the mysterious tapestry of Menzoberranzan to the spires of Silverymoon, none quite matched the one in the distance before her. The place didn't appeal to her sensibilities, but certainly Shade Enclave intrigued her, evoking both curiosity and a sense of unnerving displacement. As magnificent and incredible as the sight might be, Catti-brie didn't dwell on it.

The tents of the Desai shone white below her to the west—she could imagine the tribesmen going about their day. She thought of her parents, and reminded herself that she was due to meet with them again in just a tenday. She looked forward to it; Kavita was teaching her several potent spells to manipulate and create fire . . .

The thought couldn't hold. Not up here, free on the updrafts, gliding around as a hawk. The world looked so different to her from this vantage, and with her new insights. She looked at the river again, then off to the west, where dark clouds had gathered. She could even see the lowering darkness of heavy rain falling. The perfection of nature's design overwhelmed her, for the simple clockwork of the world was truly a beautiful thing. The rain would fall, the rivers would run, and the rising heat would lift again the moisture into the air, cleansing it that it might fall and nurture the plants and the creatures once more.

The whole of Mielikki's cycle flowed through her thoughts as her feathered wings spread wide to lift her on the winds. Life, death, the continuum of time and space. The cycle, and within it, the great wheel of civilization, rolling forward so slowly.

She could appreciate more clearly the life she had lived, the roles she had played, the gains she and her powerful companions had made for those goodly folk around them.

Indeed, hers had been a remarkable life, full of joy and adventure and purpose.

But . . . incomplete.

That thought brought her to memories of Drizzt. She hadn't seen him in so many years, yet those years had done little to douse her love for him. She remembered the feel of his embrace, the softness of his kiss, the gentle strength of his hands.

She, Bruenor, and Regis had returned in the hopes of meeting with Drizzt again, after banding together on an appointed night, but it was not a godly-ordained night. There were no guarantees, she knew. Would all three survive the two decades of their second childhoods to arrive in Icewind Dale?

Even if they did, there was no surety that Drizzt would be anywhere near Kelvin's Cairn, or that he would even still be alive.

The girl recalled her time in Iruladoon, her dance and her song. She had pleaded with Mielikki for assurance, but the goddess could not give it. That wasn't how it worked, for the clockwork of the world moved along to its own machinations; the players were not mere puppets of controlling gods. They—Catti-brie, Bruenor, and Regis—weren't pawns of Mielikki, or under her protection. Neither was Drizzt, in any direct sense. If the Netherese found Catti-brie and killed her, then so be it. If an ogre's club crushed Drizzt's skull, then so be it.

Mielikki had intervened just one time, in the face of the greater catastrophe of the Spellplague and the tumult of the pantheon. The goddess had offered great gifts to Catti-brie in the magic of her spellscar and in, of course, rebirth itself. And she had given Regis and Bruenor a chance as well.

But it was all just that, a chance. Bad luck would get them killed. Too much faith in some intervention by the goddess would get them killed. Recklessness would get them killed.

Indeed, simple circumstance could get any of them, or all of them, killed.

Mielikki had done what she could by creating Iruladoon, but that was a minor thing, after all, Catti-brie saw so clearly from this high vantage point, where the vastness of the world spread before her, where the brilliant, interweaving clockwork of the world overwhelmed her with its beauty and force.

In taking Mielikki's bargain, they were mortal once more, as Drizzt ever had been and so remained—if he even remained alive! With Iruladoon fading to nothingness, the bargain could not be renewed.

Bad luck could get them killed.

The hawk shook her head, reverting to human form as the dweomer of the spellscar wore away.

And now it was Catti-brie a league above the ground, in the empty air, and her human arms could not catch the updrafts. The world seemed to spin below her as she plummeted from on high.

Bad luck could get them killed.

CHAPTER 10

PATRON

The Year of the Third Circle (1472 DR)
Citadel Felbarr

THE OVERHEAD CHOP CAME AS PREDICTED, PAINFULLY PREDICTABLE TO the sensibilities of the seasoned warrior.

Bruenor found himself disgusted with how pedestrian his opponent proved to be. This was the top student of Bruenor's training group.

But still, Bruenor's feint had been obvious, and the idea that the dwarfling had swallowed it so fully . . .

Bruenor easily turned aside to avoid the downward strike, sliding one hand up to the middle of his fighting stick—straight poles this day—and thrusting his arm out behind him, driving the weapon hilt into the ribs of the stumbling dwarfling. Bruenor's continuing turn put him directly behind the gasping youth—and he remembered that it was, after all, just a child here, and that thought almost slowed his next merciless strike.

Almost.

His two-handed slash cracked his weapon across the dwarfling's head and sent him flying to the side and to the floor, where he abandoned his weapon and grabbed at his head with both hands, tears flowing and cries of pain echoing.

Gasps came from all around the room, along with a call from Master Muttonchops Stonehammer to two other dwarflings.

Bruenor sighed and turned around to meet the charge of not one, but two students this time.

Fist and Fury, they were called, the powerful Fellhammer sisters, considered among the top students of the training class above Bruenor's level. And

Bruenor had to admit that by the way they were coming in at him, their coordination appeared sophisticated and correct.

He settled himself calmly, feet widespread, and easily defeated the twin thrusts with a sudden down-and-over, leftward sweep of his fighting stick, at the same time hopping out to the left to further exaggerate the miss.

The nearest of the twins, though, extracted herself almost immediately and with a quick two-step, launched herself at Bruenor, swinging with one hand, punching with the other.

He dived down low, shouldering her just above the knee and launching her into a somersault past him, to thump down hard on her back on the dirt floor of the chamber. The collision staggered Bruenor a bit, but he never lost his balance, and was already into his next move, sweeping a tremendous uppercut that froze the second sister in her tracks, and just barely missed taking the tip from her nose.

She charged in right behind the uppercut with a roar.

Bruenor had known that he would miss with his wild swing; the point of the attack was to give him just an eye-blink of time to reset his footing and to get his momentum going. As his stick lifted, he veered that momentum and threw himself into a rolling back flip over the stabbing stick of the female and over her arms, as well, landing only a step back to the right, but directly in front of her.

She was just a child, a girl child, he reminded himself. But with a growl, he slammed his forehead into her face anyway, and as she staggered backward under the blow, he leaped up, flattened out, and double-kicked her in the torso.

He landed on his side, bounced right back up and parried the incoming attack from the first of the sisters.

"Bungo's Roll," Emerus Warcrown said to Muttonchops at the side of the room, correctly naming the maneuver Bruenor had used on the second charging teenager. "When did ye start teachin' the dwarflings to dance such a move as that?"

"Haven't," Muttonchops said with a shake of his head.

Emerus Warcrown turned his attention back to the fight, just in time to see one of the sisters go flipping head-over-heels to the right and to see the second cringe in pain as Little Arr Arr, working her hands, her weapon, and her attention up high, stomped down on her foot.

110

She cringed and started reflexively to double over, and a left hook sent her sprawling.

"His father's sitting at Moradin's side, laughin' at us," said the king. As he spoke, the other of the young sisters went somersaulting aside yet again, the victim of a beautifully balanced parry, hook, and throw.

"I'm guessin' that Arr Arr's jaw's hanging as open as yer own," Muttonchops replied. "Moradin's too."

They came at him in a long line, a stream of attackers, sometimes two at once, and in the end, the last four together.

This wasn't Little Arr Arr they were battling, but Bruenor Battlehammer, King of Mithral Hall, the great warrior who had held back Obould's hordes in Keeper's Dale beyond Mithral Hall's western gate.

And it was Bruenor Battlehammer who had sat upon the throne of Gauntlgrym, who had heard the words of Moradin, the whispers of Dumathoin and the battle shouts of Clangeddin. Though he wore the frame of a child's body, inferior to those of his older attackers, his understanding of balance and movement kept those attackers constantly turning and shifting, often right into each other, and always clumsily.

And whenever that happened, Bruenor's fighting stick invariably and painfully cracked against an opponent's skull.

In the very first moments of that last assault, four coming at him furiously, Bruenor had stopped their charge and tied them up with misdirection, feinting left, then right, then left again so smoothly that the edges of the foursome collapsed upon the middle.

He swept the legs out of the teenage dwarf the farthest to his left, half-turned and backhand stabbed the second in line, then pivoted the other way to parry and roll around the stabbing sticks of the remaining two. Running back out to the right afforded him a few moments of single combat with the one on that end of the line. He stabbed, pulled up short and swept across, taking his opponent's weapon and her balance with him, then reversed suddenly and snapped his fighting stick across her chin, dazing her. In a one-on-one fight, Bruenor would have let it end there, but this opponent had three allies, after all, and so he leaped up and spun, lifting his stick over his head, and came around with a resounding chop that knocked the dwarfling girl senseless, and shattered Bruenor's fighting stick in the process.

He dived to the floor, retrieving her stick—she wasn't going to need it any longer, after all—and just managed to turn sidelong and brace the butt of the stick against his hip as the next in line leaped at him.

If it had been an actual spear instead of a blunt stick, that second dwarf would have surely impaled himself. The stick bowed but did not break. The flying dwarf bowed as well, doubling over the forward end, eyes going wide, breath blasted from him. He hung there for what seemed like an eternity, feet off the floor, until the momentum played out and Bruenor's stick dipped, dropping him back to his feet.

He didn't stay on his feet for long, however, grabbing at his belly, wailing in shock and pain, and tumbling to the side.

"Are ye having fun, then?" Bruenor roared, becoming disgusted with this whole ridiculous exercise. "Are ye, damned Moradin?"

The blasphemy drew more than a few gasps around the room, but Bruenor hardly heard them. Up again, he launched himself at the remaining two, his stick whirling with seeming abandon, though in truth, in perfectly timed and aimed angles and strikes. He cried out with every hit, his voice filling the air, and soon, so too did his two opponents cry out in pain and terror. They turned and fled . . . or tried to.

Bruenor kicked the feet out from under the nearest, the same poor dwarf whose legs he had swept out at the beginning of the encounter. He ran right over the poor lad, stomping him flat. He couldn't catch the other one, though, for she was older and faster, so he hoisted his fighting stick like a javelin and let fly.

The missile caught the poor girl right in the back of the neck and sent her sprawling to the floor in a cloud of dust.

"Are ye having fun, then?" an outraged Bruenor yelled at Muttonchops and King Emerus.

"Promote him at once to the town guard," King Emerus mumbled to Muttonchops Stonehammer.

"But 'e's just a laddie."

"He'll be trainin' with the adults," the king sharply replied. "Take him to new heights of prowess." He paused and looked Muttonchops in the eye. "And humble him. Three gods as me witness, I'll not again be hearin' the son of Reginald Roundshield blaspheme Moradin."

"Yes, me king," Muttonchops said with a low bow.

And so began the next journey for Bruenor, where he would spend the next three years on the training grounds with the finest warriors of Citadel Felbarr—and where he would spend most of those brutal sessions on the floor, truth be told.

But for the angry young dwarf, that journey was not humbling.

Just infuriating.

The Year of the Final Stand (1475 DR)
Citadel Felbarr

The young dwarf, Reginald Roundshield, had gained much notice in Citadel Felbarr. Every clan in the city buzzed about "Arr Arr's tough son," no longer referring to this teenager as "Arr Arr's little boy." For though he had seen no action outside of the city guard's training grounds, his strength and battle prowess had been nothing short of amazing, given his tender age and his still small and underdeveloped body.

For the one named Reginald Roundshield, who had been named Bruenor Battlehammer in his previous existence, the whispers that followed him to the training grounds each morning and home again late each night did nothing to flatter him, and everything to remind him of how ridiculous this whole process had become.

Day after day, tenday after tenday, month after month, and now year after year, he had played the game and assumed the role: "child prod'gy," they said.

"A fittin' tribute to Arr Arr!" they whispered behind his solitary walks.

Even, "Clangeddin reborn!"

For a long while, the whispers bothered Bruenor, particularly the most outrageous, as if the dwarf gods had any part in the travesty that had put him back in Faerûn instead of granting him his due to sit beside them in his well-earned place of honor. Now, though, he didn't even hear the whispers or the applause, and when he did, he didn't let the words sink in below a cursory level of awareness. He went to the training grounds and he fought, viciously, tirelessly, and fearlessly, and came home each night battered and bruised and exhausted.

Yes, exhausted most of all, because exhaustion was his defense against the restless sleep he too often fell into. Even his dreams proved disjointed and off-balance, interspersing the experiences of his previous life with those of this existence. And worse, those dreams, like his thoughts, too often contained a scowling image of Moradin.

He sat in his bedchamber one night, wrapping bandages around the newest wounds on one forearm—how had he missed such an easy parry?

"Nah, not missed," he stubbornly told himself, for the block had been good, but his still immature muscles had not given him the strength to properly deflect the veteran warrior's blow far enough from his exposed shield arm. But he had indeed erred in not anticipating that, he reminded himself. He had gone for the kill in the sparring match, trying a complicated cross-body deflection with his wooden axe instead of the safer block with his buckler. If he had been older and stronger, he would have properly pushed that striking wooden sword out wide enough, and left himself in perfect balance to smack the fool across the face with a "killing" backhand.

But he was not older and stronger, and so he had lost the match.

"Keep tellin' yerself that," Bruenor counseled, for while little mattered to him in those dark days of his young second life, he wanted above all else to beat them all, to knock down these city guards one after another and stand atop the bleeding pile!

Why?

He came to this point of reasoning and questioning often, his anger driving his thoughts onward and onward until they reached that fantasy of seemingly pointless supreme victory.

What would he win?

"Ah, but ye got yerself a nasty one," said Uween, his mother, stepping into the room. "I heared ye fought well against Priam Thickbelt, though, and he's a good one, I know. Fought him meself . . ."

Her voice trailed off, and Bruenor knew it was because he hadn't even afforded her the courtesy of looking at her while she rambled. He winced at the realization—Uween was not deserving of his disrespect.

But still, neither was she his mother. Not to his present thinking, and allowing her to continue along with the delusion truly insulted him and reminded him of how helpless he was in the face of his errant choice in Iruladoon.

A strong hand grabbed his ear and yanked his head around, to stare into the scowling face of Uween Roundshield.

"Ye look at me when I'm talkin' to—!" Then her voice became a garbled grunt of surprise and pain as Bruenor, acting purely reflexively, acting as Bruenor Battlehammer and not Reginald Roundshield, slapped her arm back, catching her by the wrist, breaking her grasp and driving her arm down, twisting it to force her to lurch to the side.

"Oh!" she exclaimed, catching her breath when Bruenor let her go.

He looked away, embarrassed but still angry, and was not really surprised when Uween smacked him on the back of his head.

"Ye don't disrespect yer Ma!" she scolded and she poked him in the side of the head. "And look at me!"

He did, his face a mask of anger.

"I come in here givin' ye praise and ye slight me?" Uween asked incredulously.

"I'm not wantin' yer praise or anyone else's."

"By the gods!" cried the exasperated woman.

"Damn the gods!" Bruenor exploded at her. Before he even realized his movements, he was on his feet, hoisting his wooden chair above his head. With a growl he threw it across the room, against the wall, shattering it to kindling.

"Oh, but get yer head, boy!" Uween scolded. "Ye don't go cursin' Moradin in me house!"

"Ah, but it's all a stupid joke, don't ye see?"

"What's all?"

"All of it!" Bruenor insisted. "All a durned game for them to laugh about. All a puny try for puny glories that none'll remember or care about. 'Bones and stones,' so me friend used to say. Bones n' stones and nothing more. For all our cries o' glory, for all our cheers to lost kin . . . bah, but ain't it just a game then!" He kicked at some of the wood that rebounded near to his feet, and when he missed it, he scooped up the plank instead and snapped it in half, then threw both pieces, sending them spinning across the room.

"Stop it!" Uween demanded.

Bruenor froze, stared her hard in the eye, then calmly walked over and picked up another chair. With a look of supreme defiance at this dwarf who would be his mother, he lifted the chair up high and brought it crashing down on the floor, smashing it to kindling.

Uween wailed and fled the room.

Bruenor followed her only far enough to slam the bedchamber door behind her.

115

He went back to his original position, though the chair was gone, and picked up his bandage to continue his work. But then he snarled and growled and spat and threw it, too, across the room.

He glanced back at the door and only then fully realized what he had just done—and done to an undeserving and always supportive dwarf widow!

The shame overwhelmed him and sent him to his knees, where he threw his face into his hands and wept openly. Shoulders bobbing in sobs, Bruenor lay down on the stone and splintered wood.

He fell asleep right there, face wet with tears, and troubling dreams began to descend upon him, and flitter up like dark wings all around him. Dreams of Catti-brie lying dead, of Obould's orcs drinking mead with tankards marked by the foaming mug, the standard of Mithral Hall—and indeed, drinking mead within Mithral Hall, and in a room littered with dwarf corpses!

The room's door banged open, startling him awake, but it took him a long while, time he didn't have, to determine if this was reality or another image in his dream.

He finally figured it out when King Emerus Warcrown lifted him roughly to his feet and slapped him across the face.

Behind the king, Parson Glaive stood solemnly, hands intertwined before him in prayer.

"What're ye about, then?" the king demanded.

"Wh-what?" Bruenor stammered, not knowing where to begin.

"How dare ye dishonor yer Da!" Emerus shouted in his face. "How dare ye treat yer Ma as such?"

Bruenor shook his head, but could not begin to offer a response. Not verbally. Dishonor? The word screamed in his mind! Could these two even begin to understand the word? He had died a good dwarf's death—he had earned his place at Moradin's side, and it had been taken from him through guilt and a foolish choice!

Dishonor? That was dishonor, not some meaningless argument in a meaningless house in a meaningless citadel!

His previous existence, his glorious tenure as King of Mithral Hall, had been ripped from relevance! Oh, and not by his own impulsive, foolishly emotional choice, but by the mere fact that he had been given that choice in the first place. What point this—any of it!—if a god's whim could undo everything?

"Well, Little Arr . . . Reginald?" Emerus Warcrown growled in his face. "What do ye got to say?"

"What playthings we be," Bruenor replied quietly, calmly.

The king looked at him curiously, then glanced back at Parson Glaive, who opened his eyes at the young dwarf's curious words.

"Self-congratulating," Bruenor went on undeterred. He gave a helpless chuckle. "And all our great deeds be tiny spots on the altars o' the laughing gods."

"His father," Parson Glaive explained to the king, who nodded and turned back to Bruenor.

"Ye don't know me father," Bruenor snarled at him. "Nor his father afore him."

He was sitting on the floor then, flying down at the end of a fist, with the room swimming around him in uneven turns.

"Yer time on the training grounds is done, Reginald," Emerus Warcrown told him. "Ye go out and fight aside them that's keeping Felbarr free o' damned orcs, and then ye come back and tell me about yer playthings! If ye live to get back to me, I'm meanin'!"

They left abruptly, King Emerus first, and Bruenor caught a glimpse of him offering Uween a much-needed hug before Parson Glaive, with a profound and purposely loud sigh, closed the bedroom door.

Perhaps no section of Citadel Felbarr was more revered and less visited than this one, where rows and rows of piled stones stretched into the vast darkness of the huge cavern. The cemetery of Clan Warcrown encompassed many rooms, and a new one was always under construction.

Bruenor heard the solitary digger's pick chipping at the stone when he entered the main chamber of the cemetery, the heartbeat-like cadence ringing somewhere far off in the distance to his left. He moved to his right, across the huge main room, the oldest room, and through one low tunnel into the next section. This room, too, he crossed, and another beyond the next tunnel and another beyond that.

He could no longer hear the lonely tap of the worker, who was digging out a chamber that would not be used for decades. As most of this solemn place was a testament to the past, to the fallen of the clan, so that dwarf excavator was the promise of the future. Citadel Felbarr would go on and she would bury her dead with reverence and tradition.

117

The thought nagged at Bruenor as he passed into the last chamber out here on the right flank of the centuries-old graveyard.

"A testament?" he heard himself muttering, with clear distaste.

He came to the cairn of Reginald Roundshield, his father.

He didn't know what to feel concerning the dwarf. He had never really known him, though so many spoke highly of him. And surely, Uween's character spoke highly of any dwarf who would take her as a wife.

He stared at the inscription that bore his father's name, his name.

"No!" he said emphatically at the thought. Never his name! He was Bruenor Battlehammer of Clan Battlehammer, the Eighth King of Mithral Hall and the Tenth King of Mithral Hall.

And what did that mean?

"Ah, Reginald," he said, for he felt as if he should say something. He had come out here, after all, to the cairn of a respected warrior. "Arr Arr, they called ye, and with great affection. Might be that yerself was Emerus's Pwent, eh?"

The mention of his own trusted guard sent Bruenor's thoughts spinning back to Gauntlgrym and that last fateful battle. All had been lost, so it had seemed, but then in had come the dwarves of Icewind Dale, led by Stokely Silverstream, and most importantly, with old Thibbledorf Pwent in tow—nay, not in tow, never in tow, but leading the charge!

As always, Pwent had been there, fighting beside Bruenor, propping Bruenor up, helping Bruenor along. Untiring, without surrender, ever with hope and ever full of the word of Moradin and the loyalty and glory of Clan Battlehammer, Pwent had carried Bruenor to the lever, had placed Bruenor's hand upon it, and had helped Bruenor pull the lever, ending the threat of the primordial volcanic beast.

Now Bruenor was crying, but for Pwent and not for Reginald.

Nay, not for Pwent alone, he came to realize, but for them all. For traditions that seemed quaint to him so suddenly—silly, even. For homage to gods who did not deserve it.

That last thought slapped back at him profoundly.

He wanted to curse Moradin, but inevitably wound up cursing himself. "Ah, but what a fool I be," he muttered through clenched teeth. He shook his head, a stream of curses escaping his lips. "A fool's choice," he ended. "I throwed it all away."

He nodded as he spoke the words, as if trying to convince himself. For every image he conjured of his just reward at Moradin's side, he found a complementary one of Catti-brie, or of Drizzt or Regis. Catti-brie, his adopted daughter . . . how could he abandon her in this time of her greatest need?

He would see her again in a few short years, so he hoped.

"Nay," he heard himself saying, for those years would not be "short," but interminable.

He focused on Drizzt. Had he ever known a better friend? One more loyal to him, including a willingness to tell him when he was wrong? Oh, Bruenor was beloved by many, and counted among his clan hundreds of loyal minions and scores of dear friends, like Thibbledorf Pwent. But Drizzt had known him on a deeper level, he understood, and Drizzt had not treated him with the deference afforded to a king, but rather, with the bluntness often needed from a friend.

"Them was me thoughts when I chose me path out o' the forest," a sitting Bruenor said to the cold cairn. "Me friends were needin' me, and so to them was I to go."

He chuckled helplessly as he considered his audience, for if he was speaking to Reginald, then the Reginald in question was himself. He felt no kinship with this dead dwarf lying entombed before him—how could he?

So he had come here to speak to himself, and to speak to all who had gone before and to the gods who awaited them. He felt the need to explain his decision, but even as he spoke the justifications for walking out of Iruladoon instead of going into the pond to the promise of Dwarfhome, he realized how thin his words must sound to Moradin, and especially to Clangeddin, whose edict was to die a glorious death, which King Bruenor Battlehammer had certainly done.

And then he had nullified it! He had abandoned tradition, abandoned all that was dwarf—all for friends who were not of Delzoun blood. The energy of that moment in Iruladoon had propelled him along to an impetuous choice, he felt, for now, more than halfway to the appointed meeting time, the passing of years did not make him feel as if he was moving toward his heartfelt goal, but rather the years were moving him, ultimately, further and further from it.

For every passing day this abomination named Reginald Roundshield drew breath served as an insult to Moradin, and for the sake of a goddess more aligned with elves.

Guilt bowed his head. Guilt brought tears streaming from his eyes.

When faced with that crystalline moment, that ultimate decision, Bruenor had betrayed tradition, betrayed the dwarf gods, and stolen all meaning from his previous, glorious life.

The troubled dwarf wandered away, back through the tunnels, but haunting thoughts followed him, as tangible as if the spirits of the thousands of dwarf dead had risen to poke at him with their cold bone fingers.

Everything felt off-balance to Bruenor. He could blame Mielikki, but that seemed insufficient. He could blame himself, but not without feeling the pangs of his own disloyalty to those who had loved him in his previous life.

And he could blame the dwarf gods, as he had done when King Emerus had screamed in his face, "How dare ye dishonor yer Da!"

"Ah, what playthings we be," he muttered again, a pervasive sense of emptiness freezing his heart. He stopped and turned back in the general direction of Reginald's grave, shaking his head.

"Nah," he decided, "I could'no have throwed it all away, for nothin' was there to throw. Nothin'!"

Once again, Bruenor found himself circling around from blaming others to blaming himself, to the ultimate place of despair: It was not the choice that had stolen all that he had held dear, but the mere fact that he had been offered the choice in the first place!

"Damn ye, Mielikki, and yer Iruladoon," he said. He growled, and he stamped his foot upon the stone floor. "Damn ye, Moradin! Ye didn't come and get me. I earned me place and ye didn't come and get me!"

The reason for that seemed obvious enough: because Moradin didn't care.

CHAPTER 11

MENTOR

The Year of the Third Circle (1472 DR)
Delthuntle

Shasta Furfoot, proprietor of the Lazy Fisherman, the Delthuntle inn closest to the water, paused in her glass-washing and looked past the one patron currently at her bar, nodding knowingly.

That patron, Eiverbreen Parrafin, gawked at her for a few moments, not really knowing what to do. She had warned him that folks had been inquiring about him of late—one powerful character in particular, and her expression now told him in no uncertain terms that the person in question had caught up to him.

Eiverbreen lifted his glass and swallowed its contents in one courage-inducing gulp. At least he had hoped it would have such an effect, though with or without the brandy, the stubble-faced halfling couldn't quite summon the fortitude to turn around. He heard the hard boots tapping on the floor, coming nearer.

Sweating now, he glanced around, moving only his eyes, for he daren't move his head.

He felt a tap on his shoulder and looked down to see an ivory cane. He slightly turned, keeping his eyes defensively down, to see a pair of beautiful, shining black boots, neat trousers tucked firmly inside, and a sash of golden thread holding a slender rapier whose elaborate hand cage left no doubt of this one's identity.

Eiverbreen swallowed hard and managed through sheer determination to turn around farther to square up to this most famous and dangerous halfling. He noted Grandfather Pericolo's neatly trimmed goatee, and the fabulous beret he wore, a tight headband with an octagonal flare up above, fashionably tilted higher on the left and with a golden clasp buttoning down the front flap. It was made of some shiny blue material, some exotic fabric which Eiverbreen didn't know, and stitched in small squares angled to give it a flecked look as it captured and reflected the light.

"Grandfather Pericolo," he said quietly, and he caught himself and quickly looked back down.

"A bit early for the drink, eh?" Pericolo replied. "But, ah well, it is a fine day! Might I join you, then?"

So nervous was he that Eiverbreen hardly registered the words, and it took him a long while to digest them enough to nod and stutter out, "At your pleasure."

Pericolo Topolino sat on the stool next to him. "Yes, one for me," he said to Shasta, motioning to Eiverbreen's empty glass, "and another for my friend here."

"We've better libations than that," Shasta replied.

"And I've spent nights nursing my head from far worse," Pericolo replied with a hearty laugh. "If it is good enough for my friend Eiverbreen, then so it is for me!"

Shasta's eyes went wide, as indeed did Eiverbreen's, at that proclamation.

"To Jolee," Pericolo said, hoisting his glass in toast. "A pity that she was lost in childbirth."

Now Eiverbreen did look at him, curiously and skeptically. "You didn't know my wife," he dared to say.

"But I knew indeed her important work," Pericolo explained. "I am a connoisseur of the finer things, my halfling friend."

His use of that word, "halfling," settled Eiverbreen in his seat more than a little, a clear reminder that they were, after all, of the same race—a race often denigrated by those of greater physical stature. Naming another little person as such was, in the end, a salute of brotherhood.

Eiverbreen lifted his glass and tapped it against Pericolo's and they shared a drink.

"And I count the deep-sea oysters among those delicacies," Pericolo went on. "I admit that I have not known for very long the specifics of how those came to the fishmonger, but I did indeed notice their absence, or perhaps their rarity would be a better way to put it, a decade ago. Now I know why. So, to Jolee Parrafin." He toasted and took another sip.

"You must be devastated by her loss," Pericolo said.

Eiverbreen hunched over his glass. He had indeed been devastated, but not for any reason of love that he would admit, even if it was there, in the back of his darkened heart. The loss of Jolee had financially devastated him—what little wealth they'd had.

Without oysters to sell, he had become a beggar, and only now, as his boy began to realize his potential as a deep diver, had Eiverbreen's purse—and his choice of whiskey—begun to recover.

"And now the oysters have returned, and I am pointed once more in your direction as the source," Pericolo said. "Your boy, I believe."

Eiverbreen didn't look up, fearful of where this might be going.

"Spider? Is that his name?"

"Heard him called that."

"Did you ever even bother to give him a name?" Pericolo asked, and Eiverbreen's wince answered that seemingly ridiculous question quite clearly.

"We just call him Eiverbreen, after his Da," Shasta offered.

"Spider," Pericolo corrected, and the woman nodded.

"He's a promising diver, so say my sources," Pericolo said to Eiverbreen. The other halfling grunted his agreement.

"And yet, for all that talent at your fingertips, you have never managed to do more than merely, barely, survive," said Pericolo. "Do you even understand the value of the treasures you possess?"

Eiverbreen's thoughts swirled around the words, winding over and under. He feared them to be a threat—was Pericolo going to kill him and "adopt" his boy? He looked up at the other halfling—he had to—trying to get some read of that smiling, disarming face.

"Of course you don't," said Pericolo. "The oysters are merely a means to an end to you." He lifted his expensive cane and tapped Eiverbreen's glass. "This end. The only end for Eiverbreen. The all-encompassing purpose of his existence, eh?"

"Have you come to taunt me, then?" Eiverbreen said before he could find the good sense to hold back the words. He even half-turned on his stool, as if to square into position to strike at Pericolo.

Any thoughts of that disappeared almost immediately, though, as he looked into the smiling, so-confident cherubic face of the wealthy halfling who was known to all on the street as Grandfather Pericolo.

Grandfather of Assassins.

His bravado gone in the flash of that recognition, Eiverbreen's eyes lowered and focused once more on that slender blade, the fabulous rapier of Pericolo. He wondered how badly it would hurt when the tip plunged through his skinny ribs and poked at his racing heart.

"Oh, heavens no, my friend," Pericolo said, however, and in such a light-hearted tone that Eiverbreen settled back once more—until he feared the words and tone were just a ruse to put him off his guard.

Oh, he didn't know what to think!

But Pericolo kept talking. "You think small because you live small," the Grandfather explained. "Whatever goals and hopes you might possess are pushed aside for the sake of one immediate goal, eh?" Again he lifted his cane and tapped the glass, then motioned for Shasta to refill Eiverbreen's.

"Perhaps that is the difference between us," Pericolo said. "You are small and I am not."

Eiverbreen didn't know how to answer that. He felt the insult keenly—all the more so because it was obviously true—but of course, to say such a thing would leave him dead on the floor, and that wasn't where he wanted to be.

"Ah, I have wounded your pride, and I assure you that such was not my intent," said Pericolo. "Indeed, I envy you!"

"What?"

Pericolo glanced at Shasta Furfoot as Eiverbreen blurted out the question, and he laughed, for her expression clearly reflected that it might have come from her as well.

"Ah, but to be done a day's work when the sun sets," Pericolo explained. "To think small, to live small, perhaps, is to live contented. I am never that, you see. Always is there another treasure, another conquest, to be found. Complacency is not a vice, my friend, but a blessing."

Not understanding whether he was being mocked or complimented, Eiverbreen took another deep gulp from his glass, and no sooner had he placed it back on the bar than Pericolo had motioned to Shasta to pour another one.

"The world needs both of us, don't you think?" Pericolo asked. "And likely, we need each other."

Eiverbreen stared at him, dumbfounded.

"Well, perhaps not 'need,' but we can surely profit from an . . . arrangement. Consider, you have goods and I have the trade network for such goods. What does the fishmonger pay you, a few pieces of copper, a silver or two perhaps, for an oyster? Why of course she would pay you so, because there is

competition here for the things—your boy is not the only diver, although, admittedly, he seems to be quite good at it!

"But there are places, not so far from here, where an oyster from the depths of the Sea of Fallen Stars could bring a gold piece, and I know how to get to those places," Pericolo explained. "You cannot do it without me, of course, but, so it seems, neither can I without you."

"What do you mean?"

"He means that your life's about to get a bunch easier, from what I'm hearing," Shasta Furfoot dared to say.

"Indeed, my lovely," Pericolo agreed, and to Eiverbreen, he added, "Do we understand each other?"

"I give you the oysters my boy brings in?" Eiverbreen asked more than stated, for he did not really understand what was transpiring here.

Pericolo nodded. "And I reward you," he said, and he tapped his cane on the bar to make sure he had Shasta's attention. "My friend here eats and drinks and resides here for free, this day forward."

The halfling woman's face dropped in a protest she dared not utter aloud, but Pericolo took care of it anyway, by adding, "I will pay all his bills henceforth."

He motioned to his glass, which Shasta moved quickly to fill. Pericolo stopped her short, though, with a thrust of his cane. "But just for Eiverbreen, yes," he warned in no uncertain terms.

The blood drained from Shasta Furfoot's face. Pericolo moved his cane aside and she poured the brandy into his glass. Pericolo pushed it with his cane in front of Eiverbreen. With a tip of his fine beret, Pericolo Topolino took his leave.

"Seems to be Eiverbreen Parrafin's luckiest day, eh?" Shasta Furfoot said as Eiverbreen stared over his shoulder at the departing Grandfather.

Eiverbreen, who had lived day-to-day, often eating dead rats he found in the alleyways, even licking puddles of others' spilled liquor, couldn't really argue, but a nagging fear inside of him put a lump in his throat.

"Generous," Donnola remarked to Pericolo, the two of them walking down the street from the tavern where Pericolo had left Eiverbreen. Donnola Topolino was the Grandfather's actual granddaughter, a promising young thief, and more importantly, a well-heeled socialite. Her primary function in Pericolo's organization was to keep abreast of the whispers behind the power structures in Delthuntle, something the brassy and lively seventeen-year-old halfling girl truly enjoyed, and at which she truly excelled.

"He has something I want," the Grandfather answered.

"Indeed, but you could have garnered that favor much more cheaply, don't you think?"

"How much can one halfling drink? Or eat? And he'll not eat much if he's drinking excessively, eh?"

Donnola stopped, and after a couple of steps, Pericolo, too, paused in his walk and turned to regard her smiling face, a perfectly smug expression.

"And sleep?" she said knowingly. "Not just the drink he craves, but lodging as well? No, Grandfather, this is about more than Spider. You feel sympathy for Eiverbreen."

Pericolo considered the words for a moment, then scoffed. "He disgusts me. He is weak. There is no place among our people for such reinforcement of prejudice!"

"Generous," Donnola said in a leading voice.

"To Spider, then," Pericolo agreed and he started on his way once more, "for I have surely hastened the death of his worthless father."

***

In all his life, even his previous life, Regis had never felt freer than in these very moments. He slithered around, almost weightless, enjoying the crags and valleys of the uneven sea floor. He didn't even bother to keep his guide rope, tied to a buoy above, in sight because he knew that he would have no problem in slowly ascending from the watery depths.

So entranced was Regis by the multitude of small fish swimming around, the eels ducking backward into their caves, and the waving sea grasses that he had barely begun to fill his pouch with the valued oysters.

It didn't matter, he knew. In all of Delthuntle, there weren't five others who could get down to this depth, with nearly fifty feet of water between him and the air, and none that he knew of could stay down here for any length of time, or come back down after a break. The others, of course, had to rely on magical spells with typically short durations, whereas Regis, for whatever reason, had little trouble swimming along the depths and moving around for a long, long while, or in coming right back down after a quick breath up above.

Even worse for those venturing to these depths under magical spells, they had to take great care in ascending, or be wracked with sometimes fatal pains. But Regis didn't have that problem. He could swim right up with few ill effects.

Even if he lingered too long, he never felt that drowning sensation, the terror of an immediate need to gulp air. Never. No, as he considered his time underwater, it seemed more like he was getting some air from the water. He couldn't actually breathe down here as well as up above, of course, but he could still draw some tiny sustenance, enough to keep him alive, if not entirely comfortable.

There were dangers under the dark waters of the Sea of Fallen Stars, but he knew them well enough and knew how to avoid them. His fears could not outweigh his sense of adventure, the feeling of freedom, and the extraordinary beauty all around him.

He had come out early this morning, giving himself all day to swim and enjoy, and to fill his pouch—for indeed, Eiverbreen was not forgiving when Regis returned without a full pouch.

The sun was low in the sky when he walked the broken cobblestone ways of Delthuntle's lower section. Eiverbreen was not at home in the alley with the lean-to, but that didn't much bother Regis, for he was fairly certain of where he might find his poor, afflicted father.

Shasta Furfoot smiled widely at the young halfling when he entered her establishment, and Regis returned the look, but only briefly, his expression shifting to one of concern as he glanced around the common room.

"He's upstairs in his room," Shasta remarked.

"His room? Whose?"

"Your Da."

"His room?" Regis asked, puzzled, for he and his father lived in an alley, with only a few boards leaned up against a wall to call their home.

"Aye, and your own, too, I'm guessing." Shasta nodded toward the staircase. "Third floor, third door on your right."

"His room."

Shasta merely smiled.

Regis bounded up the stairs, not slowing until he came to the appointed door. He started to knock, but paused and crinkled his nose, for inside, he heard the sound of someone violently vomiting.

He had heard this sound many times before.

He gripped the doorknob and slowly turned it, slipping quietly into the room. Across the way, before a dirty window, Eiverbreen kneeled, hunched over a bucket, choking and spitting. Eventually, he became aware of Regis's presence, for he turned and looked at his son, and began to laugh crazily. Only then did Regis notice not one, but two full bottles of whiskey standing by the wall behind the kneeling halfling.

"Ah, but she's the finest of days, my boy!" Eiverbreen tried to stand, but he overbalanced, staggered, and pitched headlong into the side wall, crumbling to the floor and laughing maniacally all the way.

"Father, what . . . ?"

"You got a bag full?" Eiverbreen asked, his tone suddenly changing to one of grave importance. "Good dive, was it? Tell me so! Tell me so!"

Staring at Eiverbreen, Regis lifted his bulging pouch. He had seen his father drunk before, of course. Indeed, many times. But night hadn't even fallen, and this level of drunkenness took him aback. The two bottles of whiskey just sat there, promising to keep Eiverbreen glowing until he finally passed out.

"How?" he asked. "Where did you get the coin?"

Eiverbreen began to laugh. "Good that you filled it!" he said, spittle flying with every word. He staggered toward Regis, veering wildly across the floor, sliding down near the unopened bottles. "Can't disappoint that one!"

"What one? Father?" Regis moved over and grabbed Eiverbreen's arm, just as the older halfling reached for one of the bottles.

Eiverbreen yanked free of his grasp and fixed an angry stare on him. "You give me the pouch," he demanded.

Regis hesitated.

"Now's not the time to get stupid, boy," Eiverbreen scolded and he thrust his hand out at Regis.

"You need to sleep—"

"The pouch!" Eiverbreen shouted, thrusting his hand forth again. "And you get back out there in the morning and fill another one—no, two! We can't be disappointing him!"

"Who?" Regis asked, but Eiverbreen had apparently forgotten him and shifted around to grab a bottle instead, fumbling around with the cork.

Regis knew better than to try to take it.

He left the room in a hurry and rushed downstairs, jumping up onto a stool right before Shasta Furfoot.

"What have you done?" he demanded.

"I?" the woman innocently replied.

"We're not paying!" Regis shouted.

"Who asked you to?"

"But . . . but . . . ," Regis stammered.

"Been paid, little one," Shasta calmly explained. "Paid evermore."

Regis tried to sort it out, shaking his head helplessly. "Who?"

"Don't you bother yourself with such details," Shasta said. "You get your oysters for your Da, and do as he tells you."

"He's too drunk to tell me anything worth hearing."

One of the patrons near him snickered at that remark, and Regis resisted the urge to walk over and punch the human in the nose.

"None of my business," Shasta Furfoot replied.

"And you gave him two more bottles," Regis protested. "He will be drunk for—"

"Not my problem!" the barkeep emphatically interrupted, coming forward threateningly as she did. "Now go away before I paddle your backside."

Regis slipped down from the stool and backed away a step. "Who paid, is all I want to know," he said quietly. "I have to give these to him." He hoisted the pouch. "Me Da says so, but couldn't tell me who before he fainted away."

"Ye just give them to me," Shasta explained, holding out her hand. Regis hesitated.

"Grandfather," said the nearby patron when Shasta hesitated. "Those will be Grandfather Pericolo's oysters, then."

"Aye, and I'll get them to him," Shasta Furfoot insisted and she tried to grab the pouch from Regis, who proved too quick for her.

Regis swallowed hard. He had never met the famed Pericolo Topolino, though, like everyone in this section of Delthuntle, and surely every halfling in the city, he had heard many stories of him. Mostly stories ending with someone's untimely and violent death.

He kept backing away and before he had even realized it, he had backed right out of the tavern and onto the street. He looked up at the top floor of the building and pictured Eiverbreen, pouring another bottle down his throat, probably vomiting as he drank.

Giving him so much whiskey would prove to be a death sentence, Regis knew, for he had seen many such walking corpses in his previous life in

Calimport. The Grandfather hadn't done Eiverbreen any favors, surely, whatever deal they might have made.

Regis chewed his lip and considered the anger simmering inside him. He had to do something, had to take some action.

But what? And how?

This was Pericolo Topolino, after all, the Grandfather of Assassins.

Regis wandered the streets that night, using oysters to bribe the halflings he found milling around, and soon enough found himself in the alleyway beside the house of Pericolo—Morada Topolino, it was called—a beautifully appointed, modestly sized home with sweeping balconies and railings decorated with hand-carved balusters. It stood three stories high, but halfling-sized, which made it about as tall as the average two-story human house. In the middle of the roof was another room, a fourth story, known as the widow's walk, for it looked out, far down the hill, over the vast Sea of Fallen Stars, affording a long view to those desperately searching for returning vessels, a constant, mournful reminder to those whose spouses never returned.

He moved around to the main street and the house's gate, which was locked. He looked around for some doorbell, a horn, or a large clapper, but found none. He thought of going over the fence, but shook his head, remembering the identity of the owner.

He looked up at the structure and thought to shout out. It was late, but no matter—what did he care, after all?

In that moment, he noted movement in one window, and watched as the lovely form of a young halfling lass drifted past it, half-dressed at most. The image stunned him, though through the lace curtains the woman seemed more like a ghost, a mirage, a fantasy.

She blew out the candle in the room and there was only darkness, breaking the spell.

"Grandfather," the halfling diver whispered derisively, shaking his head and wondering what he might do next. He thought to toss the bag of oysters over the gate, but stopped himself, and wisely, for they would be ruined laying out there before morning, surely, and would probably be gathered up by a raccoon or some other nighttime scavenger. With a sigh, Regis realized that he'd hand them over to Shasta after all.

"Grandfather," he said again, and began to plot.

Within a tenday, Regis found himself delivering his satchels directly to Shasta Furfoot on a regular basis, for his father was too drunk to handle the task. Constantly too drunk.

Eiverbreen grew thinner before Regis's eyes. Regis pleaded with Shasta to stop supplying drink to his father, but she simply brushed him away. "It's not my place to become a Ma to my customers, now is it?"

"He'll die, and then where will you be?"

"Right where I am now," she answered curtly. "Except I'll have one more room back to rent."

Her callousness struck the halfling profoundly, and sent his thoughts spiraling back to Calimport, many decades before. He had seen this attitude, prominently, among the poor of that southern city, and from people—humans and halflings alike—he knew to be of good character. That was the thing about the destitute. They had so little that they couldn't offer much, even compassion. Ever were the rich folk, the pashas of Calimport, praised for their philanthropy, when in fact, the gold they so charitably gave actually cost them nothing in terms of their own standard of living. A poor woman might take in an orphaned boy, without fanfare, though the proportional cost was surely much higher.

But, heigh-ho, all must cheer for those philanthropists!

"I will stop fetching the oysters," he declared to Shasta, and he ended with a snarl.

"Then you'll be talking to Grandfather Pericolo about that."

"Perhaps I should."

Shasta looked down at him from behind her bar, her smile growing in a mocking manner.

Regis found himself swallowing hard.

"Boy, you've got it better than you've ever known," Shasta said. "You're not living in a box anymore, and you've got food aplenty. You love your work and your work's giving back to you now more than ever."

"Have you seen my Da?" Regis asked. "More than just to give him your bottles of whiskey, I mean? Is he even eating?"

"He's eating."

"And vomiting it all over your room!"

For the first time, Regis caught a hint of sympathy in Shasta's expression. She leaned forward and bid him come closer, then very quietly said, "It's not my business, little one. Your Da's got his own mind and his own way, and none are to tell him different. None—not even yourself. You be smart now, and think about yourself. Eiverbreen's been walking downhill for years now, since before you were born. I've seen this too many times to count. You can go and yell at him all you wish, but you'll not change his path to the grave."

"Stop giving him the liquor, then," Regis pleaded.

"He'd get it anyway, if not from me then on the street. Are you to tell every tavernkeeper in Delthuntle to stop? And what of those allies he finds on the street to come in to places like my own and buy the bottles for him?"

"If he doesn't have the coin, then he can't get the bottles," Regis said.

"Back to refusing your work, then?"

"If that is what it takes," Regis said, and he snorted and turned and started away.

Shasta's strong hand clamped down on his shoulder and spun him back to face her, pulling him back roughly to the bar in the turn.

"Now you hear me good, Spider," she said, "and only because I've taken to liking you that I'm even telling you this." She paused and glanced left and right, as if to ensure that no one might be eavesdropping, and that, of course, added weight to her words as she continued. "You're not for understanding Grandfather Pericolo, so let me tell you. Don't you cross that one. Don't you ever cross that one, or you'll pay in ways you cannot begin to understand."

Regis looked at her curiously. "I've seen you with him," he replied. "Full of smiles and lighthearted banter."

"Aye, and I'm meaning to stay on his good side. And you should, too, for your own sake, and for your Da's."

"My Da cannot continue like this!"

"His end will come swifter and so will your own," Shasta warned. "You work for Pericolo now. When you work for Pericolo, you always work for Pericolo. Forevermore. Get that in your head now before you go and do something stupid."

Regis stared at her hard, but had no answer. She thought him a neophyte in such matters as this, no doubt, but he had grown up on the tough streets of Calimport, where characters like Pericolo Topolino ran rampant.

He silently cursed. For a few moments, he allowed himself the fantasy of being older, in a mature and trained body, where he could take on the likes of Pericolo Topolino!

But what would he really do, he wondered? He thought of Bregnan Prus and of how he had faced his fears and gone to battle with the older and larger boy, and had done so fully expecting that he would take a beating. Yes, it had been a brave action. This, though, was something entirely different, something far more dangerous.

"You have to be upon Kelvin's Cairn," he reminded himself under his breath.

"What's that then?" Shasta asked.

Regis shook his head and walked away. He was heading for the door when a shout on the stairway caught his attention. His father entered the common room, calling out "Drinks all around!" to the cheers of the other patrons.

Shasta Furfoot was quick to tamp down that enthusiasm, though, loudly reminding Eiverbreen that his tab was only good for his own libations. That brought some jeering, and a few half-hearted insults thrown Eiverbreen's way.

Regis moved near the door. For a brief moment, he locked his gaze with his father, who smiled widely as he climbed onto a stool. Then Eiverbreen turned away from Regis, to Shasta, and he slapped his hand down on the counter.

She was already moving to fill a glass of whiskey for him.

"It doesn't matter," Regis told himself as he departed the tavern. None of this mattered. He was only here to prepare himself for his journey to Icewind Dale and his return to the Companions of the Hall. And he would be ready, he silently insisted.

Nothing here mattered.

But he glanced back at the tavern and a wave of emotions rolled over him. Eiverbreen was his father, and had been kind enough to him—in his own broken way. He had never beaten Regis, and had found occasion to show him tenderness. Eiverbreen had lived a miserable life, more miserable still since his wife had died in birthing Regis. But only once in his decade with Eiverbreen had Regis ever heard his father place blame upon Regis for his miserable predicament, and even in that instance, a sober Eiverbreen had tearfully apologized the very next day.

"It doesn't matter," Regis said again, but more quietly, and contritely, for he recognized the lie.

Of course it mattered. It had to matter. If it did not, then what claim might a miserable and ungrateful Regis ever have to stand beside the Companions of the Hall?

But what could he do?

He glanced to the north, in the general direction of the fine Morada Topolino. Shasta's warning echoed in his thoughts, and he knew that she wasn't exaggerating. Pericolo was the Grandfather to all who knew him, and that meant that he was the Grandfather of Assassins. One didn't easily attain such a title as that.

Regis entertained a fantasy of returning to Delthuntle from Icewind Dale with Drizzt and the others beside him, to properly repay the Grandfather.

It was just a fantasy, however, for Eiverbreen couldn't wait that long, and the Grandfather himself was not a young halfling.

Regis moved to a different track, wondering if he could indeed stop, or at least slow, the take of oysters. Perhaps if he claimed only a couple each day, Pericolo would see his "gift" to the Parrafins as a losing business proposition.

Even that seemed a fleeting possibility—for what then would be left for Regis and his father? If he tried it, the Grandfather would monitor them closely. They would have to remain utterly destitute or invoke his wrath.

Regis sighed. He looked again in the general direction of Morada Topolino, but hopelessly.

The situation didn't improve over the next few tendays. With a bottle ever in hand, Eiverbreen stumbled around the tavern and the streets, covered in vomit and a multitude of small wounds, from tumbling into a chair or a wall or onto the street. He had more than a few bruises and cuts from knuckles, as well, as in his drunken stupor, he often insulted others.

Regis returned to their room one afternoon, his pouch half-filled, to find his father in a very agitated state. Broken glass and a puddle of semi-translucent brown liquid near one wall offered a clue.

"Ah, good that you're 'ere," Eiverbreen slurred. He laughed and nearly fell over from his seated position near the mess. "My legs're a bit wobbly," he said, struggling to stand.

Regis helped him to his feet, though Eiverbreen fell immediately against the wall for better support.

"Be a good brat and go get me another bottle," Eiverbreen instructed.

"No," Regis replied, and hearing the word escaping his lips only bolstered his resolve. He couldn't do much about the larger situation around him, but perhaps he could resolve the problem more directly.

"No?" Eiverbreen stared down at him hard.

"Too much, Da," Regis said calmly.

"Eh?"

"You are too much in the bottle, Da," Regis said. "You need to slow down. More food and less drink, yes?"

He noted that Eiverbreen wasn't blinking.

"And you need to get out of this tavern—you hardly ever go outside anymore!" Regis said, trying to sound as cheery as possible. "Oh, but it's a wonderful season, full of sun and a cool wind off the sea. Let me get you some food. We've time before sunset for a walk to the shore—"

The last word came out with a yelp attached, for in an explosion Regis had never before witnessed, so sudden and primal in its ferocity, Eiverbreen sprang at him and slapped him hard across the face, sending him sprawling to the floor.

"Go fetch me a bottle!" Eiverbreen yelled, storming closer and stamping his foot heavily against the wooden floor. "You little rat! Don't ever tell me what to do!" He reached down and grabbed the stunned Regis by the collar and hoisted him from the floor, lifting him right up off his feet before dropping him back down. Eiverbreen didn't let go, shaking him violently and howling at him with spittle flying.

Regis hardly heard the words, he was so stunned by this abrupt transformation. Eiverbreen finally let go, sending Regis spinning back against the room's door.

"Go!" Eiverbreen demanded.

Tears welling in his eyes, Regis scrambled out of the room. He rushed down the stairs, but didn't go to the bar. Instead, he burst out of the tavern's door, onto the street.

Before he had even realized his course, the young halfling found himself in the alleyway beside the fabulous Morada Topolino.

He waited for the sun to set, waited for the dark of night to fully fall, then Spider began to climb. His love for Eiverbreen drove him upward.

He moved right to the roof and crept to the window of the widow's walk, his vision following the moonbeams inside.

"What am I doing here?" he quietly asked. What could he hope to accomplish? What difference might anything he did in Morada Topolino make to the death spiral of Eiverbreen?

He would steal—a lot—and with that wealth, he would take Eiverbreen away to a better place, and to a situation not dependent upon the whims of a heartless Grandfather and an uncaring barkeep.

"Yes," he said and nodded.

He ran his sensitive young fingers around the window encasement, feeling for trip wires or other potential traps. How he wished he had a glass cutter, and even more so when he realized that the window was locked.

Regis pulled a small knife from his pouch, one he used to pry up oysters stuck under rocks in the depths of the Sea of Fallen Stars. The window was divided into two panes that could slide past each other to allow the sea breeze to enter. The higher pane was inside the lower, he noted.

He eased his knife into the tight crease between them.

Slowly, very slowly, his face pressed against the glass below as he pushed the blade down.

And there it was: a tripwire.

Regis nodded, having seen this particular trap design many times in Calimport. The movement of the sliding windows would set it off, one or the other taking the wire with it. Each pane's frame would have on it a small sharp edge, designed to cut the wire when it pulled tight.

Regis worked his knife around the top lip of the top pane, and found just such a blade, cleverly embedded. He removed it with ease.

Back in went the knife, this time tapping the locking mechanism. With a subtle twist, Regis threw the lock.

Slowly he lowered the top pane. He would have preferred to lift the lower one, obviously, for easier access, but he couldn't easily get to the embedded blade on that one, for, as that pane was in front of the other, the blade would be between them. No matter, though. His name was Spider, after all, and it was a moniker he had properly earned.

The window half down, Regis glanced around to ensure that no one was watching, then up he went, climbing the side of the dormer, then twisting over, inserting himself into the room above the window.

He clung there, in the room at the top of the window, for some time, inspecting the floor. Likely there was a pressure trap in place, he told himself, and so, still up on the wall, he moved to the side before dropping down lightly.

The room was sparsely furnished, with just a chair facing out the window, overlooking the vast sea, and a small table beside it—for a dinner tray, perhaps.

Behind the chair was a trap door, open now, and with a secured ladder leading down into the main house.

The main house and the Grandfather's treasures.

Down went Regis, creeping into the darkness. He padded around on bare feet, getting a lay of the various hallways and doors, stopping and listening at each. Around a corner to the narrow corridor leading to the back of the house, he saw a small light peeking around the edges of a slightly opened door. Every step taken with care, every movement in complete silence, the burglar peeked into the room.

A single candle burned, and burned low. He could see a grand desk across the way, one too ornate to be that of a minor clerk. Thinking this to be the place of the Grandfather's business, the halfling dared push the door a bit further and peer in.

To his great relief, the room was empty.

To his great delight, the room was full of statues and baubles, a trio of chests, and an assortment of other interesting, and likely profitable, articles.

It had been too easy—somewhere in the back of his mind, Regis knew that. He had dealt with characters such as Pericolo in his previous life in Calimport, and never could he have come this far without some resistance. Perhaps it was just the difference between the two cities, he thought. Perhaps here in smaller and quieter Delthuntle, reputation alone was enough to ensure security.

He stood up straight, smiling widely. He reminded himself to check for a trap around the door jamb, but before he even started, he heard a low and ominous growl.

Not from inside the room, but behind him.

Slowly Regis turned his head around. His eyes had adjusted to the darkness now, but still the first image that came to him were two sets of eyes shining back at him, at a level just below his own. The halfling held his breath and moved into the room a bit farther. The opening door let the meager light spill out enough for Regis to make out the massive canine forms behind those eyes, enough for Regis to see the shining fangs of the guard mastiffs.

He didn't dare move, other than to ease his hand behind him to grab at the edge of the opened door.

The dogs growled, long and low, barely ten halfling strides away.

Regis knew that he had to move first and fast. His brain screamed at him to flee. But he couldn't, and he couldn't tear his gaze from those threatening sets of eyes.

One of the dogs barked, breaking the spell, and both mastiffs leaped as Regis fell into the room. He almost had the door closed when the nearest dog crashed into it, and there they struggled, the dog scraping and barking and pushing back hard.

The desperate halfling threw his shoulder against the door, and luck was with him, for he hit it just as the dog backed off—but only so that the beast could leap back in hard.

The door shook from the impact and Regis stumbled backward. Now both dogs barked and howled and slammed and scraped.

He had to get out of there! He ran across the room to the one window, and threw it open, but only to find the opening barred.

He fumbled for a locking mechanism, but found none. He heard more noise outside the door, down the hall.

He rushed around.

The door rattled hard.

He blew out the candle, though he didn't know why.

The door burst in.

With a yelp, Spider dived to the corner and scrambled up the wall, feeling the hot breath of pursuit. He got up ahead of the dogs, out of their snapping reach, but to what end? What might he do next?

Then it didn't matter as the darkness flew away in the thunderous retort of a fireball, all the room filling with flame. Regis saw it more than felt it, his brain screaming at him that he was surely burning.

For everything around him was burning, including the very wall where he held on. With a terrified shriek, he let go, pitching hard to the floor, nearly knocking himself unconscious.

He felt a sharp sting, and now felt the intense heat mounting all around him. He had to get out, but he couldn't. He rolled to his back and looked up at the fiery ceiling.

He thought of his poor father.

He thought of Drizzt and Catti-brie and Bruenor, of his pledge to meet them on the mountain, of the glories they would again find together.

But Iruladoon wasn't waiting for him, he knew.

Not this time.

The heavy, burning timbers collapsed atop him with a tremendous roar and rush of flame.

He didn't even hear his own scream.

CHAPTER 12

MISTRESS

The Year of the Splendors Burning (1469 DR)
Netheril

I T FELT TO HER LIKE A COMMON NIGHTMARE, FALLING HELPLESSLY, THE deafening wind thundering in her ears. She tumbled and tried to right herself, which only made her twist and spin as she turned head-over-heels.

Dizzy and disoriented, Catti-brie felt her face flapping from the pressure of her speeding descent. Only then did she realize that she was screaming at the top of her lungs, though she couldn't really even hear her voice through the drumbeat of the rushing air.

She noted the spin of colors before her, brown and blue, brown and blue, and used that to get her bearings, up from down.

She stretched out to her full length and threw her arms out wide, and gradually managed to stop her tumble.

But then, knowing ground from sky once more, another reality struck her profoundly: the ground was much closer and she was speeding toward it and hadn't the energy to transform into a bird, or anything else.

She was just a human girl, whose bones would shatter to mush when she slammed into the ground.

***

Lady Avelyere gasped and threw her hand over her mouth as she watched the scene unfolding in the waters of her scrying pool. She looked to the east, but the child was too far away for Avelyere to spot her with the naked eye.

"Go! Go! Help her!" Lady Avelyere yelled to a pair of her students who lingered nearby. The young women—Diamone and Sha'qua Bin—glanced into the scrying pool, yelped, and rushed away.

"No, no, no," Lady Avelyere said to the child who could not hear her. She didn't want it to end like this! There was something here with this young one, something magnificent and intriguing.

And now it was ending before her very eyes. She scoured her brain, seeking some spell she might throw through the scrying pool—was it even possible?

She heard a gasp from behind her and turned to look over her shoulder to see Rhyalle and Eerika, both wide-eyed and horrified. Eerika began to weep in sympathy.

Lady Avelyere didn't even want to turn back, for tearing her eyes from the horrifying scene had broken her fixation. There was nothing she could do, she told herself, and so too told herself not to watch the morbid, unfolding catastrophe.

But she couldn't resist, and bit her lip as she turned her gaze once more to the plummeting Ruqiah.

She began to cast a dweomer of levitation. It was probably useless.

But she had to try.

She didn't even feel as if she was falling anymore. It seemed as if she were standing in a strong wind, her arms out wide to catch as much of the breeze as she could.

But the ground loomed ever nearer, by the heartbeat.

The young girl began to recite a spell she had learned only a couple of tendays previously. Only because of that had Catti-brie dared to fly so high, for she was, of course, well aware that the magic of her shapechanging ability was a finite thing each day, and could leave her abruptly.

She began to whisper. She fought the tug of the wind and reached into her small pouch, producing a feather.

How Lady Avelyere's eyes widened when the girl in the scrying pool suddenly slowed her descent, drifting down, floating down, so gently!

"Mistress!" cried Eerika. "You saved her!"

But Lady Avelyere knew that she had done no such thing. In her desperation, she had fumbled her spellcasting and had started over, and was no where near completing the levitation spell. In any case, she knew it wouldn't have worked through a simple scrying device.

Lady Avelyere's thoughts whirled with possibilities—Diamone, one of the two students she had sent running, was quite proficient in the levitation spell. Indeed, Avelyere had tasked Diamone with cleaning the high windows of their keep in Shade Enclave for just that reason.

Had Diamone gotten close enough and saved the girl?

But Lady Avelyere could only shake her head as she considered the floating Ruqiah's current position. Even if Diamone had been on the ground directly below her, Ruqiah would be long out of range of such a dweomer.

There could be only one answer.

"She cast the spell," Lady Avelyere told the two behind her. "Our little Ruqiah has learned a new trick, apparently."

"More powerful than any arcane magic we have yet seen from her," Rhyalle remarked.

"But not more powerful than the druidic magic, surely," Eerika countered. "Is there such a spell as that in a druid's repertoire?"

Not knowing the answer, Lady Avelyere quickly cast a detection spell aimed at the scrying pool, sensing the emanations around the floating child. "Arcane," she announced.

"We have watched her for many tendays," Eerika said. "How could we have missed this ability, this level of arcane power? And to execute an intricate spell in the middle of such a fall!"

"We haven't witnessed it because it is new," Lady Avelyere decided, and she turned and nodded to drive home the point to her two confused students. "Our little Ruqiah is being trained."

She was still several hundred feet above the ground, but now floating down, drifting on the winds as she sank gently, as if in deep water. She did a quick estimation of her height and her descent and came to the comforting conclusion that the spell's duration would more than suffice to put her safely back to the ground.

She had another spell on her lips to control her movement, but she changed her mind and shook her head. She didn't want to be in control now.

She wanted to fly, or to float at least, and let the wide winds take her where they may.

Catti-brie noted the landmarks below her, and as the ground grew larger, she began to pick out movements here and there. She noted some wolves lying around in the sunlight, and some grazing deer far to the side.

The wind was not so strong in her ears now in the gentle descent, but there wasn't much to hear from this high perch. The absence of sound served to increase Catti-brie's sense of freedom, and she came to see this wind-inspired ride, like the bird-flight before it, as a spiritual journey as much as a physical one. She could learn from the tickling wind. On the ground, the world seemed so static and firm, but up here, drifting and floating around on the gusts, it occurred to her that the world was ever in flux, ever in movement.

She closed her eyes and let the sensations wash over her.

Soon after, she touched down, and fell into a short trot. She looked back up at the brilliant sky and reflected on the feelings of freedom, of flight, of falling, of drifting on the breezes.

This, then, was the beauty of her communion with Mielikki, she realized. Everything she experienced had the power to widen her vision, her thoughts, her possibilities.

Truly, she felt blessed.

Lady Avelyere was awakened from a nap a few days later by Rhyalle, with word that little Ruqiah was on the move.

"Eerika, Diamone, and Sha'qua Bin have been dispatched to track her," Rhyalle assured her.

Still, Lady Avelyere was fast to her scrying pool, gathering more information from Rhyalle as she went. Soon enough, she had conjured up the image of the girl. Ruqiah, it seemed, was now a wolf, loping along in the general direction of the Desai encampment. Lady Avelyere nodded, not surprised.

"She will go to look in on her tribe and her parents when night has fallen," the diviner predicted, and she, Avelyere, would be there to watch. She had already inconspicuously visited the Desai several times, invisibly, and knew the layout of the camp and the location of Ruqiah's parents.

"How long shall we play this game, Mistress?" Rhyalle asked, and Avelyere turned to regard her curiously.

"She is being trained," Rhyalle explained. "She grows more powerful by the day, it seems. She will become harder to catch, and harder to control."

The words hit Lady Avelyere with the power of truth, and she found herself nodding in agreement.

"And we grow weary of this brown plain," Rhyalle admitted.

"We?"

"All of us," said the student. "And yourself as well, I would guess?"

Lady Avelyere found herself smiling at the accusation. She had not trained her students to be mindless pets, after all, cowed into telling her what they thought she would most like to hear. No, far from it. To join the Coven of Avelyere was to pronounce opinions without fear of retribution.

And Lady Avelyere had to admit, in this instance, Rhyalle was right.

"Go to her secret garden," she instructed the younger woman. "Gather the rest of your peers, even those in pursuit of Ruqiah, and set the traps, as we discussed. It is time for us to bring little Ruqiah into our net. I have seen enough. We know her strengths and her weaknesses."

Rhyalle bowed and turned to the other two acolytes.

Lady Avelyere went back to her scrying pool and watched the wolf's progress. Soon enough, as the sun began to set, she saw through the pool the waving white and brown tents of the Desai.

She dismissed the enchantment and prepared her next spell, a teleport, which put her very near to the Desai and very near to Ruqiah. A simple dweomer of invisibility, another to prevent magical detection, and into the camp walked the diviner, confident and quite pleased with herself.

"What is it?" Rhyalle asked when Lady Avelyere joined her near the Desai child's secret garden.

Lady Avelyere shook her head and sighed. "Wizards, both," she replied.

"Both? Ruqiah and . . . ?"

"And both of her parents," Lady Avelyere explained with a wide grin. She had watched Ruqiah in the tent with her parents. She had expected a quiet night of hugs and kisses, perhaps a comforting story or two. What she had seen instead was a training session in the magical arts as regimented and trying as anything she would inflict on her own, much older students. Ruqiah's parents, particularly Kavita, the mother, had been instructing the child on "the glory of At'ar the Merciless, the Yellow Goddess, the bringer of light and fire." Ruqiah could conjure a fan of flames with ease, and the power of her spell was substantial! Clearly this little child of only a few living years was on the verge of casting fireballs.

Fireballs, though she was just a child!

The thought of it took Lady Avelyere's breath away.

"Her parents practice the Art?" Rhyalle asked. "But they are Bedine. That is forbidden!"

Lady Avelyere waved her hand to silence her student, for the point was moot, wholly irrelevant even. Lady Avelyere was well aware of the fact that the Bedine counted magic-users among their ranks, whatever the edicts of Shade Enclave. It didn't matter—to Avelyere or to the Netherese rulers—the ban was in place merely to keep these magic-users in the shadows instead of in a leading role among potentially insurgent tribes.

Rhyalle kept talking, but Lady Avelyere waved her hand all the harder, bidding her to silence. The diviner was considering their plans in light of the new information she had just garnered about Ruqiah. She worked through the expected sequence.

Speed would be the key.

Catti-brie, exhausted from her lessons, didn't return to her garden that night, or until late the next day, when she trotted among the wind-blown rock walls in the guise of a wolf once more. This had become her favored animal form. She felt so light on her . . . paws! And her senses were so keen, her hearing and smell particularly, that she felt quite safe loping around the plains.

And she liked the way the world looked through the eyes of a canine, with their broader field of vision. While she missed the vibrant colors of her human eyes, the clarity of the "duller" world amazed her in the distinct structures of the grasses and her ability to detect even the slightest movement.

Still, she saw nothing out of place as she trotted into her refuge.

But something was amiss, she realized quickly, as foreign smells tickled her nose. She glanced all around, then reverted to her human form and continued her scan, beginning a spell to detect any magic that might be around.

Before she had hardly begun it, a wave of dispelling energy washed over her, and a voice from behind her said, "No tricks, little one."

Catti-brie swung around, to see a beautiful woman dressed in flowing purple and blue robes staring back at her.

And others came into view as well, their mass invisibility dismissed, five similarly dressed but younger women floating just above her garden, their arms outstretched.

"Surrender easily, young one," a seventh woman said, coming into view beside the oldest of the group, who began to murmur, as if in spellcasting.

Catti-brie's eyes went wide in the realization that the dreaded Netherese had found her once again.

"We wish to speak with you, Ruqiah," the newest of the seven said sweetly—too sweetly, and Catti-brie felt the weight of magical suggestion behind the voice. "We are not enemies to you."

She wanted to believe it—she almost believed it!—but she realized that was the point of the magical enhancement, of course.

Seven against one—seven waiting for her. She could not fight here.

Catti-brie became a bird and flew away.

Or tried to, for she came to understand the hard way that the floating five wizards were actually anchor points. The oldest of the group released her spell and the expanse between those five filled with webbing, just as Catti-brie started to fly through it.

She slammed in to the web, quickly entangled. She thought of her mother's lesson, and knew that fire was her only chance—although she would surely get singed in the effort. Before she could launch any spells, though, she saw sparks all around her, as the five floating wizards ignited their hands, burning free of the web, which now, without anchors, fell to the ground, taking Catti-brie down with it.

She landed hard and felt the breath blown out of her, and in the stunning impact, reverted to her human form, though she found herself no less entangled.

But then the webbing was gone, only a moment later, and a trio of young women rushed over to her.

She became a bear, thinking to tear them apart—or she tried to, for even as she began her enchantment, several waves of dispelling magic assailed her.

Then came a more insidious spell, striking at her mind, numbing her body to the calls of her thoughts, holding her in place. She battled it, and even managed to keep herself somewhat free of its paralyzing grasp. The distraction cost her, though. She felt her hands yanked behind her, magical bindings immediately applied.

She cried out and struggled, but she had only recently turned six and so was no physical match for the older women. A hood went over her head and she was thrown to the ground, and she felt a thick sack being pulled down over her. She kicked out, and took some pleasure in hearing one of the sorceresses yelp in pain. She was already caught, however, and too far into the sack. The others stuffed her legs in behind her, and the drawstring tightly closed.

She struggled, and got kicked hard. Stunningly hard, brutally hard, and then again when she moved some more.

"Speak not and move not!" said the same woman who had first addressed her. "For every word and every shift will bring a beating to you, I promise."

Stubborn Catti-brie started to protest, and promptly got kicked again. Then someone sat on her, crushing her down, holding her still.

"Kimmuriel is a drow of his word," Draygo Quick informed Parise Ulfbinder through their crystal ball connection. "He studies with the illithids, and they are very aware that something is indeed transpiring."

"But they do not yet know what that might be," Parise reasoned.

"They sense a disjointedness in the multiverse. They warn of chaos and of celestial changes."

"Cryptic words are useless words."

"For now," Draygo Quick replied abruptly. "Give them time."

"Have you located your former prisoner? Have you determined if this drow, Drizzt Do'Urden, is indeed a favored mortal?"

"None have found him, though many look, including Jarlaxle of Bregan D'aerthe. It is as if Drizzt has simply disappeared from the known universe. But no matter. He was not of paramount importance to me, and surely not now when I have entered into this bargain with Kimmuriel, who will provide greater answers to me than Drizzt Do'Urden ever could."

"Do we need another prisoner who might offer answers?"

"Do we need any, or did we ever?" Draygo Quick replied. "I have not gone after Drizzt again, nor have I sought revenge on this drow organization with which we both still do business."

Parise Ulfbinder tapped his fingertips together nervously. "Have you shared 'Cherlrigo's Darkness' with Kimmuriel?"

"Surely not!" Draygo Quick answered. "Our bargain was that I would forgive the assault of Bregan D'aerthe upon my home in exchange for the information Kimmuriel garners from his time with the mind flayers. There was no reciprocating action on my part intended or offered, other than my willingness to allow our trading agreement with the drow mercenaries to continue, to the mutual profit and benefit of us both."

"But it is possible that our sonnet will hold clues the illithids might find valuable in their search for the celestial truth."

Draygo Quick paused, and Parise could see that he had caught the older lord off guard.

"Perhaps in the future, then, but only with your agreement, I assure you," Draygo Quick decided.

Parise nodded—that was what he had been hoping to hear. He bid Draygo Quick farewell, replaced his cloth over the crystal ball, then rose and turned back to the anteroom, where he had left his guest.

He poured a drink for Lady Avelyere and one for himself when he returned to that room, and took the chair across from his guest before the burning hearth.

"A Chosen or a prodigy?" he asked absently, a question he had posed in their previous discussion, before dismissing himself to attend to some business.

"I don't think we can know," said Lady Avelyere. "Truly she is gifted in the Art—more divine than arcane, it would seem."

"And divine would indicate . . ."

"It would seem," Lady Avelyere said pointedly. "There is no telling with spellscars. It is possible that this Ruqiah child is afflicted in ways we have never witnessed, at least to this magnitude, but that hardly means she is blessed by any particular god."

"She is worth watching," Parise said, and Lady Avelyere breathed a clear sign of relief.

"You thought I would have her killed?" the Netherese lord asked incredulously.

"The thought did cross my mind."

"To what end?"

"To what end in bothering with the little one at all? To what end in hunting these favored mortals you seem to fear—and if you fear them, does it not follow that you would wish to destroy them?"

Parise Ulfbinder shook his head. "I wish to learn, nothing more. You are acquainted with my friend Draygo Quick?"

"The lord who resides outside of Gloomwrought?"

"Yes."

"With whom you just spoke," she stated and didn't ask.

Parise eyed her slyly.

"You know my title and my profession," the diviner teased.

The Netherese lord could only laugh at that. He trusted Avelyere—indeed, she knew much concerning his work with the ancient sonnet and with Draygo Quick in deciphering recent events.

"Lord Draygo caught a curious drow some years ago," Parise explained. "He is called Drizzt Do'Urden, and is rumored to be a favored child of Mielikki, and also rumored to be an unwitting Chosen of Lady Lolth."

"Quite a combination of admirers."

"Indeed," Parise agreed with a laugh, and he took a sip of his liquor. "Lord Draygo lost his prisoner a couple of years ago, although after more than a year with that one residing as a . . . visitor, he had learned nothing of value, in any case."

"Perhaps our little Ruqiah is a better charm, then."

"What do we know of her?"

"She can shapeshift—a gift of one of her two spellscars, I believe, and no small feat," Lady Avelyere answered. "Only powerful druids can attain such levels of animal form."

Parise nodded.

"She killed Untaris and Alpirs, as you suspected," Avelyere added. "It was no random lightning bolt, but a directed and devastating strike by this child."

"The fools tried to murder her mother, so you said. How can I blame her for defending her family?"

Lady Avelyere obviously found her forthcoming words stolen by the surprising response. She stammered and stared at her friend Parise.

"Alpirs and Untaris were idiots, both of them," the lord explained with a shrug.

"And she saved her mother in that fight, with healing magic quite considerable."

"From the spellscar?"

Now it was Lady Avelyere who could only shrug. "She bears two curious markings. Perhaps they are relevant, perhaps not."

"You trust your bevy of students?" Parise asked.

"Implicitly," Lady Avelyere assured him. "I am, after all, a fine spy."

Parise could only laugh as he figured out her meaning, and he lifted his glass in toast to her undoubtedly considerable ability in understanding the actions of those around her.

"I would not have the knowledge of Ruqiah spreading beyond this room and your tower," the Netherese lord explained. "If word got out among Shade Enclave that this child killed two Netherese agents and that she was training in the Art under the auspices of two Bedine wizards . . . well, the implications would be dire indeed."

"You don't wish to punish her."

"I do not wish a slaughter of this Desai tribe, nor any war at all, nor anyone else taking an interest in this curious Ruqiah. This child may prove of great value to us, but she is not our enemy. Not now, and hopefully not ever. Untaris and Alpirs were not sent as assassins, but as kidnappers, the fools, and so they deserved their fate. And I only sent them, as others have gone on similar expeditions for other potentially favored mortals, because I did not anticipate such an easy look into the events that may soon be circulating around this one."

"What would you have me do with her?"

"What would you wish me to answer?" He shrugged and took another drink, seeming as if he simply did not care.

A great smile widened across Lady Avelyere's face.

She considered the potential of her newest student.

PART THREE

UNINTENDED BONDS

I could not have planned my journey. Not any particular journey to a town or a region, but the journey of my life, the road I've walked from my earliest days. I've often heard people remark that they have no regrets about choices they've made because the results of those choices have made them who they are.

I can't say that I agree fully with such sentiments, but I certainly understand them. Hindsight is easy, but decisions made in the moment are often much more difficult, the "right" choice often much harder to discern.

Which circles me back to my original thought: I could not have planned out this journey I have taken, these decades of winding roads and unexpected twists and turns. Even on those occasions when I purposely strode in a determined direction, as when I walked out of Menzoberranzan, I could not begin to understand the long-term ramifications of my choice. Indeed on that occasion, I thought that I would likely meet my death, and soon enough. It wasn't a suicidal choice, of course—never that!—but merely a decision that the long odds were worth the gamble when weighed against the certainty of life in Menzoberranzan, which seemed to me emotional suicide.

Never did I think those first steps would lead me out of the Underdark to the surface world. And even when that course became evident, I could not have foreseen the journeys that lay ahead—the love of Montolio, and then the home and family I found in Icewind Dale. On that day I walked away from Menzoberranzan, the suggestion that my best friend would be a dwarf and I would marry a human would have elicited a perplexed and incredulous look indeed!

Imagine Drizzt Do'Urden of Daermon N'a'shezbaernon sitting at the right hand of King Bruenor Battlehammer of Mithral Hall, fighting beside King Bruenor against the raiding drow of Menzoberranzan! Preposterous!

But true.

This is life, an adventure too intricate, too interconnected to too many variables to be predictable. So many people try to outline and determine their path, rigidly unbending, and for them I have naught but a sigh of pity. They set the goal and chase it to the exclusion of all else. They see the mark of some imagined finish line and never glance left or right in their singular pursuit.

There is only one certain goal in life: death.

It is right and necessary and important to set goals and chase them. But to do so singularly, particularly regarding those roads which will take many months, even years, to accomplish is to miss the bigger point. It is the journey that is important, for it is the sum of all those journeys, planned or unexpected, that makes us who we are. If you see life as a journey to death, if you truly understand that ultimate goal, then it is the present that becomes most important, and when the present takes precedence above the future, you have truly learned to live.

One eye looking toward your future destination, one eye firmly gazing on your present path, I say.

I have noted before and do so again—because it is a valuable lesson that should often be reinforced—that many who are faced with impending death, a disease that will likely take them in a year's time, for example, quite often insist that their affliction is the best thing that ever happened to them. It takes the immediacy of mortality to remind them to watch the sunrise and the sunset, to note the solitary flower among the rocks, to appreciate those loved ones around them, to taste their food, and revel in the feel of a cool breeze.

To appreciate the journey is to live in the present, even as you aim for the future.

There are unintended consequences to be found, in any case. We do not usually choose to love those who become important to us. Oh, perhaps we choose our mate, but that is but one of a myriad of beloved we will know. We do not choose our parents or our siblings, but typically these people will become beloved to us. We do not choose our neighbors in our youth, and our city or kingdom is determined for us, initially at least. Few are those who break from that societal bond. I did, but only because of the extreme nature of Menzoberranzan. Had I been born and raised in Baldur's Gate, and that city became involved in a war with Waterdeep, under whose flag would I fight? Almost assuredly the place of my birth, the place of my kin and kind. This would not be a neutral choice, and would be one, almost assuredly, influenced by past events large and small, by past emotional attachments of which I might not even be consciously aware. I would fight for my home, most of all, because it was my home!

And not one I had purposely chosen.

This is even truer regarding the followers of various gods, I have found. For most people, at least. Children are typically raised within the guidelines of their family's faith; this moral code becomes a part of their very identity, true to the core of who they are. And though the ultimate morality of so many of the gods is, when stripped of nearly irrelevant particulars, identical. Only those particular pieces, whether in ritual or minor tenet, may be at odds, and in the larger context, what should that matter? Even these seemingly minor discrepancies go to the heart of the tribal bonds of every sentient being, and few can step above their partisan outlook to evaluate a conflict at hand, should there be one, through the eyes of the opposing people.

These are journeys that we do not individually determine, full of beloved people we did not consciously choose to love. Familiarity may breed contempt, as the old saying goes, but in truth, familiarity breeds family and familial love, and that bond is powerful indeed. It would take extraordinary circumstances, I expect, for a brother to fight against a brother. And sadly, most wars are not waged over extraordinary moral quandaries or conflicting philosophies.

And so the bond will usually hold in the face of such conflict. To pass through childhood beside our siblings is to forge a special bond that those outside the family cannot enter. A wise drow once told me that the surest way to rally citizens around their king is to threaten him, for even if those same citizens loathed the man, they would not loathe their homeland, and when such a threat is made, it is made upon that homeland most of all.

I find that such parochialism is true more often for humans and the shorter-living races than it is for elves, drow or surface, and for a very simple reason: rarely are elf children raised together in a singular family unit. A child of the People is more likely to have a sibling a century older than he is to have one passing through childhood beside him.

Our journeys are unique, but they are not in isolation. The roads of a thousand individuals crisscross, and each intersection is a potential side street, a wayward path, a new adventure, an unexpected emotional bond.

Nay, I could not have planned this journey I have taken. For that, I am truly glad.

—Drizzt Do'Urden

CHAPTER 13

A CHIP OFF THE OLD . . . AXE

The Year of the Dark Circle (1478 DR)
Citadel Felbarr

Y ER DA FAVORED THE HAMMER AND THE SWORD," RAGGED DAIN SAID AS the group neared the outer gate. Dain had been so nicknamed for his scrappy fighting style, typically leading with his face, which was crisscrossed now by battle scars.

"I ain't me Da," Bruenor gruffly answered, hoisting his battle-axe to rest on his shoulder.

"Fine tone for a beardless one, eh?" Ognun Leatherbelt, the battle commander, chimed in. He gave Little Arr Arr a shove on the shoulder and a playful half-punch on the jaw. His eyes widened as he did, though, and as he took closer notice of his youngest foot soldier. "Here now! Little Arr Arr's got the beginnin's of a beard, does he?"

"Reginald," Bruenor corrected, and how he wanted to throw aside this whole facade, then and there. He was Bruenor Battlehammer, Eighth King of Mithral Hall, Tenth King of Mithral Hall, champion of Icewind Dale. How he wanted to shout that out, loud and clear!

But Ognun's observations were true enough, for Bruenor had indeed begun to see—finally—the beginnings of a beard, a fiery red one much like the one he'd worn in his previous existence. He wondered if he would look the same as he had in that other life. He hadn't really thought about it very much, but now with the beard coming in, it occurred to him that he might well indeed be a physical twin for the king he had been.

Without the scars, at this point, of course, and without, he lamented, glancing at his new axe, the many notches he had earned in battle.

He brought the axe down before him, ignoring the continuing banter at his expense, and instead studying the clean and smooth curving blade of the weapon. He thought of his first notch in his previous existence, in the great ettin adventure in the tunnels around Mithral Hall, and realized that he had been much older in that fight than he was now. Reginald Roundshield's fifteenth birthday was just three months behind him, which put him a decade and more short of Bruenor's first true adventure in his former life. Indeed, Reginald Roundshield, Little Arr Arr, was much more accomplished among the soldiers of Citadel Felbarr at this age than a teenaged Bruenor had been among the fighters of Clan Battlehammer, even though all of Reginald's exploits thus far had been on the training grounds. But of course, in counterbalance, in that previous life as the prince of Mithral Hall, Bruenor had been presented with great opportunities to do great things that he, as Reginald, would never know.

His memories swirled through the years, to the many battles—leaping upon the back of Shimmergloom, freeing Wulfgar from the demon Errtu, splitting the skull of Matron Baenre when the drow came a'calling, splitting the waves of Obould's minions like a stone against the incoming tide in Keeper's Dale—and Bruenor blew a profound and resigned sigh. Could he really live that journey again? Could he really begin over, not a scratch on his axe, and forge a name worthy of Clan Battlehammer?

And the most troubling question of all, to what end?

"So the gods can just wipe it clean and pretend it never happened, eh?" he mumbled.

"What's that now, boy?" Ragged Dain asked. "Wipe it clean? Nah, that's the real hair ye got there, yer beard comin' in thick and red. No more Little Arr Arr then! Just Arr Arr, as was yer Da."

"Reginald," Bruenor calmly replied, and Ragged Dain burst out laughing, as did the other five dwarves on this scouting patrol. They'd never give in and stop the teasing, Bruenor knew.

Not that it bothered him. What did it matter? His name could be Moradin itself and that too would become bones and stones and nothing more.

He felt a snarl coming to his lips but he suppressed it.

"One day at a time, one step at a time," he told himself, his growing litany against the whispering despair.

"Through the gate, we're turnin' north, lads and lasses," Ognun told his battle group. "Into the Rauvins and Warcrown Trail. Been word o' some goblinkin getting a bit too comfortable there."

"Heigh-ho, then, for a fight!" said Tannabritches Fellhammer, the "Fist" of Fist and Fury.

"Heigh-ho!" Ragged Dain joined in the cheer, but in a mocking way. Every patrol that walked out of Felbarr was told to expect trouble, but, alas, trouble was rarely found.

"Now, don't ye get all Mallabritches on me," Ognun Leatherbelt said with a laugh, referring to Tannabritches's twin, who was aptly nicknamed Fury. The two had been split up, and Mallabritches had been sent back for more training after she had punched a traveling human merchant in the nose when he laughed at her suggestion that he might be selling his wares to orcs.

Mallabritches's demotion had given Bruenor his spot on the battle group, something that hadn't sat well with Tannabritches, who was three years Bruenor's senior, as she had reminded him often with the constant refrain of, "Don't ye get yerself too comfortable, Little Arr Arr. Me sister's to return and ye're to be put back with yer own dwarfling friends."

"Ah, but then might I tell them all again o' how I whomped yer skinny butt, eh?" Bruenor always responded, and time and again, it had almost come to blows. Almost, for it became obvious that the blustering Tannabritches wanted no part of Little Arr Arr one-against-one.

"We'll be half-a-tenday in the mountains," Bruenor heard Ognun explain as he focused back to the present conversation. "And we'll be watchin' all about us every heartbeat o' them five days, don't ye doubt. If them goblins are up there, we're to make sure King Emerus knows it."

"By bringing back their ears, then?" Tannabritches asked.

Ognun laughed. "Aye, if we're finding the chance, I expect. But more likely we'll find goblin sign—scat and prints. We find that and King Emerus is sure to send out a bigger fightin' group, and . . ." He paused and patted his hand in the air, calming the ever-excited Tannabritches. "And aye," he went on, "be sure that I'll be askin' for a leading place for us six in that battle group."

"Heigh-ho!" Tannabritches Fellhammer cheered.

As the youngest members of the patrol, Bruenor and Tannabritches were given most of the menial tasks, like gathering kindling for the campfire. Winter had relinquished its grip on the Rauvin Mountains and all around the Silver Marches, but just barely. This high up above Citadel Felbarr's gates, there were still some small patches of snow to be found, and the night wind could still send a thick-bearded dwarf's teeth to chattering.

"Come along then," Tannabritches scolded Bruenor as they circled around one bend in the trail, moving through a channel carved by centuries of melting mountain streams through the heart of a huge rocky ledge. "They've already got the flames started," she added when she came through the pass, in sight of the camp in a wooded, boulder-strewn dell below.

"By the gods, Fist," Bruenor replied, "but me legs're aching and me belly's grumblin'."

"All the reason to walk faster then, ain't it?" she called back over her shoulder, and she ended with a curious grunt that Bruenor took as a snort.

Until her armload of kindling fell to the ground and Tannabritches tumbled backward, a spear protruding from her chest.

Bruenor's eyes went wide. He threw his own kindling aside and dived down to the ground—and not a heartbeat too soon, for a spear flew just above him, cracking off the stone across the channel.

Bruenor scrambled furiously on all fours to get to his fallen companion, and he winced at the severity of the wound, at the blood gushing around the spear shaft, deeply embedded just below her collarbone and not far above the poor girl's heart. With a trembling hand, Bruenor tried to hold the spear shaft perfectly still, seeing that every vibration brought wracking pain coursing through poor Tannabritches.

"Get ye gone," the fallen girl whispered, spitting blood with her words. "I'm for Dwarfhome. Warn th' others!"

She coughed and started to curl up, and Bruenor, trying to comfort her, looked up suddenly, hearing the approach of enemies, certain from the sound of them that they would swamp the channel in mere moments.

"Go!" she pleaded.

Had he really been Little Arr Arr, had he really been an inexperienced dwarfling of merely fifteen winters, Bruenor would have likely taken her advice—even with his experience, he couldn't deny the fear that was inside him, or the truth that he had a duty to warn Ognun and Ragged Dain and the others . . .

But he wasn't Little Arr Arr. He was Bruenor Battlehammer, who had learned through centuries to put loyalty above all else, who had passed through death itself and come back with a deep and pervading sense of outrage.

With a growl and a burst of strength he didn't realize he possessed, he grasped the spear shaft in both hands and cleanly snapped it, leaving just a stub poking from the brutal wound. As one hand threw the broken shaft aside, the other grabbed Tannabritches by the collar, and he easily hoisted her across his shoulders, starting off in a run before she had even settled.

He heard the whoops behind him and imagined a volley of spears flying his way, and that only made the furious dwarf spin to face that missile barrage head on, to keep Tannabritches mostly behind him that he wouldn't inadvertently use her as a shield.

Indeed, a trio of spears reached out at him, and their orc throwers, barely ten paces behind him, howled at the expected kills.

Bruenor managed to dodge one, take a second with his shield and deflect the third enough with his axe so that it only glanced him along the side, stinging painfully through his chainmail armor but doing no mortal harm.

The jerking movements nearly cost him his tentative hold on his companion, though, and she started to tumble. But again, Bruenor merely growled and realigned his feet, catching Tannabritches fully again and rushing off down the path.

"Orcs!" he shouted, leaping from stone to stone down the steep decline and somehow, miraculously, managing to hold his balance.

He pitched into the copse headlong, finally overbalancing and diving into a face plant, with Tannabritches bouncing over him, pressing his face harder into the ground as she rolled limply toward the fire.

"Mandarina!" Ragged Dain shouted for Mandarina Dobberbright, the group's cleric, and the female dwarf spat out a large mouthful of stew and scrambled to get her medicine bag.

"Orcs!" Bruenor shouted, spitting dirt.

As he spoke, there came a large cracking sound above and splintering tree limbs fell around the camp, and a huge stone crashed to the ground, crushing poor Ognun Leatherbelt's toes! Oh, but how he howled!

Bruenor and Magnus Leatherbelt, the sixth of the party and Ognun's third cousin on his father's side, reached the boulder at the same time, trying to push it off Ognun's foot, but unfortunately, they came to the spot on opposite sides of the stone and inadvertently worked against each other. With a groan and a growl, the two rolled around to meet at opposite sides of their commander, but that, too, proved problematic for poor Bruenor, and poorer Ognun, for when Bruenor came around, the spear shaft, the missile firmly embedded in his shield, swung around and whacked Ognun across the side of his head.

"Bother and bluster!" Bruenor cried and he dropped his axe, reached over with his free hand, and yanked the spear free. He swung around as soon as he had, and threw all of his weight and strength against the stone, and joining with Ognun and Magnus, they managed to hoist it enough for the commander to pull his foot free.

"Better ground to the west!" Ragged Dain cried out from atop a boulder just beyond the dell.

"Go! Go!" ordered Ognun.

"Ah, but I can't be movin' her!" Mandarina protested.

"Ye got yerself no choice!" Ognun insisted and he hobbled over, but his voice trailed away when he got there, for it was clear to him and the other two that Mandarina wasn't speaking lightly, and wasn't exaggerating.

Tannabritches seemed on the very edge of death.

But now the orcs were coming, and another heavy stone crashed through the branches just above them.

"They've a giant," warned Magnus.

"Run away!" shouted Tannabritches with what seemed the last of her strength.

The other three looked to Ognun—Bruenor could see the pain there on the face of the seasoned but compassionate leader. Ognun had no choice, Bruenor understood, for the good of them all and the good of Citadel Felbarr.

"To Ragged Dain, with all haste," Ognun said quietly, and somehow his words stuck out clearly among the mounting whoops of the charging orcs.

Ognun fell to one knee and handed the nearly unconscious Tannabritches a long knife, then kissed her on the cheek. A good-bye kiss, surely.

"Go! Go!" he ordered, coming to his feet.

The words prodded at Bruenor's heart more sharply than the spearhead stuck in Fist's chest.

"No!" he shouted before he could stop himself. Even as the word echoed in his own thoughts, Bruenor didn't really understand it. It was a denial, and not just of leaving the girl, but of everything. It was a scream at the gods for this tragedy, for their very mocking of the life Bruenor had given them, centuries of fealty and honor.

No! his mind screamed, at himself and at Moradin. No to everything. Just no!

And in that eye-blink of time, Bruenor could not deny the sudden and unexpected sensation. He felt as he had felt on the throne in ancient

Gauntlgrym, and heard the strategic whispers of Dumathoin, the calm command of Moradin, and felt, most of all, the strength of Clanggedin coursing through his young muscles.

"No!" he said again, more forcefully, and he tore the cape off his back and threw it to Ognun. "Make her a litter!" he ordered.

Ognun stared at him incredulously.

"Too many!" Magnus cried.

"They ain't getting past me!" Bruenor roared, and he spun around, taking up his axe and shield, and with a feral growl, he rushed up to the boulder and threw his back against it. With an exaggerated, confident wink back at the other three tending Tannabritches, he rolled around the boulder, whooping and swinging.

He caught the nearest orc by surprise just as it lifted its arm to hurl a spear at the group, his axe cracking into the beast's chest and throwing it backward. No sooner had he pulled the axe free, then Bruenor charged along, cutting back in front of the boulder.

He threw his shield up high as he skidded down to his knees, sweeping out an orc's legs at the same time the beast's mace thumped hard against the blocking buckler.

The dwarf was to his feet in a heartbeat, leaping along to the next two in line, shield-rushing, skidding short and sweeping across with his bloody axe. He didn't wound either, though he managed to rip the sword from one's grasp and cut the other's spear short by a third.

He did not relent—he would not surrender his rage and ferocity, butting and swinging, shield-charging and screaming with every step. The overwhelmed orcs scrambled back, turning right into their reinforcements and slowing the orc charge.

Into that confusion went Bruenor, wildly chopping and punching, shield-butting, and even biting when one opportunity presented itself. He got hit hard by a club, a resounding thud that nearly knocked his helmet from his head. Things didn't sort out clearly for him at that moment and for many afterward, but it didn't matter. He wasn't worried about precision or about tactics even.

He was just mad. Mad at Mielikki for tempting him, for making him start anew. Mad at Moradin for allowing it! Mad at Catti-brie and Drizzt and mostly at himself for not having the sense to step into Iruladoon's pond beside Wulfgar, to go to Dwarfhome and his just reward.

And now . . . the uselessness of it all! The thought that he had wasted a decade-and-a-half only to be cut down on a cold mountain trail in defense of a clan that wasn't his own, for the honor of a name that wasn't his own, and to the ultimate futility of his "mission" to help Drizzt.

It was too much . . . too, too much.

He felt the punches—or were they stabs?—of orc spears, and he ignored them and charged on, roaring, denying. He felt his axe dig into flesh and crack through bone. He heard the varied screams of his enemies, of rage, of pain, and sweetest of all, of fear.

He managed to glance back only once, and hardly registered the scene, though it seemed as if the three were hard at work with Tannabritches, attempting to ferry her away, he hoped.

No longer did it even matter.

He shield-rushed the next two orcs in line and down they went, all three, in a tangled ball. Even as he tasted dirt, Bruenor kept chopping, cutting the spine of one. He somehow got the edge of his shield on the throat of the other and pressed down, using the orc's neck as support to allow him to stand once more.

And then he was free, standing alone, and he hopped all around.

Orcs fled in every direction, some, to Bruenor's anger, past him. But when he glanced back, he took comfort in the fact that Magnus and Mandarina had Tannabritches up in a stretcher, and mighty Ognun was ready for the incoming enemies, and with capable Ragged Dain huffing and puffing to join him.

Bruenor turned back, just in time to dodge a huge stone flying his way. And there before him stood the giant, an enormous behemoth. Not a hill giant, as one might expect with orcs, but bigger, far bigger indeed.

"Run away!" he heard Ognun yell to him, and that, of course, was the only answer in the face of such an enemy.

The only answer for a fifteen-year-old Reginald, perhaps.

But not for Bruenor Battlehammer, King of Mithral Hall.

He charged.

The mountain giant stood more than thrice his height and outweighed him ten-to-one or more. But he charged, roaring, demanding the giant's attention as it moved to hurl another boulder.

With a stupid look and a grunt of "huh?" the giant flung the rock at the oncoming, nearly beardless young dwarf. It hit the ground a few feet in front of Bruenor and skipped up at him, and nearly clipped him as he dived to the ground.

By the time the boulder bounced against the hard ground again, Bruenor was already up and running. He thought to charge straight into the behemoth, to rush around its treelike legs and whack at its knees with his axe.

He changed his mind when the giant reached back and pulled forth its club, an uprooted tree, as thick across as Bruenor's waist!

To the left veered the dwarf, formulating another plan, for the trail rose up here, moving behind a wall of stone. He got under that cover just in time, the tree-club slamming down just behind him and shaking the ground so forcefully that he almost lost his balance.

Cursing with every step, telling himself to just run away out of spite and to the Nine Hells with them all, Bruenor kept his young legs pumping. The curses were real, as was the rage, but he would not abandon his fellow dwarves. Part of him wanted to, just to spite Moradin, but it simply was not the way of Bruenor Battlehammer.

He ran on, rounding a bend and climbing higher.

An orc leaped out before him, startling him. He threw his shield across desperately, but didn't deflect the weapon quite enough, and felt the bite of the spear tip in his belly, trading that severe hit with a downward chop of his axe that crushed the orc's skull. The creature fell away and Bruenor stumbled forward, and that action only drove the spear in deeper.

With a trembling hand, the dwarf reached down and grabbed the shaft, thinking to pull it out. As soon as he started to tug, though, he changed his mind. The head was barbed and surely his entrails would spill forth with it.

"So now ye killed me to death in battle, did ye, Moradin?" he said, sliding down to one knee and trying hard to hold his balance there. "Bah, but ain't that a fittin' end for yer games? Ye couldn't even let the giant do it. It had to be an orc . . ."

The dwarf, grimacing and trying to stop the world from spinning, considered those words for a few heartbeats.

An orc, probably an orc from Many-Arrows. An orc living around this region because of a decision Bruenor had made a century before.

Another orc appeared on the trail ahead. Spotting the wounded dwarf, it let out a whoop of delight and charged at the kneeling dwarf with a spear deep in his gut.

A huge rock crashed along the trail just behind them as they turned a bend, reminding the dwarves of the behemoth at their backs. But so too did they find trouble before them, as more orcs gathered along the trail ahead.

"By the gods, but we'll be fightin' either way, then," said Ragged Dain. "And fewer behind us!"

"But bigger behind us!" Magnus reminded.

"Aye, and better to die fightin' a giant than a stinkin' orc," Ognun Leatherbelt cried, and he wheeled around, patted his old friend Ragged Dain on the shoulder, and said, "Let's take out its knees then, and leave it limping fore'er!"

Ragged Dain grinned as only a dwarf who knew he was about to die in battle might. He was first back around the bend.

The giant saw him, and surely heard his cry and those of Ognun beside him.

The giant had just come forth from its place before the rocky peak, massive club in hand, but when it saw the dwarves, it gave a chuckle that sounded like an avalanche and turned around to retrieve another boulder.

And there on the ledge it saw, and Ragged Dain and Ognun saw, a most curious sight.

The spear came out with a tug of angry denial, and Bruenor had it swiveled around and planted just as the orc leaped upon him—or almost upon him, as it skewered itself on the bloody spear. A wild shove of the dwarf's shield had the flailing orc tumbling off to the side.

Bruenor paid it no more heed. The forearm of his axe hand tight against his spilling guts, the dwarf growled through the blinding pain and charged up the path, spitting blood with every curse.

The trail climbed up and wound around to the right, then broke into three branches, including a straight path back in the direction where Bruenor had left his friends. And at the end of that straight path, across a small ledge, Bruenor saw the back of the mountain giant's head.

All sense of agony left him then, replaced by the sheerest rage.

He charged along, lifting his axe up high and shouting "Moradin!" at the top of his lungs, as much a curse at the god as a plea for strength. How thin his voice sounded against the rumble of the giant's laughter!

The giant turned around, apparently unaware of Bruenor, and reached for a stone. Its huge eyes widened at the sight of the dwarf, and widened some more when Bruenor, the strength of Clanggedin Silverbeard coursing through his muscular arms, flung the axe with all his might, and never slowed in his charge behind it.

End over end, the newly bloodied weapon sailed, its silvery head catching the last rays of daylight in dramatic flashes.

The giant dropped both its club and the rock and brought its hands up to block, but the missile split the gap between its fingers and turned perfectly in its last rotation, the axe blade creasing the giant's nose and cracking hard into its face right between the eyes.

"Whoa," it moaned, fingers flexing repeatedly, but not daring to grab at the embedded weapon. Its big eyes tried each to look in, crossing in a confused and dizzy manner.

And so with double vision it noted the second missile, the living missile that was Bruenor Battlehammer leaping from the ledge and flying in, shield forward.

The collisions blasted the breath out of Bruenor, and sent waves of agony burning through him. He knew that he had smashed his shield against the back of the embedded axe, at least, and he knew the giant was falling, for he found himself descending above it.

He felt the second impact, the earthquake it seemed, when they hit the ground, but that was all he knew.

He didn't realize that he was bouncing away, over the behemoth and along the ground. He didn't know that he came to a stop all twisted and broken at the feet of Ragged Dain, with the other four of the dwarf scouting party close behind, and with a gang of orcs only a short distance behind them.

CHAPTER 14

CULTURED SOCIETY

The Year of the Third Circle (1472 DR)
Delthuntle

H E DID WELL TO GET AS FAR AS HE DID," PERICOLO TOPOLINO SAID TO TWO of his captains, a halfling prestidigitator aptly nicknamed Wigglefingers, and the Grandfather's most trusted advisor, his own granddaughter, Donnola Topolino.

"I had a bead on him halfway up the building," Wigglefingers protested. "I could have blasted him from the wall with ease."

"He is just a child," Donnola argued. "And it took you half the building to sight him?"

Wigglefingers ran his fingers down one end of his deliciously curling black mustache, glanced at the pretty young halfling socialite out of the corner of his brown eyes and gave an unappreciative, "Hmm."

"Has he awakened yet?" an obviously amused Topolino asked, and indeed, he was often amused by the continual banter of these two. It was all in good fun, after all, and they were the best of friends when not vying for his attention. There were rumors that Wigglefingers—Topolino couldn't even remember his real name most of the time—was even quietly training Donnola in some clever magical suggestion techniques, just to make her information gathering more lucrative to Morada Topolino.

"You shot him good," Donnola replied. "And perhaps with too much of the poison for one so little."

In response, Pericolo snapped at the handle of the weapon in the holster at his side, drawing it in the blink of an eye. As it came forth from the cleverly designed scabbard, the spring-loaded wings of the hand crossbow extended, showing the weapon to be cocked and ready to fire, a poison-tipped dart set in place.

"Just a good batch, this one," Pericolo said with a laugh.

"You still draw well, old one," said Wigglefingers, who was the same age as the Grandfather and had grown up beside Pericolo on Delthuntle's streets. Only Wigglefingers would dare to so tease Pericolo Topolino.

"Quick enough to shoot a wizard before he casts his first spell, no doubt," the Grandfather answered. He worked his hand on a hidden lever on the inside of the pearl-gripped hand crossbow, releasing the catch, and immediately the wings loosened. Pericolo gave the weapon a couple of spins, rolling the trigger guard around his index finger in a dramatic flair before spinning it right back into the holster.

"Good poison," he said again, for he, of course, had brewed it. "This Spider will sleep another day away, likely, and awaken with a mighty ache in his head, do not doubt."

"Good enough for the little thief," said Wigglefingers. "A headache well-deserved for his impudence. How dare he assault the home of Pericolo Topolino? And a fellow halfling! Ah, but Brandobaris is surely shaking his head at that one, eh?"

"A valuable little thief," Pericolo corrected. "And given the agreement I've forced from his father, I expect that Brandobaris would be shaking his head in disappointment had the courageous one not tried to garner a bit of extra recompense."

"Courageous? Or foolish? He had no chance of succeeding."

"He is just a child," Donnola reminded yet again. She rolled her hand around and a perfect pink pearl seemed to appear there out of nowhere. With a subtle movement, she flicked it to the wizard. "Another one worthy of enchanting," she explained. "Another from the deepwater oysters our little nuisance so easily and skillfully collects."

Wigglefingers caught the pearl and stared at it lovingly. "Well, he does have his uses, I suppose," he admitted.

"And think how long and low he might dive when you've put enchantments upon him," said Pericolo. "We have only begun to test the value of this one, I expect." He turned to Donnola, who returned his look with a sly one of her own, as if catching the hint that the Grandfather might have something more in mind here. "You inspected him?"

"From the hair on his head to the hair on his feet," she replied. "His teeth, as well," she added before Pericolo could. "And I used your wand upon him, twice, to detect any items or dweomers. There is no magic around him."

"As I expected."

"Then how might he dive so deep and so long?" Wigglefingers asked.

"His mother's blood," said Pericolo. "Her family has a bit of the genasi in them, several generations back, so say the rumors. Apparently, Jolee Parrafin was an equally impressive diver, although she never gained enough notice outside of her small group for anyone to properly exploit her talents, or to properly reward her."

"Genasi?" Wigglefingers said with a gasp. He thought about it for a few moments, then burst out laughing. "Planetouched offspring of human and djinn, and now playing the eight-limbed beast with a halfling? Ha, but that's grand!"

"And profitable," said Donnola, and the clever pickpocket rolled her fingers around again and produced, again seemingly out of nowhere, another perfect pink pearl, of the type Pericolo's people knew how to coax from the deepwater oysters. Pink and perfect and, because so few could get to them, quite rare. And rarer still, because Pericolo's group alone understood the true value of these particular oysters. They harvested pink pearls, while others slobbily ate the creatures!

"Let me know when he wakes up," the Grandfather instructed Donnola. "Obviously our little guest is in need of a good lesson or ten."

He looked to Wigglefingers. "You have a pair of fine pearls to prepare, I do believe," he said, and the mage seemed all too happy to comply, bowing and springing back lightly, then rushing to his work.

"This new recruit will prove to be a difficult project," Pericolo warned Donnola when they were alone. "Headstrong and angry, I fear. I came upon him when he was taunting a group of far-older children—seeking a fight he could not win. Alas, his mother died giving birth to him."

"And his father is a drunkard," Donnola remarked. "Perhaps he has a reason for his anger."

"Oh, indeed. And that, my dear granddaughter is the first thing we must coax out of him."

Donnola rocked back on her heels and took a good long gander at Pericolo. "So you think there is more value about him than just a deep diver," she stated flatly.

"He is full of talents," Pericolo admitted. "He earns the name Spider as surely as a moniker of 'Dolphin' would fit. And of those boys he taunted . . . well, let's just say that the ringleader of those bullies still walks a bit awkwardly, and though he has grown from boy to man, his voice, of late, has reverted to a childlike pitch . . ."

Regis's eyes popped open, and he frantically slapped at his arms and torso, trying desperately to put out the biting flames. He stopped abruptly, though not even realizing that there were no flames and no burns, and instead grabbed his head on either side, groaning loudly and closing his eyes very tight.

"Yes, it is not unlike the morning after a night of very heavy drinking," he heard, and he slowly opened his eyes, squinting against the pain. He glanced to the side of his bed, to see a fabulously dressed, meticulously groomed older halfling relaxing in a comfortable chair. Regis knew this one, of course, and was not surprised.

"It will pass quickly." Pericolo reached to a night table beside his chair and handed Regis a cup of water.

Regis just stared at him, not releasing his head, not reaching for the water. He did glance down at his bare arms, his expression one of puzzlement.

"Do not berate yourself too unkindly," Pericolo said. "My wizard friend has spent years perfecting that fiery illusion—and that of the dogs, as well. The explosion would fool a seasoned assassin, let alone a mere child, and with the added benefit of the magical winds he imbued upon the door, how could you guess the dogs to be an illusion?"

Regis gradually released his grip on his throbbing head and accepted the cup from the Grandfather—the Grandfather of Assassins, he reminded himself, well aware of the implications of such a title, given his previous life in the murder-ridden city of Calimport. He looked at the clear liquid suspiciously, but then realized that if Pericolo Topolino had wanted him dead, he would already be dead.

He emptied the cup in one gulp.

"I was quite surprised, though pleasantly so do not doubt, that you would be so bold as to try to rob me," Pericolo said. "Saves me the trouble of hunting you down, for you are a difficult one to find. Although I admit that I am confused as to why the sudden good fortunes of your family, at my purse, would bring you to such treachery."

"Good fortunes?"

"You lived in a lean-to of rotting wood. Your father haunted the alleyways behind taverns to find discarded scraps of food. Now you have the comfort of a reputable inn to call home, and all the food you can eat."

"And all the liquor Eiverbreen Parrafin can drink," Regis added solemnly, staring hard at the Grandfather.

"Well, that is his choice, of course."

"Your generosity will kill him."

Pericolo sat up straighter, a clear tell to Regis. The Grandfather knew the truth of his generosity and had been caught off his guard that this mere child understood that truth.

"I'm not in the habit of telling others how to live their lives," Pericolo said.

"Aren't you, then? It is said that Grandfather Pericolo controls the docks of Delthuntle."

Another surprised look came from Pericolo, and he slowly nodded . . . perhaps, Regis thought, in congratulations.

"My father was not unlike your own," the Grandfather said, and it was Regis's turn to wear a surprised look, both at the revelation and the tone of sympathy. He silently warned himself to stay on his guard, for Pericolo Topolino was certainly bound to be a master of deception, given his station.

But surely Pericolo seemed sincere as he continued, "I was more fortunate than you, my little Spider, for I did not lose my mother so young."

"I never knew her."

"I know," Pericolo said. "Which makes your ascent all the more impressive. Your work is outstanding, and truly a boon to your family."

They had walked a rhetorical circle, right back where they had started. Regis let his expression show that he did not much care for that.

"I watched you that day long ago when you taunted the older boys," Pericolo said, catching him off his guard. "The glue on the whistle! Oh, but that was a grand and clever trick!"

"Truly I feel as if I have been spied upon," Regis answered with dripping sarcasm.

"But you have, Spider!"

Regis reflexively began to correct the Grandfather regarding his name, almost blurting out his true name. Almost, but he stopped short, and not for any fear. Spider, he thought, and found that he more than accepted that particular moniker.

"What is it?" Pericolo asked, and Regis shook his head. "Your name is not Spider, then?" the too-perceptive Grandfather asked. "I have heard no other. Eiverbreen did not say . . ."

"Perhaps he doesn't know."

Pericolo looked at him curiously.

"If he did not care to give me a name, it is my right to choose my own, yes?"

Pericolo laughed heartily. "Granted!" he said. "So choose!"

"Spider," Regis replied with a wry grin and not the slightest hesitation. "Spider Parrafin."

"You do me honor," said Pericolo, and he stood up and bowed. "Indeed, I do like the name for you, given how easily you scaled the side of my house."

Regis considered it some more, but found himself nodding, fully accepting it.

"Very well then, Spider it is, as we move forward."

Regis nodded again as Pericolo sat back down, before a puzzled expression crossed his cherubic young face. "Move forward?" he echoed tentatively.

"Of course."

"You mean when you turn me over to the city guard, or when you read the judgment over me."

"Hardly," Pericolo said with another hearty laugh. "Judgment? Why, Spider, I have long judged you quite worthy! You may number me among your admirers."

"I broke into your house, and perhaps not merely to steal—"

"Loyalty to your father!" Pericolo exclaimed. "Another commendable trait, though I hope you come to accept that Eiverbreen's choices are Eiverbreen's to make, and not Pericolo Topolino's."

"You are killing him," Regis said grimly. "He is senseless most of the day, full of booze and choking on his own vomit."

"I am merely fulfilling my end of our bargain. In exchange for the oysters you fish."

"Then you will get no more oysters from me."

"You would go back to the rotting lean-to?"

"Yes," Regis answered without the slightest hesitation. The easy path didn't seem so alluring to Regis if it meant such distress for Eiverbreen.

"Well then, what would you ask of me?" Pericolo asked, seeming genuine. "I agreed to compensate Eiverbreen in return for the oysters."

"Bring him here," Regis said.

"That cannot be," Pericolo replied, and Regis began shaking his head.

"But perhaps . . . ," the Grandfather went on, pausing and tapping his finger against his lips. "There are houses farther from the taverns that I might appropriate for him."

"That would be a start."

"I cannot forbid him from his vice," Pericolo explained. "That is not my business."

"Then I cannot dive."

The Grandfather laughed. "Well, perhaps I can dissuade the local tavern-keepers from doing business with Eiverbreen. That is the most I can promise. Are we agreed?"

Regis stared at him for a long while before finally nodding his agreement.

"And what of Spider?" Pericolo asked. "What do you wish for your efforts? You are doing all of the work, after all."

"Take care of my father."

"Oh come now, there must be more. That is already agreed. But what for Spider?"

Regis didn't quite know how to answer. He could think of many rewards off the top of his head. He had been the champion of luxury in his previous life, after all, and Pericolo's lifestyle afforded such things in abundance.

"I look at you and I see myself," Pericolo said before Regis could formulate any requests. "Such potential! And more than from your extraordinary ability in the water. I rather admire your courage, and your skill is without question."

Regis shrugged and worked hard to prevent Pericolo from seeing the inner smile that beamed through him. "You have something in mind."

Pericolo laughed again. "And your perception!" he said. "So let us change the bargain, you and I. I will open my pockets deeper and purchase for Eiverbreen a home of his own, and will open them wider for you, and purchase the cooperation of the tavernkeepers in limiting, nay denying, Eiverbreen the drink he so craves. And in exchange, you work for me."

"I already do."

"Not just diving for oysters," Pericolo clarified. "You come and join in my . . . organization. There is much you should learn, and much I can teach you."

"Like?" Regis prompted.

Pericolo stood, and turned just a bit to better display the amazing jewel-studded basket of the fabulous rapier that hung easily on his left hip. "How to fight," he said. "And how to get that which you desire without fighting—that is the more important skill."

173

The jarring offer reminded Regis of his true purpose in coming back to live once more upon the sands of Faerûn, and of the resolve that had brought him here. He had spent the majority of his spare moments from the instant of his rebirth trying to prepare himself, and now it was all he could do not to openly lick his lips at the Grandfather's offer.

"Good," Pericolo remarked, for Regis wasn't that skilled at hiding his feelings, obviously. "But I do demand one more thing of you—two, actually."

Regis nodded.

"First, your loyalty. I warn you only once that if you betray me, if you steal from me, your end will not be pleasant."

Regis swallowed hard and nodded.

"And second, I will call you Spider hereafter, and you cannot choose to change it—for me at least! I rather like that name."

On the surface, it seemed quite a silly thing to Regis, but as he thought about it, as he remembered his time working for the pashas of Calimport, he understood the seemingly odd request. Pericolo was asking about controlling more than Regis's name: he was asking to control Regis's identity.

So be it, the young halfling decided. He looked at Pericolo's rapier once more and considered what he might learn from this accomplished halfling. This was the solution to achieving his purpose in stepping forth from Iruladoon, held before him within his grasp.

He nodded, smiled, and asked, "And I am to call you Grandfather?"

"I would quite like that, yes."

"Only ten," Wigglefingers explained to Regis a few days later, when the youngster was ready to dive once more. The mage had escorted him to a private wharf and a private boat, which Wigglefingers captained out from Delthuntle and to a remote location, guiding Regis as he rowed. All the way, the halfling mage kept casting spells, peering intently at the water as he finished, and often correcting Regis's course.

Clairvoyance, Regis understood. Wigglefingers was hunting for oysters with his magical sight.

Finally the mage signaled for Regis to put up the oars, and sat nodding as he unrolled a long elven cord that was secured to a metal eyelet on the craft. He tied the other end to a small harness, and handed it to Regis.

"Only ten," he reiterated as Regis strapped the harness around his torso. He noted then that a small vial hung on one side of the vest, secured with a slipknot.

"Ten?"

"Ten oysters, no more. We'll not fish them out, and ten is enough."

Regis looked at him curiously. "Then we move on to another spot?"

"Then we go home," the mage corrected.

Regis's expression became incredulous. He normally returned to Delthuntle with more than twice that number, sometimes several times that number, in his considerable pouches.

"Ten is enough to fit our needs," Wigglefingers explained.

"I could eat ten myself!"

"Eat?" Wigglefingers laughed. "Nay, on days when we intend to eat them, we'll get more, but these are not for eating."

Regis started to question the mage on that one, but Wigglefingers held up a hand to silence him. The mage began to cast a spell then, and Regis felt the soothing magical energy fall over him. Another spell quickly followed.

"You will swim faster and your breath will hold for longer now," the mage explained. "If you find that you have tarried too long down deep, do not panic, as that potion on your vest will also imbue water breathing, if necessary. If necessary, I say, and try not to make it so! Such potions are not made cheaply or quickly."

"We are far out," Regis noted, glancing back toward the distant shore.

"To keep away those who might try to steal our catch, of course. The Sea of Fallen Stars has no shortage of pirates."

"Or killer fish," said Regis. "I usually stay near to the reefs . . ."

Wigglefingers grasped him by the shoulders and moved him toward the edge of the boat. "I am watching. Be quick, then. Only ten."

Before Regis could respond, the mage shoved him overboard.

He returned in short order, ten oysters in his belt pouch, and though he was tired from the deeper-than-normal dive, Wigglefingers put him right back to the oars and started them for home.

"When we return, I will teach you to be more discerning in your choice of oysters," Wigglefingers said, examining the catch and sighing often. "Yes, you have much to learn, much to learn."

Regis kept rowing and said no more. He had stepped into it deeply, he knew then; his position with Grandfather Pericolo was not to be without serious responsibilities, so it then seemed.

So it went that Regis found his days quite structured over the coming months. Each morning, he was taken to the boat beside Wigglefingers, who, he came to learn, was quite adroit at clairvoyance and used the skill to position them far from shore, always over beds rich with oysters.

Their return had him doing the bidding of the mage for the rest of each morning, and there he learned the truth of the oysters Pericolo desired. The Grandfather wasn't selling them as exotic food delicacies, for these particular deepwater shellfish had the highest rate of producing pearls, beautiful pink pearls that Wigglefingers knew how to entice from them.

That first day back with the catch, Regis was taken to one of the mage's private laboratories, where watery tanks lined several tables. Another table sported a complete alchemy lab, it seemed.

Wigglefingers taught Regis to gently cut a slit in the mantle tissue of the oysters, and to then gather a small dropper and smoothly add in the potion of irritant. As the days moved along, he even taught Regis how to brew the irritant, and then began to instruct him in many other aspects of alchemy.

What had seemed a chore each morning, other than the diving, which he loved, quickly became an entirely new and important talent for the youngster to perfect.

When the sun reached its zenith each midday, Regis was handed off from Wigglefingers to Donnola, to become her personal page and attendant. So began his training with weapons, and Donnola was quite the swordswoman! And devilishly clever with a knife, too.

"Fighting is about your balance and your position," she told him early on in their sessions.

Regis nodded, allowing himself to become a sponge for all that she had to say, although, having lived and traveled beside one of the finest finesse warriors of the Realms for most of his previous life, he realized that he would find much of her philosophical lessons redundant. He listened to them anyway, carefully cataloguing Donnola's insights alongside his own experiences.

There was no small amount of drudgery involved in the lessons. Every day, Regis had to stand against a doorjamb for a long, long while, merely thrusting his rapier into the wood before him, into the other side of the doorway. The wood at his back forced him to hold his posture perfectly upright. Again and again, a thousand times a thousand times, month after month and into the passage of years, he would thrust that rapier.

His speed improved. His aim tightened.

The Year of the Dark Circle (1478 DR)
Delthuntle

One day early in his sixth year at Morada Topolino, Donnola came to Regis while he worked on his repetitive lessons.

"Continue," she bade him as he paused to consider her, and consider the bundle of fancy clothing she had brought, all rich green and golden edged.

"Then go and bathe and put this on," she explained.

Regis paused again with his rapier work and stared at her curiously.

"There is a ball tonight at the house of one of the city's most important lords," Donnola explained. "I am invited—I am always invited. You will accompany me, this night and from now on. It is time you learned the finer aspects of our . . . business."

Regis smiled, her words throwing him back to the days when he had accompanied Pasha Pook to all of the grand social gatherings among the landowners and moneylenders, the fat merchants and the most important ship captains, back in Calimport.

"Donnola Topolino the socialite?" he asked with a laugh, and realized his error immediately when the woman scowled and considered him with obvious surprise. How would Spider, the little boy from the alleyways and grown under the bloodshot eye of a destitute alcoholic, know such a word, after all?

Regis swallowed hard.

"Yes," Donnola replied cautiously, never blinking. "Do you find that . . . trite?"

Regis swallowed hard and almost expected her to slap him across the face, given her look.

"You will learn, little Spider," Donnola said. "Of all the things I might teach you, in the eyes of Grandfather Pericolo, this lesson will be the most important one of all. If you are to ever rise beyond the rank of foot soldier and fisherman in Morada Topolino, then it will be determined by how well you learn to play these events for your—for our gain."

"Yes, of course," Regis said, lowering his gaze, but barely had he dipped his head before Donnola grasped him by the chin and forced him to look up at her.

"Grandfather has selected you," she said. "Understand what that means. Appreciate the great honor he has bestowed upon you, and the great opportunity you can make for yourself. You train in his very house, with his most powerful and trusted wizard, and with his most beloved, trusted, and powerful advisor. That is no small thing, Spider. He expects more from you than a life as a mere oyster-diver."

Regis didn't know what to say.

"Do not disappoint me tonight," Donnola warned, and she let him go and took her leave.

Regis looked at the pile of expensive clothes. He wasn't really worried about disappointing Donnola, for unlike the physical skills he worked so hard to perfect, the skills he would need as her page among the folk of society were well known to him, and long-practiced in another life. He didn't expect to learn much from Donnola, and figured he might even teach her a thing or two.

He immediately realized that his assumption was wrong when she gathered him up for their coach ride to the ball, however, for when he glimpsed Donnola Topolino in her fine silken gown, her light brown hair curled and fashionably tied up on one side, her button nose and freckled dimples, her wondrously wide brown eyes accentuated by just a hint of black liner, he learned that she was easily the most enchanting and beautiful and intriguing halfling woman he had ever seen. He thought back to his first night prowling around Morada Topolino, and the beautiful ghostly figure he had seen crossing the room to blow out the candle.

Yes, he realized then, it had been this very halfling girl, barely a woman, but clearly a woman.

And Regis realized right then that he would not much longer be a boy.

CHAPTER 15

NOT WITHOUT A COST

The Year of Splendors Burning (1469 DR)
Shade Enclave

SETTLED ALONG THE WESTERN WALL OF THE NETHERIL'S FLOATING CAPITAL city of Shade Enclave was a compound that seemed as out of place within that city of harsh black spires and foreboding walls as the city itself, which sat atop a floating inverted mountain of stone, seemed out of place in a world that obeyed the basic laws of nature.

This compound was called the Coven, and Catti-brie found it a most interesting keep indeed. Here Lady Avelyere and her devoted followers, all female, and all except for Catti-brie, Netherese, practiced and studied, engaging in contests throwing lightning bolts as archers might compete with arrows. Here, in protected rooms with cautious oversight, sorceresses of varying skill dared to try out new spells, or combinations of known dweomers pieced together for new and greater effect.

In the basement was a summoning room of careful design and meticulous crafting, lined with powerful runes to prevent some demon or devil from breaking free of the room even if it managed to overpower the summoning wizard.

The Coven stood as a testament to magical learning, and as functional as the place might be, it was surely beautiful, crafted with a woman's eye and a cultured vision of comfort and sophistication. The exterior view was not dominated by a large central tower, as was so often the case in this dour city, and often the case among the abodes of wizards in the Realms, particularly with male wizards, which led, of course, to no small amount of lewd joking among the sorceresses of the Coven, but by several domes leafed in various precious metals. Leering gargoyles did not stare down from every corner of every roof, but gutter spout statues of shapely sirens and nymphs, and cheerful brownies overlooked the compound.

The keep's interior proved no less appealing to the eyes, with fine fabrics all around, as rugs and tapestries gaily decorated and vibrant with color dominated the decor. Sweeping stairways lifted the imagination and large windows, many of colored glass, brought in ample light for study in most of the many rooms. The place was airy and clean, with the younger students assisting the many Bedine servants, often magically. Indeed, the first spells Catti-brie learned in her first tendays at the Coven involved conjuring a magical invisible servant, and creating water, wind, and magical light: four especially useful practices for illuminating cobwebs, blowing them away, and cleaning up after them.

Strangely, to Catti-brie, this keep in particular, and Shade Enclave in general, evoked memories of both Silverymoon and Menzoberranzan all at once, for they held the sweeping and grandiose beauty of the former and the magical decorative improvisation and sheer otherworldliness of the latter. Surely the Coven stood far apart from the other structures of the teeming city of Shade Enclave, and seemed perfectly out of place among the shadowy and hard-edged dark structures that otherwise dominated the city.

Her first few tendays in the keep of Lady Avelyere were not unpleasant, with an easy combination of chores and studies—studies Catti-brie was more than happy to devour. Her goal was to grow strong in the Art, and this place afforded her that exact opportunity. Her training under her parents had been acceptable, if limited, but this . . . this was a grand academy with instructors quite proficient in the various schools of magic, from fire-throwing, explosive evokers, to diviners, to those skilled at summoning creatures from the nether planes.

She was not mistreated. The beating she had taken upon her capture seemed an anomaly, an initial warning and nothing more, and the other women of the Coven welcomed her now, particularly Rhyalle, who assigned Catti-brie a room very near to her own.

Yes, this place would suffice, and indeed help her in her ultimate goal. Catti-brie went at her studies with great determination—and with far more insight and previous experience and training than her mentors could ever anticipate.

She excelled, and the sorceresses of the Coven pushed her all the harder.

And she excelled, still.

To her surprise, however, within a short while, Catti-brie did not find any real level of contentment with this arrangement, for uneasy feelings gnawed at her through the days. She could not speak with Mielikki, could not offer worship to the goddess who had given her this second life. Shade Enclave was a city devoted to magic, and in an empire that had once tried to unseat a goddess and claim supremacy over magic for its own spellcasters. In her very first days in the Coven, Catti-brie had been asked repeatedly about her proficiency with healing powers, from whence they had come, and her apparent druidic abilities.

She had deflected the question with shrugs and incredulity, wisely insisting that she didn't even know that the two types of magic, arcane and divine, were of different sources. That had apparently satisfied her captors, but not in any way that made her comfortable to even attempt any contact with, or to offer any prayers to Mielikki in the home of Lady Avelyere.

She thought of Niraj and Kavita constantly, and prayed that they were well. Lady Avelyere had hinted that she knew of Kavita and Niraj's secret, which came as a veiled threat to Catti-brie.

So it was one night that Catti-brie crept from her room and made her way quietly on bare feet to the back wall parapet of the Coven. There she looked up at the city wall, not so far away, and saw that it was unguarded. She closed her eyes and began a spell.

"If you become a bird and attempt to fly away, I will loose a bolt of lightning that will blow you out of the sky," came the voice of Lady Avelyere behind her. The young girl froze, the hair on the back of her neck standing up.

Catti-brie swallowed hard, trying to sort out her next move. She reflexively glanced up at the sky and wondered how long it might take her to create enough of a disturbance above for a lightning bolt to come to her call. It was a ridiculous thought, though, for even if she managed such a thing, powerful Lady Avelyere would easily destroy her.

"Do not make me regret taking you in, little Ruqiah of the Desai," Lady Avelyere went on, coming closer.

"N-no, Lady, of course not," Catti-brie heard herself stammer.

"You have no permission to leave," the diviner insisted. "I spared your life on condition of your acceptance into my school, and now that you are here, the rules apply, dear little Ruqiah, and without exception."

"I wasn't leaving," Catti-brie replied.

"Oh, but you were. Do not take me for a fool, I warn. I heard your thoughts as easily as I watched you walk from your room."

Did Avelyere know, then, of Catti-brie, and not just of Ruqiah? Did she know of Catti-brie's devotion to Mielikki? Had everything Catti-brie feigned when captured just unraveled?

"Then you know I meant to return," Catti-brie said, more forcefully and evenly now as she found her determination, her courage, and her grounding. If Avelyere knew everything about the girl's secret thoughts, she wouldn't be confronting Catti-brie on the wall of the Coven at this time, with so much at stake.

"You are not allowed to leave at all," Lady Avelyere replied.

Catti-brie turned to face her directly. "I want to see my Ma," she said.

"Your mother is fine, and of no concern to you."

There was little severity in Avelyere's tone, but Catti-brie knew enough to make it seem so, and thus, she began to weep, and wail, "I want my Ma!" repeatedly.

Lady Avelyere moved right beside her and to Catti-brie's surprise, embraced her and hugged her close. A moment later, the diviner dropped into a crouch and looked Catti-brie directly in the eye, brushing her reddish-brown hair back tenderly.

"I know the secret of Niraj and Kavita," she said quietly. "They are outlaws, upon my word, and the Twelve Princes of Shade Enclave will not deal with them mercifully, should they ever learn the truth."

Catti-brie cried all the louder and fell into Lady Avelyere's embrace, whispering still, "I want to see my Ma."

After a long while, Lady Avelyere pushed the young girl back to arms' length. "You meant to become a bird and fly to the Desai," she stated.

"Just for a bit," a sniffling Catti-brie assured her. "I meant to be back before dawn."

"Why should I believe you? You wish to escape."

"No, Lady, never!" Catti-brie insisted with all the diplomacy she could muster—it helped that she was speaking truthfully.

"Then leave this place in the morning, forevermore," Lady Avelyere said suddenly, spinning away. "Be gone from me, never to return!"

"No, Lady, please! No!" Catti-brie pleaded. "Then I won't go at all. I want to see my Ma, but not to leave this place! Never to leave this place! I learn so much here! Rhyalle is my sister now!" She kept her voice on the edge of panic, playing the part of a little girl, and Lady Avelyere's smile back at her in response to those words showed to be a look of sympathy and not distrust.

"I am going back to bed now," she said after a bit. "I expect you awake and alert in the morning." She spun on her heel and started away.

Catti-brie caught the implicit permission that she could go, but just as she started to begin her spell anew, she realized that the child, Ruqiah, would likely miss that subtlety.

"I may go, then, Lady?" she asked, all filled with hope and bubbling gratitude.

"Child, I will see you in the morning," came the answer, but then Lady Avelyere stopped suddenly and spun around, looking fierce once more. "And if not, then know that your parents will suffer the consequences of their crimes."

With that, she was gone.

Catti-brie stood on the wall for a long while, trying to make sense of the encounter. Avelyere was letting her fly away, but to what end? Did she expect a more devoted student because she would allow this transgression, or was it perhaps the simple truth that this accomplished Netherese woman was not a merciless beast?

The latter, Catti-brie, decided, even when a flash of terror crossed her mind in the fleeting thought that Avelyere was teasing her.

She became a bird and flew away, and found soon after that her fears were unfounded, that Niraj and Kavita were safe in their tents, though certainly not "fine," as Avelyere had insisted. Nay, they were distraught, mourning the loss of their beloved daughter.

How abruptly that changed when Ruqiah appeared before them! Changed in the flash of smiles, in the warmth of hugs, and in her assurances that all was well, and all would remain well.

The next morning, Catti-brie was hard at work on her studies when Lady Avelyere came to her again and pulled her aside.

"You have expectations to fulfill," she explained to the child. "Goals to meet, and I will hear no excuses when you fail me. You may go and visit your parents, once a tenday, but only on condition that you do not disappoint me."

Catti-brie couldn't contain her smile, and it truly surprised her, yet again, at how much she wanted to play her childhood games with Niraj, and how badly she wanted Kavita to brush her thick hair and tell her tales of the Bedine, of her ancestors who were not even really her ancestors. Somehow that particular truth of her heritage didn't seem to matter.

She promised Lady Avelyere that she would be the best student the diviner had ever known, and she meant it sincerely, for all the reasons she had returned to Faerûn, and also out of sincere gratitude for this extraordinary gesture.

She would meet and exceed every expectation put before her.

The Year of the Dark Circle (1478 DR)
Shade Enclave

The small flicker of flame flew out from the young woman's hand, into the midst of her orc enemies, and there exploded into a fireball, immolating the group.

Her blue eyes squinting against the glare, the sorceress mentally reached into that fire and brought forth a sprite of flame, a living ally fashioned of the fiery element. The sorceress only focused on it for a moment, binding the flames, creating the sprite, and then she turned aside. But the sprite knew what to do, and leaped and skipped across the rooftop, leaving a line of wisps of smoke and sparkles before springing into the chest of the next nearest orc.

The sorceress turned left and swept her arms down and across from left to right, and as if she had thrown forth flaming liquid, a line of fire rushed along the edge of the roof, sealing that flank with a wall of hot-burning flames.

She kept turning left, ducking and spinning, then coming up fast to meet the approach of a handful of orcs. Her thumbs together, her fingers spread wide, she called forth her fourth spell, and a fan-shaped sheet of flames flew out over the enemies. The sorceress dropped low, as if to avoid any swings or thrusts, and kicked out with one foot into the knee of the nearest orc, just for good measure, and just because she enjoyed the sensation of a physical strike.

A slow clapping sound began behind her, from the doorway of this one flat rooftop in the Coven.

Catti-brie stood upright, straightened her clothes, took a deep breath, and slowly turned to face Lady Avelyere.

"An interesting display," the diviner said. "You fancy yourself a battle-mage?"

Catti-brie stumbled a bit. "I . . . I like to be prepared."

"For battle."

"Yes."

"You understand that you live in a city, surrounded by your sisters in the Coven and the forces of Netheril? An unparalleled city guard and the great Twelve Princes?"

Catti-brie lowered her gaze. She had expected something along these lines, given Avelyere's tone and rather sour expression. A sudden pop from the side startled her as the flames biting at one of the orc training dummies found some life in an air pocket, or a bit of sap in the wooden base pole, perhaps.

"You'll spend far more time in social gatherings than on battlefields," Lady Avelyere remarked, moving over to join her. "You will find your missions in service to the Coven more those of information gathering and coercion, as I have repeatedly told you."

"Yes, Lady," she said. "I practice those spells as well . . ." As she finished, Lady Avelyere cupped her by the chin and forced her head up that they could look each other in the eye.

"Dear Ruqiah, what is this fascination you have with flame?"

Catti-brie licked her lips, honestly considering the question, for in truth, she had wondered that herself. Of all the schools of arcane magic available to her in her training, she admittedly found herself most comfortable with, and most proficient with, those of evocation, shaping spells of explosive and deadly force. And of those many spells, she did indeed fancy those concerned with the element of fire—at least for her arcane studies. She already knew how to bring down a bolt of lightning, after all, and had been able to do that with lethal force since her earliest days. Indeed, ten years had passed since she had killed two Netherese agents with such a bolt from the cloudy heavens above.

Perhaps that was it, she pondered, though she would not tell Avelyere, of course, but deep inside, Catti-brie sensed that perhaps it was even something more. Her divinely inspired spells, which she still kept secret from Lady Avelyere and the others at the Coven, exercising her powers only on those occasions when she went to visit Niraj and Kavita, and even then, only in secluded places where she created gardens to honor Mielikki, allowed her formidable protection from the elements. In that advantage, she found fire especially appealing. She needn't worry about unexpected blowback from a fireball with Mielikki's protection wards glistening around her frame.

Besides, she found that she truly enjoyed the eruption of a fireball, the flash of warmth and brilliance back at her, the explosive and cleansing power. She smiled, even though it wasn't an appropriate response to Lady Avelyere, for she was thinking of Bruenor, her adoptive father. In her true formative years, Catti-brie had been raised as a warrior, a woman of action who would not shy from, who would indeed charge into, battle. The power of a fireball enthralled her, for it wasn't subtle and it wasn't quiet. Not in nature, but in nurture, Catti-brie had more than a bit of the dwarf in her.

Lady Avelyere's sigh brought her back to the present situation, to realize that the older woman was shaking her head in obvious disappointment.

"I had hoped for more sophistication from you, my young protégé," she said. "You remain the youngest student I ever allowed into my guild, and my hopes were high indeed. But you waste your time with explosions and kicking dummies in the knee. Perhaps I should send you out to train with the town guard!"

That remark, obviously intended as an insult, sat quite well with Catti-brie. How she would love to hold a sword in her hand once more, or to let fly with Taulmaril, her magical bow from another life!

Lady Avelyere's visage softened and she came forward a step, reaching out to run her hand through Catti-brie's thick reddish-brown hair—hair that had grown more auburn, as in her previous life, as she had grown into adolescence. The great woman's touch didn't make Catti-brie recoil at all. She had come to trust Avelyere, after all.

"My power is knowledge," Lady Avelyere explained. "And with the help of that knowledge, with coercion, I get what I want without the blasts of flame and lightning, you see? My way suits us in Shade Enclave, in the world in which you now live."

The way Avelyere explained things, the tone of her voice in particular, informed Catti-brie that this was about more than her penchant for explosive spellcasting. Lady Avelyere—and the title bestowed upon her was certainly fitting—was more disappointed in Catti-brie's lack of decorum and her willful ignorance of the etiquette of the social circles. Dignitaries often visited the Coven, after all, and Ruqiah had never impressed them. Amused them, perhaps, and brought more than a few deprecating chuckles from time to time, but never impressed. It was not the kind of life that Ruqiah, that Catti-brie, had either fancied or in which she had, even in her previous existence, thrived.

She thought of her first encounters with Lady Alustriel of Silverymoon—indeed, Lady Avelyere somewhat reminded her of Alustriel. Catti-brie had been so uncomfortable, had felt so diminished, beside that woman, whose social graces seemed so easily brought forth, shining ever brightly.

Again Catti-brie thought of Bruenor, and again she was comforted. Bruenor could hoist a tankard of ale with anyone, but put him in a room of fine wine glasses with the gentlemen of, say, Waterdeep, and . . . well, it was not a calm and gracious scene.

A comical scene, likely, but never gracious.

"You find my disappointment humorous?" Lady Avelyere asked.

"No, Lady, no," Catti-brie blurted, and she meant it, of course. "It is only . . . you are so beautiful and so graceful. You float through ballrooms as easily as the shadows of dancers, and every head turns your way. Every woman is jealous of you and every man wants to possess you."

She could tell immediately that her flattery had diffused any anger, and even though she was using the pretty words as a dodge against revealing her memories, she wasn't lying.

"But I am no such swan," she went on. "And so perhaps my choice in magic is more fitting to who I am. Your appearance and grace enhances your skills with the spells you describe, for few could resist your charms even without the magic you employ. But I am afraid that my own . . ." She paused and held up her hands, as if to let her appearance speak for itself. "My own graces and charm would hinder such a devotion to schools of coercion."

Lady Avelyere, her hands on her hips, looked Catti-brie over from head to toe. "Well, you are a bit gangly, and no more shapely than a young boy, but you are barely a woman." She reached out and grabbed at Catti-brie's shirt and ruffled it a bit. "Indeed, I believe you will fill out nicely as you move into womanhood. And you are not ugly, though a bit, well, ruddy. Yet you hardly resemble the beastliness so common among those your heritage—in many lands, none would even think you Bedine."

Catti-brie could only reply with a smile against that prejudiced viewpoint, for in her own estimation, Kavita was among the most beautiful women she had ever seen, in both lifetimes, with her smooth brown skin, impossibly thick and long and lustrous raven-black hair and those dark eyes that could pierce and even mock the soul of another with their implied depth.

"Thank you, gracious Lady," she said, and dipped a polite curtsey.

"Go and practice your more subtle repertoire," Lady Avelyere instructed. "None in our sisterhood has found need of a fireball in many years. I daresay that your impressive and explosive display shows me that you are already capable in this arena, in the unlikely case that such need befalls you."

"Yes, Lady," Catti-brie replied, and she started to bow, caught herself, and curtseyed again, then rushed away, glad to be done with that confrontation.

It occurred to her, though, that this would not be the last uncomfortable conversation she would have with Lady Avelyere, and thoughts of the trial that might come in a few years, when it was time for her to abandon Shade Enclave and the Coven, sent chills through her spine.

CHAPTER 16

DISMAYED GLORY

The Year of the Dark Circle (1478 DR)
Citadel Felbarr

Bruenor's heavy eyelids eased open, leaving a fuzzy grayness where before there had been only darkness. Gradually, painfully, the air around began to take shape, images coming into view in the low firelight, including two wide-eyed faces leaning in close, looking back at him intently.

Bruenor noted an older dwarf male and a younger female, both dressed as clerics. The names Parson and Mandarina hovered around his thoughts, just out of reach. The two continued to study him, their expressions shifting from surprise to concern to, finally, relief and joy.

"Blessed by Moradin," said the woman, and she bent low and kissed young Reginald Roundshield on the cheek. "I'd thought we'd lost ye."

The other dwarf nodded his agreement. "And she's been with ye since yer fall," he explained to the dizzy and dazed dwarf lying on the cot in Citadel Felbarr. "Ain't left yer side for a moment, that one."

"Arr Arr saved us all out there, don't ye doubt," said the woman—yes, it was Mandarina Dobberbright. "What a sorry and ungrateful friend meself'd be if I left him with healing to be done!"

The other, Parson Glaive, nodded again. "Aye, but I thought ye'd be meetin' yer father, me young friend."

"Bangor?" the confused Bruenor whispered under his breath, his lips sticking together with dryness.

"Eh, what's that then?" asked Parson Glaive, leaning forward.

Only then did Bruenor's sensibilities begin to return to the present. He considered what the female cleric had called him, "Arr Arr," and remembered then that he was not King Bruenor, son of Bangor, anymore.

At least, not yet.

That last thought bounced around in his head for a little while, slowly replaced by the returning details of the battle in the mountains, particularly those last few desperate moments when all had seemed lost in the shadow of a towering mountain giant.

"Been days," Parson Glaive went on when no answer seemed forthcoming from the patient. "And Mandarina's been at yer side the whole time, all the way back from the mountains."

"The others?" Bruenor managed to whisper more audibly.

"Ye won the day," Mandarina said, though it didn't seem to Bruenor as if she was doing so in response to his question. "When that durned giant tumbled down, how the ground shook! And how them orcs turned tail and run away! Bwahaha, but ye should've seen 'em, I tell ye, fallin' all over each other and screeching every step. And Ragged Dain, he weren't about to let 'em go, but chased them a mile an' more, choppin' and kickin' and bitin' all the way!"

"Ognun Leatherbelt's talked to King Emerus about ye," Parson Glaive added. "Ye get yer rest, I tell ye, because ye've a party waitin' in yer honor."

Bruenor, still trying to sort out the fight—he remembered throwing his axe and charging the giant, but what he recalled most of all was the explosive pain in his gut—tried to prop himself up on his elbows.

He realized immediately that that was a bad idea.

Waves of agony laid him low, replaced only gradually by waves of nausea. He began to cough and choke, and Mandarina and Parson Glaive were quick to roll him to his side so that he could safely throw up.

He looked at the puddle on the side of his bed with shock and even fear, for more than a little blood was mixed in with the bile.

"It's all right, boy," Parson Glaive said as they settled him onto his back. "Better than it's been. Not to worry."

"Aye, we'll have ye up and about in a tenday or two, but we'll hold yer party off for a month, I'm thinkin'," added Mandarina.

"Aye, a month at least afore this one can drink the toasts he'll be getting!" Parson Glaive agreed with great zest and a wide smile. He looked down at Little Arr Arr and nodded, then produced a small vial, which he moved to his patient's lips. "Ye drink it, boy," he coaxed, tipping the sweet-tasting liquid in.

It did not make Bruenor gag—quite the opposite—it felt warm and soft and steadying. And as the magical potion went down, so too did Bruenor's eyelids, the darkness taking him to a land of confusing and troubled dreams.

Bruenor was the last to arrive of the six battle group members who had gone scouting in the Rauvin Mountains, and to the loudest cheers of all—of all the others combined, those in attendance understood. For this was Reginald Roundshield's moment of glory, with hundreds of Felbarr tankards hoisted high as Parson Glaive led him into the Hall of Ceremony, a grand and high, partly natural, partly carved cavern. On one wall loomed a giant hearth, a bonfire blazing within, lighting all the place with great waves of orange glow, and to the side of it, far enough to avoid the blast of heat from the conflagration, sat King Emerus Warcrown on a great throne on a raised dais.

A second throne had been placed beside his own, less ornate, perhaps, but no less high in position or stature. To this second chair, Parson Glaive led the hero of the evening, and when Bruenor went to respectfully bow to the king, he found that Emerus dipped first.

The king then stood and turned the hero around to face the community, who raised mugs in toast and voices in a great "Huzzah!"

And there in the front row of that crowd, her face wet with tears, stood Uween Roundshield, nodding and sniffling.

Bruenor knew the decorum and ignored it. He wasn't quite sure why Uween's face touched him so at that particular moment, but he could not resist the urge. He broke from King Emerus's grasp and leaped from the dais and across the way to wrap Uween in a tremendous embrace.

"For your Da," she whispered to him amidst the thunderous applause.

Bruenor shed a tear, the first for his dead father. And he hugged Uween all the more and for a long, long while, lifting her from the floor and swaying her back and forth gently.

When he finally broke and turned back for the dais, a dozen hands reached for him, to pat him on the shoulder, and one voice lifted above the others to draw his attention.

"Ye saved me sister," said Mallabritches Fellhammer. Bruenor locked gazes with her. "She told ye to leave her, but ye would no'." The tough warrior aptly nicknamed Fury had more than a little moisture in her eyes as she solemnly nodded her gratitude and approval.

Back on the dais, King Emerus signaled for Bruenor to take his seat, then called for the testimonials. One by one, starting with Ognun Leatherbelt, the other five members of the Rauvin scouting group stepped up to stand before the king and the hero, and offered to the gathering stirring tales of the battle. And each of those tales outdid the previous—clearly, they had rehearsed the roles each would play in this historical retelling. Ognun set the stage, then Tannabritches told of the opening volley, and of Arr Arr's great courage in saving her. Mandarina came next, to confirm that "Fist" would have died if Arr Arr had chosen differently.

Magnus Leatherbelt brought out the "oos" and "ahs" with his description of the arrival of the giant, and the great behemoth surely sounded even bigger in his retelling than it had loomed on the field that day!

Last came Ragged Dain, the old warrior. He looked Bruenor in the eye, to offer a nod of respect and a wink of salute.

And then, with the sobriety of a veteran who had fought a hundred battles, the temperance of a dwarf who had seen many enemies killed, and the grim resolve of a dwarf who had fully expected to die in the foothills of the Rauvins, Ragged Dain showed himself to be as fine a bard as he was a warrior. He had the crowd hushed for a long while, hanging on his every word, and when he finished with, "And so I'm tellin' ye here and tellin' ye true, if not for Little Arr Arr . . ."

His dramatic pause right there brought an audible gasp from the crowd. "Nah," he corrected. "Ain't no 'little' left in that one."

This pause brought the most raucous cheers of all.

"If not for Reginald—son o' one o' me dearest friends, Moradin keep him drunk!—then know that not one of us'd be standing with ye tonight, and ye'd not know that orcs and a giant prowled just to the north o' Felbarr's gates!"

The room exploded as Ragged Dain walked over to Bruenor and presented him with a flagon of Gutbuster, as sure a passage into adulthood as any dwarf could offer a teenager. He took Bruenor's arm and coaxed him out of the chair, leading him to the center of the stage.

With a wink at Uween and a nod to Ragged Dain, then to King Emerus, Bruenor drained the flagon.

Up came Emerus, and from a pouch he produced a grand golden medal, fashioned in the shape of a round shield, and hung it around Reginald's neck with a fine mithral chain.

"Grant a wish!" Mallabritches Fellhammer cried from the crowd, and the chant was taken up all across the hall.

"Grant a wish!"

King Emerus wore a surprised expression, but it was feigned, Bruenor could tell. The king had expected this, as Bruenor surely would have in one of the similar feasts of honor he had presided over in Mithral Hall. And indeed, Bruenor had granted more than a few such "wishes."

The most common request, of course, would be for a tub of beer, a flask of brandy and the hand of a lovely lass for a dinner date, or a sturdy lad when a female was being so honored.

"Take the girl, Little Arr Arr!" someone yelled out from the back, and all started laughing at that.

"Ain't so little if he takes the girl!" another cried.

"Fist!" yelled one.

"Fury!" argued another.

And so it went, with both Fellhammer lasses furiously blushing, and Bruenor wearing a little grin through it all.

"Might be the pair o' them, if Fist 'n' Fury're meaning anything!" Ragged Dain shouted and the room exploded with laughter, King Emerus most of all.

Finally, Emerus quieted it all and put his arm around the hero. "Well there, Reginald," he said. "It's seemin' that we're all in agreement here. Ye're deservin' of a wish, be it a weapon or a suit o' mithral or a tub o' beer, as I can order. If it's a girl yer wantin' for a dance or a dinner, well, that's for her to agree, course, and if it's for the two o' them Fellhammers, then I'm thinking their Da might have a word with ye."

That brought more laughter, and even Bruenor joined in this time.

"But the wish is yers to ask and ourn to grant," King Emerus proclaimed. "Ye name it. Moradin's blessed ye and who're ourselfs to argue?"

The smile left Bruenor's face in the blink of an eye at that, replaced by a frozen expression as he tried to hide his grimace. Emerus's words, "Moradin's blessed ye," bounced around in his head with the force of a giant-hurled boulder, assaulting his sensibilities, reminding him of the futility, the sad joke, that was the reality of Little Arr Arr.

A roiling anger twisted his belly and stabbed at his heart. Moradin's blessed ye? It was all Bruenor could do to keep from cursing Moradin in front of all of them, then and there!

"Reginald?" King Emerus asked, and Bruenor only then realized that a long while had passed. He looked up from the king to the gathering, to Uween, then to Ragged Dain and Ognun and the others of the battle group, including Fist and Fury, standing side-by-side and smiling widely at him, their eyes sparkling with anticipation.

He looked at Parson Glaive and wanted nothing more than to run over and dress the priest down, to tell him that it was all a joke, that Moradin played with them and ridiculed them, and laughed at their victories and failures equally!

But he didn't.

And he knew what he wanted, above all: to be back in Iruladoon to bid farewell to Catti-brie, Regis, and Wulfgar, to enter the pool and go to his earned rewards in Dwarfhome.

But King Emerus couldn't give that to him, and so another notion came to him suddenly.

"To go to Mithral Hall," he said. "That's me wish."

King Emerus was smiling widely, and started to respond, but caught himself as he clearly digested the young dwarf's demand, and just stared blankly at the hero of the night. The gathering in the hall around them went silent, with many shoulders lifting in a shrug.

"Mithral Hall?" the king asked.

"Aye," Bruenor confirmed, and just to break the confusion, for indeed it was a surprising request, he added, "and a keg o' this," and held up his mug of Gutbuster.

That was what the gathering had expected to hear, of course, and their confusion flew away in the burst of a great cheer.

"Two wishes, then!" King Emerus declared. "And so it will be!" And the crowd cheered more, except for the Fellhammer sisters, Bruenor noted, who both seemed a bit disappointed.

Bruenor continued to smile, and took a hefty gulp of Gutbuster, but it was all for show, designed to keep up the charade of his feigned identity. He was truly looking back inside his own thoughts, and weighing the emotional cost of fulfilling his request to return to Mithral Hall, where he had twice been king.

His gut had told him to return there, but he wasn't quite sure why.

Spring came on in full and turned to summer, but Bruenor did not get his wish in those seasons, or in that year at all. Parson Glaive overruled him, insisting that the young dwarf's injuries were too severe for him to make that always-dangerous and burdensome trip. Bruenor wanted to argue; now that he had proclaimed his plan to return to Mithral Hall, his desire to be on with it had only grown. But he could not, for Parson Glaive had told him, and told King Emerus, that Reginald could well prove a liability on such a trip.

And so King Emerus had counseled patience, and Bruenor had agreed without complaint.

In truth, what did a few months, even a year, matter?

So he focused on getting healthy and strong once more, and was back to training by the end of the summer. He spent as much time as he could with Uween, as well, for her presence at the gathering had taught him something important: Perhaps he would never see himself as her son, as a Roundshield of Felbarr, but poor Uween could never see him as anything but. He had a responsibility to her, owed a debt to her, and he would not forsake it. For all of his anger at Moradin and the other gods, he would not show hostility or indifference to this dwarf woman who had offered him nothing but the unconditional love of a parent.

By the turn of the winter of the Year of the Dark Circle, though, the darkness began to descend upon Bruenor once more, and when came the turn of Dalereckoning 1479, the Year of the Ageless One, the red-bearded dwarf's patience had fully run out.

Day after day, he prodded his elders on when the first caravan out from Citadel Felbarr to Mithral Hall would commence, and he confronted Parson Glaive many times to ensure that the priest would not reverse his recent determination that Reginald was ready for the road.

In his whole life, this one and the previous, Bruenor had never felt himself more ready for the road.

He knew that he was becoming more and more testy, his patience long gone. Fist and Fury began avoiding him.

In a sparring match one day early in the second month, Alturiak, Bruenor nearly split the skull of his opponent, so hard was his chop with his practice weapon.

"Ah, but that's enough of ye," Ragged Dain said a short while later, coming into the training grounds all red in the face, eyes wide and lips full of froth. He moved to the weapons rack and grabbed out a wooden axe, then stormed over to Bruenor.

"Yerself and me, then," he said.

"My session is done," Bruenor replied, and he turned away—and Ragged Dain whacked him across the back, sending him into a forward stagger.

Bruenor straightened and took a deep breath. He noted all the other warriors moving to the side of the room, staring at him. He slowly turned around to face Ragged Dain.

"Come on, then," the old veteran demanded.

Bruenor held his hands out wide, as if to ask why.

"Ye been grumpin' and spittin' and kickin' all the year!" Ragged Dain said. "Ye so durned determined to get out o' here, are ye?"

Bruenor rubbed his face and didn't blink.

Ragged Dain threw the axe and a round shield at Bruenor's feet, then pulled a second set from the weapon rack.

Bruenor looked at them, snorted, then glared up at Ragged Dain.

"Clangeddin's wantin' this," Ragged Dain assured him.

Bruenor snorted again.

And walked away.

He didn't say a word to Uween when he entered his home, just moved past her to his private chamber, where he began stuffing his clothing into a sack. He knew that there would likely be repercussions for his actions on the training grounds, but he knew enough of dwarf tradition to understand that they couldn't stop him from his promised journey to Mithral Hall.

"Clangeddin," he spat, stuffing the bag. "Hope ye enjoyed the show, then!"

"Are ye so determined to be away from me?" came Uween's voice from his door, and Bruenor glanced over to see a sad face indeed.

Bruenor closed his eyes and looked down, trying hard to separate his intense rage from his feelings for this gentle dwarf woman, to separate the pain of the false promises of Moradin and the other gods from those real joys involving innocent dwarves.

"Not yerself," he whispered, and he looked back at Uween, now with tears of his own rimming his gray eyes. He shook his head and dropped the sack, then rushed over to hug the woman. "Ye been all to me an' more," he said, and he held her for a long while, until her sobs subsided.

"Mithral Hall?" she asked after she had composed herself. "What's in yer head, then?"

Bruenor tried to figure out what he might say to her—a task made all the more complicated because he wasn't even sure of the truth of the matter. Why had he declared his wish as such? What was there for him but more painful reminders of the silly game that he and his people played seriously, as if anything at all actually mattered?

"I heared stories o' the place," he replied. "Of a hero named Thibbledorf Pwent and the Gutbuster Brigade—finest in all dwarfdom."

"Thibbledorf Pwent?"

"An old battlerager, long dead. Shield dwarf to King Bruenor Battlehammer hisself."

Uween shrugged and stared at him, clearly confused.

"They train 'em differently at Mithral Hall," Bruenor explained, improvising with every word. "Were ye proud o' me when me group returned from the Rauvins?"

"Ye saw me in the hall," Uween replied. "Ye done yer Da well!"

"Well, I mean to do him better," Bruenor said. "I'll be trainin' with them Gutbusters if they'll be havin' me, and then I'll come back to Felbarr and pass it on. Don't ye worry, Reginald Roundshield'll be takin' his place at King Emerus's side afore many more years've gone by!"

That cheered her, and this time she threw a happy hug around Bruenor.

Bruenor hugged her back and whispered more reassurances. It bothered him to lie to Uween, but he figured it would bother him more to wound her.

He had no intention of ever returning to Citadel Felbarr.

Not as Reginald Roundshield, at least.

That he knew for sure, though he knew not what path might now be pulling him from this place.

He had been quite ready to lift the weapons and battle Ragged Dain, relishing the thought of laying the old veteran low, confident that he could do so. For Bruenor had more battle experience than Ragged Dain, and he carried it in a body young and strong. Yes, he had initially thought the challenge a grand idea, but then his would-be opponent had invoked Clangeddin.

Their fight would be nothing more, then, than yet another show for the pleasure of the dwarf gods.

Nay, Bruenor would be no part of that. Indeed, if Clangeddin Silverbeard had shown up in that room, Bruenor would have picked up the wooden axe and swung it at Clangeddin's face!

Because there was no point.

Because there was no truth.

Because the dwarf gods did not reciprocate the loyalty of their foolish subjects.

Because everything that had sustained King Bruenor throughout his centuries of life and his dedication to the tenets of his clan was a fraud, a game, a play without consequence.

He realized that he was crushing Uween against him by then, but she didn't understand that anger, not love, drove his muscles, albeit unintentionally. She didn't seem to mind, however, so Bruenor held on, needing something, someone, solid and dependable.

Alturiak became Ches, and by the end of that third month, the first caravan was organized for the journey to Mithral Hall.

Reginald Roundshield was named as second guard of the fourth wagon, serving under none other than Ragged Dain.

CHAPTER 17

COMPLICATIONS

The Year of the Grinning Halfling (1481 DR)
Delthuntle

THEY HAD BEEN AMONG THE BEST YEARS OF EITHER LIFE FOR REGIS, AND mostly because of this very dance, with this very opponent.

The tip of the blade came at him in a series of rapid thrusts, Donnola's lead foot tapping solidly on the matt as she strode and maintained perfect balance.

Regis countered with an upraised blade, tapping each thrust off to the left, Donnola's rapier turned only a couple of degrees, but enough to barely miss the mark.

"Both ways!" she scolded, for she had warned Regis against falling into a dangerous parry rhythm, and to accentuate her point, she held her next thrust just an eye-blink longer, then stabbed in behind Regis's waving rapier, her eyes and smile wide at her apparent kill.

But up came Regis's dirk, left arm rising behind his right, the small blade angling Donnola's attack to the right. And in that movement, Regis began his rapier retraction, bringing it down and dropping his right shoulder back, throwing himself right around, right behind left, farther from Donnola's turned blade.

He came around with a devastating thrust that brought a yelp from his opponent, who nearly tripped over backward, so fast did she retreat.

But Regis stayed up with her, thrusting high, thrusting low, and always maintaining his perfect fencing posture, with his back foot perpendicular to the line of battle, his front foot aiming the way forward.

Donnola ducked off to the right, and as Regis turned to keep the pressure, she quickly skipped back to the left. This wasn't the way she typically

199

fought, and Regis understood that she was testing him, using techniques he would more likely see from an opponent with a heavier blade, or a slashing or bludgeoning weapon. She was moving him, turning him, to see if he could react without losing his posture.

It went on for many strikes and parries, Regis gaining a clear and lasting advantage for the first time in their years of sparring.

"Well done, but hold!" Donnola demanded, leaping back and lowering her blade.

"Oh, fie!" Regis argued, for he had her. He knew it!

"You have shown your agility and ability to hold your balance," Donnola said. "But you could not close."

"I did not have to close," Regis protested. "You use rapier and dirk, as do I!"

"Close," Donnola challenged, assuming a ready position once more. "You can never win without it. Do you think you'll be fighting a halfling with a rapier? Nay, Spider, you'll be battling an orc or a human, bigger and stronger, and able to smash your skull from afar!

"Haha!" she added with a deft parry as Regis rushed ahead with a series of sudden, balanced steps, never crossing his trailing foot before his front, the perfect fencing "charge."

"You can't win from there!" Donnola laughed, and when Regis came on more ferociously, the woman twirled away.

"Oh, but here comes the club for your head!" she said, or started to say, for then she was rolling back and away once more as Regis kept up the pursuit. Now he moved her deliberately, cutting the room down, guiding her to a corner.

She saw it, he knew.

"Can't catch me!" she declared, spinning out to the side, but Regis had anticipated it and moved even as she did, his rapier reaching out for her. She fended it brilliantly, as usual, with a rolling block and a riposte, but Regis was ready for that sudden turn of events, and he, too, rolled his blade, back up and over, then down under and suddenly up, lifting Donnola's arm as he rushed in.

He slammed against her, pressing her back into the wall, and they were so close, face-to-face, Donnola's sword arm up over her head, pinned to the wall by Regis's trapping blade.

The tip of her dirk came against his ribs at the same moment his own found her ribs.

He had taken her breath away, and lost his own in the process, for he could not draw any air so close to this beautiful creature.

They stared at each other for a long moment.

Donnola kissed him suddenly, passionately, and pressed out from the wall.

Regis felt his knees go weak and it was all he could do to hold his balance. But then Donnola broke the kiss and he nearly overbalanced forward once more, and might have fallen on his face.

Except that the woman's rapier prodded into his chest in what would have been a clean kill.

She laughed at him. "You will learn," she said, and she spun away as gracefully as any butterfly and skipped out of the room.

Regis just stood there, his blades lowered, feeling positively naked, his thoughts spinning helplessly. He tried to focus on the fight, on the flow that had garnered him such an advantage. He tried to learn from this moment, but that was a useless exercise with the heat of Donnola's kiss so warm in his mind and body.

To think that she had kissed him so!

She was only eight years his senior, in her mid-twenties, and so smart and beautiful and brilliant with the blade, and brilliant in her diplomacy . . .

Brilliant in her diplomacy?

Regis shook his head to clear the cobwebs and looked at the door where Donnola had departed—had departed after disarming him with an unexpected kiss and defeating him in the match!

Brilliant diplomacy?

Pericolo's index finger jabbed down onto the map spread wide on a table and a wry smile came over his face.

Donnola looked at the map, a nautical chart of the Sea of Fallen Stars, and perhaps the most complete one in existence. For this had been a project Pericolo had been pursuing for years now, as long as Donnola could remember and more. The Grandfather had spent a small fortune on the detailed nautical chart, at one point offering any boat that went out a small bounty on soundings around the various reefs and shoals. And years earlier, Pericolo had hired the best known cartographer of this sea, and had brought him to Delthuntle, giving him a fine set of rooms and all the charts they could purchase to compile this one grand work.

When Wigglefingers took Spider out for his morning dives, the wizard knew well where they were going and how deep the water would be.

Donnola looked up from the map to regard the mage then, as he stood to the side passively, having obviously already received Pericolo's big announcement, and when Donnola shifted her gaze to consider her Grandfather, she found there the most contented and satisfied grin she had ever seen from the man.

And then she understood. "You found it," she said breathlessly.

Pericolo just kept grinning.

"The Lichwreck," Donnola whispered, looking back to the pointing finger, settled just south of Aglarond.

"Ebonsoul," Pericolo added, referring to a powerful lich, reputedly sealed inside a silver coffin aboard his boat, Thepurl's Diamond. According to legend, the ship had been sunk by pirates around the time of the Spellplague. It was rumored to hold crates stuffed with the great magical treasure hoard of Ebonsoul, taken from his lair in the Chondalwood.

All around the southeastern stretches of the Sea of Fallen Stars, mariners whispered about the Lichwreck; it had been a topic of conversation at many of the parties Donnola had attended. She had always thought of it as rumor and legend, a source of intrigue and daydreams, and fantasies of great power and wealth. She had always considered the stories greatly exaggerated, a way for idle noblemen to puff up their peacock feathers with feigned adventure, but Donnola knew well that Pericolo truly believed in the stories of Thepurl's Diamond's treasure hoard. He hadn't pursued his search for any gain of power or wealth even, but because he considered this to be his ultimate adventure.

He would be the man who salvaged Ebonsoul's treasures, and in doing so, Pericolo Topolino would forever etch his name among the legends of the Sea of Fallen Stars.

"How do you know it's . . . ?" Donnola started to ask.

"It is there," Pericolo answered flatly. "Settled in a trench twelve leagues southwest of Aglarond's southwestern-most point."

Donnola swallowed hard and stared back at the map. "How do you know?"

"I have suspected it for a long time," Pericolo answered.

"I have summoned water elementals around the area to investigate for us," Wigglefingers added. He stepped to the side of the room, to a hutch covered with astrolabes and rolled charts and a pair of spyglasses. From a drawer he produced an item covered in a black cloth and returned to the table.

Donnola and Wigglefingers stared each other in the eye as the mage slowly removed the cloth, revealing a daggerlike shard of glass—no, not glass, Donnola realized, but a piece of a broken mirror. She tilted her head not sure what to make of the curious item.

"Go ahead and look into it," Pericolo said. "You are too large for the shard's magic to activate in any substantive way."

Donnola took the glass from Wigglefingers and peered at her reflection, or what part of it she could see in the shard, which was not more than three fingers' breadth at its thickest point.

She saw half her smile and one brown eye . . . no, half her frown and a bloodshot brown eye. Perplexed, she drew back and looked at her companions.

Wigglefingers, smiling, held out his hand for the shard and Donnola handed it over.

"Were it the complete mirror and not just a sliver, I would never have allowed you to peer into it," Pericolo said.

Donnola shrugged, growing more curious still as she looked to the wizard, who produced from one of the many pockets in his grand robe a small rat. The creature climbed around his hand as he rolled it over for Donnola to see. Wigglefingers bent to the floor at the side of the table, rat in one hand, mirror shard in the other, and placed both down so that the rat could get a look at itself.

Donnola gasped and nearly jumped out of her shoes as a second rat, identical to the first, ran out of the mirror, rushing wildly right for the first, who responded in kind. With sudden, seemingly insane ferocity, the rodents attacked each other, biting and rolling in a confused ball that quickly became bloody. Rat screeches filled the air.

"Stop it!" Donnola pleaded, horrified by the sight. She looked to Wigglefingers, who was already living up to his nickname, his hand waving in the air.

He cast a spell, a dispel actually, and the air shimmered with magical energy and one of the rats simply disappeared.

"What?" the young halfling woman asked with a gasp.

"A Mirror of Opposition," Pericolo explained. "Any who look into it will find a replica of themselves stepping forth, and to do battle."

"And it teems still with considerable magic, though it has obviously been shattered and has lain at the bottom of the sea for a hundred years," Wigglefingers explained.

"Ebonsoul had one, so say the tales," Pericolo remarked.

"And you found this . . . ?" Donnola paused and poked her finger down on the spot on the nautical map.

Pericolo nodded somberly. "It is the Lichwreck. I have suspected it for some time. And now I have the means to get to it."

Donnola nodded as she digested the words, then her eyes went wide as she came to understand them, as the end of that statement, "the means to get to it," rang clear in her mind.

"You have come to love him as a son," she protested, barely able to find her voice.

Pericolo looked at her, at first seeming surprised by her remark, but then with a clever smile. "And you more than that?" he retorted.

Donnola laughed it off, but her grandfather didn't stop grinning.

"Do you deny that you love Spider?" Donnola asked.

"Why would I? I brought him into our family as truly as if he were my own chil—grandchild," Pericolo replied. "His father resides in a house I purchased and survives on funds I deliver."

"Yet you mean to send him to do this," Donnola said dryly. "You will send him to the depths in search of this shipwreck."

"Danger is a part of life, my girl, and an important part. Never forget that!"

"You will send him to his death!"

"I deny your description! For years, I have searched for Ebonsoul's lost treasure, and now it is mine, within my grasp."

"Because of Spider."

"Yes."

"So you value this treasure more than you value—" Donnola started to accuse, but a flash of anger in Pericolo's eyes stopped her short.

"It is precisely my love of the boy that leads me to offer this to him," the Grandfather argued. "Oh, but that I had his gift of the genasi! Of all the adventures I have known, of all the victories and the plunder, this would eclipse them as surely as a giant moon could block the sun!"

"And eclipse them in danger?"

Pericolo snorted at the thought. "I send you into the lair of sand jackals every tenday and I love you more dearly than any other."

"That is different," Donnola replied. "I am older and more worldly."

"Not when you started," Pericolo shot back. "Think back, my pretty granddaughter. How old were you when you attended your first ball in

Delthuntle? It was before your sixteenth birthday, I believe, and Spider is nearly two years beyond that mark. By the time you had reached his age, you had attended scores of such festivities in the pits of intrigue, and more than one of those balls ended with a body found in a nearby alleyway, yes? And by your eighteenth birthday, you had, with my blessing and encouragement, robbed a dozen palaces, pickpocketed half the lords of Aglarond, and killed a trio of assassins, including two in one fight! Should I have hidden Donnola in a room as we do Spider?"

She sputtered but had no real response.

"Or do you now believe that I did not care for you, and was reckless?"

"That was different," she said softly and without much conviction.

"He is ready to earn his way, to step up to a position of authority and responsibility."

"Different," she whispered again, shaking her pretty head and swallowing hard.

"How so, girl?"

"I went to the homes of nobility, but you would send him to the depths in pursuit of the treasure vault of a lich."

Pericolo looked at the nautical map spread before him, at the spot where his poking finger had dented the parchment, the spot where he believed Thepurl's Diamond lay. For a long while, he said nothing, but then he looked up at Donnola and nodded.

"The greater the risk, the greater the reward." He wore a determined smile.

"The risk to Spider, the reward to Pericolo?" she replied sarcastically.

The Grandfather narrowed his eyes. Donnola sucked in her breath, unused to seeing a threatening expression from him directed at her. "All glory to Spider if he succeeds," he said evenly. "All glory and a pick of the treasures. What might I need with them, indeed? Nay, it is the adventure, the conquest, and I shall oversee it, and forevermore, when my name is spoken along the coast of the Sea of Fallen Stars, it will be mentioned that it was I, Pericolo Topolino, who salvaged the Lichwreck! And Spider will be mentioned, as well.

"Do you not understand, my girl?" he asked with great exasperation. "I offer Spider a chance at immortality, a chance to make a name that will resound around Aglarond for centuries hence!"

"And if he fails?"

"We mourn him and find another who might be up to the task," the Grandfather answered without a moment's hesitation. He gave a little chuckle and shook his head, staring hard at Donnola. "I will not live in a walled fortress, nor will you. Look past your personal feelings for Spider. Is caution what you truly desire, my beloved granddaughter? Have I taught you nothing, then?"

Donnola swallowed hard.

"What do you feel when you enter the window of a rich fool's house unbidden?" he asked. "What does Donnola feel when the shadows around her reveal the presence of an assassin, or a deadly blade comes forth against her?"

The young halfling woman didn't blink.

"Alive," Pericolo answered for her. "You feel alive. This is what I have taught you, this is how you have lived. Indeed, this is how I have lived! Is there any other way?"

Donnola lowered her gaze in shame. The adventures she had known over the last decade came flooding back to her—how many times had she stood at the edge of her own grave? And Pericolo had known the razor-thin edge of disaster more than she in those last ten years, by far. From everything she had ever heard of her grandfather, of the Grandfather, the last ten years had been the quietest decade of his most adventurous life.

"Do you doubt my love for you?" Pericolo asked.

"Never," Donnola answered without the slightest hesitation, her gaze shooting up so that she could look Pericolo in the eye as she answered him.

"If I could offer you this dive, would you take it?"

The woman licked her lips. She didn't answer, but both she, the Grandfather, and Wigglefingers, who was quietly chuckling, knew the answer, of course.

"Then do not doubt my love for Spider, either," Pericolo begged. "I offer him the grandest adventure of all, Thepurl's Diamond!"

"A cursed ship of mighty undead."

"A sunken ship of grand treasures," Pericolo corrected. "And I know where it is, and Spider, with the help of Wigglefingers, can get there. Ah, but how I envy the young one!"

Donnola started to reply, but stopped short. Would she make the dive to Thepurl's Diamond, if that were possible?

Of course. Without hesitation.

A smile, not of defeat, but of acceptance, began to spread over Donnola's face, and she found herself envying Spider more than a little, as well.

Regis entered the small but well-appointed cottage with a bit of trepidation, as he always did when he came here. He couldn't shake the memory of those early days, when he had often found Eiverbreen passed out on the floor, smelling of whiskey.

He came upon his father in the living room, fast asleep in a chair, but by the look of his clothing—only a bit disheveled—he seemed to be taking an honest nap. Regis, who had lived his previous life lying on the banks of Maer Dualdon in Ten-Towns with an un-baited fishing line tied to his toe, could certainly relate to that.

He quietly stoked the fire in the hearth and took a seat opposite Eiverbreen, then patiently waited. His duties at Morada Topolino were done for the day, so he was in no hurry.

He watched the halfling across from him, studying Eiverbreen's expressions. The man was dreaming, though not contentedly.

Had Eiverbreen Paraffin ever known contentment?

Regis silently chastised himself—a typical sensation of late—as he watched the man. He recalled when Eiverbreen had dunked him in the sea—and truly he thought that he would drown!—to learn if Regis was possessed of the same blessing as his lost mother. And then had come the dangerous dives in any and every weather. Eiverbreen had thrown his son to the sea, and above all else, Regis had to get the oysters—that single obsession fueled by the man's need for drink at any cost to himself or to his son. For a long while, Regis had resented Eiverbreen, as any child born of such a troubled father might.

But Regis had been no child in Delthuntle. He had seen poverty before, and had felt the sting of hopelessness that so often accompanied it. In Calimport, in his first youth, Regis had known many Eiverbreens, indeed had quietly championed them even while he was rising within the guilds of the ruling pashas.

He couldn't help but smile when he recalled one particularly lucrative heist: He wasn't about to get away with it, he had soon enough realized, for the golden coins of the pasha he had robbed had all been cleverly marked. So Regis had taken that sack of coins to one of the most destitute reaches of Calimport in the dark of night and had strewn the treasure up and down the lane! The next day, every tavern and bakery in that region of the city became flooded with the dirty and the downtrodden.

Regis had known, and shown, mercy and compassion to the unfortunates of Calimport, and yet it had taken him many years to acquire the same level of compassion for this halfling now sitting before him.

The resentment had only worsened in the first years Eiverbreen had lived in this house, for Pericolo, on Regis's demand, had indeed made it harder for Eiverbreen to purchase alcohol. No tavern would sell the liquor to him, on order from Pericolo, and Eiverbreen hadn't taken well to that demand, and had blamed his son, Spider, most of all. Oh, he still found liquor, to this day, despite every attempt by Regis to tamp down the sources.

Only gradually had the two settled into a truce. They didn't discuss Eiverbreen's drinking, for there was no common ground to be found there, but Eiverbreen had stopped blaming his son, openly at least, and had even occasionally expressed gratitude that Regis had cared enough to try. And Regis had stopped resenting the downtrodden halfling, instead coming to see Eiverbreen in the same manner he had viewed those poor souls on the dirty streets of Calimport. He couldn't "fix" Eiverbreen, but so be it.

The realization that Eiverbreen wasn't actually his father had allowed the reborn halfling the emotional room he needed for objectivity.

Eiverbreen snorted and licked his lips, moving his head side to side suddenly, then opened one lazy eye to look back at Regis.

"Hey boy," he said through sleep-sticky lips.

"Father," Regis lied.

Eiverbreen rubbed a hand over his face, sitting up straighter in the process.

"I'm seein' you less," Eiverbreen slurred.

"I've much to do now."

"With them Topolinos."

"Yes."

"Aren't you the fancylad!" Eiverbreen said with a laugh, but one that was only half-mocking. He sat up straighter still, rubbing the sleepiness from his eyes. "You still dancing with that pretty girl, are you?"

"She trains me with the blade."

Eiverbreen issued a coarse laugh that sounded more like a wheeze than anything mirthful. "Well, I'd be stabbing that one, given the chance!" he said with a howl.

Regis steeled his posture and shut his mouth, reminding himself that Eiverbreen was harmless, that his crudity served as cover for despair.

"She's a friend," Regis said instead.

"Aye, you and your important friends," Eiverbreen said with a derisive snort.

"They've done well by you," Regis said before he could bite it back.

Eiverbreen snorted louder and turned to look at the hearth.

"I'm sorry, Father," Regis said. "But you seem well."

Eiverbreen pulled himself to his feet, grabbed the poker, and began prodding at the logs. "I get by, boy," he said absently.

"My name is Regis." He wasn't really sure why he had said it, but there it lay.

"So says you," replied a clearly confused Eiverbreen.

"Indeed, and is there any other to argue my choice?"

"Not your choice!" Eiverbreen said harshly, even lifting the poker to aim its tip Regis's way. "Your Ma's choice!"

"She's dead."

"My choice, then! You could have spoken to me first, boy, to see if I approved."

"You had your chance, but you didn't bother," Regis said, and Eiverbreen's expression flashed with anger.

"You forgetting your place?" the older halfling asked.

Regis shook his head, denying Eiverbreen. The discussion had reminded him of why he had come here; he was eighteen years old now. The west was beginning to call, the bargain of Mielikki sounding louder and louder in his thoughts.

"Might that I'll call you Earnst," Eiverbreen said. "That was my brother's name, your dead uncle, drowned in the storm of 1445. Just a boy, you know. Aye, I should have named you Earnst to honor him!"

"You should have, perhaps, but you didn't."

"Your name is what I tell you it is!" Eiverbreen growled, and he prodded the poker Regis's way—or started to, for the halfling's rapier came forth in the blink of a surprised eye, quickly parrying and rolling over the poker, where its blade caught under the item's hook. With a subtle twist and shift, Regis pulled the poker from Eiverbreen's hand and sent it bouncing aside.

Eiverbreen stared at him dumbfounded, then looked at the fallen poker. He began to laugh heartily. "Oh, but that Topolino lassie's teaching you well, boy!" he said. "And what else is she teaching my boy?"

He fell back into his chair, his shoulders bobbing with amusement.

"Much," was all Regis replied, and he did so with a wide grin, thinking there was no reason to dissuade Eiverbreen from his undoubtedly lewd notions.

Eiverbreen shrugged and snorted, waving his hand dismissively. "Where did you find this name?"

Regis paused and looked down from Eiverbreen, who was leaning forward in his chair now, seeming suddenly interested in the conversation. Perhaps it was time to tell Eiverbreen the truth.

"It's a name I heard, a long time ago," he started, unsure.

"Where? With them Topolinos?"

"Longer back."

"Well, where then?" Eiverbreen said, his tone sharpening.

Regis considered that question for a few moments. What would be gained by telling Eiverbreen? The old drunk probably wouldn't even believe it, and if he did, well, to what gain? Others had told Regis that Eiverbreen was proud of him, in his own way, whispering about "his boy with the Grandfather" between bites of his meals at the local common rooms. Perhaps, Regis mused, he had just wanted to hurt the man, to steal from him the one boasting point in all of his miserable life.

But why? Because of the neglect? Because Eiverbreen had been a fairly pathetic father—even though Eiverbreen wasn't even his father at all?

No, Regis decided then and there. He was allowing his own pettiness to sway him, but there was no place for such things. His entire purpose for returning to Toril awaited him just a trio of years down the road—the long road to Icewind Dale.

He looked at Eiverbreen and offered a disarming smile. He really didn't want to hurt the halfling. It was that simple.

He laughed. "Grandfather calls me Spider. Spider Parrafin, son of Eiverbreen, student of Grandfather Pericolo Topolino."

Eiverbreen looked at him even more curiously at first, as if wondering what in the Nine Hells had just transpired, and to what end. But then he nodded, even laughed a bit, echoing, "Spider, eh? I like that much better."

Regis felt proud of himself for rising above pettiness, for being able to separate his own wounded feelings enough to find for this poor soul Eiverbreen the same compassion Regis had shown to others in his previous life.

The smile couldn't spread too widely, though, as Regis reminded himself that he would indeed be wounding Eiverbreen, perhaps mortally, when he left Delthuntle, and that unsettling thought had him chewing his lip.

How could he do this? How could he go to Icewind Dale, thousands of miles away, when he was needed here? How could he walk away from this life he had built on the shores of Aglarond?

He thought of Drizzt, then, and of Catti-brie and Bruenor. It would be grand to see them again, of course.

But he thought of Eiverbreen and Pericolo and of Donnola—yes, mostly of Donnola!—and of all that he had come to love about his life here in Delthuntle.

The halflings of Delthuntle had been good to him, and to Eiverbreen. Even before Regis had signed on with Pericolo Topolino, he and Eiverbreen had known kindness from fellow halflings.

And to think that here, in this city of tall and hardy men, a halfling like Pericolo could rise to such stature and prominence! Even the more formal thieves guilds in the city, including the most powerful of all, the Three-Fingered Ring, an organization known to frown upon any lesser guilds, afforded Pericolo and his halfling Morada great respect. Regis himself had witnessed the respectful bows of the Delthuntle Lord's Guard, the Hobgoblins, whenever Pericolo Topolino walked past them.

The halflings of Delthuntle were not treated as curiosity pieces, or lessers—whether that was because of Pericolo, or an attitude that had helped facilitate Pericolo's rise.

"A good halfling community," he said aloud, though he was speaking to himself and not to Eiverbreen.

The older halfling heard him, though. "What's that?" he asked.

"A good halfling community," Regis stated more loudly. "Here in Delthuntle, I mean. As good as any I have ever known."

That brought a curious look from Eiverbreen.

Regis laughed at his own foolishness. As far as Eiverbreen was concerned, Delthuntle was the only place Regis had ever known!

Regis nodded, though he was not looking at Eiverbreen, and not even hearing the actual words as the older halfling pressed him on the point. He was considering his unexpected status, and to his surprise, he found that it was no small thing. Here in Delthuntle, halflings were not second class, and here in Delthuntle, he personally was not the tag-along. Far from it! Here he was the protégé, growing strong and skilled under grand tutelage.

His thoughts careened to a lonely mountain rising into a starlit sky on the northern tundra. That image had been so prominent in his thoughts on that day he had walked out of Iruladoon. He had never imagined how difficult this twenty-one-year journey back home would prove to be. When he had walked out of Iruladoon, he merely thought that he would bide his time, training, always training, and would return to the Companions of the Hall as if nothing had ever interrupted their heroic journey.

Not so, he knew now.

He looked at Eiverbreen, who needed him.

He thought of Pericolo, who had taken him in and shown him great kindness and opportunity.

He felt again the softness of Donnola's kiss.

Not so, he knew now.

Regis couldn't reason his way out of it. He couldn't pretend it had never happened, and he couldn't even sublimate it by reminding himself of the higher purpose this second chance at life had given him.

He thought about it when he went to his bed at night. He dreamed about it. He thought about it when he woke up each morning.

He tried to attribute it to youthful exuberance, but even if that were the case, it didn't seem to matter.

No, that kiss from Donnola had overwhelmed Regis; in both of his lives, he had never experienced anything quite like it. But the lingering taste of it wasn't all joy for the halfling as he pondered it through the hours and days, for there were things about Donnola . . .

Four days after the incident, he readied for his daily sparring match with his instructor. Donnola came in smiling, in a grand mood. She lifted her blade and tipped it in salute.

But he dropped the tip of his rapier to the floor and shook his head.

"Are you troubled?" Donnola asked, similarly dipping her blade, and wearing an expression of honest concern.

"Why did you kiss me?" Regis asked bluntly, unable to contain his unease.

Donnola fell back a step, as if she had been slapped. "What?"

"You kissed me,"

"You kissed me back!"

"Of course I did! You're beautiful!" Regis lowered his gaze as he felt his cheeks blushing.

Donnola's laughter followed him, and finally he looked back up.

"Thank you," she said, and dipped a curtsey, and she, too, was blushing.

"But why?" Regis asked.

"Why what?"

"Why did you kiss me?"

She started to answer, but Regis's expression turned dark and he continued, "What did you hope to gain from it?"

Donnola fell back another step, but then came forward aggressively, dropping her blade and putting her hands on her hips. She stood barely inches from Regis, staring at him coldly.

"You cannot be mad at me!" Regis insisted. "You have shown me—you have taught me! You have taken me to those noblemen's grand parties and shown me how you use your charms to manipula—"

Donnola's hand came up faster than Regis could react, and slapped him hard across the face.

She huffed and swung around to run away, but Regis caught her by the shoulder and tugged her back around, throwing himself at her. And when they crashed together, he hugged her tightly. He saw the moisture in her pretty brown eyes, and kissed her.

She twisted to get away. She pulled her mouth back. But Regis pressed in harder and rejoined the kiss and Donnola's tension gradually melted away, and then she was kissing him as passionately or more.

"Do you doubt me?" she asked, and she twisted suddenly, dropping them both to the floor, her atop him.

"Have you never kissed any of them? Isn't that part of the game you play?" Regis asked.

Donnola's brown eyes flashed with anger, but it passed quickly, and with a burst of laughter, she said, "Aye, they like the little ones like us, you know. It makes them feel so big and strong."

"So you have kissed a Delthuntle lord or two!" Regis cried, clearly feigning outrage, and with a sudden burst, he rolled Donnola onto her back.

Donnola smiled up at him, her moist eyes twinkling in the sunlight streaming in through the room's lone window. "Aye, that's the tease, and aye, I have," she admitted, and with a sudden twist, she rolled Regis onto his back. "A kiss and a tease and nothing more," Donnola insisted. "And nothing more ever, with any . . . until now."

The sun was long set, the moonlight streaming in through the window, when Regis awakened in Donnola's arms. He felt the fool for ever doubting this amazing halfling lass. She was playing no game for him; her feelings were honest.

As were his own.

But lying there in the dim light, Regis couldn't help but think of Drizzt and the road to Icewind Dale.

It had all become so very, very complicated.

CHAPTER 18

THE CHARMING NET

The Year of the Ageless One (1479 DR)
Netheril

THE STARS TWINKLED, A CLEAR DESERT SKY, AND THE SLIVER OF A MOON cast a thin glow over the woman's private garden, but enough of one for the moistened soft petals of her many flowers to sparkle like the stars above.

Catti-brie was in a fine mood—how could she not be when she felt so close to Mielikki?

Her days of dancing in Iruladoon, of communing with the goddess, had taught her so much about the ways of the celestial spheres and the eternal cycle of life and death. And the goodness of life, taken as a whole. She was part of those stars above, she understood, as were the flowers before her.

She was at peace.

And yet, she was not, for this place, this moment, reminded her of why she had returned to Faerûn, and of the task before her, in not so many years. This day, the spring equinox of 1479, marked her sixteenth birthday, or "re-birthday," as she had privately named it. She had spent some hours with Niraj and Kavita in the Desai encampment, and she was not due back at the Coven until the next morning.

"Five more years," she whispered to a flower before her. She lifted the plant's wide and soft petals and gently brushed them. "Only five."

She conjured an image of Drizzt in her thoughts, and she smiled widely. She had been gone from him for just over sixteen years by her measure, but more than a century in his lifetime. Had his feelings faded for her? Would he even remember her in any meaningful way?

215

Would she find him happily married, to an elf perhaps, and raising children of his own?

The woman shrugged, not happy about the possibility, but accepting it as just that, a possibility, and one that she could not control. She thought of seeing him again, of his smile, of his touch. How she missed that touch! Many things could seem trivial to Catti-brie now that she had been in the arms of a goddess, now that she had looked at the multiverse with such profound understanding. But Drizzt's touch was not one of those trivial things; their bond seemed as large as that of the celestial spheres, and as eternal as the cycle of life and death, no matter the interfering practicalities.

If Drizzt had another wife, then so be it. Catti-brie knew that he still loved her, that he would always love her, as she would always love him.

She would be no less dedicated to the coming battle Mielikki had described to her in her days of communing with the goddess in the enchanted forest. If Lady Lolth or her minions came for Drizzt, they would have to fight through Catti-brie to get to him!

She pictured Kelvin's Cairn in Icewind Dale, under a sky as sparkling as this one, the unending wind tossing her hair, the chill breeze tickling her skin.

"Five more years," she whispered again.

"Five more years for what?" came a sharp voice behind her. Catti-brie froze in place, smile vanishing, eyes going wide. She knew that voice, too well!

"For what?" Lady Avelyere asked again. "And do face me, child."

Catti-brie took a deep breath.

"Your magic is no match for my own, child," Lady Avelyere said, as if reading her thoughts. "And you'll not shapechange fast enough to be away from me."

Catti-brie slowly turned around. Avelyere stood at the entrance to her secret garden, dressed in rich traveling robes of purple and white, and she seemed taller to Catti-brie at that moment, much taller and more imposing.

"You lied to me," she said quietly, but each word resonated in Catti-brie's mind as if it had been shouted into her ear.

"No, Lady . . . ," she stammered.

"I took you in, opened my house to you, and you lied to me," Lady Avelyere insisted.

"No . . ."

"Yes!"

Catti-brie swallowed hard.

216

"You didn't know where your power of healing and shapeshifting came from, you told me," Lady Avelyere went on. "You didn't know that they were divinely inspired or different at all. But you have deceived me all along, worshiping this . . . god?"

"Goddess," Catti-brie managed to say.

"I spared your parents!" Lady Avelyere screamed at her. "A mere word from me about their magical activities and Shade Enclave would have captured them and tortured them in the town square. And this is how you repay me? By lying to me?"

She swept forward as she spoke, moving very near to Catti-brie, staring down at her from on high.

"This does not concern them," Catti-brie stammered, rising, but keeping her head bowed. The thought that Avelyere might take out her wrath on Niraj and Kavita horrified the woman—how would she be able to live with herself after bringing such ruin on those wonderful people?

But a comforting thread wove into her mind then, an assurance that Lady Avelyere would do no such thing, that Niraj and Kavita were not Avelyere's concern and would not be exposed.

Catti-brie looked up at the woman. Lady Avelyere reached out a hand and gently stroked Catti-brie's thick hair. "Oh, dear girl," she said, her voice as smooth as the flower's petal. "Do you not understand that I have come to love you as if you were my own daughter?"

"Yes, Lady," Catti-brie heard herself replying.

"I'm merely wounded, truly wounded, that you did not trust me with your secret."

"I didn't think you would understand."

"Faith, child, faith," Lady Avelyere cooed. "I am your mentor, not your enemy." She drew Catti-brie to her side and looked all around. "Tell me about this place. It is your shrine to this . . . goddess, yes?"

"Mielikki," Catti-brie whispered.

"Yes, well do tell me more. Surely you have been blessed by her! I have seen the marking."

Catti-brie's hand reflexively went to her opposite forearm, to the unicorn-shaped spellscar she carried.

"Your spellscar, yes, and the powers it affords you," Lady Avelyere said, though Catti-brie noticed that Avelyere had not even looked down or followed Catti-brie's inadvertent movement.

"Tell me of it. Tell me of Mielikki," Lady Avelyere purred. "And tell me of this dark elf and the mountain under the stars."

Had she been of her reasoning faculties at that moment, Catti-brie would have understood that Lady Avelyere had garnered much more information than she could surmise by the garden, for Catti-brie had not spoken openly of Drizzt, had merely thought of him and pictured him.

"Tell me, Ruqiah," Lady Avelyere prompted.

"Catti-brie," the disciple of Mielikki corrected.

Lord Parise Ulfbinder sat in his grand chair, his hands together and before his pursed lips. He didn't blink as Lady Avelyere poured forth the wild claims of young Ruqiah of the Desai.

"She is Chosen of Mielikki," Parise said a long while after the diviner had finished her lengthy tale.

Lady Avelyere could only shrug. "It would seem."

"And you believe her?"

Again the woman shrugged, but this time she added a nod.

"A Bedine child, a Chosen of Mielikki, who is not a Bedine goddess?" Parise asked skeptically.

"But she says she is not a Bedine child," Lady Avelyere said. "She claims her name is not Ruqiah, but Catti-brie."

It was Parise Ulfbinder's turn to shrug, for the name meant nothing to him.

"A woman from another time, before the Spellplague."

"That is quite a claim. Is it not more likely that she is merely trying to protect her outlaw parents?"

"So I thought," Lady Avelyere replied. "But her claims—"

"Desperate claims for a desperate young woman . . ."

"She was adopted by a dwarf in this previous life," Lady Avelyere interrupted. "A dwarf king."

The end of his intended sentence caught in Parise's throat. "A dwarf king?" he asked instead.

"King Bruenor Battlehammer of Mithral Hall," Lady Avelyere explained. "She told me this under my charm dweomer, under a spell of hypnosis, under the power of magical suggestion."

"She completed the concocted story," Parise argued.

"There is record of such a king in the library of Shade Enclave."

"So the girl visited the library."

"And a mention of his adopted daughter, Catti-brie—"

"So the girl went to the library!" Lord Parise Ulfbinder shouted.

" —who was taken in the night by the ghost of Mielikki's unicorn," Lady Avelyere talked over him.

Parise fell back in his chair and meekly asked, "What do you mean?"

"This human daughter of King Bruenor, driven mad by the Spellplague, died in the night and was spirited away from her bed by a celestial unicorn, so goes the legend." She paused and painted a wry grin on her face. "Away from the bed of her dark elf husband, Drizzt Do'Urden."

Lord Parise Ulfbinder was among the most composed and dignified men in Shade Enclave, but the gulp and squeal that issued forth seemed more the cry of a startled child. He leaped up, his chair flying out behind him.

"A name you have mentioned before, yes?" Lady Avelyere said, grinning wider still.

"This is madness," said Parise, rushing and stumbling around his desk to take a seat on it right before the woman. "Are you sure that you have not mentioned this name to her? Perhaps you inadvertently put her on the road to concoct this wild story!"

"I don't know that I have ever spoken that name before, or heard it, other than in this very room."

"But the child is magical. Perhaps she has slipped an insidious dweomer past your guards and read your thoughts."

"That would be quite a scouring. I do not concern myself with the dark elf. I did not even recall the name until Ruqiah—until Catti-brie spoke it to me, and even then, it barely sparked recognition. It was not until she mentioned this Drizzt creature's race that I even recalled our long-ago conversation about Lord Draygo's drow prisoner."

"His lost prisoner."

"We may find him, then, for this child is determined to find him sometime after the Year of the Awakened Sleepers. Indeed, she has fellow conspirators in this, who she intends to rejoin on the night of the spring equinox in that same year."

"Bedine conspirators?"

Lady Avelyere shook her head.

"1484," Lord Parise mumbled. "Five years, almost to the day." He scratched at his goatee. "Interesting indeed."

"What do I do?"

"Let her go!" Parise cried immediately. "And watch her, every step. We may witness a battle of Toril's goddesses, and what a sight that will be!"

Lady Avelyere didn't openly respond to that, but her expression spoke volumes, most of all revealing her relief.

"Why Lady," Parise said teasingly, "you have come to love the girl."

Lady Avelyere rocked back on her heels and considered the words. Her first impulse was to staunchly deny the accusation, but she quickly put that aside and honestly searched deep within herself. "She has such promise and skill," she replied. "A curiosity and a hope, from her earliest days."

"It is more than professional curiosity," said her friend, who knew her well.

Lady Avelyere nodded.

"You think her a protégé."

"Thought," Lady Avelyere was quick to reply, correcting the tense. "Now I understand that is impossible. Her loyalty is not to me and never has been."

"But she has not crossed you."

"True enough," said Lady Avelyere. "And thus I am content to do as you say, and not to punish her for her duplicity and secret devotion to this foreign goddess."

Parise Ulfbinder wore a sly grin, which elicited an exasperated sigh from Lady Avelyere. He was seeing right through her, of course. He recognized that she was wounded to think that this girl she had brought in and all but raised as her own might have a higher loyalty than to her and the Coven. To think that Ruqiah would walk away after all that she had done for her! And to think that Ruqiah would accept so much training, diverting the precious resources of the Coven toward one who knew that she would not remain!

So indeed there was a measure of anger within Lady Avelyere, a sense of being wronged by this girl. But more than that, she had to admit, there was sadness and disappointment. Ruqiah had been quite the project for her, and yes, quite the protégé! Lady Avelyere had great affection for all of the sisters of her Coven, but none more than the curious little Bedine girl she had captured in a web years before.

It would not be easy to let her go.

Catti-brie rubbed the sleep out of her eyes and moved to the window, surprised that sunlight was streaming in. It was a west-facing window, after all, and usually remained quite dark until late in the day.

She pulled aside the sash and stared at the sun lowering in the western sky.

The woman backed up a step and turned to regard her unkempt bed. How could it be late in the afternoon? How could she have slept throughout the whole of the day?

She thought back to the previous night and tried to recall going to bed. But she could not.

She tried to recall what day it was, and when she was supposed to meet again with her parents in the Desai encampment. She had a vague recollection of speaking with them recently, but that didn't make any sense to her.

She dressed quickly, brushed her hair, and headed out, ready to apologize profusely for abandoning her duties that day.

Just a short way down the hallway, she ran into Rhyalle, who greeted her with a big smile and a gentle touch.

"Oh, but you are up!" Rhyalle said before Catti-brie could begin her apology. "We have been so worried about you."

"I was only in my room," Catti-brie replied hesitantly. She half turned to point back the way she had come.

"For a tenday," Rhyalle replied. "We feared that you would never awaken, though Lady Avelyere assured us that your affliction would pass."

"Avelyere? Affliction?" Catti-brie stammered.

"Yes, of course—oh, but you probably remember little of your fevered dreams. It was the spellscar, Lady Avelyere believes." She grabbed Catti-brie's arm and pulled back the sleeve, revealing the spellscar that resembled the seven stars of Mystra. "Others with such marks have suffered similar afflictions recently, from what we've been told. But it will pass—indeed, it has passed. You look so well!"

Catti-brie couldn't begin to sort through all of that confusing information. One thing did leap out at her, however: The last memory that would come to her was that of her parents, in their tent. Was it there that she had fallen? And if that was the case, how had she come back to her bed in the Coven?

Catti-brie half-turned back the way she had come, then changed her mind and pushed past Rhyalle. "I must speak with Lady Avelyere," she explained.

But Rhyalle tightened her grip on Catti-brie's arm and held her back, then shifted to block her way.

"You need to remain in your room," she said. "Lady Avelyere will come to you presently."

"No, I—"

"Yes!" Rhyalle forcefully corrected. "I was coming this very moment to check in on you. Lady Avelyere has made these instructions quite clear. Come, back to your room."

Catti-brie hesitated.

Rhyalle pushed her more forcefully. "No argument," she insisted. "You are to await the lady in your room. You are not to leave your room until she has granted you permission."

She pushed again and Catti-brie relented.

A few moments later, she was sitting on the edge of her bed, alone in her room, her thoughts spinning, her memories drifting in and around.

"A tenday?" she asked aloud, and she couldn't begin to sort that out. Even her memory was playing tricks on her now—first she had thought her last memories to be of the Desai encampment, but now she wondered if those were older recollections. For it seemed now that her most recent memories were of doing her chores around the Coven and anticipating her next visit to the Desai encampment. Yet even these seemed strangely removed, or had greatly receded at least.

None of it made any sense to her. Something was wrong, very wrong. She pulled back both her sleeves and looked at her scars, even running her fingers over each. Nothing seemed amiss with them.

Lady Avelyere came to her some time later, rushing to embrace her. She reiterated everything Rhyalle had told her, pausing every so often to gently kiss the young woman on the cheek and stroke her hair.

"I don't . . . ," Catti-brie started to say, and she paused and shook her head. "Nothing of the last days . . . of the last . . ." She shook her head again. "Nothing makes any sense."

"I know, dear," Lady Avelyere replied. "Fevered dreams. You were quite ill, though I am not sure of your affliction. I sense it was tied to the spellscars you carry. We have heard of others—"

"Yes, I have been told," Catti-brie interrupted.

"In all of those cases, the affliction passed quickly and showed no sign of returning," Lady Avelyere added. "So it will be with you, I expect." She kissed Catti-brie on the forehead again. "Now back to your rest, I demand."

Catti-brie didn't resist as Lady Avelyere eased her back onto the bed.

"I am expected soon in the home of my parents," Catti-brie said.

"Oh, no, no, no, girl," Lady Avelyere replied. "You will not be going out of the Coven for many days. No, no. Not until I am certain that your affliction has truly passed. You were fortunate that you were struck down here, among friends with great means to help you to heal. Had you been outside of here, you likely would have died."

"They will worry—"

"I will find a way to get word to them that you are well and will visit when you are able," Lady Avelyere promised. She gave Catti-brie one last hug and quietly left the room, leaving Catti-brie alone with her jumbled thoughts.

She chewed her lips and kept looking at her window, wanting nothing more than to be out of there and off to one of her secret gardens, where she might commune with Mielikki to garner some answers. Beyond the confusion of her apparent loss of memory, and of a tenday, something seemed wrong; somewhere, just below her consciousness, contradictions nagged at Catti-brie's sensibilities.

Catti-brie searched through the conversations with Rhyalle and Lady Avelyere over and over again, seeking some clues. One thing stood out: Why would Catti-brie have likely died had she been struck with her affliction outside of the Coven? Hadn't both Rhyalle and Avelyere just told her that others had been similarly afflicted, and that in those instances, the affliction had passed with no serious ramifications?

Catti-brie winced. Had Avelyere just lied to her?

She focused her mind, determined to remember more, or to at least put some of the flitting memories floating through her thoughts into some sort of context and order.

She looked to the door again, then to a small, decorative plant set in the corner of the room.

Her gaze went back to the door as she chewed anew on her lip. Dare she?

Caution bade her not to do it. The projection of Ruqiah bade her not to do it.

But the wisdom of Catti-brie nagged at her, told her that something was truly amiss.

She went to the plant and dragged it across to the opposite wall, out of sight of the door, which opened into the room and would shield anyone entering from that particular corner for a moment at least.

She glanced around again. In all of her years here, she had never attempted anything this dangerous.

But she needed to know.

She began to whisper a long and solemn spell. From inside the Coven, in the floating city of Shade Enclave, she called to Mielikki.

She asked for guidance, asked for some divine intervention to clear the confusion in her mind. The unicorn-shaped spellscar began to glow, a bluish light wafted over her forearm like the mist enveloping a mountain stream on a cold autumn morning.

She found no answer immediately, but the notion of a simpler spell came to her.

She cast a spell to dispel magic, first as a divine spell, then again in the arcane school of magic. She cast it upon herself, repeatedly, and more assuredly each time as she came to recognize that yes, indeed, the fog in her mind was magically inspired.

That twisting fog began to clear, just a bit, but that one piece of the puzzle, a memory of Lady Avelyere out in the desert, at her secret garden, was all that Catti-brie needed in order to piece the rest of the damaging story together.

Avelyere knew!

She knew!

All of it!

Catti-brie's breath came in short gasps as she tried to sort out her last conversation with the woman in light of this new realization. She had told Avelyere of her previous life!

What did that mean for her plans? What did that mean for Drizzt and the others?

She couldn't focus on that, however, as other issues pressed in on her. Lady Avelyere's parting words spun over and over in her thoughts.

Then she unwound it, and looked at the door with her mouth hanging open, as Lady Avelyere's last promise echoed in her thoughts. Her heart beat faster as she replayed those words.

Catti-brie had been with Niraj and Kavita immediately preceding her encounter with Lady Avelyere in her secret garden. The timeline of Avelyere's explanation of Catti-brie's affliction didn't work. If Catti-brie ever again spoke with her parents, she would discern that lie.

"Oh no," Catti-brie mouthed. Lady Avelyere would surely go to Niraj and Kavita, not to comfort them, but to make sure that Catti-brie never again had the opportunity to speak with her parents.

"Oh, no," the woman whispered, breathing hard. She felt moisture gathering in her eyes.

She thought of Drizzt and the clear risk to her mission. She thought of her duty.

But she thought of her duty to her parents, too, to Niraj and Kavita who had shown her nothing but love and kindness.

She had to leave, she knew, then and there.

"Forgive me, Mielikki," she whispered, crying openly now.

For she knew what she must do.

"What is she doing?" Lady Avelyere asked Rhyalle, who stood beside her on the high balcony, huddled under a blanket against the driving rain. Down below and in the distance, they noted Ruqiah's movements, the young woman darting from corner-to-corner, glancing back over her shoulder again and again as if in fear that she was being followed.

"Fleeing Shade Enclave?" Lady Avelyere asked.

"The wall is the other way," Rhyalle replied.

A peal of thunder shook the ground and the rain intensified.

Lady Avelyere had hit Ruqiah with a barrage of spells to confuse her, to block her memory, to suggest things were other than what they were. Still, she couldn't deny her surprise that Ruqiah—Catti-brie—had found the wherewithal to leave her room, let alone the Coven's compound.

"If she leaves Shade Enclave, bring her back in chains," Lady Avelyere instructed.

"And if she goes to the encampment of the Desai?"

"Do not let her."

"She is . . . difficult to contain," Rhyalle admitted.

Lady Avelyere started to respond, but paused and nodded for Rhyalle to look back at Ruqiah. The young woman rushed across a clearing and into a small storehouse, glancing around one last time before closing the door behind her.

"A curious choice," said Rhyalle.

"You know that building?"

"Storage," Rhyalle answered. "Oils and lanterns and torches mostly. Is it possible that Ruqiah plans to search the sewers of Shade—"

A tremendous bolt of blinding lightning interrupted her, and had both Rhyalle and Lady Avelyere falling back in surprise. The thunderous, stone-shaking retort following immediately, indeed almost instantly, because the bolt had struck only a short distance from the balcony on which they stood, and with such power that it jolted them into the air and both nearly tumbled down.

They clutched at each other for balance, and both stared out from the balcony to the small storage building, which had been hit directly by the blast.

Smaller explosions rocked the area, no doubt as casks of oil ignited, and flames leaped up against the driving rain.

"Ruqiah," Rhyalle breathed.

A final, massive explosion shook the square, shook the entire section of Shade Enclave, and a huge fireball curled up from the storehouse like some fiery mushroom, lifting skyward, to dissipate into steam and smoke. Below it lay the utterly destroyed building, a pile of smoldering debris sputtering in the driving rain.

And Ruqiah did not come forth.

CHAPTER 19

GODLY INSIGHT

The Year of the Ageless One (1479 DR)
Mithral Hall

THE TORCHLIGHT FLICKERED, CASTING WILD SHADOWS IN THE VAST EMPTY chamber as the solitary figure made his way along the narrow bridge. A massive drop to his left and right only accentuated the loneliness of the scene: a single dwarf, walking hesitantly, his torch only barely chasing away the darkness.

His step slowed even more as he approached the central platform on this great bridge that spanned the chasm known as Garumn's Gorge. His footsteps echoed, hard boots on stone. The shuddering torchlight showed that he was trembling.

He paused at the front rim of the circular platform. Across from him, in the darkness, he heard the sound of water—Bruenor's Falls—which marked the final run to the eastern gate of Mithral Hall.

For Bruenor, the return proved only bitter, not bittersweet.

He had come this way with the caravan only a tenday before, but hadn't slowed and hadn't even dared look at the podium on the northern side of this ceremonial platform. In his short time in Mithral Hall, he had not come back this way to the east, spending his days in the great Undercity, and even venturing to the western gate and to Keeper's Dale beyond, arguably the place of his greatest triumph.

Keeper's Dale was heavily guarded now, with fortified positions and war machines all around the higher peaks. Guarded against orcs, Bruenor . . . Reginald Roundshield of Citadel Felbarr . . . had been told, for the troublesome creatures had become very active of late.

Yet again.

How strange it had been for Bruenor to hear the discussions about him, questioning his own judgment as king that century before, when he had made peace with King Obould Many-Arrows. Back and forth went the arguments, and they sounded to Bruenor much like the same debates he had heard, and had been party to, in the days of the treaty!

Nothing had been resolved. The land had known relative peace, but to many of the current dwarves of Mithral Hall, it clearly seemed more the crouch of the tiger before the killing spring than any true and lasting alliance, partnership, or even tolerance between Mithral Hall and the orcs. And worse, they whispered, now the orcs had made inroads into the kingdoms all around their own land, and knew the defenses and, perhaps, how to exploit those defenses.

Bruenor's gaze locked on the podium, on the parchment spread atop it, secured by a heavy piece of clear crystal. He swallowed hard and inched up.

He saw the signature, his signature, and the crude mark of King Obould.

"Did ye lead me wrong, elf?" he asked quietly, as if speaking to Drizzt, who had counseled him on this very important decision, who indeed had lobbied him strongly to sign the treaty.

"Ah, but I can'no know," Bruenor whispered.

"What's to know then, eh?" came a voice behind him, startling him—and all the more surprising because it was not accompanied by the light of a second torch. He turned around to see Ragged Dain, who had obviously followed him out here, secretly and stealthily.

"If this paper'll hold in these times," Bruenor replied.

"Bah, that treaty," said the old warrior. "I remember when it was signed. Never did much like it."

"King Bruenor was wrong, then?"

"Hush yer mouth, boy!" Ragged Dain scolded. "Ye don't be talking ill o' the king o' them whose hall ye're walking about!"

"It was a long time ago," Bruenor replied.

Ragged Dain came up beside him and put his hand on the crystal mount, sliding his fingers slowly over the signatures of Bruenor and Obould. "Aye, it was, but be sure that I'm rememberin', and so's King Emerus Warcrown, don't ye doubt, particularly now when these new orcs are in a fightin' mood all across the Silver Marches."

"Are ye thinking it was wrong for King Bruenor to sign the treaty?"

Ragged Dain didn't answer for a bit, but just stared at the parchment. Then he shrugged. "Who can know? Meself was arguin' against it, to be sure. Told King Emerus that personally, though I was but a young fighter of little renown at the time."

"King Emerus stood here for the signing," Bruenor said, and he remembered well the look Emerus had given him before he had moved up to add his signature, an expression more of resignation than of antipathy.

"Aye, he did," said Ragged Dain. "Weren't his choice, mind ye."

"He would have preferred war."

"Most dwarves would've!"

"But not King Bruenor." Bruenor purposely said it in a way that could be construed as accusatory, to gauge Ragged Dain's expression.

The old veteran merely shrugged and wore no such agreeing scowl. "Alas for King Bruenor, then. He weren't for findin' any support for a war. Not from Silverymoon, not from Sundabar." He paused and took a deep breath, and Bruenor knew well what was coming next. "Not even from Felbarr."

"King Emerus wouldn't stand with Mithral Hall?" Bruenor asked, trying to feign surprise.

Ragged Dain offered another shrug. "Without Sundabar and Silverymoon, we wouldn't've been doin' much again them orc thousands," he said. "Tens of thousands! Tens of tens of thousands!"

"So you don't blame Bruenor?"

Ragged Dain paused again and looked at the treaty for a long while. "If I've any anger, lad, know that it's for the human kingdoms o' the Silver Marches, and them elves o' Silverymoon and the Moonwood. We could've put an army on the field that would've shaked the whole o' the world! We could've chased that durned Obould back into his hole, ne'er to come out again!"

"I've heard the tales of what's now what," said Bruenor. "Might that we'll be doin' just that, in short order!"

Surprisingly this time, Ragged Dain offered another shrug, one halting and almost resigned.

Bruenor's eyes went wide. "So ye've lost the love o' the fight, ye old dog?"

"Bah, but if ye say that again, I'll pitch ye into the gorge, don't ye doubt," said Ragged Dain.

"Then what? Ye heard the rumors of orcs stirring as surely as I have. Ye know them orcs're pushin' for a fight."

Ragged Dain glanced all around, as if ensuring that they were truly alone. "King Connerad . . . ," he said, shaking his head.

"A good dwarf, by all accounts, and son of a hero, King Banak," said Bruenor.

"Aye, but with no reach," Ragged Dain explained. "Not to his fault, but true nonetheless. When Bruenor talked, th'others o' the Silver Marches listened. Proved in battle, he was, and oh, beyond anything anyone now might know! Even King Emerus would'no stand atop any pedestal higher than that one! King Connerad's a good dwarf, as ye say, and his people love him, don't ye doubt, but he ain't no King Bruenor. Ain't no King Bruenor nowhere, and if the Marches ain't fightin' as one, the legions o' Many-Arrows'll run us all down."

Bruenor felt proud and overwhelmed all at once. The fleeting moment of pride held him up, but only briefly until the weight of the world descended upon his young and sturdy shoulders.

He didn't know what to say, but knew what he wanted to say. He wanted to grab Ragged Dain by the collar and shout the truth into his face.

Or was that the plan of the gods all along, Bruenor suddenly wondered?

"What do ye know?" Ragged Dain asked.

The words jolted Bruenor and made him aware that he was gasping for air under the weight of emotions. "Wh-what?" he stammered back.

"What do ye know?"

"Nothing," Bruenor answered, and indeed, he was in no position to answer that or any other question at that moment, his mind spinning with the possibilities. He considered his anger toward the gods, toward Moradin in particular, for allowing him to be so manipulated by Catti-brie and Mielikki, for stealing the meaning and the reward of his life right out from under him.

But then he thought of Dumathoin, God of Secrets Under the Mountain, and it occurred to him that his step from Iruladoon, though facilitated by Mielikki, might not have been for Mielikki at all.

He looked again at the treaty, at his signature. His greatest achievement or his greatest folly? Indeed, that had ever been the question, and now, with the specter of war looming over the Silver Marches, the answer seemed clear before him.

Through the power of Mielikki, he had been given rebirth, but perhaps— yes, more than perhaps, he then convinced himself—through the power of Moradin, he had been delivered here, to this place in this time, with this crisis looming.

Mithral Hall, indeed the Silver Marches, needed a King Bruenor, so Ragged Dain had just declared.

Bruenor Battlehammer alone knew where to find one.

The party was on in full, as was customary whenever a large caravan from one of the three dwarf communities in the Silver Marches—Mithral Hall, Citadel Felbarr, and Citadel Adbar—prepared to head for home from one of the others. In addition, the train from Citadel Adbar had arrived the night before, giving the dwarves of Mithral Hall an added reason to break out the Gutbuster this fine day, and so they did.

They toasted to Citadel Felbarr. They toasted to Citadel Adbar. They toasted to Mithral Hall. They toasted to the Delzoun brotherhood. They toasted to the demise of Many-Arrows. They toasted to toasting!

Watching the merriment from the crowd proved to be a strange experience for Bruenor, so used to being upon the dais and leading the libations was he. He couldn't help but smile as he considered the many times he had done that, Drizzt and Catti-brie, Regis and Nanfoodle, and of course, Thibbledorf Pwent by his side, filling his foaming mug, rapping him on the back with a hardy "huzzah!" with every call for a drink.

He recognized King Connerad, and remembered him as a good lad, and remembered his father as a great general and leader, and as brave a dwarf as he had ever known. Banak Brawnanvil had been instrumental in the defense of Mithral Hall against Obould's minions in the days before the signing of the peace treaty.

As was customary in these gatherings, each of the departing Felbarr dwarves was able to climb onto the raised dais and tap tankards with the King of Mithral Hall. Bruenor fell in line right behind Ragged Dain.

"Ye know him?" he whispered to the veteran.

"King Connerad?"

"Aye."

"Aye," Ragged Dain replied. "Knowed him for a hunnerd years and more."

"Introduce me afore ye leave then."

"And tell him o' yer glory?" the older dwarf asked sarcastically.

"Aye," Bruenor answered without shame and without hesitation, and he held up the golden medal that hung from a mithral chain around his neck. "I'll be askin' him for a favor, and that's suren to help me cause!"

"What?" Ragged Dain asked incredulously, turning around and fixing Bruenor with a curious stare.

Bruenor just waved him on, for it was then Ragged Dain's turn to ascend to tap flagons with the king. And he did, and drank a hearty toast, then put his arm around King Connerad's shoulder—they were indeed old battle companions. Ragged Dain turned the king to regard the young dwarf next in line.

"Little Arr Arr," Ragged Dain explained.

"Arr Arr's boy?"

"Aye, King Connerad, that there be Little Arr Arr, Reginald Roundshield the Younger, and a true scrapper! He come to Mithral Hall as part of his valor wish."

"A valor wish, at his age, then?" King Connerad said, and Bruenor recognized that he was feigning surprise for the sake of flattery. "And the medal, indeed!" the dwarf king added.

"Aye, for 'twas Little Arr Arr that sliced the orcs and felled the mountain giant, and a bunch of us, meself included, would've been killed to death in the Rauvins were it not for Little Arr Arr!"

He spoke loudly and many heard, and so it was in the embrace of a chorus of cheers that Bruenor went to stand beside the king of Mithral Hall, beside the dwarf who was king because Bruenor himself had named his father as successor with full knowledge that the throne would fall to Connerad.

"I lift me tankard aside a hero, then!" King Connerad declared, tapping Bruenor's drink.

He paused though, as the mugs clinked together, for Bruenor fixed him with a stare, and such a look that Connerad Brawnanvil had surely seen before from the dwarf who had been his king. A spark of recognition flickered in Connerad's eyes, but it was overwhelmed by a look of confusion.

"Ah, but good King Connerad, ye might be doing me a higher honor than tappin' yer cup with me own," Bruenor said.

The crowd hushed quickly, caught by surprise at the forwardness of this obviously very young dwarf.

"Ah, so ye say, and do tell," King Connerad prompted.

"I been hoping to go to the west, to Mirabar, might be, or all the way to Luskan," Bruenor explained. "I been told that Mithral Hall sends such caravans, and I'd be honored to serve aboard one."

That brought more than a few gasps from around the dais, including from those dwarves Bruenor had accompanied to the hall from Citadel Felbarr.

"What are ye about, then, boy?" Ragged Dain demanded, coming forward, but King Connerad held up his hand to hold the old veteran back.

"I'm wantin' to see the sea, good king," Bruenor replied. "Ye send such trains, I been telled."

"Aye, we do, but not so late in the year as this. Next'll be out in the spring."

"And I'd be honored to be aboard her."

"A long wait."

"Then might I be asking ye a second favor?"

"Oh, the set o' iron on this young one!" a dwarf yelled from the crowd, to rousing laughter and more than a few huzzahs.

" 'E'll be asking for the king's daughter in his bed any time now!" another roared, and the laughter grew.

And King Connerad, too, seemed quite amused, and not at all insulted, as Bruenor, who knew him well, had fully expected.

"I been wantin' to train with yer Gutbuster Brigade," Bruenor explained. "For me Da, who always spoke well o' the band, and of a dwarf by the name o' Thibbledorf Pwent . . ."

"For the Pwent!" came a cry from the crowd—a cry that became a roar, that became the loudest toast of all, and how it did Bruenor's heart good to hear such cheers for his dear old friend, who had died so heroically defending him, and helping him in concluding his most important mission in the faraway ancient kingdom known as Gauntlgrym.

"I would train in his name, and for his memory, to bring his strength back to Citadel Felbarr to best serve King Emerus," Bruenor explained.

King Connerad glanced over at Ragged Dain, who wore a perplexed expression just a moment longer before nodding his agreement.

"So it is done!" the king proclaimed, hoisting his mug once more. "To Little Arr Arr o' the Gutbusters!"

"Arg, but if he can take it," snarled an ugly dwarf at the side of the dais, another one Bruenor recognized from a century before, though he could not recall his name. This one had served in the Gutbusters under Pwent, Bruenor recalled.

"Arg, yerself," said Ragged Dain. "Little Arr Arr'll teach ye all a thing or three!"

"Huzzah!" cried the visitors from Citadel Felbarr.

"Huzzah!" roared the hundreds from Mithral Hall.

And so it went, the boasting and the toasting—anything for a drink.

Bruenor woke up in that hall early the next morning, his head throbbing from a few too many huzzahs, and far too many heigh-ho's. Barely sentient, he crawled to a nearby table, where eggs and bacon and muffins and berries had been put out aplenty.

"Ye do us proud," Ragged Dain said to him, crawling up beside him.

"Me thanks for yer blessin' and yer help," Bruenor replied.

"Bah, but I'm owin' ye at least that much, eh? But don't ye think me making light here, Little Arr Arr. Ye do Citadel Felbarr proud. Them Gutbusters're called the finest battle group in all the land, and I'm not one to argue the point. King Emerus'll be thinking well o' ye when he hears o' yer choice, but know that he'll be a'fearing it too, for ye're now to make us all proud, ye hear?"

"Aye, and aye," Bruenor assured him.

"And are ye really meanin' to go to the west, all the way to the sea?"

"Aye, again," said Bruenor. "Something I'm needin' to do."

"Ye'll be gone from Felbarr for two years and more, then!" Ragged Dain said.

"And I'll still be a kid when I get back, in yer gray old eyes."

Ragged Dain smiled, patted Bruenor on the shoulder, and promptly passed out, his face falling into a bowl of porridge.

Bruenor paused at the graves of Catti-brie and Regis, set in places of honor, side-by-side. Here, under piled stones, lay the cold mortal bodies of those two beloved friends. They would be decayed now to skeletons, perhaps even dust, Bruenor realized, for a hundred years had passed.

Bruenor had always believed that there was more to the soul than the body, that shedding the mortal form would not be the end of existence, but having it now laid out before him with such clarity was nonetheless jarring. He remembered the day he and Drizzt had buried them. He had kissed Catti-brie's hand, one last time, and her skin had been cold on his lips. He remembered how he wanted to crawl between the rocks beside her, and breathe his warmth into her. He would have changed places with her, taking her cold and giving her his life, if that had been possible.

It had been the worst day of Bruenor's life, the day his heart had broken.

Standing here now, tears formed once more and dripped from his gray eyes—and yet he knew that Catti-brie, and Regis, too—lived on, indeed that they had lived on in bodies reminiscent of the height of their health. The Catti-brie he had seen in Iruladoon was the Catti-brie he had known as his daughter, in the prime of her youth and strength.

Nearby lay his own grave, one of two, though it had never been inhabited, and had been enacted and sanctified by the priests of the hall as a ruse and nothing more, a way for Bruenor to quietly abdicate the throne of Mithral Hall to Banak Brawnanvil in true and secret dwarf tradition. Bruenor went to the elaborate cairn and stared at it, but found himself strangely devoid of emotion. The piled stone sarcophagus was quite the affair, surely befitting that of a king, and even included a small sculpture of King Bruenor in his battle stance, standing at the top of the flat stone. On a sudden impulse, he lifted his medal from around his neck and hooked it over the one good horn of the statue's carved helm.

He smiled as he considered the gesture, thinking that it somehow had added weight and meaning to the grave. He watched the spin of the golden medal as it settled into place, and thought it appropriate, for here and now the past had joined the present in common goal.

With a final salute to what had been, the young-again dwarf wandered the catacombs and came at last to the grandest tomb of all, the grave of Gandalug Battlehammer. And there Bruenor found a kindred spirit, he realized, for Gandalug, too, had returned from death, from imprisonment by Matron Mother Baenre, to become the king of Mithral Hall once more, and in a time and a place far removed from his previous existence.

"Ah, but now I'm seein' what ye went through, me oldest king," Bruenor whispered in the darkness. "How out o' sorts ye must've been, eh?"

He put his hand on the stones covering the body of Gandalug, and closed his eyes as if in communion with the spirit that had been laid to rest in this place. "Are ye with him now?" he asked. "Have ye found yer seat at Moradin's table at long last, me old king?"

Bruenor nodded as he asked the questions, confident of the answers, and a smile spread on his face. He wanted to go back to the other graves, to apologize to Catti-brie and to Regis, and to Drizzt by extension. Perhaps he would visit there on his way out of the catacombs.

For he no longer intended to go to Icewind Dale, he knew then, he accepted the fact that he had voided his pledge to Mielikki and to his friends.

He was Bruenor Battlehammer, Eighth, Tenth, and soon to be Thirteenth King of Mithral Hall, sent back by Moradin to finish the task he had started.

He was going west to claim his regalia and his stature, to become again recognizable as King Bruenor. Then he would return to unite the Silver Marches. This was Moradin's gift to him, he decided, and his responsibility to Moradin. Moradin's gift and Moradin's deception, as it was Bruenor's responsibility and Bruenor's deception.

He nodded. "So be it," he whispered. He wondered if perhaps when he was done with his work here, he might find Catti-brie, Drizzt, and Regis—he would have scouts at his disposal, after all, and with Stokely Silverstream and his boys still in Icewind Dale, Bruenor might well find his way to them.

Too late perhaps to aid in whatever plans Mielikki had concocted. His choice could cost his friends, and dearly.

"So be it," the tough dwarf said again. He could have gone into the pond in Iruladoon, abandoning the quest before it had ever begun, after all. Wulfgar had chosen that course—could Wulfgar rightly be blamed if Drizzt was not saved from the Spider Queen?

Bruenor took a deep and steadying breath as he stood upright. "I know yer pain, me old king," he whispered to Gandalug. "Out o' yer time, aye."

He nodded, and kept doing so as he turned to walk away, tying to convince himself that he was right.

He stopped before he had taken a step and swung back, his face twisting, his expression shifting.

"Has to be," he said. "Or it's all a game." His bearded jaw twisted as he tried to translate his thoughts into words, as he tried to enunciate the gut feeling that held him fast.

To have been denied his seat at Moradin's table for the sake of Mielikki's concern, for the sake of Drizzt alone, seemed a trite thing to him somehow. Were there not many living disciples of the goddess who could have fulfilled this mission, after all?

In light of that nagging and obvious truth, Bruenor had come to know that his choice to leave Iruladoon had mocked everything that he had accomplished, had mocked a life of centuries of courage and achievement, and most of all, of loyalty to traditions and to a trio of gods that were not Mielikki.

But in light of his newfound epiphany, that Moradin had used Mielikki's enchantment to return the great king of Mithral Hall, who alone might rescue the Silver Marches from the encroachment of Many-Arrows . . .

For Bruenor Battlehammer, the logic and righteousness rang clear. He could forgive Moradin's delay in rewarding him with a seat of honor in Dwarfhome in light of that epiphany.

And perhaps it was more than that, Bruenor realized, and he smiled at the grave of Gandalug.

"I been a good servant," Bruenor whispered, "to kin and kind and to gods alike! So they give me another chance, ye see? Aye, but I choosed wrong when I put me name on that damned treaty! But they give me a chance now to tear it up and do what I should've done a hunnerd years afore."

He gave a little chuckle and remembered standing atop a stone in Keeper's Dale, swatting aside orcs with abandon.

"Aye, orcs, ye sleep with one eye open, ye hear? Because that monster under yer bed's holding the axe o' King Bruenor Battlehammer."

CHAPTER 20

A TASTE OF EBONSOUL

The Year of the Grinning Halfling (1481 DR)
Delthuntle

His headband had been enchanted with a continual light spell, illuminating the water all around him. While that light enabled Regis to see where he was swimming at this substantial depth and in murky waters, he was also keenly aware of the fact that it made of him quite the target.

Did sharks lurk in this area, miles from the Aglarond coast? Or minions of Umberlee, perhaps, like the vicious sahuagin or dangerous mermen?

He carried some formidable weapons with him, and he knew how to fight, even underwater, but this dive did not carry with it the usual feeling of freedom. He was much farther out, in much darker water, and diving deeper than ever before.

He stayed with the anchor line as he made his way carefully and slowly down. He could still make out the outline of the sizable boat above, where Wigglefingers, Donnola, Pericolo, and a few other crewmen waited. He came to another band that had been strapped around the anchor line, this one telling him that he had fifty more feet to go to the bottom. He paused there and stared downward into the darkness, the ocean floor still well beyond the lighted area.

Down he went, slowly, hesitantly.

Too long, he realized, and he shook his head and started back up, again slowly to allow his body to more easily adapt to the changing pressure. He surfaced right beside the boat, gasping for air.

"Well, did you see it?" Pericolo demanded immediately, coming to the rail and leaning over eagerly.

239

"Wasn't deep enough."

"Then why have you returned?" the Grandfather snapped. Donnola put a hand on Pericolo's shoulder to calm him.

"I was gauging the depths and the distance," Regis explained, spitting water with every word, for the sea had grown somewhat rougher now.

"You will run out of daylight," Wigglefingers warned.

"There is none down there in any case," Regis was quick to reply. "I will get to the bottom on this dive, but whether the shipwreck we seek is there, I cannot say."

Pericolo sighed loudly.

"It will take many dives, likely, and many days of searching," Wigglefingers reminded the old halfling.

"More if Spider doesn't even get to the bottom with each!" Pericolo said.

"It is a long way," Regis said, but he did so resignedly, for he knew that these halflings could not understand the trials of the depths, however he might try to explain them. He was going half-again deeper than he had ever done before, and in water far more dangerous, with stronger currents and limited visibility.

He swam over to the anchor line and checked the loop on the second line tied to it, and also fastened to the harness he wore. A hundred feet of elven cord, light and strong, would secure him to the lifeline. Once he got to the bottom, he could search in a radius of that length and no more, unless he dared to free himself from the tether in these dangerous waters.

Pericolo started to protest again, but Regis didn't stick around to hear it. He inhaled deeply and disappeared under the dark water, moving more swiftly this time so that he was very soon at the marking on the line, fifty feet from the seabed and anchor, and thrice that distance and more from the surface.

Down the halfling went, hand over hand. He felt the pressure in his ears, but felt, too, his body quickly adapting. This was the gift of the genasi bloodline, the gift of long breath and of a body more malleable to the pressures of the depths.

He spotted the anchor set against a rocky ridge. He was surprised at how much colder it was down here, suddenly, and knew that he wouldn't be able to stay for long. He tested the safety line on the main anchor line again, then set off, swimming to the end of its length, then circling around.

This was the spot, Pericolo had assured him, but he saw no signs of a wreck. He came to a smooth and sandy bed among the rocks and glided across it. Feeling quite vulnerable, he shifted his gaze this way and that as if he expected a giant shark to sweep in from the darkness and gobble him up in a single bite.

The surprise came from below instead, as the ground suddenly erupted, sand flying up all around him. He thrashed and gurgled with surprise, and nearly swallowed the seawater.

His eyes went wider still as a gigantic flat fish flapped its mighty wings and rushed away, its powerful wake spinning him around. Regis had never seen such a beast, with massive mandibles and a stringy tail running out behind it.

The sand settled and so did he as the ray moved out of sight.

On he went, more cautiously now, watching the ground and rocks, particularly the small caves in those rocks, more carefully than looking ahead, more concerned with keeping himself alive than with any shipwreck.

The big winged fish returned, and it was not alone.

Regis held himself very still as the gigantic rays glided all around him. He could sense their curiosity, and knew at once that it was his illuminated headband attracting them. They glided in from the darkness, appearing all of a sudden, their white underbellies bright in his eyes. One after another, they floated past, and despite the fact that every one of them—and there had to be a dozen or more—was much larger than he was and could likely buffet him to death with ease, the halfling found himself giggling at the surreal scene. He felt as if he wasn't in the water then, but rather, floating up in the night sky, with magical celestial behemoths flying around him.

After a long while, he reminded himself of his mission, and of the tremendous amount of water between him and the surface. On he went, the giant winged fish hovering around like a protective escort—and indeed, the halfling came to think of them in that manner, for he came to understand that they meant him no harm, that curiosity, not aggression or hunger, kept them near to him.

He had almost completed his wide circuit of the anchor line, coming over one dark ridge, when he found the seabed falling away from him, farther into darkness. Worse, the current in this ravine proved quite strong, and Regis held onto the rocks of the ridge and thought to backtrack instead of continuing along.

He was just about to do exactly that when he noted a crossbeam against the stones just below and before him. It hardly registered to him initially, and he started back, and indeed had gone some distance before he even realized what he had seen.

A mast.

Regis rushed back to the ridge and moved lower, toward the beam. Yes, it was a mast, lying against the stone. Using its reclined angle as a pointer, the halfling crept farther, to the very end of his tether. He couldn't quite make out the markings, but it seemed to him that there was something there, a hull, lying on its side against the rocks before and below him. He reached back and pulled the elven cord, but it had no more length to give to him.

He looked up, at the long and dark ascent, at the rays gliding all around.

It would take a long time to get back up there, hoist the anchor, and reposition the boat, and the thought of coming back down here after the sun had set was not a comforting one.

Regis fiddled with his harness, producing one of Wigglefingers's potions. How many times had the wizard told him not to use these unless absolutely necessary? They were expensive and took a long time to brew, after all. But Regis wasn't about to return to the surface and come back down this day. He put the vial in his mouth and bit off the cork, the cool liquid affording him the ability to breathe underwater. Even with that, it took all of his courage to continue. He untied his tether line and started down, holding the rocks as securely as if he was scaling down the side of a mountain. The current tugged at him, and if it caught him, he feared he would be washed far, far away, and probably held under long enough that he would drown.

But now he saw the hull, battered and broken, cracked amidships.

He couldn't be sure that this was the boat he had been seeking, of course, for the Sea of Fallen Stars was littered with shipwrecks.

And yet, he was sure.

And it called to him like a siren's song, but caught in the entrancement of the magical melody, Regis merely thought it his own curiosity pushing him along.

He crept closer, but had no direct path to the broken hull. He planted himself against the ridge and pushed off, swimming furiously.

The current grabbed him and rushed him along to the shipwreck, then right past it! At the last instant, the halfling lunged out with his hand and caught the taffrail and held on for all his life.

Finally he pulled himself aboard and spider-walked along the side of the hull to the wide crack.

He peered in, his light shining on a scene that had known only darkness for many decades.

Fish scampered all around, and past their flickering scales, Regis noted crates lying around the hold, many broken, but some intact, and one in particular catching his eye, for it gleamed of silver in his headband's light.

He pulled himself into the hull and, relieved of the current's pull, rummaged around. He opened a bag Pericolo had given him, a magical bag of holding, and eased into it a pair of small boxes and a coffer, all the while making his way to the large silver crate.

No, not a crate, he realized as he arrived just above it.

A coffin.

A coffin made of silver, and with chunks of broken mirrored glass atop it and beside it. Regis caught his own reflection in one large shard, but looked away immediately, remembering the story of bloody rats Donnola had told him.

Too late.

A halfling, a copy of Regis himself, slid out from the mirror, drawing a rapier identical to the one on Regis's belt.

Regis cried out, bubbles escaping, and fell back, crashing against crates and boxes, thinking only of escape. But he couldn't get away; the magical image was too close, and too intent on destroying him.

He saw the tip of the rapier, darting for his face.

"He's been gone too long." Donnola crouched down at the rail, peering intently into the dark water.

"At ease, lass," Wigglefingers interjected. "Yer little friend's got potions if he needs them. He's been down longer than this just catching shellfish."

Donnola didn't respond, other than to shake her head. She knew that Wigglefingers was stretching the truth, for Spider had never been down this long, she was sure.

"Can you enlighten us with a magic vision, perhaps?" Pericolo asked his wizard, clearly as nervous as his granddaughter.

Wigglefingers nodded and fumbled around his cloak, producing one scroll tube after another until he settled on the appropriate one. He pulled the parchments forth, cleared his throat, and began his incantation. A few moments later, an eye, huge and bulbous, its pupil alone as large as the halfling's head, appeared in the air beside him, floating as if in water.

Wigglefingers cast an enchantment upon the eye, giving it light, then sent it forth into the sea, and willed it down along the anchor line. Soon after, it neared the bottom.

"I see his tether," the wizard announced, for only he could view the scene through his wizard's eye. "Spider is on the bottom, out that way." He pointed to the northeast, back toward the coast, though the hills of Aglarond were long out of sight. At the same time, the wizard eye rushed along the tether.

The wizard could see that the rope was slack, but he kept that information quiet for the moment.

"He is off the tether," Wigglefingers finally announced, and Donnola and Pericolo both gasped, and a couple of the others nearby began whispering in ominous tones. "A ledge . . . the water goes deeper."

"Follow along the directional line of the tether, then!" Pericolo demanded, but indeed, Wigglefingers was already doing exactly that.

"Thepurl's Diamond!" the wizard gasped. "And Spider's light within!"

Regis fell back in a swirl of bubbles and thrashing arms, trying desperately to keep the rapier away. He felt its bite and started to yelp reflexively, throwing himself backward with abandon. He crashed into a pile of crates, old wood breaking apart at the impact, and tumbled backward into a narrow cubby.

He could barely move and had nowhere farther to retreat, and no way to dart out to the side.

And the doppelganger Regis came on methodically, unemotionally, rapier leading and thrusting.

Fear reached up around Regis like dark black wings, enveloping him, paralyzing him. He wouldn't get to Icewind Dale! All of the training and preparation he had done would be for naught.

He would never see Donnola again.

Half-standing, half-sitting, he managed to draw out his rapier and awkwardly lift it in defense. But his opponent, a mirror image of himself, was equally skilled and had the upper hand. As soon as Regis's blade came up, the doppelganger's rapier matched its angle, rolled around it in a watery swirl, and stabbed Regis hard in the hand. A subtle turn and flick took the rapier away.

Regis tried to back-paddle, churning splintered wood and the contents of the broken crates—and he hardly even noticed those treasures! Gems and jewels rolled aside on piles of coins. Silver plates and golden goblets danced and bounced away.

Regis reached back, trying to feel his way along, but he was out of room. His fingers closed on the ridged top of a crate and as the rapier darted forward, he yelped again and instinctively brought his arm defensively around, the broken crate cover in hand.

The makeshift shield blocked the doppelganger's thrust, the rapier tip prodding through and stabbing Regis hard in the finger. He let go of the wooden plank, but it stayed up before him, stuck fast to his enemy's blade.

An image of Donnola flashed through his mind—if he ever wanted to see her again, he had to move now!

He brought his right hand down atop the debris and half-turned, thinking to bull his way forward out of the tight cubby. He felt a cylindrical grip under that hand, a hilt, and instinctively closed his fingers and brought the item around.

It was a dagger, a three-bladed parrying dagger, with a long, silvery, double-edged main blade flanked by a pair of exquisitely designed side blades that seemed as if they were made of jade or some other deep green crystal. Carved as serpents, they rolled out from the pommel to form a crosspiece, then curled back around, one going before, one behind, the main blade. Out to the side they went a second time, then curled forward so that the open maws of the carved snakes reached fully a third of the way up the length of the main blade, which was as long as a halfling's forearm.

Regis didn't have time to admire the craftsmanship, of course. Desperate and running out of time, he leaned against the stuck plank of wood and bulled forward, stabbing out wildly with powerful overhead chops.

The doppelganger retreated, but the water quickly darkened with blood between the combatants.

Regis pushed forward, coming into the clearer liquid, but realizing that his opponent had moved cleverly to the side. He turned, waving his arms to control his floating movements, and pressed forward, then tried to stop as the doppelganger freed its blade, the wooden plank fluttering aside.

In came the rapier, the doppelganger going right back on the offensive.

Regis stabbed across with his newfound dagger to parry, and caught the rapier between the main blade and one of the snakes. He started to twist, hoping to lock the blade, and his eyes went wide indeed as the snakes on his dagger came alive, or animated somehow at least, and tightened the catch on the rapier.

Regis turned his wrist hard, and the dagger twisted to help him, and the rapier blade snapped in half.

He retracted and charged in at the doppelganger. Now, as if sensing that he was going for the kill, the snakes of his dagger rolled back over his hand, forming a defensive basket.

Regis felt a dull thud against his belly, but didn't slow. Again and again he pumped his arm, his long dagger striking home and gliding easily though flesh and bone.

The water darkened once more, but Regis didn't relent, stabbing furiously. Over and over again, driven by terror, afraid to stop, Regis plunged home the blade.

And then like an illusion, the doppelganger was gone, folding in on itself until it was nothingness, even taking the blood from the water with it. Gone, all of it, all trace of it, even the broken rapier tip, as if it had never been, except for Regis's own blood, trailing up from his hand.

Regis looked at the wound, but instead found himself staring at the dagger, at the altered dagger. He pictured its previous, three-bladed form, and as if to his call, the snakes unwound from his hand and curled across and forward once more into their original form.

And there they hardened, inanimate side-blades once more. Intrigued, the halfling continued his focus on the weapon and changed the image in his mind, thinking then that he preferred the stronger and reinforced grip. The serpentine side-blades of the dagger complied, coming to life and curling tightly but comfortably around his right hand. He had found quite a prize, he knew, but he knew, too, that he had no time to consider that now. He had to get out of there!

He turned for his rapier, but it was back in the cubby area, which was all a mess of broken woods and tumbled crates. He glanced to the side, to his dropped bag lying near the silver coffin. He picked up the plank of wood instead and made his way carefully back to the coffin, placing the plank down atop the enchanted glass.

He had to get out of there, he knew as he retrieved the bag of holding and slung it over his shoulder. He had to . . .

He had to open the coffin.

The thought seemed ridiculous to him, of course, but he found that he couldn't easily dismiss it.

It was not a fleeting thought, he learned, as he tried unsuccessfully to turn away.

He stared at the coffin. Was this the resting place of the great lich Ebonsoul? He had to open the coffin. He had to know.

He treaded water just above the tomb. Only then did he realize how long he had tarried, and he reached for the second potion on his belt, understanding then that the first was nearing its end.

But even as he brought the vial up before him, he noted that the silver coffin cover seemed to thin out below him, growing less and less opaque. To his shock, he made out a form within the casket.

The cover became translucent.

He looked upon the corpse, the leering, rotted, bloated, horrific form.

It smiled at him, dead eyes opening.

It reached for him, a skeletal arm, flaps of flesh waving in the watery currents, coming forward for him, coming out of the tomb, as if the cover of the coffin was no more!

Regis dropped the vial and scrambled wildly for the break in the hull, his breath bursting forth in a rush of confusing bubbles. He thrashed and he swam, and had the snakes of the dagger not been curled around him, he surely would have dropped the blade!

Out in the open water, caught in the current, he paddled upward with all his strength. He rose too quickly, but didn't care. He knew better than to come up fast from such a depth, but at that moment, he knew nothing except that he had to get away!

"There! There! Oh, dear child!" Wigglefingers yelled, jumping up and down and pointing to the northeast. He was still looking through his wizard eye, and had seen Spider come forth from the hull, trailing blood and eyes wide with terror, and lungs near to bursting, if his expression was to be believed.

"Up anchor!" Pericolo yelled and the other halflings grabbed the line and began hoisting.

The wizard eye dweomer expired.

"Faster!" Wigglefingers implored the crew, slapping his forehead and silently cursing his spell's ill-timing. "Oh, Spider!"

He and Pericolo leaned over the rail, staring off into the distance. The water roiled as Spider broke through, gasping and splashing, and sinking right back under.

"Faster!" Pericolo demanded. "Hold on, boy!" he cried. He and Wigglefingers turned, hearing a thump behind them, and they had barely registered it as Donnola's boots falling to the deck as the young woman rushed between them and dived overboard.

"Donnola!" Pericolo cried. He turned to the crew and yelled at them to go faster, then jumped down beside them and began pulling in the anchor line.

"Do something, mage!" he yelled at Wigglefingers.

"I have nothing to offer, Grandfather!"

"A servant! A rope trick! Speed for Donnola! Something!"

But the mage could only shrug helplessly. "Nothing," he said in a defeated tone, but he perked up immediately and cried, "She has him!" jumping up and down on the deck with glee.

Pericolo scrambled back to the rail and got there just as he heard the anchor come up over the side.

It didn't matter, though, for Donnola was now approaching, one arm locked tightly around Spider's chest.

"Is he dead? Oh, child!" Pericolo wailed, for the younger halfling showed no signs of life.

"Help me," Donnola begged, spitting water and clearly exhausted. She shoved Spider forward, where Pericolo and Wigglefingers grabbed him by the tunic and roughly pulled him aboard.

Despite the immediate concerns, neither failed to gasp at the sight of the fabulous dagger affixed to Spider's hand. They laid him out in the bottom of the boat, while others helped Donnola aboard.

"Row fast, sail fast, to Delthuntle!" Pericolo demanded. "We must find a priest for the boy."

"Spider, Spider," Donnola pleaded, climbing across to lie atop the prostrate halfling. "Oh Spider, don't you die on me!"

Regis, falling backward into a great darkness, could not ignore that plea. He opened one eye, coughed up some seawater, and managed a little smile.

Then he fell into unconsciousness, letting go within the tender embrace of Donnola Topolino.

"It saved my life," Regis said, taking the three-bladed dagger from Grandfather Pericolo. "I had lost my rapier."

"Easily replaced," Pericolo said. "And not worth the effort to return to the wreck to retrieve it."

"I won't go back there," Regis said flatly. Beside him, Donnola put a comforting hand on his shoulder.

"No, no, of course not. Be at ease, my dear Spider," Pericolo replied with a warm smile. "Your extraordinary courage and competence soared beyond my expectations—my high expectations, I assure you! I would not ask you to return, and have no plans to do so, in any case."

He grinned wryly.

"You will sell the location of the wreck," Regis said, and both Donnola and Wigglefingers looked at him with surprise, but then nodded their agreement and turned to Pericolo, who was smiling even wider.

"You see?" the Grandfather asked. "My faith in Spider is not misplaced. Well reasoned, my boy! Yes, we have our treasures"—he waved his arm to the side, to a table covered in gems and jewels, potion bottles and assorted trinkets—"and likely the best of the lot to be found. I have all the proof of the wreck I need to auction the location, and no matter what comes further from it, I have—"

"You have secured your legacy as the person who discovered Ebonsoul's resting place," Regis interrupted.

Pericolo nodded and patted his young protégé's other shoulder. "You were promised your pick of the treasures, and surely you earned that, at least."

Regis turned and glanced at the table.

"The dagger is powerful," Wigglefingers said. "More so than you have yet discovered. It is possessed of many enchantments, I suspect, and better than that, it is not possessed of its own identity and pride, which is oft the downfall of mighty weapons."

Regis nodded, and marked well the truth of the wizard's words, remembering Khazid'hea, the Cutter, and what it had done to Catti-brie more than a century before. She hadn't been ready to do mental battle with the blade, and the evil thing had overwhelmed her.

"What else might it do?" Regis asked, but Wigglefingers just shrugged and shook his head.

"For your second choice, I suggest this," said Pericolo, and he brought forth a curious ring, iron-banded and set with a prism-shaped gemstone. "You will find it useful in many of your tasks, I expect."

Regis took it and lifted it up before his eyes, and found one use immediately, for turning the triangular prism stone just so and peering through it greatly magnified the immediate field of view.

"Again an item full of magic," said Wigglefingers. "And quite useful."

"What else will it do?"

"You will sort it out when you need it," the mage assured him. "That is the way with magic rings."

Regis slipped the ring on and shivered, for a chilly wave of energy flowed through him. He looked down at the ring with some concern.

"There are spells which see heat and creatures who view the world in that way," Wigglefingers explained, something Regis knew well, of course, but that Spider likely would not. "With that ring, I believe that you are invisible to such dweomers."

"Not very snuggly, though," Donnola remarked, hugging herself as she backed away from Regis, and they all laughed.

Regis closed his eyes and called to the ring, and the chill passed, and he heard the hints of other possibilities contained within. It occurred to him that when he enacted the chill, he would find himself protected from heat, from fire even. And there was more within that gemstone prism, he realized, and he couldn't help but smile.

⋯◆◯◯◆⋯

A bank of fog wafted up from the depths and gathered atop the Sea of Fallen Stars, above Thepurl's Diamond, in the dark of night. It hovered there for some time, its edges rolling in the sea breeze, but not dissipating in the least.

Then it began to drift, but not on the breeze—indeed, counter to the breeze, making its way slowly to the northeast, toward the shore of Aglarond and the city of Delthuntle.

⋯◆◯◯◆⋯

Regis awakened to the sound of the most horrific, bloodcurdling scream he had ever imagined. So jarring was it that the halfling tumbled out of his bed and onto the floor, tangling in his blankets and bedclothes.

He finally extricated himself, grabbed his dagger, and crouched in the corner, trying to figure out his next move. He didn't dare light a candle.

250

He looked out the window, thinking to go outside and circle around for a better position. He tried to sort out the scream. Who was it? From where had it emanated?

He caught his breath as his bedroom door burst open, torchlight spilling in from beyond. He recognized the silhouette of Donnola, stumbling in, and rushed to her.

"Run!" she said, and she thrust some items at him.

"Quickly, Lady," said Donnola's guard, coming into the room with the torch.

In the light, Regis noted the gifts Donnola had offered: a sword belt and pouch. His eyes widened indeed when he noted Pericolo's fabulous rapier hanging in that belt, and across from it on the right hip, the smaller holster for the magical hand crossbow.

"Run, and do not look back," Donnola said, thrusting the gifts into Regis's hand.

"The Grandfather?" Regis asked breathlessly, and he understood then who it was that had screamed.

"And this," Donnola added, producing a blue beret, the prized cap of Grandfather Pericolo Topolino.

Without doubt, then, in that terrible moment, Regis knew that the great halfling was surely dead.

"I cannot leave," he whispered.

"You have no choice, boy," said Wigglefingers, coming up to the door. "For your sake and for all of our sakes!"

"What is the meaning of this?" Regis demanded.

Donnola grabbed him by the shoulders and squared him up to face her, then gently kissed him. "Ebonsoul," she whispered, pulling back. "He is here . . . for you. Be gone, I beg! Out your window, out of Delthuntle, at once."

"No time, boy," Wigglefingers added. "We cannot contain him, we cannot defeat him."

His expression reflecting his shock, the dumbfounded halfling took the beret from Donnola and glanced at his window.

Donnola threw herself over him, kissing him again, deeply and passionately, sweetly and sadly.

How could he leave her?

But he thought back to the image he had seen in the Lichwreck, the leering, emaciated form of the lich, and his legs went weak beneath him.

He strapped the sword belt around him, set his dagger into it opposite the grand rapier and right beside the hand crossbow, and was out the window quickly, scrambling along the side of the mansion as nimbly as any spider. He didn't go straight to the ground, as he should have, but instead, seeing a light from within, he crept along the side of the second story to the master chamber.

He spotted Pericolo immediately when he looked in, the old halfling sitting before the hearth. Old indeed! The Grandfather's silver hair had thinned greatly, and turned pure white, and his face! All wrinkled it was, as if Pericolo had suddenly aged decades.

It took Regis a long while to realize that he was gasping for breath.

He noted then a fog slipping under the closed door of Pericolo's room, and a great chill swept through him, and not from his ring.

"Ebonsoul," he whispered, and he scrambled away, jumping down into the hedges and staggering off across the small lawn and down the lane. He didn't look back for many strides.

But his thoughts surely did.

He had abandoned Donnola! He had left her in a house with the lich Ebonsoul!

Tears of shame streaked down his face. Was he that same Regis once again, the tag-along halfling who had more often been a burden to his friends than a valuable companion?

He skidded to a stop and swung back to look at the house.

"No!" he said determinedly, hands going to rapier and dagger. He would not abandon his friends, would not flee in fear, leaving them to face this great foe alone!

He took a step back toward the mansion, but stopped and fell back immediately, for he saw a fog collecting outside of Pericolo's house, a small patch up by the window.

No ordinary fog, he knew without doubt.

Coming for him, he knew without doubt.

"He is here for you," he whispered, recalling Donnola's words.

Regis turned and fled.

Spider sat alone behind the captain's quarters, on the deck of a sailing ship, the very next afternoon, the coast of Aglarond long out of sight behind him.

He wore Pericolo's hat, though he called upon its magical qualities to change its appearance to that of a simple black cloth beret. That hat had also altered his appearance, making him seem much older, and with blonde curly hair instead of brown. He had even added a thin mustache for effect, and the tip of a beard at the point of his chin. And his rapier, that fabulous and distinctive blade, looked much more like the mundane one Regis had carried to the Lichwreck. He had secured the hand crossbow safely away, for that item was too unique, its craftsmanship alone speaking of a king's treasure, for him to properly disguise it. His three-bladed dirk fit well into the hand crossbow's holster anyway, and he was skilled at the two-handed fighting technique.

He glanced around to ensure that he was alone, then turned to the pouch that was set upon the belt. He knew it well, and knew, too, the key words to activate it—indeed he had done just that to hide the hand crossbow within. Anyone without those magical words would think this a normal pouch with a few coins inside, but once Regis whispered, "For the love of pink pearls," to it, his hand slipped in deeper. Much deeper, up to his elbow and with no sense of being anywhere near the bottom, though the magical container still outwardly appeared as no more than a small belt pouch that would barely hold his fingers.

Regis thought of coins and felt a pile of gold under his hand.

He cleared his thoughts and let the pouch speak in his mind, communicating its contents. He saw clothing, mostly, some fit for the muddy road, other outfits that would serve him well among the grand parties of the lords of Waterdeep. One garment in particular caught his attention, and he called to the pouch and pulled it forth, recognizing it as Pericolo's battle armor, a mithral-lined white shirt. He glanced around once again, and quickly donned it, putting his own sweater over it, then thrust his hand back into the pouch of holding, immediately happening on another garment, a specialty item known as a housebreaker harness. He smiled and left that one alone . . . for now.

He had coins and jewels aplenty, enough to secure his passage and board for years to come, he guessed. Donnola had done well by him before coming to him that dark night.

He imagined a tome and pulled it forth, and as soon as he had glanced at its contents, the halfling eagerly thrust his hand back into the pouch.

"Indeed!" he whispered with a gasp of delight and astonishment as he noted another item, or set of items: a portable alchemy lab to go along with the book of recipes he had just brought forth.

He was well trained and now, well equipped. He could look ahead with hope.

This boat was bound for the Bloodstone Lands, for the city of Procampur, though Regis knew that to be a stopover only, for his road away from Delthuntle would only begin there. He meant to catch the first boat out of Procampur bound for the Dalelands on the western edges of the Sea of Fallen Stars. It was time for the eighteen-year-old Regis to look west, far west.

Donnola lingered in his thoughts. Eiverbreen, too—how would his father get on without him? And he hadn't even said farewell to the man, fearing to bring the lich anywhere near to the helpless halfling.

"Donnola will see to him," he told himself, and he believed it, for he believed in her as much as he had believed in anyone he had ever known.

That thought struck him profoundly, particularly considering the road upon which he had embarked, the road to his friends, to the Companions of the Hall.

He would return to Delthuntle, he told himself. He had to have faith in Donnola now, that she would escape Ebonsoul. She would assume Pericolo's rank, with a faithful Wigglefingers at her side.

Yes, he had to have faith in her.

But he would return to her, he thought, and he nodded with determination.

First, though, he was less than three years from a date with destiny in a far-off place called Icewind Dale.

He managed a little chuckle as he recalled his first journey to Icewind Dale, in another body and another time, decades before. Then, too, he had thought himself living the life of luxury, well-fed, well-housed, settled, and content in the far-off city of Calimport.

And then, too, he had been chased out, with deadly pursuit close behind.

The smile left his face as he considered the last image of Grandfather Pericolo, sitting in his chair, so suddenly a withered corpse.

Tears streamed down his cherubic cheeks, and he wanted nothing more than to pay back the murderous lich.

He sucked in his breath at that notion, though, recalling the horrid image of Ebonsoul.

To his astonishment, he found himself wishing that it was a hunter as mundane as Artemis Entreri on his trail again.

CHAPTER 21

THE RUSE

The Year of the Ageless One (1479 DR)
Shade Enclave

THE TINY MOUSE LOOKED BACK WIDE-EYED AT THE BURNING BUILDING. The roof fell in and the remaining kegs of lamp oil exploded, sending another massive fireball rolling up into the air.

The mouse silently prayed for the corpse within the building. She felt it her duty to witness this, and yet she knew that she should not, and when reason at last overruled emotion and her sense of obligation, she scurried away.

Down the alleyway, the mouse became a bat and flew off into the night, to the wall of Shade Enclave and away from the floating city.

Catti-brie didn't dare revert to her human form. Lady Avelyere wouldn't be easily fooled, or easily deterred from seeking her out with every magical trick and spell she could muster.

Catti-brie could only hope that her explosive diversion and her placement of the dead woman would hold the diviner off her trail long enough for her to make a clean getaway.

She thought of that woman. She had gone to the graveyard and raised a zombie. She had desecrated a grave and disturbed the sleep of the dead.

The notion grated on her uncomfortably, for surely such an action was not a goodly deed. But it was a necessary one, and the zombie had been raised through the power of Mielikki, though such a spell was anathema to the very tenets the goddess represented, that of the natural cycle of life and death.

These were extraordinary circumstances, and Catti-brie had to accept the granted power of animating the dead as confirmation that Mielikki

255

understood and approved of her choice. The mission was paramount and the mission had been severely compromised. Charmed and hypnotized, Catti-brie had revealed far too many secrets to Lady Avelyere. That recollection reminded the young woman that she could be caught again, and would be helpless in such an event. She sprouted larger wings from her rodent form, transforming yet again. Within a few moments, an eagle fluttered down to the desert floor and became a wolf, loping off on padded paws, silently into the night. Catti-brie couldn't keep this up for much longer, she knew, for her magical energy was fast depleting, so she had to find a sheltered spot and properly ward it from intrusive, magical eyes.

She would say a prayer to the poor woman whose corpse she had abused with magical animation, of course.

As she settled in for the night within the shadows of a rocky overhang, she hoped that the many blessings and wards she had placed on the dead woman would hold against Avelyere's certain magical intrusions, for her own sake as well as for the dignity of the deceased.

"I do not believe it," Lady Avelyere remarked, standing on the edge of the smoldering ruin. "That was no coincidental lightning strike. We have seen this play before!"

"We had compromised her, and all that she meant to do," Rhyalle dared to say. "Perhaps Ruqiah became worthless . . . nay, less than worthless, even dangerous, to the designs of her professed goddess, Mielikki."

"So she went into a tinder keg and obliterated herself with a blast inspired by the goddess?"

"A divine blast greatly enhanced by the elements contained within that location, it would seem," said Rhyalle.

But Lady Avelyere was shaking her head through every word of the feeble explanation. "That would be more the play of A'tar, or Lady Lolth. I doubt that Mielikki would support . . ." She paused, hardly able to throw out the word, and waved her arm out at the blasted and burning building, and finished, ". . . this."

A thin form approached through the hazy smoke.

"We have found her, Lady," Eerika said quietly, and she glanced over her shoulder toward the far corner of the blasted building. "What is left of her."

Lady Avelyere took the lead and strode across the smoking rubble, joining a trio of her other disciples at the spot Eerika had indicated. She followed their gazes and glanced down, then looked away quickly from the disgusting sight.

Blackened and blistered and shrunk to half its size, the ruined corpse rested on its side, one arm splayed out, one apparently burned to nothingness.

Lady Avelyere took a deep breath, which, she quickly realized, was not a good idea, as the smell of charred flesh nearly doubled her over with nausea.

"Get a blanket and collect . . . this thing," she ordered. "Bring it to the Coven."

"Ruqiah?" Eerika asked, clearly confused by the reference.

Lady Avelyere waved her arm angrily at the corpse. "That!" she stated flatly, and she rushed away, unwilling to tag it with Ruqiah's name.

Yes, she had seen this trick before, outside the encampment of the Desai. A thin smile cracked through Lady Avelyere's angry and disgusted expression, for she knew indeed that the dead did tell tales.

Wings spread wide, the eagle glided on the updrafts of hot air, circling lazily above the Desai encampment. The form afforded Catti-brie enhanced vision, so even from this great height, she could clearly make out the faces of those moving around below her. She had already noted the tent of Niraj and Kavita, and focused on it most of all. She had arrived early in the morning, after all, and it was unlikely that the two were already out and about.

How she wanted to go down there, revert to her human form, and accept one last warm hug from her parents!

But she could not, she understood. Lady Avelyere would surely visit the couple, and would wield her insidious magic to get into their thoughts. If they tried to cover for Catti-brie, they would be discovered and heinously punished, no doubt, and in either case, just letting them know the truth, that she was alive, would likely put Avelyere back on her trail.

Catti-brie repeatedly reminded herself of that dark reality, but then she saw the brown, bald head of Niraj come out of the tent, and before she even realized it, she had dipped her wings and circled lower.

She caught herself and fought back, truly heartbroken. The feeling only intensified when the raven-haired Kavita came out beside Niraj.

He draped his arm around her casually, affectionately, and the two turned to stare out to the north, Kavita shading her eyes against the morning glare.

They were looking toward Shade Enclave, Catti-brie realized. They were thinking of their daughter. As with every morning, she sincerely believed.

The eagle circled lower, but tried to stay behind the couple, that Catti-brie might hear their conversation without distracting them.

"She is well," she heard Niraj assert, and he hugged Kavita closer.

A second cry demanded Catti-brie's attention, from a tribesman who had noted her, soaring just above the tops of the tent poles. She couldn't stay, she knew—the farmers would treat her as a threat to the livestock.

She swooped across the encampment, issuing a loud shriek as she closed in on Niraj and Kavita. They swung around, eyes going wide as the large eagle bore down upon them.

Catti-brie dipped her wings one after the other, then broke fast to her right and pumped her wings, gaining speed and height. She heard Kavita gasp, "Ruqiah?"

Catti-brie was satisfied with that. She had to be, for she could offer no more than the hint, for their sakes and for her own. She raced out across the desert, flying west, quickly leaving the Desai encampment far behind.

She doubted she would ever look upon it, ever look upon Niraj and Kavita, again.

When she landed in a sheltered dell, her magic exhausted, she came back to human form with tears streaming down her cheeks.

"Try harder," Lady Avelyere implored her warlock friend.

"Lady, I have nothing more to offer," the older man said with a wheezing laugh. "I have used every spell at my disposal. The corpse will not speak to me!"

"Pry her spirit back from the netherworld then," the woman argued.

"Look at the wounds! It would just fall over dead again, in short order."

"Do it anyway," Lady Avelyere coldly ordered.

"You should hire a priest," the dark magic-user replied.

"I already have," the woman assured him. Lady Avelyere had gone after the corpse with her own spells, to no avail. She could get no communication at all from the curled and charred body. Then the priestess had come—at no small expense—and that woman, too, could only shake her head, unable to communicate with the deceased. And when that had failed, the priestess had tried unsuccessfully to resurrect the charred corpse. Resurrection was among the most powerful spells in the repertoire of any priest, and indeed, very few could even try to perform such a divinely brilliant dweomer. It was not a spell expected to fail, and yet it had, and failed miserably, not a movement or flicker of life within the charred corpse.

"The corpse has been warded," the priestess had claimed. "Consecrated and mightily blessed." Lady Avelyere had implored her to try again, but she would have no part of it and had abruptly departed. Indeed, the priestess had gone further than her personal refusal, so Lady Avelyere had learned, for no other priest would subsequently come to her call and perform any rituals over this particular corpse.

And now this man, Derenek the Dark, known throughout Shade Enclave for his expertise in the handling of undead, had proven similarly useless.

"And what did the priest say?" Derenek inquired.

"Priestess," Lady Avelyere corrected, but otherwise just stared at the body and did not elaborate or answer.

"Sanctified?" the warlock asked. "This body has been powerfully warded against desecration."

"Ruqiah's spells," Lady Avelyere said sourly.

"Or Ruqiah herself," came an unexpected voice from the door, and the diviner and the warlock turned to see Lord Parise Ulfbinder enter the room. "One would expect that a Chosen of a god would be so protected in death, correct?"

"Of course, Lord Ulfbinder," Derenek said deferentially, and he bowed low.

"Stay with her," Lady Avelyere instructed the necromancer. "Find a way."

"I have attempted all of the appropriate spells, Lady," Derenek replied.

"Then try them again!" Lady Avelyere demanded. "And again after that! I will have my answers." She moved from the room, collecting the grinning Lord Ulfbinder in her wake.

"Terribly smelly," he remarked when they were out of the chamber.

"That is not Ruqiah," Lady Avelyere insisted.

"But you agree that she would be so protected from desecration."

"No," the woman reflexively responded, though she quickly changed it to, "Yes, but it is not her!"

"How do you know?"

"I have seen this ruse before. It would seem to be the way of the Desai. They used a dead child to hide the truth of Ruqiah those years ago." She offered a derisive snort. "And that, too, was a death supposedly caused by a random stroke of lightning."

"The bolt that hit the warehouse was no coincidence," Parise agreed.

"Nor was it suicide," Lady Avelyere insisted. "She would not do that. What goodly goddess would accept such a thing?"

"If her purpose was greater than her life," Parise remarked leadingly, "would she not willingly sacrifice herself for the greater good?"

"We were no threat to that."

"But how could she know that?"

"She should know none of it!" Lady Avelyere insisted. "Not that I discovered the truth of Ruq—Catti-brie, or that she had divulged any hint of the coming rendezvous under my magical influence."

"If you think her ignorant of it all, then why would she kill herself? Or why would she create such an elaborate ruse? Isn't this more likely a tragic accident, then? Perhaps not a coincidence, but a miscalculation by the confused young woman? And if she had somehow unwound the mental webbing of Lady Avelyere, is it not as likely that she would kill herself rather than jeopardize the entire purpose of her return to Toril? She had been reborn precisely for that reason, so you declared."

"She had," Lady Avelyere admitted. She paused and glanced back at the door to the room, trying to sort it all out. She couldn't deny Parise's reasoning; whether this was a fake suicide or an actual one, in either case, it would have to have been precipitated by Catti-brie discovering her own breach of secrecy.

"That is not Ruqiah," she stated flatly a moment later. She turned and faced Parise directly, her expression set, strong and determined. "She has tried to trick us, and has set out from Shade Enclave."

Parise shrugged, not ready to argue the point.

"And I will find her," Lady Avelyere vowed.

"I certainly won't dissuade you from trying," said Parise. "If the goddesses Lolth and Mielikki wish to do battle over the soul of Drizzt Do'Urden, I would dearly love to bear witness."

"And you shall," Lady Avelyere promised. "And if she survives that trial, know that our little Ruqiah will answer to me."

Summer had begun to blossom in the Silver Marches, lines of cherry trees lining the banks of the great rivers, their petals all fluffy and white.

The image struck a tender chord in Catti-brie's heart, reminding her of days long past, of times long lost, and for a moment, the first in a long time, the woman was free of the emotional burden. For a moment, just a few heartbeats, Catti-brie was able to move her fears and regrets for Niraj and Kavita into the back of her mind and bask in the promise of the Companions of the Hall, of her father Bruenor and friend Regis, and most of all, in the arms of Drizzt.

She was a great bird again, a graceful hawk, perched on the branch of a naked, dead tree hanging over the eastern bank of the Surbrin just a short distance downstream of the stone bridge that spanned the river. She could see the decorated walls bordering the road beyond that bridge, winding back toward the rocky hillsides, leading to, Catti-brie knew so very well, the eastern gate of her beloved Mithral Hall.

She wanted to go in there! How she would have loved to see again the hallowed rooms she had called home for so many years.

She shuddered as she considered the possibility of standing before her own grave and that of Regis. Her previous body would be in that grave, though no doubt rotted to bones.

The thought weighed heavily on her, but only for a few moments. For she was a favored child of Mielikki now, and had seen the world through the philosophy of the goddess, the endless cycle, the eternal existence within physical boundaries to hold the spirit and give it substance and shape.

The rotting corpse within the cairn in Mithral Hall could not define her. Not anymore.

But still, the thought unnerved her. Despite her devotion and faith in the song she had learned in Iruladoon, the way of Mielikki, Catti-brie didn't want to stand before that grave.

Not then. She simply wasn't ready.

The hawk spread its wings and lifted off into the air, across the river and beyond.

To the west, ever west.

Catti-brie was barely out of sight, flying off, when a caravan rolled along the road on the eastern bank.

The dwarves across the bridge called out as the lead wagon made the bridge, but they were cheering, not demanding identification. For the lead wagon flew a pennant well-known to the folk of Mithral Hall.

Beside the driver of the fourth wagon sat a young red-bearded dwarf who had to remind himself to breathe as they rolled across that bridge, as they wound their way to the great doors of Mithral Hall, the kingdom he had twice ruled.

PART FOUR

THE ROAD TO KELVIN'S CAIRN

Is there any greater need within the social construct than that of trust? Is there any more important ingredient to friendship or to the integrity of a team?

And yet, throughout a person's life, how many others might he meet who he can truly trust? The number is small, I fear. Yes, we will trust many with superficial tasks, but when we each dig down to emotions that entail true vulnerability, that number of honest confidants shrinks dramatically.

That has ever been the missing ingredient in my relationship with Dahlia and in my companionship with Artemis Entreri. As I consider it now, I can only laugh at the reality that I trust Entreri more than Dahlia, but only in that I trust him with matters of mutual benefit. Were I in dire peril, would either rush to my aid?

I think they would if there were any hope of victory, but if their help meant true sacrifice, wherein either of them had to surrender life to save mine . . . well, I would surely perish.

Is it possible that I have grown so cynical that I can accept that?

Who am I, then, and who might I become? I have forgotten that I have known friends who would push me out of the way of a speeding arrow, even if that meant catching the missile in their own bodies. So it was with the Companions of the Hall, all of us for each of us.

Even Regis. So often did we tease Regis, who was ever hiding in the shadows when battle was joined, but we knew with full confidence that our halfling friend would be there when the tide turned against us, and indeed, I have no doubt that my little friend would leap high to intercept the arrow before it reached my bosom at the willing price of his own life.

I cannot say the same of this second group with whom I adventured. Entreri would not give his life for me, nor would Dahlia, I expect—though in truth, with Dahlia I never know what to expect. Afafrenfere the monk was capable of such loyalty, as was Ambergris the dwarf of Adbar, though whether I had earned that level of companionship with them or not I do not know. And Effron, the twisted warlock? I cannot be certain, though I surely doubt that one who dabbles in arts so dark is a man of generous heart.

Perhaps with time, this second adventuring group will grow as close as the Companions of the Hall, and perhaps in that tightening bond there would come selfless acts of the highest courage.

But should I spend a hundred years beside them, might I ever expect the same level of sacrifice and valor that I had known with Bruenor, Catti-brie, Regis, and Wulfgar? In a desperate battle against seemingly unwinnable odds, could I move ahead to flank our common enemy with full confidence that when it came to blows, these others would be there beside me, all in to victory or death?

No. Never.

This is the bond that would never materialize, the level of love and friendship that rises above all else—all else, even the most basic instinct of personal survival.

When I learned of Dahlia's affair with Entreri, I was not surprised, and not merely because of my own role in driving her away. She made of me a cuckold, something Catti-brie would never have done, under any circumstance. And I was not surprised at the revelation, for this basic difference between the two women was clear for me to see all along. Perhaps I deluded myself in the beginning with Dahlia, blinded by intrigue and lust, or by the quaint notion that I could somehow repair the wounds within her, or most likely of all, by my need to replace that which I had lost.

But I always knew the truth.

When Effron told me of her dalliance with Entreri, I believed him immediately because it resonated with my honest understanding of my relationship and of this woman. I was neither surprised nor terribly wounded. However I lied to myself, however I tried to believe the best of the woman, this was who I knew Dahlia to be.

I wanted to remake the Companions of the Hall. More than anything in all the world, I wanted to know again the level of friendship and trust—honest and deep, to the heart and to the soul—that I had known for those years with my dearest friends. The world can never brighten for me until I have found that, and yet I fear that what I once knew was unique, derived of circumstances I cannot replicate.

In joining with Entreri and the others, I tried to salve that wound and recreate the joy of my life.

But in considering the new band of adventurers, there entails the inevitable comparison, and in that, all that I have accomplished is to rip the scab from the unhealed wound.

I find that I am lonelier than ever before.

—Drizzt Do'Urden

CHAPTER 22

CAIRN FOR A KING

The Year of the Tasked Weasel (1483 DR)
Neverwinter

Inever knew a dwarf who wouldn't come out for a fest on payday," Jelvus Grinch said to the promising young Neverwinter guard.

"Went out two tendays ago," the dwarf answered. "And sure that I'll be goin' again soon enough. Ye ain't for taking it personal, are ye?"

The aging citizen of Neverwinter smiled warmly. "Not to any son of Bonnego Battleaxe," he replied, wearing a wistful look for days long past. Jelvus Grinch had long ago been the de facto leader of the city, the First Citizen, battle hardened. All of the hardy settlers fighting for the fledgling city in those dangerous days had looked to him for guidance.

Now Jelvus had been given a minor position, out of courtesy, it seemed. General Sabine was in charge of all the many sellswords hired on to protect the city, but she allowed Jelvus to handle a few of them, though just a few. It was a gesture of respect and nothing more, Bruenor had quickly realized upon coming into Neverwinter, but at least it was something.

Humans were so quick to lift up their heroes, and just as quick to toss them aside to make way for new ones.

"Not to any whose family is naming Drizzt Do'Urden as a friend," Jelvus Grinch went on, nodding.

"Aye, me Da spoke o' that one often. Strange fellow, I be hearin'."

"Unique," Jelvus Grinch corrected.

"Ye e'er seen him about?" asked Bruenor, who had come into Neverwinter early in the year of 1483, utilizing the same alias he had in his previous visit to the region. When he and Drizzt had come this way in search of

Gauntlgrym decades earlier, Bruenor had traveled under the same name, Bonnego Battleaxe, as now, except that now he was claiming to be the progeny, Bonnego, son of Bonnego.

"Drizzt?" Jelvus Grinch asked. "No, no, and there's been word that he's no more to be found anywhere."

"What do ye know?" Bruenor asked past the lump in his throat.

"No one has heard from Drizzt in many years, so it is told," said Jelvus Grinch. "Though many have searched for him. Strange characters," he added with a chuckle. "Another drow elf—I don't remember his name, but quite the extraordinary figure! That one seemed quite anxious to find him, as I recall."

"Eye patch?" Bruenor asked.

Jelvus Grinch looked at him curiously for a moment. "Yes."

"Jarlaxle," said Bruenor. "Me Da's told me much o' that one. Strange dogs, them drow, and ye never can trust 'em."

"Not true of Drizzt," Jelvus Grinch was quick to reply. "By all accounts, there have been none of any race with a greater claim of loyalty."

Bruenor couldn't help but wince, stung by the reminder. Stung and shamed, given his present course and intentions.

"Here's hopin' that one's still about," Bruenor replied. He took his tenday pay from Jelvus Grinch and dropped the coins into a belt pouch. He gave the pouch a lift, feeling its heft, and nodded as he walked away, confident that he had sufficient funds now to close the deal.

The city of Neverwinter had still not fully recovered from the devastation of the volcanic eruption four decades previous. The area down near the river and the Winged Wyvern Bridge had been rebuilt and was thriving, but beyond the new walls there remained many ruins of the old city. Every night, lights would be spotted out there, among the ruins, as honest travelers and rogues alike took refuge in the unclaimed skeletons of houses long dead.

And every night, Bruenor was up on the wall, spying out those ruins, looking to one building in particular for signs of inhabitation. The night before, he had seen firelight in the empty window, and so it was again this night, the appointed night.

The dwarf went out from the wall, making his way through the desolate boulevards and past the black and empty portals. He knew that many eyes were upon him, from vermin to highwayman to innocent traveler and more. But he was known as a formal mercenary tied to the the Neverwinter garrison, and he carried an axe over his shoulder with practiced ease. Indeed, the frustrated and angry dwarf would almost welcome an ambush.

He made his way to the appointed building, paused before the broken doorway, and gave three sharp whistles. He didn't even wait for the appropriate response, which came as he crossed the threshold into the place. Down the corridor and through a makeshift door, he found his associates, a pair of men, halfling and human, and an elf lass.

"Ah, but there's young Bonnego with our coin," said the human, Deventry, a thin man with a sharp face and a full beard marked by several angry scars. "Mayhaps we'll be sleeping in a proper inn this night!"

"Waste of coin," said Vestra, the elf. She wore a green hooded cloak, much like the one Drizzt used to wear, Bruenor recalled. Her long blonde hair was gathered in the hood, all in a tangle, and her delicate features showed the dirt of the road. But still, she was a pretty thing, Bruenor thought, at least for those who considered the lithe elves attractive.

"My back aches," Deventry argued. "One night in a bed, I say."

"Sharing the sheets with lice, no doubt," Vestra replied with a chortle.

Deventry waved her to silence. "Twenty pieces of gold, then," he said to Bruenor.

"When I see the map, ye'll be seein' the gold."

Deventry smiled and nodded to the third of the group, the halfling they called Whisper, so named because, as far as Bruenor could tell at least, he never said a word.

Whisper produced a scroll tube while Deventry brushed aside the plates and remains of their recent meal, clearing a spot between the three.

"There's your map, as ordered," Deventry said, helping Whisper unroll it.

Bruenor bent low, but the man leaned over to block his view. "Thinking to put it in your mind for free, are you?" Deventry scolded. "We spent half the summer building it, and on good faith!"

"Good faith and twenty pieces o' gold already," Bruenor reminded. "And no, don't ye fear, I ain't for puttin' the whole of it in me head. Now move aside, for there's one or two things that'll tell me the truth of it, and when I see them where they should be, ye'll get yer coin."

Deventry looked to Vestra, who nodded. He slid back from over the map.

Bruenor noted immediately the rocky dell, and how that sent his thoughts careening back through the years. Drizzt and Dahlia had fought a rearguard action there against Ashmadai zealots, while Bruenor, Athrogate, and Jarlaxle—an unlikely trio!—had found the vale and the cave that had led them to the Underdark and Gauntlgrym. The dwarf's scan of the map widened; it all seemed to fit together properly.

"Ye found the stony ravine," he said.

"Aye," Deventry replied.

"And what was beyond it, to the east?"

Deventry looked at him curiously, then glanced at Whisper, who pointed to the map.

"A wide dell," Vestra answered.

"Full o' rocks?"

"Aye, and full of caves."

Bruenor nodded and couldn't contain his grin. His scouts had succeeded. They had found the entrance to Gauntlgrym. He reached into his pouch and pulled forth a handful of assorted coins and sifted through them, counting out twenty pieces of gold, which was, in truth, the vast majority of his wealth. Indeed, when he removed the payment, he had only one remaining gold piece in his pouch, along with handful of silver and coppers.

He reached forth toward Deventry, who moved to take the coins, but Bruenor didn't immediately let go. He locked stares with the man, weighing his options here, then offered, "More for ye if ye take me there."

He handed the coins to the man, then glanced at all three alternately.

"Take you there and leave you?" Vestra asked.

Bruenor considered the possibilities before him. The journey to the caves might be perilous, and the journey into the Underdark even more so. Did he dare reveal the entrance to wondrous Gauntlgrym to these three?

He smiled and nodded as he considered the ghosts within the ancient city. Stokely Silverstream might even be in there now, he mused, along with a hundred dwarves from Icewind Dale—though none in Mithral Hall had known anything of Gauntlgrym other than the old tale of a battle when Bruenor had inquired of it in his time there.

Still, the dwarf understood that many had crossed into the place, no doubt. The Ashmadai zealots knew of it, surely, as did Stokely and his boys.

"Mayhaps," he answered Vestra. "Or follow me into the tunnels. Ye'll find the journey worth yer time, don't ye doubt."

"Fifty gold to take you," said Deventry.

"Ye'll get ten and not a copper more," Bruenor replied, and he wished that he actually had ten to give! He couldn't wait for the next tenday and next payday to pass, though.

"Twenty or nothing," said Deventry.

Bruenor shrugged and retrieved the purchased map, rolling it back into the scroll tube and tucking it away inside his vest. "Then nothing," he said, and he turned and walked out.

"Ten, then!" Deventry called after him.

Bruenor didn't turn around. "Northwest gate at sunrise," he said, then he departed. He had to find Durham Shaw, Captain of the Wall, and resign his commission. His time in Neverwinter was at its end, with Gauntlgrym before him and Mithral Hall after that.

King Bruenor Battlehammer had a war to fight.

The night breeze carried on it the unmistakable chill of late summer, a reminder to Bruenor that his window for traveling back to the Silver Marches was quickly closing. He wondered if he might go to Baldur's Gate or Waterdeep instead, and employ a wizard to use a teleportation spell upon him. Or perhaps he could find a powerful enchantress to make him a flying chariot of living fire.

The dwarf shook his head at the notion, remembering all too well the last time he had tried something like that.

"Well, are you to share your insights, or will you just sit there grumbling the rest of the evening?" Vestra asked.

"Eh?" Bruenor replied, caught by surprise, so deep was he in contemplation. He looked around at the campfire and the two sitting across from him. "Where's the little rat, then?"

"Scouting the road ahead," Deventry replied.

"Whisper thinks there's a quicker way to the valley of caves," added Vestra.

"How much quicker?" Bruenor replied.

"Getting a bit anxious, are you?" asked Deventry. "Our pay's the same, whether it's a tenday or a two-day!"

"I got me a long road ahead," Bruenor replied quietly. "And when we find what we're looking for, ye'll come to understand. Ye might even be wantin' to go along on me next journey." He nodded as he spoke, working through the possibilities. If he could get to Mirabar, some two hundred miles to the north, but along well-marked and fairly stable roads, he would find allies, powerful ones including a sizable number of dwarves. Once he revealed his true identity to them, the winter's snows wouldn't stop them in crossing the Lurkwood to Mithral Hall.

"I'm here for your coin and nothing more," Deventry reminded, in a tone that was also reminding Bruenor that he didn't much care for this aggressive lout. But the dwarf quickly suppressed his personal feelings toward the man. The mission was more important. He was alone out here, other than these three, and good help was hard to find in these wild lands.

"I'm bettin' ye'll be changin' yer mind," he replied, but casually, and with a wide grin. "But if not, then know that me coin's more than ye could e'er carry."

"Quite a hint," Vestra remarked.

"Get me to the valley of the caves, and follow me down a tunnel for a couple o' days, and ye'll understand, elf," Bruenor replied, nodding.

"Down a tunnel?" Vestra replied, seeming none-too-thrilled with the prospect.

"Didn't sign up for any of that," Deventry remarked.

Bruenor merely closed his eyes, smiled, and began to whistle a little tune, mentally reciting the words to the old song, one dwarves sang of lost lands and deep mines and treasures piled high.

When he awoke the next morning, he found all three of his companions gathered together, the halfling scraping in the dirt with his dagger.

"What'd he find?" Bruenor asked.

"The caves . . . today," Vestra replied.

Off they went, cutting around the south side of a hill, then across a wide vale. The flat-topped mountain loomed in the distance to the north, the sight of it taking Bruenor back across the years, to the eruption of the volcano and the destruction of Neverwinter. That event was seared into his memory, across two lifetimes now, and he could picture it again as if it had happened only the day before.

Whisper led them at a great pace. They broke for a very short midday meal and set off again through the forest. Bruenor didn't know where they were, specifically, for nothing seemed familiar, and he finally grasped it when they came through a line of trees to the southern edge of the rocky valley.

Bruenor scanned the rim, nodding as he noted, far to the northwest, the approach he had taken on his last journey to this place.

"Well?" Deventry prompted.

The dwarf studied the valley walls, trying to picture them from the vantage point across the way. "That one," he decided, pointing to one of the many cave openings visible from this angle.

"You said for us to take you to the valley, and now we have," Deventry replied, holding out his hand.

"Don't ye be a fool, boy," said Bruenor. "Come along and hear me tale, and see a sight that'll change yer life."

"Ten pieces of gold," demanded Deventry.

Bruenor nodded his hairy chin toward the distant cave. "I'll double it," he said. "Double it for each of ye."

"What, twenty pieces of gold for each?" asked Vestra.

"You pay up, Bonnego!" Deventry demanded.

"Sixty I just promised, and if ye knew me real name, ye'd know it ain't but a pittance," Bruenor answered with a chuckle, and he started away, leaving his three companions looking from one to the other.

Deventry grabbed the departing dwarf roughly by the shoulder and yanked him around. "Ten!" he demanded.

As he turned, Bruenor rolled his arm and shoulder up high, bringing it up and over Deventry's reaching arm and down suddenly to lock the man's wrist in his armpit. The dwarf turned and twisted fast, pulling his shoulder back, yanking Deventry into a forward lunge that crashed him up against Bruenor, who didn't budge a step.

With his free hand, Deventry reached for his short sword, but Bruenor was quicker, grabbing him by the front of his tunic and giving him a good shake. The dwarf thrust out his arm with surprising strength, throwing Deventry back a few steps—a few steps that took him over the lip of the valley. Overbalanced, the man couldn't hold his footing, and he tumbled to the ground and rolled down the grassy slope.

"Offer's still there," Bruenor called back, marching off for the cave entrance. The other two would hold Deventry back and talk some sense into him, Bruenor believed. And if he was wrong, he'd just lay the fool low with his axe and carry on alone.

He found out just a few moments later that he wasn't wrong.

"What is that place?" Vestra asked breathlessly, staring across the small underground pond to the worked wall of what appeared to be a castle. A castle underground! They were in a large hall, illuminated in a greenish tint by strange glowing lichen. Natural pillars liberally pocked the large cavern, many with worked railings winding up around them. Sprouting mostly along the pond's edge, giant mushrooms completed the strange scene, the orange underside of the huge caps catching, amplifying, and distorting the lichen glow.

"Home o' the Delzoun dwarves," Bruenor explained.

"Your kin are in there?" asked the elf.

"Might be some or might be empty. And might be that we won't be goin' deep enough to know. What I'm wanting's just beyond that open door."

Bruenor hoisted his axe and made for a nearby mushroom. A few swings felled it, and the dwarf began to sever the huge circular cap.

"He's making a raft," Vestra explained to her cohorts.

"Ye're welcome to come in if ye're wantin', or might that ye'll stay out here. I'll not be long."

Whisper was already by his side, helping to hollow out the mushroom cap, and from that action and the look on the halfling's face, Bruenor knew that he wouldn't be going into the complex alone.

Indeed, all four entered together, though it took three trips to ferry them all across the dark water.

Bruenor led the way, but his pace slowed considerably as he crossed the threshold to Gauntlgrym, his every step weighted by solemn and powerful memories. Vestra carried a torch behind him and his shadow reached out before him, wobbling in the flickering light, and somehow, that insubstantial dancing shadow seemed appropriate to him, as ethereal and unreal as this entire adventure. The burden on his shoulders only increased as they moved along the entry corridor and into the grand audience hall of Gauntlgrym. To the right, upon the dais, rested the throne of Gauntlgrym, the seat that had magically, but temporarily, imbued upon Bruenor the leadership of Moradin, the insight of Dumathoin, and the strength of Clangeddin in his battle with the balor Errtu. He remembered that vividly now, the ultimate victory to put the fire primordial back in its watery cage.

The dwarf focused on that throne as he made his way across the huge chamber. His three companions whispered impatiently behind him, but they did not cross before him.

He neared the throne and slowed to a stop, coming into view of the two rocky cairns that had been erected beyond it. He remembered the claim of Catti-brie in the magical forest and knew at once what these were, and who might be interred within: one for Bruenor, one for Thibbledorf Pwent.

The stones of one had been pushed aside, leaving an empty hole. Was that his grave, he wondered? Had his grave, his corpse, been desecrated and robbed? He swallowed hard in a moment of panic, at the notion that his entire purpose in coming here had just unraveled.

So caught up was he that he hardly noticed Vestra, Deventry, and Whisper moving past him, toward the throne.

"Keep yer hands off, for yer own sake!" Bruenor yelled in warning at the last moment, even as Whisper reached out to the burnished wood of the throne's ornate arm.

"You took us here to threaten us?" Deventry came back at him angrily. "If there are treasures to be had, then they are ours as much as your own, dwarf, even if I have to cut out your throat to get my due!"

Bruenor stared hard at Deventry and moved past him. "A throne for dwarves, ye fool," he said, and he marched up and sat down upon the great chair. Anticipations of enlightenment, assurance, and strength accompanied him, but they were shattered immediately when he felt the anger of the chair, a tangible emotional and physical rejection that launched him into the air, flying from the dais to land hard on the floor in a bouncing tumble.

Horrified, King Bruenor rolled to a sitting position and stared back at the throne.

Moradin had rejected him!

His three companions laughed at him.

"So it's full of magic, then!" Vestra said. "Beneficent or malevolent, or more likely a bit of both."

"But not so fond of dwarves, it would seem," said Deventry with a mocking laugh.

Bruenor didn't know how to respond. His thoughts spun around in confusing circles. Surely he had cursed Moradin and the others mightily in these twenty years of his second life, but that was behind him now. He had come to see the truth: that he had been returned to undo the wrongs of King Bruenor, that Mielikki had been but a pawn for a greater purpose. He had found the error of his ways, and had found contentment and purpose once more.

But then why had the throne rejected him?

Was it due to the physical changes, he wondered, the fact that his blood now was not that of a king, but of a guard captain? He looked like young Bruenor, to be sure, but the blood in his veins had come from Reginald Roundshield and Uween, and not the line of Gandalug.

It seemed so trite, almost mocking the purpose of the gods and the throne. He was King Bruenor. He had seen the truth and mended his ways and had corrected his attitude toward the gods who gave power to that throne.

"Ye mock me," he whispered to his gods, dark thoughts climbing up from the floor around him where he sat, burying him in melancholy's hopeless shadow. So lost was he that he almost didn't notice his three companions standing around the throne in close discussion, drawing lots from a piece of broken straw bedding.

Bruenor pulled himself to his feet and staggered toward them. "Don't ye dare," he said.

"A throne for dwarves?" Deventry replied, turning around with a scowl. "It seems that the chair did not agree with your description."

Bruenor shook his head, trying to find the words to properly explain. He noted Whisper rubbing his little hands together eagerly, and Vestra pushing him toward the seat.

"Don't!" Bruenor warned.

"We're all to take our turns!" Deventry shouted back.

The halfling leaped up into the seat and spun around, hands on the arms. His expression remained one of eagerness for a few heartbeats, but then turned to a confused look that quickly showed discomfort. He began to jerk spasmodically, as if bolts of energy were stabbing at him from behind, which indeed they were! He tried to cry out, his mouth twisting weirdly.

"Get him off o' there!" Bruenor yelled, staggering forward.

Vestra spun back on Whisper and lunged for him, but as she did, the chair ejected the halfling—not as it had done with Bruenor, but much more forcefully, heaving poor Whisper through the air. He clipped Vestra as he launched, bloodying her face and spinning her around and down to the floor. Off he flew, high and far, ten long strides and more from the throne. He landed awkwardly, one leg extended below him, and the snap of bone echoed through the chamber. Whisper cracked his shoulder and the side of his head on the stone, and rolled long and hard into the stone wall, where he thrashed in agony. Oh how the supposedly mute halfling screamed!

The other three ran to him, Vestra trying to turn him to his back, and from her own spasms it was clear that it was all she could manage to not vomit at the mere sight of the halfling's wound. His shin had broken in half, the bones protruding through his ripped skin.

"What did you do?" Deventry shouted in Bruenor's face.

"I told ye to stop!" the dwarf yelled back.

But Deventry shoved him, and Bruenor only took a step back to better balance himself as he retaliated with a fearsome right hook that sent the man flying sidelong to the ground.

"Next time'll be with me axe!" Bruenor warned.

"What do you know?" Vestra demanded, standing up from the halfling and moving in front of Deventry to hold the man back.

"I know that yer friend was thinkin' o' robbing this place, and he told it to the throne that guards it, and he got what a thief deserves!"

Deventry started to shout at him, Whisper continued to scream and wail, but Vestra spoke over the tumult, "No, Bonnego, there's more!" she insisted. "What do you know, of that throne, of this place?"

Bruenor swallowed hard. "Me name's not Bonnego," he said, but the others didn't hear. He turned and motioned with his head for them to follow, then started off, angling to the right of the throne, toward the cairns.

"What are we to do with him?" he heard Deventry say behind him.

"Carry him along," Vestra ordered.

Despite his desperate need to inspect the graves, to see if it was his own or Pwent's that had been desecrated, Bruenor turned around to regard the trio. They should let Whisper rest for a bit, should make a splint for his leg and pop his shoulder back into place, of course, before trying to move him.

But Deventry wasn't that smart, apparently, or compassionate. He moved to lift the halfling, who thrashed and screamed even louder. Whisper's flailing hand poked the big man in the eye, and how Whisper screamed even more when Deventry dropped him back to the stone.

"He'll bring the whole place out against us!" Vestra cried. "Whisper, silence!"

Deventry clutched at his eye, his face a mask of rage. His free hand grabbed at his sword and pulled it from his belt, and before Vestra could even yell at him, to call him back to his senses, the man brought the blade down hard and sure.

And Whisper screamed no more.

Bruenor trembled with disgust and anger at himself for bringing these three monsters into sacred Gauntlgrym. He looked at the throne—perhaps that was why it had rejected him.

He started for his grave more determinedly, but heard Deventry's call behind him, "Stand and be counted, dwarf!"

He kept walking.

"Bonnego!" Deventry called, sounding much closer now, and Bruenor spun around to meet the challenge, axe in hand. He found both Deventry and Vestra facing him, weapons drawn and ready.

"Me name's not Bonnego," Bruenor said through gritted teeeth. " 'Tis Bruenor, Bruenor Battlehammer. King Bruenor Battlehammer of Mithral Hall. Might that ye've heared o' me."

The two looked to each other and shrugged, clearly oblivious, then turned back to the dwarf, brandishing their blades.

"And what will you offer in exchange for your life?" Vestra asked. "As recompense for the death of Whisper?"

"Ye should be asking yer big friend on that last part."

"Chair killed him!" Deventry retorted. "This place killed him, and was you that brought him here."

"Stupid killed him," Bruenor corrected with a wry grin. "And 'tis yerself that's stupid."

Deventry growled and lifted his blade, coming ahead with an overhand chop. Up came Bruenor's round shield, easily intercepting. In the same movement, the dwarf slashed across with his axe, forcing Deventry to suck in his belly and throw himself backward. The man landed solidly, leaning forward, no doubt thinking to come right back at Bruenor behind the slash, but the dwarf was far too seasoned a warrior for such an obvious counter. Bruenor pulled his axe up short as it went across and turned his wrist over, breaking its momentum and sending it slashing back the other way as he stepped forward.

Again Deventry retreated, but not quite enough this time, the axe blade scraping across his chain armor and tearing his shirt and skin below it, drawing a welt and a line of blood.

"Circle right!" the grimacing Deventry called to Vestra. "Flank him."

"Aye, flank me and give me the choice which o' ye dogs I cut down first!" said Bruenor, and on he came with a ferocious routine, nearly overwhelming poor Deventry before the fight had even truly begun. The man fumbled with his sword, putting it out left to block the axe, then staggered backward as Bruenor's round shield slammed against his ribs.

"Vestra!" Deventry called, stumbling backward, and he managed to glance her way, and although Bruenor had the clear advantage and was certain to make quick work of Deventry, the shocked look on the man's face gave Bruenor pause, and he too glanced at the elf.

Vestra stood staring off into the distance, her face bloodless.

She whispered one word, "Drow."

Bruenor heard it keenly and he swung around, for some reason thinking it had to be Drizzt come to his rescue—because hadn't Drizzt always come to his rescue?

He spotted the two figures immediately, moving in slowly, determined, arms extended, hands bent like claws, eyes glowing red.

"More!" Deventry called, and Bruenor followed his voice, then his gaze, to see another pair walking in at them. Something was wrong, the dwarf knew, for these enemies were not moving with the grace and speed of dark elves. Far from it!

He watched in astonishment as a large bat flew up beside the pair coming in at Deventry, rolled over itself in midair, and elongated as it did, coming out of the spin as another dark elf.

"Vampires," he heard Vestra say.

He turned to look at her, but she wasn't looking back. Torch in hand, she fled for the exit.

"Aye, go!" the dwarf called, turning to Deventry, to see the man already engaged with two of the undead. Surprisingly swift, they dodged his wild attacks, and when one managed to get in behind an attack and swing its arm against the man's shoulder, Deventry was lifted from the ground and thrown to the side by the sheeer force of the blow.

Bruenor growled and started to charge to the big man's aid, but he skidded to a stop, and called out a warning to Vestra as more large wings filled the air around her. She thrashed with her torch, first at bats, then at vampires, and the torch went flying to the floor as a trio of forms fell over the screaming elf woman, bearing her down.

Bruenor didn't know where to turn. He swung back for Deventry, but found the man flailing, a drow creature upon his back, biting him around the neck and head. Deventry swung around and thrashed and kicked, and managed to get his sword up and over his shoulder, driving it deeply into the creature, which fell away with an otherworldly shriek, but taking Deventry's sword with it. The man started after, desperate to retrieve his weapon, but he had only gone a step before two more of the creatures tackled him, clawing and biting ravenously.

Bruenor didn't see that last part, for now he found another pair of undead dark elves coming in at him, reaching for him with cold, clawing hands.

His axe hit one squarely and turned it aside, but he could not win. He knew that, particularly from the screams of Vestra, who was surely in the last moments of her life.

Bruenor ran for the throne, calling to Moradin, demanding the strength he had known before.

He couldn't win and he couldn't escape. Two pursued him, nipping at his heels.

If he leaped upon the throne and was rejected, he would be killed before he ever regained his footing. He knew that.

So he veered, around the throne toward the two graves, though he knew not why. The pursuit was too close!

He stopped and turned, launching a heavy slash that caught the nearest creature in the side and buried the axe head halfway through it, sending it flying away. Bruenor barely held on to the weapon, and found himself turned and off-balance as the second vampire closed in hungrily.

He caught himself, planted his foot, and pivoted back fast the other way, hardly thinking of the motion as he let fly the battle-axe, spinning it end over end.

It hit the charging drow square in the chest with tremendous force and drove it backward into the darkness.

Bruenor didn't pursue, instead turning for the graves, for the unopened cairn.

His grave, he hoped, and prayed too that his weapon would be in there. He slid down to the floor, grabbing the nearest cairn stone and rolling it aside. Vestra had gone silent by then, and Bruenor tried to block out the frantic calls of Deventry, tried to focus on his desperate, seemingly hopeless task.

"They're eating me!" the man screamed and Bruenor swallowed hard and tossed another stone aside.

He heard scuffling behind him as he reached for the third rock, and instead of just pushing it off the cairn, he hoisted it, turned, and heaved it into the face of the charging vampire, knocking it aside.

Bruenor spun and dropped to his knees, and understood that it was indeed his grave, for he saw a portion of the skeleton within then, its bone hands wrapped around the handle of a weapon he surely recognized.

He dived for it, reaching desperately, confident that if he had that many-notched axe in hand once more, he would fight his way through this, leaving severed pieces of drow vampires in his wake.

He almost had it!

A heavy boot slammed down on his forearm, crushing his arm against the rocks, stopping his progress cold.

And the vampires gathered around him, on all sides now, reaching for him, red eyes leering, white fangs shining even in the dim light.

CHAPTER 23

THE GRINNING HALFLING HERO

The Year of the Grinning Halfling (1481 DR)
Elturgard

THE WAGON BOUNCED ALONG THE TRADE WAY, MORE THAN A HUNDRED miles northwest of the town of Triel, and five times that distance, still, from Waterdeep.

Regis sat in the back, huddled under a heavy winter blanket, for the season grew late. His legs dangled off the tailgate, peeking out from under his cover and showing fabulous high black boots that had miraculously escaped the dirt of the road thus far.

"Smoke in the west!" came the expected call from one of the riders flanking the merchant caravan, and the halfling nodded at the confirmation of their location. Regis had been this way before, though many decades had passed since then. By his estimate, they were approaching the river called Winding Water and the famous span known as the Boareskyr Bridge.

The sun lowered before them, and looking back beyond the Forest of Wyrms and the Reaching Woods, Regis noted the aptly named glistening peaks of the Sunset Mountains, far in the distance. The halfling nodded again, taking measure of the journey that had begun on a dark late-summer's night in Delthuntle.

On the far side of those mountains in the distance, their eastern foot-hills reached down to the westernmost banks of the Sea of Fallen Stars, the great sea that had been in his sight for every day of his second life until this very journey. He had sailed from Delthuntle to Procampur in the kingdom of Impiltur on the northern banks of the sea, and from there to the city of Suzail, seat of power for the great kingdom of Cormyr. Regis

283

could only sigh now as he thought of that grand and bustling place, with its fine markets and the stirring parades of the armies of Purple Dragons. Thousands of people called Suzail home; truly Suzail stood among the greatest of Faerûn's cities.

And the palaces! Ah, but Regis could only smile and nod and pat his belt pouch, wherein rested his housebreaker harness, as he thought of those gilded mansions. He had seen the interior of many of them, though usually in the dark of night and without use of a torch.

He nodded more confidently, assuring himself that he would return there someday. Indeed, Regis would not have left Suzail so abruptly, except that a particular lord of the city also happened to be an accomplished wizard. If only Regis had known that before paying a visit to the man's house one night . . .

Disguised as the gnome Nanfoodle—for indeed, his wondrous beret could even make him appear as a different race—a friend from another time and another life, Regis had departed the city by the end of the summer of the Year of the Grinning Halfling, buying passage on a caravan bound a hundred miles down the western road to Proskur and a hundred more after that on to the town of Irieabor, the very western edge of the kingdom of Cormyr.

And there Nanfoodle had simply disappeared, and so had come into being the dwarf Cordio Muffinhead. Cordio had traveled the length of the kingdom of Elturgard, riding the Trade Way to Triel, where again, it had been time for a change of identity.

And so, with the tip of a blue-speckled beret, Spider Pericolo Topolino, great nephew of the Pericolo Topolino of Aglarond, had been born.

What a year it had been, Regis mused! What a journey, full of sights and sounds and smells and foods any traveler would envy. He had lived as a street orphan, a gnome potion-maker, a dwarf adventurer, and now a halfling dilet-tante, dabbling in artwork, overpaying for all, then, of course, retrieving his spent coins in the dark of night.

He had traveled a thousand miles as the crow flies, and likely twice that distance in his meandering but enjoyable western journey.

Enjoyable, but only when he wasn't looking back to the east, as he was now, images of beautiful Donnola Topolino so clear in his thoughts. When he closed his eyes, he could see her more clearly, and could feel her touch, her gentle fingers brushing his skin, her warm breath whispering into his ear. He could smell her sweetness, taste her . . .

"Runt!" he heard loudly, shattering his memories, and Regis nearly fell off the wagon as he wheeled around to regard the shouter, the dirty man driving the wagon.

"Get me some water, and be quick!" the man, Kermillon by name, ordered. "Or I'll slap ye in the mud and suck the water out o' yer ears!"

"Aye, and might be taking a bit of your brains with it, then, eh?" said Kermillon's co-pilot, Yoger, a burly man who was dressed and bathed a bit cleaner, but by all accounts remained no less a ruffian than the other.

Regis climbed fully into the wagon and inched his way along the right-hand rail to the back of the driver's seat, where Yoger handed him a waterskin. He quickly filled it at the tapped keg, then handed it back.

"Ye listen better and move quicker!" Kermillon warned.

Yoger took a deep drink, but never stopped staring at the halfling.

"You know my namesake, I trust," Regis said.

"Can't say that I do," said Yoger.

"They call him Grandfather Pericolo."

"Thought he was your uncle."

"Everyone calls him Grandfather," Regis said slyly, but he could only snort and shake his head, for the obvious reference to Pericolo as the head of an assassin's guild was clearly lost on this ignorant peasant.

"Get back and sit down and shut yer mouth," Kermillon told him. "Ye paid for a ride to Daggerford, and ye might be getting there, but if ye're too much the bother, I'm dropping ye in the mud and leaving ye."

Regis was more than happy to comply. He started to turn, but paused just long enough to view the smoke of campfires rising above the trees not far ahead. He nodded, remembering the Boareskyr Bridge, and the merchant encampments perpetually set on either side.

"It is a good place," he said, hardly thinking, and only realized he had spoken it out loud when both men turned to regard him curiously.

Regis just tipped his fabulous beret at them and moved to the back of the wagon.

The white tents dotted the sides of the road long before the mouth of the bridge, a virtual city of merchant kiosks and open markets. The ten wagons of the Daggerford caravan pulled up into an open field along the right side of the road, where corrals had been set up and smoke rose from blacksmith fires. This place was well-suited for resupply, for shoeing horses and even buying new ones if necessary, though, since the roads were empty for scores of miles on either side of the bridge, such services and goods did not come cheap.

Regis was glad to be away from his thuggish drivers, and glad to be wandering around the bustle of a marketplace. Dressed in silken finery, all purple and blue, with blue-dyed lambskin riding gloves, and with his beret and bejeweled rapier both prominently displayed, he played the role of halfling aristocrat perfectly. Donnola had trained him well, after all, and that after decades of his previous life in the palaces of the pashas of Calimport. Many of the merchants around Boareskyr Bridge were from the kingdom of Amn, and Regis knew the traditions and customs of that land very well.

He was the perfect blend of experience and seeming innocence, floating around the tents with smiles and tips of his beret. He wandered from kiosk to kiosk, feigning approving looks at many trite trinkets and baubles, but then stopped at one table, his eyes locked on a square piece of whitened bone.

"You fancy the ivory?" said the chubby merchant dressed in the white robes and colorful vestments common in the southern deserts. "Very rare. Very rare! From the great beasts of Chult!"

Regis moved his hand toward the block, but paused and looked to the merchant for permission. The man nodded eagerly.

Regis rolled the block around his hands, the feel bringing him to another place and time.

"Ivory from the jungles," the merchant proclaimed.

But Regis knew better. "Trout bone," he corrected. "From the northern lakes."

The merchant started to argue, but Regis fixed him with a look that brooked no debate. The halfling knew this material intimately, and just holding it now brought his thoughts careening back to the banks of Maer Dualdon in Icewind Dale.

"How much?" he asked, for he needed to have this piece. His gaze roamed the table and out to nearby tents. He had some items on his housebreaker harness, small-tipped knives and tiny files, that would suffice for many of the cuts, but he would need a true carving knife, he decided.

"Ivory," the merchant insisted. "Five pieces of gold."

"Knucklehead trout bone," Regis corrected, "and I will give you two."

"Two and twenty silver!"

"Two and five," said Regis. "It is only impatience that makes me offer that, as I will be along the Sword Coast soon enough, traveling north, where the material is plentiful."

"You are a carver then?"

Regis nodded. "I was."

"Was? When you were a child?" the man said with a laugh, and Regis joined in, reminding himself silently that he wore the body of a young halfling, barely an adult.

"You make something pretty and I will sell it for you, yes?" the merchant asked, taking the coin and handing over the block. "You will find me here—I will sell your wares, sixty-forty!"

"Seventy-thirty."

"Sixty-one."

"Seventy-one!" Regis said, more than matching the merchant's zest, his halfling eyes sparkling. This was all about the arguing, he knew—the bargaining was worth more to these merchants than the extra coin they sometimes gained or saved.

"Ahaha!" said the merchant. "Sixty-five then, but you must promise to be quiet so my other vendors will not carve me into something not so pretty, yes?"

"Spider Pericolo Topolino," the young halfling introduced himself with a slight bow.

"Adi Abba Adidas," said the merchant with a much more flowery dip. They shook hands and the merchant patted the halfling hard on the shoulder. "We will do very much good business, yes!" he declared.

Spider moved around the tents, always politely feigning interest in this or that. He walked with the air of importance and confidence, one gloved hand always resting on the sparkling hilt of his magnificent rapier, the other ever-ready to tip his beret.

Across the road, following directions Adi had given him, he found a kiosk that held many herbs of interest to him. He had no intention of giving up his alchemy training, after all, particularly with a small still and other needed alchemy items safely tucked away in his magical belt pouch. To Regis's delight, the merchant herbalist also had several scrolls for sale, details for various concoctions Regis did not know, including a recipe for a potion of healing.

That lightened his supply of coin considerably, of course, but Regis left with a lighter step and a sincere grin. Yes, this day was moving along splendidly, all the more so because it had brought him a reprieve from the annoying Kermillon and Yoger.

That thought almost was prophetic for coming around the corner of one row of tents, Regis spotted the drivers talking to a pair of scruffy-looking fellows, a one-eyed dwarf and a tall man dressed in clothes that might have once been fine but had seen far too much of the open road. The tall man had long black hair and a thin mustache, with golden earrings on both ears. Regis thought he'd look more in place on a pirate ship sailing the Sword Coast than here at Boareskyr Bridge.

Not quite sure what to make of the parlay, if there was anything at all to it, Regis ducked back out of sight. He felt a bit uneasy when he saw Kermillon hand over a small purse to the tall man, at the same time as Yoger held out his hand, palm down, just above his waist level, as if describing someone of about Regis's height.

"Probably nothing," he told himself, scurrying back across the road to the more fashionable tents.

Soon after, full of the sounds and smells and the bickering of the auctions, he had forgotten all about it and once more realized the fine mood that so befit his current persona and dress. He bought no more, though he showed interest in many items at many different kiosks, and he entertained offers of his own as various merchants sought to purchase his wondrous beret—although they didn't know how wondrous it might be, Regis silently mused—or mostly, inquired about his rapier.

"Five thousand pieces of gold!" one woman offered, pointing to the weapon without ever having even held it.

"Good madam," Regis replied, "it may be no more than an unbalanced stick bedecked with imperfect stones!"

The woman smiled at him and shook her head knowingly. "I know a stone," she said, and she held forth her hand.

Regis considered it for a moment, then gave a little shrug and drew out the blade, graciously handing it over.

The woman took it and whipped it around gracefully—she knew how to handle it, the halfling realized, and that thought shook him a bit as he realized his vulnerability. But no, he told himself, this was an honest market, and she would not skewer him.

The woman handed back the blade, nodding. "I had thought my offer generous," she said. "Perhaps not."

"Indeed," said Regis, replacing the rapier inside his belt loop at his left hip, after performing a couple of practiced moves himself.

"It is worth that ornamentally alone," said the woman. "Those are perfect gems."

"You have a good eye."

"It keeps me thick with coin. Ten thousand, then?"

Regis smiled, tipped his cap and shook his head, but politely.

"Fifteen!" she said, "for I know your secret. The blade is powerfully magicked."

"Indeed," Regis agreed. He wasn't sure of the dweomer upon the rapier, for he hadn't much used it outside of simple practice. He had sensed nothing unusual in the blade, unlike his strange and powerful dagger, to be sure, but the rapier seemed far lighter than it should have been and struck with tremendous effect, its fine tip boring through most armor with ease.

"Sentimental value," he answered, graciously kissing her hand before starting away.

He had barely gone a dozen strides when another vendor hailed him. "Here, then," called the merchant, and Regis looked up, then fell back a step reflexively at the sight of the vendor, a one-eyed dwarf standing before a large tent.

The hairs on the back of Regis's neck stood up as he recalled his earlier view of this one—now only coincidentally hailing him? He thought of running away, or of politely responding from afar and slipping off into the bustle of the marketplace.

"That's what the old Regis would do," he whispered to himself, as he approached the waving dwarf.

"Sure that a little one as finely cut as yerself ain't thinking o' sleeping in the wagon, then!"

"I hadn't thought of it at all, good fellow," Regis replied. "But then, I have slept in the wagons these last days, have I not? Indeed, all the way from Suzail. And in an open boat for tendays before that."

"Yer clothes look none the worse for wear, eh?"

"New clothes, some," Regis answered.

"Well, put 'em in a bed tonight, then," said the dwarf. "Got many open, I do—them drivers are pinchin' tighter, I say!—and I'll put ye up on the copper."

Regis knew it was a trap, of course, and again his instincts told him to just walk away. But again he reminded himself that he wasn't that halfling anymore, shying from trouble, or in this case, from a likely fight. He thought of his many lessons with Donnola, and of the years he had spent training his body for a situation just such as this.

He wouldn't be any good to Catti-brie and Drizzt if he was killed, he reminded himself, and he wavered.

So I won't be killed, Spider Pericolo Topolino stubbornly determined. "The copper, you say? And pray tell how many coppers you might be looking for, good Mister . . . ?"

"Tinderkeg," the greasy dwarf replied. "Mister Tinderkeg at yer service, Mister . . . ?"

"Topolino. Spider Pericolo Topolino."

"Aye, but that's a mouthful o' i's an' o's, haha!"

"How many?"

"What?"

"How many coppers for a bed, Mister Tinderkeg?"

"Oh, yeah, that." The one-eyed dwarf paused and seemed at a loss for a bit, as if he was only then calculating an answer—yet another clear hint to Regis that it was more than coincidence that had brought him together with this particular dwarf, at this particular time.

"Just a few, then," Tinderkeg stuttered. "Whatever good Mister Perico . . . Perica . . . er, yerself, can spare."

Regis reached into his pouch and pulled out a few coins, silver and copper, and handed them over. He looked to the west, where the sun was very low now, long shadows darkening the kiosks as the merchants began to close up their wares for the night.

"Show me to my bed, then," he bade the dwarf. "It has been a long and dirty road."

"Dirty, eh? Well, I can draw ye a bath for a few copper more," said the dwarf. "And I'll get the water from the east side of the bridge, eh!"

That last reference almost slipped by Regis, who hadn't yet looked into the river Winding Water, but he recalled some tales of this place that he had heard soon after the Time of Troubles. According to some bards who had performed in Mithral Hall, the water upstream of the Boareskyr Bridge was clear, but downstream, below the bridge, the flow was foul indeed, the result of a battle between gods, it was said. Regis didn't recall the full fable of it, but whatever magic had soiled the Winding Water beyond Boareskyr had brought about an oft-heard curse in these parts of, "Go drink from the west side of the bridge!"

The halfling almost declined the dwarf's offer, but quickly changed his mind, seeing an opportunity to turn the tables on his would-be assailants. No dwarf, certainly not this smelly fellow, would volunteer to draw a bath for anyone, and especially not for such a pittance, considering the labor involved.

But what better way to get a victim away from his weapons and armor than to catch him by surprise in a tub of water?

"Yes, a bath would well suit me," Regis said, handing over some more coin. "And do throw some hot stones about the tub, good fellow, that I might ease the ache from my road-weary bones. I think I'll take a last quick look at some of the wares about, and will return in short order to retire."

And with that, he went off into the marketplace, resisting the urge to assume yet another identity with his hat, hard though it was.

"So ye come to pay visits and a beer for a tale!" Regis sang, and he splashed his hand around the water in the tub beside him. "Well we'll take yer wishes, a song for an ale! And if ye've a burner that's epic indeed, we'll toss out the hops and give ye a mead!"

He couldn't remember any more of the words, so he hummed instead, occasionally throwing out a syllable or two that sounded rather Dwarvish in inflection. And he kept splashing his hand around, trying to make it sound to anyone outside the curtain as if he were actually in the tub.

Sure enough, the curtain flew aside suddenly and a tall man with a thin mustache and long black hair rushed in, saber raised for a strike.

Regis lifted his hand crossbow and shot him in the chest. "You look like a bad pirate," he said as the man fell away. In behind the stumbling fellow came Tinderkeg, leaping forward with a mighty swing of his heavy hammer.

Regis dropped his hand crossbow, drew forth his rapier, and jumped back in the same movement. He came forward almost immediately and stabbed behind the blow, scoring a hit on the dwarf's arm. His rapier tip didn't fully penetrate, though, for this one was heavily armored, but the dwarf did indeed yelp and fall back.

Regis drew out his dirk, though he didn't know how much good it would do him here; certainly he wouldn't try to block or catch that huge hammer with it!

On came Tinderkeg furiously, driving the halfling back with another wild swing. Again the dwarf came in short of his mark, but this time smashed the weapon into the side of the tub, smashing the wood, and the water rushed out.

Tinderkeg tore the hammer free, splintering more of the planks, and whipped it across again, then back the way it had come, left-to-right before the halfling.

Seeing the tall man rising behind the dwarf, Regis knew that he had to move fast. He reversed his grip on the three-bladed dirk and quick-stepped to Tinderkeg's left—and how he quick-stepped! The prism on his ring lit up as he started the movement and he felt its magic within him suddenly, along with an imparted thought: "warp step." Indeed, it seemed to Regis as if time or distance or perhaps both had warped to his favor in that instant, the dwarf turning far too slowly to keep up with his movement as he bolted behind Tinderkeg's left shoulder.

Not sure of what was happening, but certainly not about to surrender such an opportunity, Regis drove his dagger out behind him, hard into the dwarf's back. It bit in through a seam in the armor and dived deep into the dwarf's flesh, and Regis turned as Tinderkeg turned, the dwarf lurching and reaching behind himself in pain.

All of those hours standing in a door jamb, reading his alchemy books while practicing with his rapier, brought on the halfling's next movement without him even thinking about it, his right arm snapping forward, the tip of his thin blade perfectly aimed.

"Ah, ye blinded me!" Tinderkeg screamed, leaping back and dropping his hammer, both his hands slapping over his one eye. He dropped his hands almost at once, blood and ichor streaming from the stabbed eye, and shook his head weirdly, as if only then understanding his understatement.

"Ye killed me," he corrected, and he fell over dead, face first to the floor.

Regis didn't see it, for he was fast at work against the second murderer, and this one was no novice with the blade, the halfling quickly realized. He noted the pinpoint of blood on the man's chest, just below the collar of his shirt. Regis had scored a solid hit indeed with the hand crossbow, but as he had feared, the drow poison had apparently lost most of its efficacy in the months since he had left Delthuntle. This one's movements showed no sign of sluggishness, Regis recognized to his horror, his rapier working frantically to deflect the flurry of saber strikes.

He could hardly keep up. Even when he got his feet properly aligned, front foot pointing, trailing left foot perpendicular, he could barely match the tall man's movements, and certainly couldn't match his opponent's reach.

He mentally called to his ring again, looking for a bit of magic, but it wasn't ready for another maneuver quite yet, he could sense.

He batted the thrusting saber to the left and rolled his rapier over it, thinking to stab for the tall man's hand. But his opponent was ready, and disengaged almost as soon as Regis's blade struck the flat of the saber. The riposte came hard, right for the halfling's face.

Regis yelped and threw his left hand up and across, catching the saber between its main blade and the one catch prod.

The one catch prod?

Regis didn't understand as he noted the dirk, with only one of its jade snake catch blades showing. As he turned the saber out, he noticed the second jade serpent, and thought for a moment that it had magically curled down around his hand to secure his grip.

He yelped again, though, and much louder and with more fear, when he realized that the second snake was detached altogether! Detached and alive on his hand!

The tall man bulled forward, throwing the halfling backward, and out of sheer desperation, Regis stabbed his dirk hand forward and flung the small snake free. The halfling tumbled backward to the floor as the serpent flew, and he and his opponent both cried out when it landed on the tall man's blouse. Hardly slowing, the snake slithered up fast, ahead of the man's slapping hands and up to his neck.

And there the tiny thing—no longer than Regis's forearm—wrapped around the tall man's throat front to back, and when the ruffian reached to grab at it, he was tugged backward suddenly, arched over as if someone were behind him, choking him with a garrote.

A cold sensation flooded through Regis then, a profound and deathly chill.

And he saw a face leering at him from over the tall man's shoulder, a withered face, a dead man's face, the face of a ghost or a lich—Ebonsoul! Wide-eyed, the halfling cracked his boots against the floor and backstepped furiously. Regis couldn't breathe, and neither, of course, could the tall man, who dropped his blade and grabbed at the snake with both hands, struggling mightily, his eyes bulging.

And the leering dead face seemed to be laughing, puffs of cold steam coming out of its mouth.

Then, with a burst of rolling gray smoke, the specter was gone.

The tall man fell over, quite dead, the snake lying limply now across his throat.

"Collect yourself," Regis whispered through gasps. "Compose." He pulled himself to a kneeling position, then glanced at his dirk. The one catch blade remained, and across the hilt to where the other had been, he saw the bud of a snake's head, just beginning to sprout.

It would grow anew, he understood, much as the prism ring on his hand would recharge its magic. It was the magic of the blade that had slain the bad pirate, not Ebonsoul, though likely this had been the lich's own dagger, Regis figured as he came to understand its value and power.

He went to his two enemies to ensure that they were dead, and relieved them of their coins, gems, and jewelry in the process. He prodded the serpent with his dirk, even rolled it over, but there was no life left in it.

He looked at the weapon once more, and it seemed to him as if the second blade had already grown a tiny bit more.

"It's a magic item, not a curse," he told himself. He recalled Wigglefingers's claim that the dirk had other powers, and more importantly, that it had no sentience or ego, as so many powerfully enchanted weapons were known to possess. He thought of the leering specter and was glad of that.

The halfling took a deep breath and steadied himself. He had fancied himself a hero, had determined that he would be one this time around, that he would be a valuable member of the Companions of the Hall and not a tag-along to be protected. He nodded, looked to his weapons, and looked at his handiwork.

This was what it meant to be a hero. He wouldn't shy from a fight, and he darned well meant to win them.

He nodded again, reminding himself that this fight was only half over.

The finely dressed halfling strode confidently around the wagons and into the light of the blazing campfire. He grinned back at the stupefied expressions of the two men—of course they were shocked, since they had paid to have him murdered, and yet, here he was!

As he walked past the burly Yoger, Regis pulled his hand crossbow out from under his traveling cloak and shot the man in the face, then dropped the weapon. It jangled down by his legs, for he had tethered it to his belt. With a flick of his wrist, Regis tossed a small serpent at the groaning man. It bounced against his belly and magically caught there, then slithered up fast, before the fool could begin to react.

Yoger cried out, then began to gasp and choke, but Regis never looked at him. Regis just kept walking toward Kermillon, his rapier and dirk still in his belt. Kermillon grabbed a small log from near the fire and began shouting out, warning the halfling back.

But Regis kept coming.

He heard Yoger fall over behind him, thrashing and kicking. He heard others from the nearby wagons calling out, confused, but he kept his focus on Kermillon, who waved the log threateningly.

Just as he stepped into range, just as the man began to swing, Regis activated his prism ring and warp-stepped past. Regis knew what to expect from it this time, and he leaped and twisted as he moved, spinning around. He landed just behind and to the side of Kermillon, and with his rapier in hand. He promptly stabbed up under the man's ear, puncturing the skin, but just barely.

"Kindly drop the log," he said, and when Kermillon hesitated, he stabbed the rapier in a bit more.

"Oh, please, Sir Spider!" Kermillon gasped, leaning over away from the pressing rapier tip.

"Kneel," Regis ordered, and Kermillon slumped to his knees.

Regis looked past him then, to Yoger who continued to thrash and kick and squirm for all his life, but to no avail. Others came into the firelight just as Yoger went straight out, his legs twitching in the spasms of death.

"Here now, what?" another driver called to Regis and Kermillon. Others ran to Yoger.

"What's this about then, little one?" another man demanded.

"Tell them," Regis said to Kermillon.

The man said nothing.

"Tell them or I will slide my blade into your head, and explain my actions to them while I am wiping your brains off onto your shirt."

Drivers, passengers, and merchants from the marketplace alike began to gather, forming a wall around the small fire and the combatants.

"You best be talking," one demanded.

"Aye, and we best like your explaining!" another added.

Regis prodded his blade and Kermillon gave a little cry.

"Speak truthfully and I will lobby for leniency," Regis said.

"I don't know . . . ," Kermillon started.

"Two dead across the way!" announced a newcomer, a halfling dressed for the road and for battle it seemed. He walked into the light, a trio of other halflings similarly adorned right behind him. "Stuffings is dead in his tent," the halfling went on. "Stuffings and the tall one. It would appear as if they tried to take advantage of a guest this night, and would I be right in assuming that we have that guest standing right before us?"

"Stuffings?" Regis asked.

"Stuffantle Tinderkeg to any who cared," the halfling replied. "Just Stuffings to all the rest."

"Aye, he coaxed me into his lair with the promise of a bed and a bath, and on coin from these two." He prodded a bit and Kermillon yelped and leaned to the side. "Do tell them."

"On your life, driver," the other halfling said and he drew out a gleaming short sword.

"We did! We did!" Kermillon babbled. "But not to kill him! No, just to rob . . . and this one!" He fell away as the rapier was withdrawn, and turned back, poking a finger Regis's way. "This one! All boasts and endless coin! Ah, but he's a rat, I tell you! Insufferable rat!"

Regis laughed and snapped his rapier across, taking the man's poking finger before tucking it away in his belt as Kermillon curled up on the ground, howling in pain.

"Well, this one's dead," said a man over by Yoger.

"Three less murderers to worry about," Regis said, and he looked at Kermillon as he added, "And likely, soon to be four."

Some of the other drivers came in and grabbed up Kermillon and dragged him away.

Such scenes were not uncommon in the markets around Boareskyr Bridge, and the interest died away quickly, the onlookers moving off, some discussing which would inherit Kermillon's wagon and goods, while others, merchants, talking about the prime tent that would now be open if the one-eyed dwarf was really deceased.

The quartet of halflings came over to Regis, though, the leader bowing before him gracefully. "You handle yourself well, Master Topolino," he said.

"You know my name," Regis replied. He locked gazes with the halfling, while quietly lifting the hand crossbow and deftly slipping it away into his magical belt pouch.

"Knew it before we ever met you, though didn't know you wore it," the other replied.

Regis looked at him curiously.

"Grandfather Pericolo," said one of the three behind him. "I have been to Delthuntle on many occasions and know him well."

"Ah, but where are my manners?" said the leader. "I know your name, but have not offered my own. I am Doregardo of the Grinning Ponies." He bowed low.

"The Grinning Ponies?" Regis asked, trying not to laugh.

"Named for our mounts and the year," answered the one who had claimed knowledge of the Grandfather.

Regis thought about it for a moment, then realized the reference to 1481, the Year of the Grinning Halfling.

"And I am Showithal Terdidy," the halfling went on.

"He rode with the Kneebreakers," Doregardo explained, and Regis shrugged, not getting the reference.

"Ah, you've not been to the Bloodstone Lands, then," said Showithal.

"Impiltur once, but only for a season," Regis answered.

"If ever you return, venture to Damara and know that you'll have friends in the famed Kneebreakers."

"Kneebreakers!" the other two cheered, lifting their gloved fists into the air.

"We claim allegiance to that band, brothers in the cause," said Doregardo.

"The cause?"

Doregardo walked over and draped his hand comfortably on Regis's shoulder. "You understand the dilemma of our people, of course, always thought of as thieves, or worse, as children. But not the Kneebreakers, who ride the roads of Damara and neighboring Vaasa. When they ride through, highwaymen cower in dark holes and townsfolk take note and cheer!"

"Doregardo spoke for you here, among the merchants who have come to know and trust the Grinning Ponies well in the few months we have been together," added Showithal. "And so your side of the story was not doubted."

"Because you're like the Kneebreakers," Regis reasoned.

"We ride the Trade Way from Memnon to Waterdeep, and east and back the length of Elturgard," Doregardo explained.

Regis looked at the group, one after another. "All four?"

"Eleven of us," Doregardo explained. "And we would welcome a twelfth." He glanced over at Yoger, lying dead by the wagon. "Particularly a twelfth who can handle himself so . . . effectively."

Regis chuckled at the flattering offer. "I can hardly ride a pony," he said, for his first reaction was to politely decline.

"Easy to learn," said Showithal, and his tone sobered Regis and made it quite clear that this was neither a casual offer nor an empty one. They were serious.

"I have business in the far North," Regis said. "Do you ride as far as Luskan?"

"Waterdeep," Doregardo replied. "But we could go farther, and perhaps help you with this business of which you speak."

Regis shook his head, trying to sort it out. He had two and a half years before his appointed rendezvous.

"I am in need of sleep," he said. "Might I spend the night in your no-doubt secure camp and give you an answer in the morning?"

The halfling known as Spider awoke to the smell of cooking bacon and eggs, and with a fine rich coffee aroma drifting around his nostrils. He propped himself up on his elbows and did a quick count of the halflings moving around the encampment, quickly discerning that most of the band was in attendance.

"Well met, Master Topolino!" Doregardo greeted when he noted Regis sitting up.

"Spider," he corrected. "My name is Spider." He looked around some more, feeling quite at home and comfortable, and adventurous! "Spider of the Grinning Ponies," he said.

"Huzzah!" the halflings cheered, gloved fists rising into the air.

"I suppose I'll need a pony," Regis said.

"Plenty across the bridge," answered Doregardo.

"I've the coin to purchase one," Regis answered.

Showithal came over, bearing two plates heaped with food, and balancing a steaming mug of coffee on each.

"A gift for a tale of Delthuntle," he said, sitting on a keg near Regis's bedroll. "Tell me of Morada Topolino!"

The fact that he had referred to the house with that obscure name confirmed to Regis that he had indeed been to Delthuntle, as he had claimed. Regis nodded and took the plate and mug, and between bites told Showithal stories of deep diving and pink pearls. He thought to tell the interested halfling of the Grandfather's demise, but changed his mind. Not yet.

"Do you know of the Grandfather's primary associate?" he asked as Doregardo came over, plate in hand, to join them.

"The mustached mage?" asked Showithal.

Regis shook his head.

"Donnola," Showithal realized, and said with all the appropriate breathlessness of any male halfling thinking of that one. "Beautiful Donnola! Aye, none who have looked on that one would ever forget her!"

"Donnola!" another cried from across the camp, lifting his mug, and all joined in the toast.

"Showithal's spoken of her," Doregardo explained.

"I am sure that his words, no matter how pretty, could not do her justice," Regis replied, and he meant it, and how it stung his heart to be away from Donnola Topolino! He turned to Showithal. "If ever you return to Delthuntle, find her, I beg, and tell her that you saw me . . . Spider, and that I am well, and that I will return to her one day."

"Spider?" Doregardo said, shaking his head. "Such a curious name."

"One earned," Regis decided. "One given to me by Grandfather Pericolo himself, when I was but a small child."

"I have heard of one called Spider," another of the band said from a short distance to the side. The three turned to face the speaker, and Regis feared that he might have given away too much information. "That's you?" the other one asked. "The climber, trained in Pericolo's own home?"

Regis stared at him, unsure how to proceed.

"We've added a valuable companion here," that halfling told Showithal and Doregardo.

"We already figured as much," the leader replied.

"And one who owes you a great debt, for taking my word and speaking for me last night," said Regis.

"An easy word to take," said Doregardo. "I've had my run-ins with Stuffings many times, and I don't regret his passing." He gave a little laugh. "Did I ever congratulate you on your fine aim with that one?"

Regis thought back to the fight, to the image of his rapier tip sliding so easily through Stuffings's one good eye. He shrugged, a bit embarrassed.

The Grinning Ponies rode out soon after, Regis on a pack mule until they could procure a proper mount on the other side of Winding Water. They passed under the tree where Kermillon was hanging by the neck, and noted the gravediggers cutting four holes in the small clearing behind it.

CHAPTER 24

WEAVING

The Year of the Ageless One (1479 DR)
Luruar

THE EAGLE RODE THE UPDRAFTS OF AN INCOMING FRONT, GLIDING EASILY
to the west, and now with the hilly region known as the Crags in sight.
Beyond those rolling hills sat Luskan and the Sword Coast, Catti-brie knew,
and the mountain pass that would take her home to Icewind Dale.

Given the limitations of her magic, she expected to pass by Luskan within
a few days, and into Icewind Dale to Ten-Towns merely a tenday beyond that.

She was thinking of her more recent home, of Niraj and Kavita, and
hoping that they were all right. Had they heard of her death? Had Lady
Avelyere gone to the Desai encampment to interrogate them? Or worse, had
Avelyere punished them?

The thought unsettled Catti-brie and stole from her the peace of this
moment of high solitude. Maybe she should have stayed in Netheril to protect
her parents, she thought, to fight, and likely die, beside them if Avelyere
came calling.

Certainly die, she nodded. With that slight movement of her head, Catti-
brie noticed a strange twinge, a pressure in her limbs akin to what she felt
when executing the shapeshifting. Her vision shifted suddenly, too, as if
from eagle eyes to human, or something strange in between, and for just a
fleeting heartbeat, the sky around her darkened, then seemed backlit, and in
the moment between blue daylight and nighttime stars, she saw or imagined
a great web of giant strands enwrapping the whole world.

She didn't know what to make of it; she couldn't begin to unravel the
meaning of the strange sight or of the pressure in her limbs or the strangeness

of her vision. The world below seemed suddenly so much farther away then, and for a moment, the woman wondered if some great updraft had lifted her higher.

But no, it was an illusion, Catti-brie realized, and one facilitated by the change in her vision, back to mere human eyes.

Her shapeshift was failing!

She focused then on her arcane magic, putting her memorized levitation spell into her thoughts—but they were jumbled thoughts, and she couldn't sort through the haze. The spell wasn't making sense to her, the words weren't coming clear. Something was wrong, very wrong! The flight became strained—she could feel her wings crackling with reversion.

Normally, Catti-brie would have climbed before the reversion, giving her farther to fall, and thus more time to enact her levitation. But the words to that spell simply wouldn't come to her.

It was Lady Avelyere. The diviner had found her and was attacking her magically, dispelling her dweomers, jumbling her thoughts.

Down she sped, angling steeply, even tucking her wings in a full stoop, knowing that she had to get to the ground as quickly as possible. She noted a stand of pine trees and soared out that way while maintaining the dive.

She felt the magic evaporating and pulled up with all her strength to break her dive. It worked, but a moment later, she felt her arms, not wings, at her sides. Still some fifty feet from the ground, she began to tumble, a human again, and in a place where no human should be. She fought to recite the levitation, but couldn't remember the words in any sensible order, and hadn't the time anyway.

She crashed into a thick pine, breaking branches and limbs, bouncing down through the tangle to the lowest branch, where she caught a handhold, but only for a moment before falling free the last dozen feet, to land flat on her back on the ground, where she knew no more.

"The city is in disarray!" Rhyalle reported, bursting into the room alongside Eerika.

Lady Avelyere regarded them briefly before turning back to the window, and offered no immediate response. She could see the tumult in the streets below the Coven, with couriers running all around, no doubt delivering messages from one lord to another.

Something had happened. Something powerful and dramatic, and not just within the Coven, where they had felt the shift keenly.

"What does it mean, Lady?" Eerika dared to ask.

"We don't know what it is, so how could she answer that question?" Rhyalle scolded.

"Have you done as I asked?" Lady Avelyere asked, turning around to aim her question at Eerika. The younger woman nodded. "Then proceed."

Eerika looked to Rhyalle for support. They hadn't started their run to Avelyere's chambers together, but had met up in the wide foyer of the main building, Rhyalle returning from the streets, Eerika from the old library.

"Lady, the words do not easily form—" Eerika started.

"Try," Lady Avelyere ordered. "It is a minor dweomer."

Eerika took a deep breath, then lifted her hand up, palm upward, and began to quietly recite a spell. A few heartbeats later, a burst of light formed in her hand, glowing brightly for just a moment, then growing dimmer. Eerika lowered her hand, but the globe of light remained, hovering in the air before her.

"By the gods," Lady Avelyere breathed, and she turned back to the window, but looking up to the sky and not to the streets below. Earlier that day, the sisters had found confusion, where spells they had prepared had become jumbled and useless. If that wasn't curious enough, now Eerika, a young magic-user unskilled in the old ways, had just enacted a spell of light creation, and from an incantation a century and more thought lost to the world.

"What does it mean, Lady?" Eerika asked.

"We are a magocracy," Lady Avelyere quietly replied. "It means that we will know confusion, then we will find transition, then we will know renewed power."

The two younger women looked to each other with great concern.

"Mental agility," Lady Avelyere said to them, turning around to offer them a comforting look. "The Empire of Netheril stands above because we are wiser and more clever. We have felt such cosmic . . . curiosities, before." She nodded and motioned to the door. "Go and rest, and when you are renewed, prepare your spells anew. Let us see what tomorrow brings."

The two women bowed and departed, and Lady Avelyere turned back to her window. Something was going on here beyond her comprehension, beyond anything she had known in her life, she sensed, and feared, and hoped. The world was always in flux—her dear Parise had shared some concerns of "Cherlrigo's Darkness," had even hinted that the fabric of magic might yet grow unsteady. Yes, something was in flux, and had not Lady Avelyere herself discovered the rebirth of this favored mortal of the goddess Mielikki?

And now this confusing day, and what it would ultimately mean, Lady Avelyere could not be sure.

But whatever might come from this magical hiccup—for that was the only word she could think of to describe this day's events—Lady Avelyere meant to benefit from it.

The clever ones always did.

Painful spasms drew Catti-brie back to consciousness. She lay on the ground, blood all around, one leg bent weirdly, surely broken, and one arm throbbing, likely also broken. The sun was very low in the western sky, so she understood that she had lain there for many hours. She was lucky to be alive, she realized.

Her levitation had failed her—why hadn't she been able to recall the words and cadence of the spell? And why had her spellscar power of shapeshifting worn away so quickly?

The spinning questions brought her back to her fear that Lady Avelyere had found her, and had brought her down. She propped herself up on one elbow and looked all around, desperate, though turning her head caused her more discomfort.

Catti-brie used all of the discipline she could muster, training earned in two lifetimes, forcing aside her fears, forcing herself to focus. She thought of other incantations she had prepared, but none seemed helpful at that moment, and worse, none came clear in her thoughts. If Avelyere arrived before her, would she even be able to muster the slightest of cantrips to defend herself?

She fell back to her greatest safeguard, her most favored dweomer, and concentrated on the weather. She would bring in a storm, yes, and if any enemies appeared, she would strike them dead with powerful bolts of lightning.

She enacted the magic, so she believed, but she needed time for the clouds to gather and the storm to coalesce.

And more than that, she realized, as she began to swoon, she needed to stop her bleeding.

She began to pray, calling to the goddess for spells of healing, and to her great relief, unlike the arcane magical spells, these words, these prayers, did flow through her. She saw the light blue mist gathering at her wounded right arm, flowing from under the wide sleeve of her robe.

The spell came forth and Catti-brie felt a rush of gentle warmth, smooth as satin and decidedly comforting, flowing through her body, sweeping through her like a cresting wave and then breaking with a burst of hot energy upon her broken right arm, upon the very spellscar of the goddess whose favor had granted her this power.

With a trembling left hand, Catti-brie pulled back the sleeve of her robe. She looked upon the spellscar, the head of Mielikki's unicorn, as the mist dissipated, and she blinked repeatedly, wondering if it was a trick of the light, perhaps, or of her own light-headedness with her loss of blood. For while the scar remained, it seemed even more distinct than before, more like a tattoo now than a birthmark, a unicorn's golden horn and with the creature's head similarly outlined in gold.

Another wave of pain brought a grimace and a reminder, and Catti-brie began again her chant, asking the goddess for more. The mist came forth from the unicorn, her divine powers intact and, she thought, even more powerful than before.

She cast a third minor healing spell, and then, her thoughts clearing, brought forth a spell to heal more serious wounds, focusing her energy on her leg. She felt better immediately within the warm cocoon of the blue-bathing light, like the softest of ocean waters sweeping away the weeds. She sat up straighter, and even flexed her knee as the leg straightened out before her.

She would survive her fall. And she would likely walk again the very next day, once her divine powers had renewed, and she could enact further healing upon her battered form.

Catti-brie took a deep breath and held it, then peeled back the sleeve of her left arm.

The seven-pointed star remained, and like the unicorn head, it seemed more distinct now, like the work of an ink artist, except that its sketching was not golden, but blood red, like a web of angry veins pulsing out the marker of Mystra.

What did it mean?

Catti-brie tried to recall an arcane spell from her repertoire, but alas, like the levitation earlier, those memorized dweomers were lost to her, a jumble of nonsensical words.

On a hunch, she considered one, her favored fireball. She closed her eyes and thought back to the very first time she had cast that spell, in another body a century before, and she tried to fight her way through the incantation jumble.

Now the words sorted, and she heard her own chant, part ancient, part new, and a fiery pea appeared in her hand. She threw it out and willed it out from her, into the air and away from the trees, and there it exploded appropriately, a burgeoning fireball, and the blue tendrils of magical energies glowed around her left arm, around the symbol of the seven-pointed star.

Catti-brie stared at it and shook her head.

What could it mean?

As she continued to stare upon the spot, the flames dissipating to nothingness, something else caught her eye, and brought her more questions. She saw the first twinkles of starlight as twilight descended upon the land.

But where was her conjured storm?

She looked all around. The sky was perfectly clear. Her spell had failed, utterly.

What could it mean?

"What does it mean?" Lady Avelyere asked Lord Parise Ulfbinder the very next day. She and her minions were managing to enact some magical spells, but only barely and only selectively.

"Instability," Parise replied, and he seemed, and sounded, quite shaken, Lady Avelyere noted. "I spoke with Lord Draygo Quick this morning. It is, perhaps, as we feared."

"Explain."

The Netherese lord shook his head. "Something is upon the world—both worlds!—but there is nothing I can yet explain. The Twelve Princes have sought out the wisdom of the priests."

"The old ways? The old gods?"

"Where is your former student?" Parise asked. "You have located her?"

"Ruqiah?" Lady Avelyere held up her hands helplessly.

"You said that you did not believe her to have perished in the fire."

"No, certainly it was not her withered body that we found among the rubble."

"Then where is she?"

"Nowhere near to us, I am sure," Lady Avelyere replied. "I have magically surveyed all of Netheril—"

"West," Parise interrupted. "Search in the west. The Sword Coast. Luskan. Icewind Dale."

Lady Avelyere looked at him curiously. "What do you know?"

"Of course I did my own research and inquiries after you came to me with that most interesting tale," he answered. "A lone mountain, you described."

"It could be anywhere."

"It could be Icewind Dale."

Lady Avelyere shrugged, for the name meant nothing to her.

"A stretch of barren tundra through the Spine of the World Mountains north of the city of Luskan," Parise explained. "Few live there, fewer still travel there, but it was once the home of Drizzt Do'Urden, Bruenor Battlehammer, and his adopted daughter, Catti-brie."

"As was Mithral Hall . . ."

"And the towns of Icewind Dale are built in the shadow of a singular mountain, rising from the tundra."

Lady Avelyere licked her lips and digested the news. It could be.

"Direct your search between Shade Enclave and Icewind Dale," Parise commanded. "You will likely find this missing girl."

"And then?"

"Watch her. Do not return her to Shade Enclave. Let us learn what we may, but safely from afar."

"We remain five years from her appointed meeting," Lady Avelyere reminded him.

"A speck of time in the cosmic calendar. But more than enough time for clever Lady Avelyere and her Coven to find this wayward child, yes?"

The woman nodded.

"The libraries of Shade Enclave are being opened to all practitioners," Parise added as Lady Avelyere turned to go. "We must once again adapt our magic, it would seem."

"The old ways?"

The lord shrugged. "Who can know?"

"Ruqiah, perhaps," Lady Avelyere quipped, and she shook her head and smiled resignedly, helplessly, and Parise responded in kind.

Catti-brie felt much better the next day, even before she bathed herself once more in the healing magic of Mielikki. Her arcane spells remained a jumble and she discovered that she could barely understand the delicate inflections of the incantations outlined in her spellbook. She felt as if everything magical had shifted several degrees, with different pieces going in different directions. She couldn't make any sense of it.

"So be it," she said, and she walked out from under the pine tree boughs that had served as her bedroom. She looked at the rising sun, then all around, to the distant Crags and north, where sat the high peaks of the towering Spine of the World, though she could not see them from this vantage.

She considered her approximate location and the year and season. She had plenty of time to get to Icewind Dale—years even—so perhaps a change of course would be in order here.

"Waterdeep?" she whispered. The lords of that greatest of cities would certainly be investigating the strange happenings—but how might she, a dirty girl from another part of the world, garner any information from those haughty ones? For she was not Princess Catti-brie of Mithral Hall any longer, but merely little Ruqiah of the Desai, and no one of note.

She thought of Candlekeep, the famed library along the coast south of Waterdeep. If any in all the Realms were going to figure out what was going on here, it would be the sages of that most learned of places. But again, how might she gain entrance to such a place?

She lifted her arms and shook them, her sleeves falling back. Her spellscars? Would they get her in?

But they didn't even look like scars any longer. Any skilled tattooist along the Sword Coast could create the markings inside Catti-brie's forearms.

The woman blew out a deep breath and called upon the spellscars then, thinking to shapeshift and be on her way, whichever way she might decide. Catti-brie closed her eyes and focused on the markings, willing herself to again become a great eagle.

Nothing happened.

She opened her eyes and looked down at her arms. No mist began to form, no hint of magic to be found.

She couldn't shapeshift. She couldn't become an eagle, a mouse, or a wolf. The notion struck her profoundly. She remained hundreds of miles from Icewind Dale, and now, so suddenly, the road appeared much more perilous and uncertain.

Catti-brie forced herself to calm down, and rationally played through her options. Even without the shapeshift, and without the storm calling and lightning bolts, she was a disciple of Mielikki, with powers divine. And she was a mage, trained in Silverymoon, trained in Shade Enclave. She was not a lost little child on the open road. She was Catti-brie, who had passed this way before, in another life. She could fight and she could enact magic both divine and arcane. She glanced around, then began to climb one of the pines for a better view. Her injured leg ached for the effort and the deep bending, despite the magic she had enacted upon it.

She thought back to the previous day, when she had been flying on high. Just to the west of her lay a road, she recalled, and she nodded, for she knew that road, the Long Road, it had once been named.

And she smiled as she considered where that road might take her, and what she might learn when she got to that particular destination.

She found an appropriate length of wood to use as a walking stick and set out determinedly. She was Catti-brie. She had returned by the will of Mielikki and for a great purpose, and she would not falter.

She made the road, or what was left of it—for now it was an old and little-used trail—that afternoon and turned to the north. Her leg ached, but she did not stop and did not slow.

The sunlight began to fade, the night descending upon the land, and Catti-brie began to search for an appropriate campsite. She moved off the road, up the side of a small hillock. She had just begun to construct a fire pit, complete with rocks around its edges to shield flames from distant eyes, when the sky to the north lit up suddenly with a great burst of orange flames.

Catti-brie rushed to the northern edge of the hillock and peered off into the distance.

A lightning bolt split the night sky. A fireball followed, and then a star-burst of multicolored sparks and flares of such magnificence that it made the woman giggle in appreciation.

She heard the distant sound of the explosions a few moments later, along with what sounded like a cacophony of cheers.

Another fireball ignited, this one lower to the ground, illuminating the land below to reveal a large mansion set upon a hill.

"Longsaddle!" Catti-brie cried, and it wasn't so far. All thoughts of camping flew from her then, and she started off with renewed determination.

The night darkened around her, the Long Road seemed in places little more than a wagon rut, but the explosions continued in the north, guiding her way, and soon after she entered the village of Longsaddle, home of the Harpells, a place she had visited in her previous life on several occasions.

All of the townsfolk were outside, it seemed, hundreds of people cheering and dancing at the spectacle on the hill, the spectacle on the grounds of the Ivy Mansion, home of the Harpells, where the wizards plied their trade in a grand celebration, it seemed, throwing fire and lightning and all sorts of spectacular dweomers up into the air in a great and splendid display.

"What is it?" Catti-brie asked a young couple she encountered at the base of the hill.

"None seem to know," the man answered. "But our Harpell wizards appear to be in a festive and fine mood this evening!"

Catti-brie moved around the gathering, gaining the road that led up to the gate of the house on the hill. It appeared as no more than a ten-stride reach of fence, unattached on either end, but Catti-brie knew better. For stretching out from either side was an invisible wall encircling the whole of the hill and mansion.

She arrived at the gate and called out, but none heard or reacted. She could see them, then, wizards atop the hill, many on the mansion's roof, cheering and throwing their spells, one after another.

Catti-brie called out again, and when that didn't work, the woman began to whisper a spell of her own. Up in the air above flew the fiery pea, erupting into a fireball of her own making.

The people below her cried out and fell back in surprise—and fear, no doubt. And from above her came shouts and warnings, and the wizards scrambled. In short order, she was confronted by the town guard from below, and soon after that, by a group of Harpells from the other side of the gate.

"Who are you, who throws magic unbidden in Longsaddle?" one wiry old mage in rumpled robes asked.

In response, Catti-brie lifted her arms and shook them, her sleeves falling clear of the markings. "A friend," she said. "Though I've not been here in many years."

The wiry old mage came closer and looked her over. "I don't know you."

"No," she agreed, shaking her head. "But I know of you, of the Harpells, at least, and some once knew me as a friend. When I tell you my tale, you will understand."

"Go on, then!" he demanded.

Catti-brie glanced over her shoulder at the town guard, then back at the mage doubtfully.

"Come along then!" demanded a man behind her, but as he approached, the wiry wizard held up his hand.

"Once I knew of Harkle," Catti-brie dared to admit, hoping that name from yesteryear would spark some recognition. "Once I knew of Bidderdoo."

"The Bidderdoos?" the man behind her gasped, and fell back, shaking his head.

Catti-brie glanced at him curiously, not quite understanding the reference, or why he had used the plural form of the name. She shook her head and looked back to the mage, to find him already fumbling with the gate. He and the others waved her in and escorted her up the hill.

"I am Penelope," the middle-aged woman introduced herself, coming into a comfortable room where the others had left Catti-brie, bidding her to be at ease. Catti-brie started to rise from her chair, but the older woman waved at her to remain seated and took the seat opposite.

"Ca—Ru—" Catti-brie started to respond, but she had to pause and laugh at herself, for what should have been a simple greeting apparently was not. To use her real name would be to open potential questions much larger than her arrival here at the Ivy Mansion, and to use her Desai name might well make it easier for Lady Avelyere to regain her trail.

"Delly," she replied with an inviting smile, borrowing another name from her distant past. "Delly Curtie."

"Well met, then, Ca-ru-delly," Penelope Harpell replied, smiling knowingly.

"Delly Curtie," Catti-brie said flatly.

"And what brings Delly Curtie to Longsaddle, pray tell?"

"Your display of magic this night, mostly. I was on the road and noted it, and since I, too, am practiced in the Art—"

"Then you already knew of Longsaddle, no doubt, and needed no fire and lightning display to lure you here."

Catti-brie stared hard at the woman, who returned the look. She started to concoct some explanation, but realized that she was only digging herself deeper with her lies, beneath the careful gaze of Penelope. These were the Harpells, Catti-brie reminded herself, goodly folk, if quite . . . eccentric. Ever had the Harpells been allies of the Companions of the Hall, and of Mithral Hall. Indeed, they had come running to Bruenor's aid when the drow had invaded the dwarf tunnels.

"I was bound for the coast," Catti-brie said. "But recent events slowed me, and perplexed me, I admit."

"Do go on."

"Changes," Catti-brie replied. "With magic." She shrugged and threw in her chips, once again pulling up the sleeves of her robe to reveal her two spellscars, now seeming as different colored tattoos.

Penelope's eyes narrowed as she stared at the woman's marked forearms, and she leaned out of her seat and moved closer, even reaching down to turn Catti-brie's arm a bit to get a better look at the seven-pointed star on the left arm.

"What artist did this?" Penelope asked.

"No artist."

Penelope looked her in the eye once more. "They are spellscars?"

"Or were."

Penelope stood straight and glanced around. She moved to the door and closed it, then walked back to stand before Catti-brie. She hiked up her robe and turned sideways, revealing a marking on her left hip, a blob of brown and blue discolored skin.

"Would that my own had taken a more attractive appearance, as have yours!" she said. "You did nothing to touch up the scar?"

"It only just happened, when I was alone on the road."

"And what were you doing alone on the road?"

"Heading for the coast, as I told you."

"These are dangerous lands for anyone to be traveling alone, even a mage."

"I was flying," Catti-brie admitted. "Through the power of the scars, I was flying as a bird. And then I was falling."

Penelope sucked in her breath.

"What is happening?" Catti-brie asked.

"Are you going to tell me your real name, Delly Curtie?"

"You would not believe me, so no, not yet. In time, perhaps, when we have both come to a place of greater trust."

Penelope walked around her chair. "You mentioned the Bidderdoos, I am told."

"Bidderdoo," Catti-brie corrected.

"A Bidderdoo, then. Which?"

Catti-brie gave a confused little laugh. "Bidderdoo," she replied. "Bidderdoo Harpell."

"There is no Bidderdoo Harpell."

"There was. And what are Bidderdoos, then?"

"Bidderdoo has been dead for a century," Penelope answered. "His legacy lives on, in the forest around Longsaddle."

Catti-brie thought about that for a few moments. "Werewolves," she whispered.

"Yes, the Bidderdoos, so we call them. The townsfolk are quite afraid of them, but in truth, they guard the town and do us no harm. I am surprised that you were not confronted on the road, coming in at night so suspiciously, as you were. But then, perhaps the Bidderdoos were enjoying our celebration."

"It was quite extraordinary," Catti-brie agreed.

"An extraordinary display for exciting times," Penelope admitted. "Strange things have been happening all across the Ivy Mansion."

Catti-brie laughed at that understatement. "The reputation of the Harpells precedes you, good lady."

Penelope paused as if to consider her reply, then couldn't suppress her own grin. "Yes, I expect it does. A well-earned reputation." She sat in the chair again, her expression growing serious.

"How could you know of Bidderdoo Harpell? And you mentioned another at the gate."

"Harkle."

"How could you know of Harkle?"

"I was raised in Mithral Hall."

Penelope sat up straight and took note. "Raised among the Battlehammer dwarves? And you learned the ways of magic?"

"I am fairly trained," said Catti-brie. "No archmage, certainly!"

"I saw your fireball," Penelope replied. "You favor evocation?"

"I like blowing things up," Catti-brie said with a wry grin.

"Spoken like a Harpell!"

"I like blowing things up when I'm not standing next to those things I blow up," Catti-brie clarified, and Penelope laughed aloud and slapped her knee.

"Maybe not a true Harpell, then," she replied. "Tell me, have you any other spells in your repertoire this day?"

Catti-brie thought for a moment, then nodded. "A fan of flames," she said, tapping her thumbs together and waggling her fingers.

Penelope looked around, then motioned for Catti-brie to follow her to a clear spot in the room, where she might enact burning hands without setting the place on fire. "One moment," the older woman said, then left the room, returning a short time later with two others, a man around the same age as Penelope and one much older.

"My husband, Dowell, and Kipper Harpell, the oldest of the clan."

Both nodded cordially, and Dowell unrolled a parchment, holding it up before Kipper with a nod to Penelope.

Penelope motioned to the empty space before Catti-brie and bade her, "Please proceed with your spell."

Catti-brie lifted her hands and began the incantation.

"Louder, please, dear child," Kipper requested.

Catti-brie cleared her throat and went at it again, and a few moments later, a fan of flames spread out from her fingers, a solid dweomer, if not overpowering. She turned to regard the three witnesses, to find them all grinning, and Kipper nodding.

"And look at her arm!" Penelope said, noting the blue mist gathered around Catti-brie's left forearm. She rushed over and tugged Catti-brie back to the others, pulling back the sleeve to show the seven-starred marking.

"What?" Catti-brie asked.

"Mystra," Kipper said reverently and bowed his head.

"It is true, then," Dowell added, grinning widely.

"What?" Catti-brie asked again.

"Your spellcasting," Penelope started to explain, but Kipper cut her short.

"You drew your power from the old ways," he said. "Is this how you were trained?"

Catti-brie didn't know how to respond. It was how she had been trained, but in another life. In this one, not so. "What does it mean?" she asked, deflecting the other's question.

"The Weave, girl," Kipper asked, "do you feel it?"

Catti-brie thought back to the moment when her spellscar magic had failed, that flash in the sky, like an eclipse, like a web.

Like the Weave of Magic.

She looked at Penelope, her expression quite dumbfounded. "Your celebration," she managed to whisper, and she put it all together. "Has the effect of the Spellplague ended?"

Penelope hugged her suddenly and unexpectedly. "So we pray," she whispered. "So we pray."

Catti-brie glanced out the window of her room at the Ivy Mansion months later, looking back to the east, toward Netheril. Her spellscar powers, the shapeshifting and storm-calling, like those of the other marked wizards at the Ivy Mansion, had not returned, and by all indications, the Spellplague was indeed no more. At long last.

But what did that mean for Niraj and Kavita? Or, Catti-brie wondered, for Avelyere and the Coven?

The Harpells seemed quite overjoyed by the news, even though they had all begun retraining. The library of the Ivy Mansion dated far back before the Spellplague, of course, and so they were well-equipped for this strange shift of magic. And when she thought about it, Catti-brie realized that she was better equipped than almost any! For she had been trained in the old ways initially, after all, and could any other mages in the Realms, other than elves and drow, say the same?

A few, she realized, for the Harpells had not fully abandoned their previous ways.

There were other differences of note between herself and the other wizards around her, and Catti-brie could only attribute it to the special days she had spent in Iruladoon. When she called upon her magic, her spellscars reacted, but that was not true for Penelope or the few others similarly scarred. Even for Catti-brie, the reaction seemed a cosmetic thing only, for her magic was not exceptionally potent—indeed, were she to engage in a spell battle against Penelope, Catti-brie was certain that she would be obliterated in short order.

Still, Catti-brie had a lot to teach the Harpells, even as they invited her to stay on and train under their masters. She was more adept at converting the spells back to the old ways than any, and Kipper and the others truly appreciated her efforts in that regard, and shared some of their best dweomers with her in return.

So for the fourth time since Catti-brie had moved from her warrior ways to that of a wizard, she had found a new school. First she had trained with the great Lady Alustriel of Silverymoon, then with Niraj and Kavita, then at the Coven, and now here at the Ivy Mansion. What student of the arcane arts could ever ask for more? She had been fortunate indeed!

"No, the fifth time," she said aloud, correcting the thought as she recalled her greatest instructor, the one from whom she received her divine abilities. She looked down at her right forearm, at the unicorn head, and heard again the magical song of Mielikki.

The young woman nodded determinedly, thinking of her coming reunion with her beloved Drizzt, and thinking, too, of the purpose of her return. What might be in store for her, she wondered? Might the demon queen actually come hunting for Drizzt, and there to battle the avatar of Mielikki? What might she do in the face of such bared power? Would it be a proxy fight, perhaps, minions against minions? Aye, but in any such battle, Catti-brie surely liked the odds for the Companions of the Hall.

Catti-brie realized that she was smiling widely—indeed, she felt as if her grin would take in her ears! To be on the road again with Drizzt! With Bruenor and Regis—and oh, how she hoped they would find their way to Kelvin's Cairn on the Spring Equinox of 1484! In that moment, she was certain that she would find Drizzt; in that exhilarating moment, Catti-brie found courage and heart, and indeed her own heart pounded in her chest.

She knew that Drizzt could be long dead, of course, or either Bruenor or Regis might have fallen along their journey. She knew her own path was far from secured, with many dangerous miles to go and her powers reduced, and perhaps with a dangerous sorceress and her many minions close on her trail.

But in that moment, Catti-brie knew that she would find her love. And she would stand beside him, prepared to do battle. Her expression shifting from joy to a look of grim resolve, the young woman dived back to her studies.

Summer turned to autumn and autumn to winter, and the Year of the Ageless One became the Year of Deep Water Drifting. Bruenor rode a caravan out of Mithral Hall, bound for Mirabar, and Regis crossed the Sea of Fallen Stars, but Catti-brie couldn't know any of that.

The year turned again, to the Year of the Grinning Halfling, and the seasons turned once more, with Bruenor crossing through Mirabar and bound for Baldur's Gate, while Regis rode with the Grinning Ponies along the Trade Way, neither of them so far from Longsaddle. But Catti-brie's eyes remained in her books—furthering her power served her goddess's wishes, and would serve her and Drizzt well.

She would stay in Longsaddle another year or two, she hoped, and perhaps even a bit longer if she could approach the level of proficiency needed to master a teleportation spell that could set her immediately into Icewind Dale.

That was her plan, at least, but one gray morning before the turn of 1483, Penelope called her to her chambers, where Catti-brie found Penelope's husband and old Kipper already seated around the sorceress's desk.

"We have come to think of you as a friend, even family," Penelope told her as soon as she had taken the indicated seat. "Many have whispered that you should be formally ordained as a Harpell."

Catti-brie thought to ask if that meant she would have to turn herself into a statue, or a werewolf, or burn herself with an errant fireball or some other such catastrophe, but, gauging the somber atmosphere around her, she wisely kept her jokes private.

"We have opened our home and books to you," Kipper added.

"You have been most generous, all of you," Catti-brie agreed.

"Do you think it is time to tell us the truth of Delly Curtie?" Penelope asked bluntly.

Catti-brie stood and stared at Penelope, her friend and mentor, unsure, and not because she hadn't come to trust and care for her hosts. Far from it!

"You hesitate."

"Does that particular point of truth matter?" Catti-brie asked.

"It does," Dowell said with unexpected and jarring seriousness.

"Kipper has detected some unwanted magic, aimed at the Ivy Mansion," Penelope explained. "Detection spells, divination, distance vision. Someone seeks something here, or someone."

Catti-brie closed her eyes and took another steadying breath. Even though the years had turned, she knew in her heart that it had to be Lady Avelyere.

"So will you tell us the truth?" Dowell asked.

"No," Catti-brie answered without hesitation.

"For our own sake?" Penelope asked, and Catti-brie nodded.

"You are being hunted by a powerful adversary then," said Kipper, and he nodded when Catti-brie looked to him. "Good that you are here, then. You are among powerful friends."

"No," Catti-brie replied, again without having to even think about it. "Good for me, perhaps, but not so for you."

"We are formidable—"

"It matters not," said Catti-brie. She was thinking beyond the walls of the Ivy Mansion. If Avelyere was hunting her, the woman and her Netherese cohorts wouldn't move on the Ivy Mansion. They would watch and they would learn, and they would have a hot trail to follow when Catti-brie at last departed.

"I am not in danger," Catti-brie explained. "Nor are you in having me here. But it is best that I take my leave, for now at least. I had never meant to so detour from my journey, though I would not trade the last years. The generosity of the Harpells exceeds even the eccentricities of the Harpells, and that is no small thing!"

"You have a great tale to tell!" Penelope argued. "Of Harkle and Bidderdoo and Mithral Hall and Delly Curtie. I wish to hear—"

"A tale for another day," Catti-brie interrupted. "And that is my promise. I shall return to Longsaddle one day and repay all of your generosity with tales that will make you smile. I know that is meager payment for the training you have offered."

"It was an arrangement of mutual benefit," Dowell said. "Your unique skills with the old ways served us as well as we served you."

"It is generous of you to say so," said Catti-brie. "Then I am free to leave?"

"Of course," said Penelope. "Ever so, though we would prefer that you remain."

"I will return," Catti-brie said, looking her in the eye, meaning every word. "But may I indulge one more favor?" She looked to Kipper, the most skilled of the bunch. "Magical transport?"

The old man raised a bushy eyebrow.

"And secrecy," Catti-brie added. "I will tell you alone my destination, and you will divulge it to no one, not even your Harpell colleagues, on your word."

"And we do not even know your name," Penelope remarked.

Catti-brie turned to her and shrugged, then wrapped her in a warm hug.

After gathering up items for the road and doing a bit of research on the current geography of the region west of Longsaddle, Catti-brie settled on a location that seemed as if it would prove hospitable enough, and within reach of her ultimate goal. She would not bid Kipper to put her down in Icewind Dale, for she did not want him or anyone else to know her final destination.

She stepped out of the old mage's portal onto a mountain pass overlooking a small town nestled in the westernmost reaches of the Spine of the World, a town called Auckney, that traced its line of lords back to days before the Spellplague, and so in the line of Meralda and Colson, the little girl Wulfgar had taken in as his own child for a short period of time, in days long past.

CHAPTER 25

FIDELITY

The Year of the Tasked Weasel (1483 DR)
Gauntlgrym

WITH ALL THE STUBBORNNESS OF A DWARF, BRUENOR IGNORED THE reaching monsters and fought against the press of the boot, driving himself with every ounce of his strength toward the many-notched axe. If he could just get his hand around it . . .

But he could not, and he let out a little grunt as the boot crushed down harder, pressing him with supernatural strength, grinding his arm into the stone. Clawed hands tore at his clothing and skin, and the otherworldly shrieks of hungry undead dark elves echoed off the cavern walls.

"Get ye back!" Bruenor heard, and the gruff voice and accent gave him pause. The hands stopped clawing at him then, but the boot held him fast. He managed to turn enough to get a glimpse of his captor, and he gasped in shock and was too numb from that shock to resist as a thick hand reached down and grabbed him by the collar and hoisted him roughly, and so very easily, to his feet.

"Ye're breathin' still only because ye're a dwarf, thief, but know that ye're not long to be breathin'!" the vampire, an undead dwarf in ridged armor, said. "I'm wantin' ye to know the grave ye're robbing afore I break yer neck."

"The cairn of King Bruenor," Bruenor breathed, and he added, his voice thin from absolute shock, "Pwent."

The vampire gave him a quick shake, so roughly that it rattled his bones. "What'd ye call me?"

"Pwent . . . oh, me Pwent, what've ye become then?"

The vampire dwarf, Thibbledorf Pwent, stared hard at this young dwarf, looking him up and down, then settling on his eyes. They locked gazes and stared silently through many heartbeats—heartbeats from Bruenor, and not from the dead battlerager.

"Me king?" Thibbledorf Pwent asked. He let go of Bruenor's collar then, his hand visibly trembling as he retracted it. "Me king?"

All around, the drow vampires hissed and shuffled uneasily, clearly wanting to leap back in at the living dwarf and tear him apart.

"Bah! Get ye gone!" Pwent demanded, shouting at them and waving his arm menacingly. The group retreated into the darkness, falling back, hissing in protest, and soon falling on Bruenor's three companions to feast on their still-warm blood.

"What are ye doing?" Bruenor asked incredulously, looking around in obvious horror. "Pwent, what—?"

"Ye died pulling the lever," Pwent replied, and there seemed to Bruenor to be a bit of resentment in his tone. "Meself did'no. Aye, but that damned vampire friend o' Dahlia's got me on the neck and put his curse into me."

"A vampire," Bruenor muttered, trying to piece it all together, trying to make some sense of this craziness. Pwent was a vampire haunting the halls of Gauntlgrym, and with a drow troupe in support? "Pwent," he said with sympathy and concern and clear confusion, "what are ye doing?"

"A pack of damned drow took home in this place," the battlerager answered. His face turned into a fierce scowl and he issued a feral snarl, and Bruenor feared for a moment that Pwent would fall over him in murderous rage—and Bruenor knew in his heart that such fear was not unfounded. Thibbledorf Pwent was on the edge; the struggle showed clearly in his dead eyes.

"I'm holdin' 'em. I'm fightin' 'em!" Pwent said. "Aye, but that's all I got left, me king. All that's left o' Pwent. And suren that it's a sweet taste when I get me fangs in their skinny necks, don't ye doubt. Aye, but that's the joy, me king!"

As he said it, he advanced a step and flashed his elongated canines, and for a moment, Bruenor again expected him to leap for his king's throat!

But Pwent pulled back, obviously with great effort.

"I'm yer king," Bruenor stated. "I'm yer friend. E'er been yer friend, and yerself me own."

The vampire managed a nod. "If ye was me friend, ye'd kill me," he said. "Ah, but ye cannot, and I'm not about to let ye." He glanced down at the cairn and kicked at it, and with his great strength sent a pile of large stones bouncing away.

Bruenor looked upon his own corpse, upon his many-notched axe, surviving the decades intact as if nary a day had passed. He noted his old armor, fit for a king, and a buckler set with the foaming mug of Clan Battlehammer, a shield that had turned the blows of a thousand enemies. He stared at the skull, at his skull, grayish white with flecks of discolored dried skin, and so shocking was the realization that he was looking at his own rotting head that it took Bruenor a long while to realize that his one-horned helm was missing. He tried to remember where he had lost it. Had it fallen into the primordial pit when he and Pwent had dragged themselves across the chasm, perhaps?

It didn't matter, he tried to tell himself.

"Tried to kill meself," Pwent went on, clearly oblivious to Bruenor's inner turmoil. "Thought I could, ah, but when the sunlight came into that cave and burned at me . . . I runned off. Runned down here into the dark. Runned into the madness, I did, but meself's not surrendering, me king. I be fightin'!"

Bruenor eased his trusty old weapon from the skeletal grip.

"But me king?" Pwent asked suddenly, and from the tone, Bruenor understood what was coming next.

"H-how?" Pwent stuttered. "Ye can't be!"

Bruenor turned to regard his old friend. "Ah, but I be, and that's the durned part of it. I got a tale to tell, me old friend, but it's one that's as dark as yer own, I'm fearin'." As he finished, he looked at the throne of Gauntlgrym, the conduit to divine power that had so forcefully rejected him. He had come here all full of hope, and with renewed faith in Moradin, and admiration in the dwarf god's clever ruse to use Mielikki.

But now, after the rejection, Bruenor didn't know what to think.

"Help me get me armor and me shield," Bruenor said.

Thibbledorf Pwent looked at him skeptically.

"It's meself, ye dolt, and I don't think I've seen such a look from ye since Nanfoodle poisoned me so's I could get meself out o' Mithral Hall."

Pwent blinked in shock, sorting out the words. "Me king," he said, nodding, and he moved to help Bruenor with the corpse.

As he donned his old outfit, Bruenor told Pwent the tale of Iruladoon, of the promise to Mielikki and the assigned rendezvous atop Kelvin's Cairn. It occurred to him that the vampire wasn't interjecting much, as he would have expected from Thibbledorf Pwent, who always had an opinion to share, but it wasn't until he looked closely at his old friend that he understood the truth of it: Pwent wasn't even really listening. Indeed, the way in which

Pwent regarded Bruenor at that moment warned Bruenor that the vampire was struggling even then against the urges of his affliction. Bruenor could see that Pwent was thirsty for blood, any blood, even Bruenor's blood.

"So now ye're here killin' drow, eh?" Bruenor said sharply to distract him.

"Aye, but not much killin' now that them below're knowin' o' me," Pwent replied. "Got me a few, as ye seen, and a few more killed to death, but most o' me time's in th'upper halls now and not near the Forge and them damned drow elfs."

"The Forge?"

"Aye, they be usin' it."

Bruenor winced at the thought of the Forge of Gauntlgrym, among the most hallowed workshops in his Delzoun heritage, in the hands of dark elves.

"Ye should be going," Pwent said, and he seemed to be struggling with every word. "I failed ye, me king, don't ye make me fail ye more."

"But ye still guard this room," Bruenor replied, and he moved closer and put a hand on his friend's sturdy shoulder. "Even as ye are, ye guard this room, me grave and the throne."

"It's all I got," Pwent answered, his voice thin. "Last thread holding . . ." His voice trailed away.

Bruenor patted him and nodded, understanding. "Me loyal Pwent," he reassured the dwarf. "To the end, ye hold true."

Pwent started to shake his head.

"All any dwarf's got," said Bruenor. "Loyalty. All honor's in loyalty, to yer word and to yer friends. Ain't nothing more to give and ain't nothing more asked of us."

As he heard those last words escape his lips, Bruenor glanced over at the throne and considered his rejection. "Drizzt," he said, more to himself than to Pwent.

"Aye, seen him in me early days of affliction," Pwent answered unexpectedly, and Bruenor turned back to regard him. "Was him that left me in the cave with the risin' sun, but he thought better o' me than me was." He shook his hairy head and looked down at the floor dejectedly.

Bruenor tried to sort it out, but other thoughts pressed in on him. "He'd've been a good dwarf, eh? That Drizzt."

"Too skinny," Pwent replied. "But aye, in heart. Ain't none more loyal to ye except meself."

"Loyalty unrepaid," Bruenor muttered under his breath, suddenly feeling quite ashamed. He looked back at the throne. "A good friend," he added more loudly.

"Aye, but if he was, then he'd've killed me to death in that cave," Pwent said, his inflection suddenly strong once more. "Ye can't be trustin' the heart of a vampire."

The words hit Bruenor hard, and as he sorted them out, he understood completely. He spun around, axe at the ready.

But Thibbledorf Pwent was nowhere to be seen.

Bruenor hopped all around. "Pwent!" he called. "Ye huntin' me, dwarf? Pwent!"

No answer.

Bruenor banged his axe against his shield. "Pwent?"

He heard something over by the throne and leaped around just in time to see a dwarf-sized fog floating away from it, then seeping into the cracks in the floor. Bruenor ran to the spot, but Pwent was not to be found. He looked at the throne, the seat of it now in view, and there upon it sat his one-horned helm.

"Ah, Pwent, me Pwent," Bruenor whispered, a tear in his eye. He rested his axe against the front of the throne and reached for the helm, the only crown he ever wore, with trembling hands.

"Loyal Pwent," he whispered, thinking that even under the affliction, the curse of vampirism, Thibbledorf Pwent had shamed him about what a dwarf was supposed to be.

Fidelity.

And then Bruenor understood, more clearly than he had since the day he had walked out of Iruladoon. All thoughts of Moradin tricking Mielikki flew from him. He, Bruenor, had given his oath in exchange for rebirth, and that oath to go to the aid of as loyal a friend as he had ever known. Drizzt Do'Urden had fought for Mithral Hall, for Bruenor, as fiercely as any.

"The Companions o' the Hall," he said. "What I fool I been."

He put the helm upon his head, took up his axe, and with a determined growl, leaped up to sit again on the throne of Gauntlgrym.

"The wisdom o' Moradin," he recited. "The secrets o' Dumathoin. The strength o' Clangeddin. And all for them dwarves that's loyal. Ain't nothing more for a dwarf than honor. Me word and me heart. Fidelity!"

He sat back and closed his eyes, and felt his wounds beginning to heal.

He thought of Catti-brie and Regis, and of course, of Drizzt. He thought of his boy, Wulfgar, and wished him unending peace in the Halls of Tempus. He considered poor Pwent and knew he must return here to put his friend to rest.

But not alone.

The Companions of the Hall would grant peace to Thibbledorf Pwent.

Aye, and then they'd go east to Mithral Hall, and fight the war that needed fighting.

Aye.

"He thinks himself the only master," came a voice, pulling Bruenor from his thoughts. He sat up and noted three forms approaching. Dark elves and vampires, he knew at once, for two walked stiffly. The third, though, in the middle, seemed more at ease, more natural, and Bruenor wondered for a moment if this one was still alive.

"Your dwarf friend, the master vampire," that drow said in a halting command of the common tongue, his words uneven and stilted so that it took Bruenor a few moments to even decipher. "He thinks us his mere minions, but perhaps that is not true of all of us."

Bruenor didn't even have to fully decipher that claim to understand this one's murderous intent.

Put me at 'em, he imparted to the throne, bracing himself, and much like before, but this time beneficially, the throne of Gauntlgrym expelled him forcefully, launching him through the air, flying and crying out with full throat and full heart, "Moradin!"

He crashed down into the two lesser vampires, sending them sprawling aside, and landed in full balance, using his momentum to heighten his swing. The drow vampire tried to scream out a protest, but before a single word left its mouth, its head left its shoulders, severed cleanly and spinning away into the darkness.

Bruenor roared and spun to his left to meet the charge of one of the lesser creatures. The strength of Clangeddin flowed through his arms—he could feel the gods within him, approving—as he brought his axe swinging mightily across.

The undead drow fell in half.

Around Bruenor went, to see the third of the group fleeing, leaping into the air to transform once more into a bat.

"No ye don't!" he screamed and let fly, his axe spinning end over end, the missile flying true.

The vampire crashed to the floor, and when Bruenor arrived, he found it quite destroyed, caught halfway between drow form and that of the bat, one-armed, one-winged, its head a grotesque twist of bone.

326

The dwarf reached down, grabbed his axe handle, and ripped it free.

"Fidelity!" he yelled into the darkness. "Hold strong, me Pwent! I'll be findin' ye, don't ye doubt, and I'll be puttin' ye in Dwarfhome where ye belong!"

But not then, he knew. The season was late already and the pass into Icewind Dale, at least a tenday's journey north, would soon close. If he didn't beat the first snows, he would not get to Ten-Towns for many months, and likely not in time to fulfill his oath.

He grabbed a torch from his pack and lit it off the low-burning one lying beside the ravaged corpse of Vestra. He said a quick prayer to his fallen companions, all three, but he couldn't pause to build them cairns and they didn't deserve it anyway. The prayer was generous enough.

And off he went, in his one-horned helm and foaming mug shield, his many-notched axe over his shoulder, with the wisdom of Moradin, the secrets of Dumathoin, and the strength of Clangeddin flowing through him.

King Bruenor Battlehammer of Mithral Hall.

But more importantly, he now understood, friend Bruenor Battlehammer of the Companions of the Hall.

CHAPTER 26

FANCY SPIDER

The Year of the Tasked Weasel (1483 DR)
Luskan

THE SMALL FIGURE IN THE GRAY TRAVELING CLOAK LEANED LOW AGAINST the rain as he slowly walked his dark bay pony toward the distant gates of the City of Sails. Spider hadn't looked back over the miles of road since he had split with the Grinning Ponies, with Doregardo taking the band back to their usual haunts in the south. His road lay before him now, he continually reminded himself, resisting the urge to turn around and ride hard to catch up with his fellow riders.

So much had he left behind him in the years of this young second life . . . friends, including a very special one in Delthuntle, friends along the Trade Way . . . He would see them all again, he vowed.

But now his road lay before him, not behind.

"Speak your name and your business!" a guard called down from a squat tower beside Luskan's closed southern gate.

The halfling looked up and pulled the hood of his cloak back, revealing his blue beret, which he wore slightly off kilter to the left and now fastened flat in the front with a golden button shaped like a running pony. His curly brown hair, wet with drizzle, hung to his shoulders and he had grown a thin mustache and a goatee that was little more than a line of hair from his bottom lip to the middle of his chin, so similar to the one his mentor, Pericolo Topolino, had worn.

"Spider Topolino," he replied without hesitation, without even the urge to call himself Regis, a name he had long abandoned, "who rode with Doregardo and the Grinning Ponies."

The guard's eyes widened at that, just for a moment, and he looked back and whispered to someone unseen behind him.

"Never heard of them," he said, turning back to Spider.

The halfling vigilante shrugged, hardly believing the man and hardly caring.

"And your business?" the guard demanded.

"Passing through," said Spider, "to the north. I've family in Lonelywood, in Ten-Towns. The last caravans of the season will be leaving soon, I expect." From his past life, he knew the schedule here well enough to know that he was speaking the truth, for the eighth month, Eliasis, of 1483 had just begun, and the pass through the Spine of the World was often closed by snows before the end of the ninth month. He should have come to Luskan a couple of tendays earlier, perhaps, but leaving the Grinning Ponies had proven a difficult thing. He had left two full lives behind, both that he had come to love, and now approached a third existence, and one he could only hope would prove no less full of such love and friendship.

"And you've the gold to get a caravan to carry you?" the guard asked, a bit too slyly for Spider's liking.

"Since I wish to travel north in any case, it is my expectation that the merchants will have the gold to afford my company," Spider answered.

The guard gave him a skeptical look.

"Pray open your gate," Spider said. "This rain has gone to the bone, I fear, and I would dearly love to find a warm hearth and a fine meal before retiring."

The guard hesitated and looked down on him from above. The halfling sat up straighter and loosened his cloak a bit, shifting his left arm so that the covering fell back behind his hip, thus revealing his rapier in all its bejeweled glory. Clever Spider made sure to turn his pony a bit to the right to afford the guard a good view.

The man finally glanced back and said something Spider could not hear, and the gates began to creak open soon after.

Spider Pericolo Topolino sat up very straight as he walked his pony through, his cloak off his left shoulder, his left arm hanging easily at his side while he guided his mount with his right hand alone. He tried to project an air of confidence—competence was the best deterrent against would-be robbers and murderers, after all.

As far as he could tell at first blush, and from the information he had garnered over the last months riding in the south, the city had changed very much for the worse in the century since he'd last been here. Luskan was still ruled by five High Captains and their respective "Ships," pirates and cutthroats all, and thoroughly unpleasant sorts. She was a city of scurvy vagabonds, where a body lying on the side of the road was not an uncommon sight.

Spider could see the masts of the many boats in the harbor over to his left. Most would be sailing for the south soon enough, likely, and so their crews might be willing to take greater risks within Luskan, figuring that they would be out of port before the magistrates could catch up to them.

With that thought in mind, Spider moved along the right-hand, eastern lanes, the inland sections, staying in sight of the eastern wall as he made his way toward the city's northern gate. Much of Luskan lay in ruins now, and when he came in sight of the Upstream Span crossing the River Mirar to the city's north gate, he saw that the bridges, too, were in heavy disrepair, so much so that he had to wonder if caravans even left from Luskan any longer, bound across the river to the north.

One compound on the riverbank just south of the Upstream Span caught his eye, and he breathed a sigh of relief to learn that Baliver's House of Horses was still, apparently, in operation. He walked his pony over to where a pair of young men and a woman loaded hay into the back of a wagon.

"Well met," he greeted, dismounting, and he was glad to see the three smiling—and was surprised at how much a little thing like a smile could brighten up this thoroughly miserable ruin posing as a city.

"And to you, goodsir," said the young woman, a handsome lass of less than twenty years. "Stabling or renting, or both, perhaps?"

"Stabling," Regis replied, and he handed the reins to one of the men who came forward. "Name's Rumble, or Rumblebelly to his friends. Handle him well, I beg. He's been a good and loyal pony." He pulled his saddlebags from Rumble's back and flipped them over his shoulder, then dug into his pouch. "Three silver a night?" he asked and offered.

"Aye, that'll do."

"Then here's a tenday, though I doubt I'll be in town that long, and a bit of extra for special care to my always hungry pony." He handed the young man four pieces of gold. "And a bit more when I collect him," he added as the happy man led Rumble away.

"I'll need to find an inn, and a caravan to Icewind Dale," Regis added, turning back to the woman. He looked to the north, to the structures along the northern bank, and pointed. "Is the Red Dragon Trading Post still in operation?"

331

It was clear that they had no idea what he was talking about.

"Might mean One-Eyed Jax," the remaining young man remarked.

"There is a tavern over on the north bank," the woman explained. "Comfortable enough, so I've heard."

"He'd be better sleeping in our hayloft," said the man.

"Well, which is it?" Regis demanded.

"Comfortable," the woman replied. "And the place you'd best find any news of caravans to the North, surely, but . . ." She looked to her doubting companion.

"I see you wear a sword," he said. "Can you use it?"

"Will I have to?"

The young man just shrugged.

"It's the safest place and bed he'll find," the woman told her companion, and she turned to Spider. "Drow are not uncommon about One-Eyed Jax," she explained. "But Ship Kurth claims ownership of the place, and none in the city are about to cross Ship Kurth. One-Eyed Jax is as safe a bed as you'll find in Luskan."

"Not saying much," said the man.

"I was not expecting much," Regis assured him. He looked to the bridge, the Upstream Span. "Will it fall out from under my feet?"

"They are repairing it," the man replied. "Have been since before I was born. Safe enough if you're careful where you step, but if there's a gang working it, they'll ask you to reach into your purse for a toll."

Spider of the Grinning Ponies just smiled and shook his head. That grin hid a true sorrow, though, for what might have been in once-proud Luskan. For he, Regis, had been here in 1377, when Captain Deudermont had tried to wrest control of the city from the Arcane Brotherhood and the High Captains. If Deudermont had won, Luskan might now stand as a smaller version of mighty Waterdeep, a shining jewel on a coast full of thriving ports. But alas, Deudermont had failed, and had fallen.

And so had begun the fall of Luskan.

The halfling flipped a silver piece to the woman, thanked her for the information with a tip of his beautiful hat, and then started off toward the bridge.

He picked his path carefully as he stepped out onto the Upstream Span, for the stones were crumbling all around it, and in places he could see down through it to the filthy waters of the River Mirar. More than filthy, he realized, for they shone inky black and their foul smell drifted up to assail him. So focused was Regis on carefully marking his steps that he was more than a third of the way across before he even noticed that there were indeed others on the bridge, a trio of dirty men sitting beside a pile of stones and wooden planks, wearing the colors of a Ship's crew he did not know.

The group stood as he neared, each reaching for a shovel or pick, and a fourth appearing from behind the pile.

Regis fought his instincts, reminding himself not to slow, not to show any concern.

"Now, what've we got here?" asked the nearest of the group.

"A visitor to your fair city, bound for One-Eyed Jack in search of a room," Spider answered pleasantly.

"Jax, you mean," the man corrected.

"Jacks, then," the halfling agreed.

A second man came up beside the first, holding his shovel like a battle-axe diagonally across his chest.

"Have ye enough coin, then?" the first asked.

"Would I seek a room if I did not?"

"Enough for the room and for the toll?" asked one from the back, and only then, at the sound of her voice, did Regis realize that it was a woman.

"I see no signs for any toll, nor was any mentioned by the guards at the southern gate," the halfling answered casually.

"Don't need no signs and don't see no guards, eh," the first man said, and he hoisted his pick-axe up over his shoulder, and moved near enough to bring it down onto Regis's head.

"Aye little one, open yer purse and we'll let ye know if it's enough to get you across," said the brute with the shovel.

"Hmm," Regis mumbled as he considered his options. He had some coins in his pouch, and many more in the secret compartment below it, which this crew would never find. It probably wouldn't cost him more than a few silver to get across.

A few silver and more than a bit of his self-respect.

"No," he said. "I do not think I will pay any toll."

"Wrong answer," said the woman from behind.

"Kindly move aside," Regis said, and he lifted his left arm, throwing his cloak back over his left shoulder and revealing his fabulous rapier.

"Ah, ye runt!" said the first, moving to strike with his pick-axe.

But Regis was quicker, his right hand sweeping across to grab his rapier and draw it in one fluid motion, and his left hand coming across the other way right behind the lifting blade, moving just under the right fold of his cloak, where his third weapon sat ready just in front of his right hip, the holster angled back toward his center for an easy and quick draw.

Out went the rapier and out came the hand crossbow, unfolding as it went, and as Regis's rapier tip went against the throat of the man with the pick-axe, just under the chin, his hand crossbow aimed out perfectly toward the man with the shovel, leveled for his face.

"Once I politely asked, but now I insist," Regis said. "Move aside."

The two men glanced to each other. Regis prodded with the rapier, drawing a bit of blood.

"Ye know what Ship ye're threatening, do ye?" the woman protested.

"I know that one High Captain might find his crew short three men and a woman," Regis answered. "Unless any of you survive the fall, of course, and the swim in those most-unappetizing waters below."

That last part seemed to have a great effect, he noted, with the blood draining from the woman's face.

"I'll not ask you again," Regis assured them.

They moved aside and Regis crossed the river, his grin from ear to ear.

Bolstered by his bravery, the halfling confidently strode into the tavern known as One-Eyed Jax a short while later. He was surprised by the spelling of the name, thinking, of course, that the place had been named after the two particular cards in a standard deck, but he just shrugged it off, realizing that few up here could even properly spell, likely, and fewer still would understand the difference between "Jacks" and "Jax."

Barely inside the door, many eyes turning to regard him, he threw back his cloak and swept the water droplets from his beret. He knew that he cut a heroic figure, quite dashing, and didn't try to hide that in the least. Boldness would get him through, he reminded himself continually, as it had on the bridge. He could not, would not, appear the least bit vulnerable.

He wore three weapons on his belt, which had been looped with a blue sash to match the color of his hat. His rapier sat on his left hip, the hand crossbow in front of his right, and his dagger in a new scabbard just behind the hand crossbow at the side of his right hip. He wore a black leather sleeveless vest and a white shirt, unbuttoned in the front just enough to reveal an undercoat of soft cloth lined with glistening mithral strands. His breeches were light brown and his boots, high and fashionable, shined of black leather to match the fine material of the vest, and indeed, had been crafted by the same leatherworker, one considered, and certainly priced like, the finest in all of Baldur's Gate.

As he pulled off his riding gloves—leather, but dyed blue to match the hat and belt sash—he scanned the room, nodding politely at those who seemed most interested. Tucking the gloves into his belt, he moved to the bar to order some wine and inquire about a room.

"And how long might you be staying, master?" asked the barkeep, an attractive young woman with gray eyes and rich brown hair just a shade lighter than the halfling's.

"Master Topolino," he answered, and he tipped his beret to her. "Spider Topolino of Aglarond. And I would like the room until I find an appropriate caravan setting out for the North."

"Mirabar? Auckney?"

"Icewind Dale," said Regis. "I am bound for Ten-Towns."

She put the glass of wine before him on the bar. "And what business might you have in that forsaken place?"

"My own," he answered, thinking it strange that anyone living in Luskan at this time would label anywhere else in all the world as "forsaken."

"Good enough for ye, then," she replied. "Just making conversation."

Regis offered her a smile. "My apologies," he said. "I am unused to friendly conversation. The north road has precious little of it now, I fear, where more oft must I speak with my blade than my charm."

"Then might be you need to be more charming," said a man beside him, but rather playfully, he noted, so he laughed and told the barkeep to buy the man a drink on his tab.

"You'll not need your blade in here," the barkeep explained.

"You are the owner?"

"Me?" the woman said with a laugh, one that was shared by all others near enough to hear. "No, no. Just a drink-maker and coin-taker."

"And a pretty eye-full to be enjoyed by the crews," the man beside Regis added, lifting his glass in toast to her.

Others joined in and the barkeep curtsied and gave a little smile, then moved to the other end of the bar to the call of some other patrons.

"But you beware, little friend, that it's just an eye-full," the man warned. "Serena's spoken for, by One-Eye himself, and he's not one you're looking to anger, no matter how well you can work those pretty weapons you carry."

"One-eye is a man, then?" Regis asked. "I had thought it a card in a deck."

"Not a man," the other patron said cryptically, and the others nearby chuckled.

The halfling left it at that. He moved to a table near the blazing hearth and ordered some food, and was quite pleased at the quality, as he was at the quality of his room when he went up to the second story to retire for the night. He found the posting board at the foot of the stairs, but there was only one caravan listed, and it was bound for Port Llast in the south and not to Icewind Dale.

"They'll be another before the season's turn," Serena called out to him when she noted his disappointment as he stood before the board.

He smiled at her, tipped his hat, and bowed gracefully, then climbed the stairs, knowing full well that more than a few patrons were likely talking about him in the common room below.

He set a trap upon his door, using a shim stuck into the top crease of the jamb to hold a vial of acid he had brewed. Anyone coming through uninvited would be in for a painful surprise.

He moved his small bed to the corner across the room that would be most sheltered by the inward swing of the door, then laid his hand crossbow out in easy reach. He re-coated the loaded dart in poison, and set another nearby, nodding approvingly at his handiwork. He had served the Grinning Ponies in many capacities. He was their finest housebreaker when they needed to gather information in places like Baldur's Gate, and also served well as the group's alchemist, providing potions of healing and speed and heroism, and this poison he had learned to brew. It was not as effective as the drow sleeping poison it had replaced, for he had no access to the mushrooms unique to the Underdark, but he had found a substitute fungus that grew in the forests around the Crags. The poison might not put anyone of considerable constitution to sleep, but it often made an enemy's movements sluggish, and as an added benefit, the clever Spider had added some particularly nasty pepper juice that made the small puncture wound of the tiny bolts feel as if it were brought about by a hot poker.

Quite a fine distraction, and thus an advantage, he had learned in fights against those so bitten by his clever weapon.

Before he settled in, the halfling scanned the room, peering closely at every crack in the wall through the magnifying prism of his ring in search of secret doors or murder holes.

Still, despite his thoroughness and precautions, he didn't sleep much that night, fully expecting an ambush, and more than that, trying yet again to reconcile himself to these two very different identities, Spider and Regis. In the south and the east, he had been Spider Parrafin and then, after his flight from Delthuntle, Spider Pericolo Topolino, and hadn't he made a grand name for himself!

But with Ten-Towns looming before him, not so far and not so long, was he to remain Spider? Or to be Regis again? He laughed as he considered that he had given his pony the same name Bruenor often used for him.

"A little of both and neither of one, then," he decided, and he tried to sleep. But of course, moving from his contemplations only reminded him of his vulnerability and the potential for an ambush, and with that unsettling thought in mind, his sleep came in fits and starts.

No ambush came, however, and the halfling went downstairs the next morning to find a smiling Serena and a fine breakfast set out for guests of the inn.

What a collection those guests proved to be; ragamuffins, one and all, road-weary, or more likely sea-weary, cast-offs looking for work wherever they might find it. Regis sat in the far corner of the common room, near the hearth and close enough that he could leap through one of the few windows in the place if need be. He had his back against the wall, and kept his head up while picking through his food, his eyes scanning.

It occurred to him that any of the dozen others in the room would kill him for the price of a few pieces of silver.

That realization sent his thoughts back to the heady days of Captain Deudermont, when the goodly man tried to wrest control of the City of Sails from the pirates and the Hosttower of the Arcane. Deudermont had failed miserably, and his loss was Luskan's loss, as was clearly evident by the decay in both structures and citizens. "Alas . . . ," Regis heard himself whisper.

All but a couple of the inn's guests departed soon after the morning meal, but others entered, particularly after Serena took her place behind the bar.

Regis just sat back and watched. Knowledge was his most important ally. Information would keep him alive.

He was no less careful that night, no less attentive the next day, and no less careful the third night at the inn.

The following morning, soon after breakfast, One-Eyed Jax filled with patrons, all milling around.

Regis dared to move to the bar, where Serena warmly greeted him.

"Ah, Master Spider, but you've found the gumption to come out of your corner," she said. "I told you already, you need not be afraid in here, and will not be needing your weapons."

"I have learned the hard way to be vigilant," he said.

"Aye," she agreed. "And that would do you well in most corners of Luskan, and surely in Ten-Towns, when you get there."

He tipped his blue beret, surprised and quite impressed that she had bothered to remember that little fact about his intended destination. "Busy day," he said.

"Postings," she replied, nodding to the board. "For crews, mostly. Many boats putting out to sea in the next tenday."

"Any heading north?"

Serena laughed. "Might be one or two planning a stop at Auckney, but not to the dale, if that's what you're asking."

"Only asking in jest," Regis replied. "I have been there before, and know well the ice floes floating about to scuttle any who dare sail there."

"You've been there?" Serena asked doubtfully. "And you're from Aglarond, so you said."

"Aye."

"Quite the traveler, then. Have you even passed your teens?"

The halfling laughed and lifted his wine. "I am older than I look, I assure you."

"Still, I would have thought that one of your . . . cut, would have gained some notice in coming through Luskan before, yet I've not heard tell of Master Spider Topolino until four days ago, nor have any that I've spoken to."

"You have told others of me, have you?"

Serena shrugged. "Luskan's full of eyes and full of ears. You made an entrance not often seen. If you hoped to escape notice, then know that you failed."

Regis shrugged and lifted his glass once more. He hopped down from his seat and went to the board, waiting patiently for the taller folk perusing it to move aside, then took his place. Several postings had gone up that morning, mostly for crews, and only one for a caravan, but alas, to Mirabar and not to Icewind Dale.

"It will happen," Serena consoled him when he returned to the bar.

Soon after, Regis was back in the corner, enjoying his lunch, the common room bristling with patrons. All seemed in a fine mood, and indeed, most of the groups within One-Eyed Jax that day were sharing parting drinks before putting back to sea. Regis enjoyed the spectacle and the many toasts, and found that he was more relaxed in the place now. Indeed, he spent most of his time looking out the window, and held his breath on several occasions when he noticed dark elves strolling by. At one point, a pair of drow came into One-Eyed Jax—and how the other patrons offered deference to them!

They took note of the finely outfitted halfling, their stares lingering on him, making him wish that he had dressed a little less colorfully and less richly this day. Indeed, one of the drow went to Serena and began a quiet discussion, and pointedly looked back his way as he did, making no effort to hide the fact that he was inquiring about Master Spider Topolino with the barkeep.

"Wonderful," the halfling muttered under his breath, and he pondered going over to join the discussion openly.

Any thoughts of that went away almost immediately, however, when a tall red-haired man entered the room, flanked by several capable-looking brawlers. Clearly, given the parting crowd, men stumbling quickly to get out of the way, this was someone of importance.

The redhead moved to the bar and Serena rushed to serve him, and the dark elves toasted him and drained their drinks, then hastily departed.

Regis noted it all, trying to sort out the hidden relationships. When the redhead moved to the posting board by the stairway, Regis dared to return to the bar.

"High Captain Kurth," Serena whispered to him, bringing him a drink. "I think you have found your caravan, little friend."

Regis stared at the man, who held a posting in his hand, but hadn't tacked it up yet, as he was reading the others recently placed. He was still focused there when the crowd in the common room went quiet once more, then gave a common "huzzah!" Regis looked all around in confusion, seeking the source of the cheer.

And then he nearly fell off his bar stool, for he realized that the patron of the establishment had entered. A drow, and not one-eyed, Regis knew, though this one did indeed wear an eyepatch.

"Jax," he whispered under his breath. "Jarlaxle?"

He noted with concern that the drow turned to him sharply upon mention of the name, and Regis huddled over his drink, silently berating himself for forgetting how keen drow ears might be, and how much keener still, likely, Jarlaxle's would be.

Regis held his breath and didn't dare look up as he heard the magically amplified sound of hard boots striking the wooden floor coming toward him.

"Do I know you, goodsir?" Jarlaxle asked, moving right beside him and motioning for Serena to bring them both a drink.

"No, goodsir," Regis answered, not daring to look up into the face of that most dangerous mercenary.

"Spider Topolino of Aglarond," Serena said, moving over with the drinks. "He came to us a few days ago, passing through and hoping to score a ride with a caravan to Icewind Dale."

"Icewind Dale?" Jarlaxle asked with clear, though feigned, obviously, it seemed to Regis, surprise.

Regis dared to glance up at the drow, who was smiling. Jarlaxle was always smiling. "I have family there," the halfling meekly explained.

Jarlaxle didn't immediately reply, but he did stare, and seemed a bit surprised. Regis tried not to audibly gulp—was it possible that Jarlaxle had recognized him? It couldn't be, the halfling silently told himself, for he hadn't seen Jarlaxle in more than a century, by the drow's accounting of time.

But still, that penetrating, knowing look . . .

"I told him that he might be in luck, since word's that High Captain Beniago is posting a caravan to the dale this very day," Serena said.

Jarlaxle continued to stare at Regis, looking him up and down.

"You are well-appointed for one looking to serve as a mere guard on a caravan," he said quietly when Serena had moved away.

"I don't wish to ride into Icewind Dale alone," Regis said. "Yetis and goblins and such."

"That is a fine hat."

Regis swallowed hard, suspecting that Jarlaxle had already discerned its magical properties.

"My family was well-appointed," he answered. "Perhaps you have heard of Grandfather Pericolo Topolino of Aglarond."

"Grandfather?" Jarlaxle replied, his tone marking the title appropriately. "No, I have not . . . yet."

Just shut up! Regis silently berated himself. He couldn't get into a cryptic conversation with the likes of Jarlaxle. This master spy would know more about him than he knew about himself in short order!

"You have enjoyed your stay at my establishment?" Jarlaxle politely asked.

"Miss Serena is a fine hostess, yes," Regis answered.

"Well then, good travels to you, sir," Jarlaxle said, and he tipped his outrageously huge, wide-brimmed hat. "May you find a road worth riding, to a hearth worth watching, and with friends worth toasting."

"And to you," Regis replied, and he breathed easier when Jarlaxle moved along to other patrons, then soon after left the establishment.

Shortly after that, High Captain Beniago Kurth made his posting and similarly departed, and Regis was fast to the board, and was quite relieved that it was, indeed, a call for drivers and guards for a merchant caravan departing at the end of the tenday for the town of Brynn Shander in Icewind Dale.

As Beniago had expected, Jarlaxle was waiting for him a short ways down the lane from One-Eyed Jax.

"An interesting halfling, yes?" asked Beniago, the lieutenant of Bregan D'aerthe, magically disguised as a human and serving the drow mercenary band as High Captain of the most powerful Ship in Luskan.

"He will apply for your caravan," Jarlaxle replied. "Give him passage, and see to it that he is not bothered while in Luskan."

Beniago didn't hide his surprise. "You know him?"

Jarlaxle shrugged. "He reminds me of someone, perhaps. I cannot place it, and could not be certain, in any case, given the beret he wears."

"A hat of disguise?"

Jarlaxle nodded. "That hand crossbow on his belt is worth many thousands of gold, and there is no shortage of magical items about that one, the unusual hat included."

"And that rapier," Beniago agreed, and he seemed impressed.

Jarlaxle nodded, but couldn't help himself as he looked back toward the distant tavern, musing.

"What do you know?" Beniago prompted.

"Little," Jarlaxle admitted. "And I never enjoy knowing little."

"I could inquire . . . ," Beniago started, but Jarlaxle shook his head, cutting short that train of thought.

"He is not to be bothered," Jarlaxle ordered.

"But watched?"

The leader of Bregan D'aerthe nodded again. "Watched when he returns as well."

"He intends to remain in the North throughout the winter, so he told Serena."

Jarlaxle mulled that over for a bit. For some reason he could not sort out, some reason lost to distant memories, it seemed fitting for this one to be in Icewind Dale. "I would know where he settles, then."

Beniago nodded, and assured his master, "His every move."

On a warm autumn day, five tendays later, Regis reclined on the banks of the lake known as Maer Dualdon, his boots removed and set on the moss beside him, a fishing line tied around one toe. Behind him, nestled among some pines, sat the comfortable cottage he had purchased on the outskirts of the small town known as Lonelywood.

Little had changed here in a century, and Regis was glad of it. He had lived in this town for many years in his previous existence, and in a house barely a hundred strides away. Despite his regrets at the roads left behind, he felt as if he had come home.

He lay on his back and watched the puffy white clouds drifting lazily across the deep blue canopy of an Icewind Dale autumn sky.

He thought of Donnola, and how he wished that she could be here beside him, fishing and carving scrimshaw, living quietly and enjoying the passing of lazy seasons.

"He remained in Icewind Dale," Beniago reported to Jarlaxle in the underground caverns of the ancient ruins within the city of Luskan, a place of ghosts known as Illusk, which Bregan D'aerthe had taken as its headquarters in Luskan. "It is possible that the little one is an outlaw—perhaps he double-crossed Doregardo's Grinning Ponies, for he rode with them these past couple of years, I have learned."

"They have come as far north as Luskan to inquire of him?"

"No. If Doregardo seeks him, we have heard no whispers."

"But this one, full of wealth, full of magic, and with apparent skill, has chosen to retire to Icewind Dale?"

"To broker a deal?" Beniago reasoned. "Perhaps there are interests further south desiring trade with Ten-Towns."

Jarlaxle shrugged. The one named Spider had mentioned a Grandfather, which was a title usually reserved for leaders of assassins guilds. Might this little one be an advanced scout? But then, how did that fit with him riding with the Grinning Ponies, a vigilante band, and surely no friends of an assassins guild?

"Keep an eye?" Beniago asked, correctly reading Jarlaxle's expressions.

"Half an eye," Jarlaxle ordered. "And send inquiries to Aglarond of one Grandfather Pericolo Topolino."

Beniago's eyes widened at mention of the title.

"Quietly," Jarlaxle explained.

Beniago nodded.

CHAPTER 27

A CONFLUENCE OF EVENTS

The Year of the Narthex Murders (1482 DR)
Icewind Dale

Not a smile greeted Catti-brie when she walked into the lone inn in the town of Auckney, a windswept, salty village nestled among the southern shores and high rocks of the Spine of the World's westernmost peaks, overlooking the great ocean.

She moved to the main table and surveyed the menu items.

"Lots of fish," she said lightly to a nearby man, whose apron identified him as the cook or owner, or likely both.

"You get that when you live on the edge of the sea," another man not far away answered, and with no warmth in his tone. Catti-brie turned to regard him, to find him staring at her body and surely not looking into her eyes.

"Three pieces of gold and take your pick," the man with the apron said.

Catti-brie started a bit at the exorbitant price. "Three?"

"You came in with a caravan?"

"No, alone."

"Three pieces of gold and take your pick," the man repeated gruffly.

"I am not that hungry."

"Three for a nibble, three for a stuffing," said a woman's voice from the other end, and Catti-brie turned to regard the speaker, who seemed a fit in age and demeanor for the owner and was likely his wife.

"Are there rooms for rent?" Catti-brie asked.

"Anything's for rent, if you've the gold," said the other man. He winked at Catti-brie rather disgustingly. "Yes?"

"Five gold a night," said the owner.

Catti-brie held her hands up, somewhere between surrender and disbelief.

"Not many visitors to Auckney," the man replied.

"There's a wonder for a mage to unwind," Catti-brie replied with dripping sarcasm. "Is there another common room in town?"

"You think I'd tell you if there was?" the owner replied.

"There's not," said his wife.

"But there are rooms to rent," said the other man. "Though you'd be sharing!" He ended with a dirty laugh that followed Catti-brie all the way back onto the street.

She looked around at the passersby, all huddled under heavy cloaks against the chill breeze sweeping in off the water. There loomed a dourness around this place, a cold chill as palpable as the burgeoning wintry weather.

She moved to what seemed to be the town's main avenue, a wide boulevard weaving around an open market. She meandered around that marketplace, inspecting the wares—late-season fruits and vegetables mostly, along with cartloads of fish. She pretended to be interested, but in truth, she could call upon her divine powers to magically create better food than she found before her. She had only inquired about a meal in the tavern to warm up the conversation in the place, for though she was only passing through Auckney, she held a lingering curiosity about the town.

Wulfgar had been here, and indeed had found quite the adventure here, one that had left him with an adopted child, though for a short time only before he returned the girl to her mother, Meralda, who was back then the Lady of Auckney.

"Don't you be touching what you aren't buying," one woman merchant snapped at her as she reached for an apple.

"How am I to judge the freshness?" Catti-brie asked.

"You'll know when you bite it, and you'll bite it after you pay for it."

Catti-brie shrugged and retracted her hand.

"Pray, tell me, who is the oldest person in Auckney?" she asked.

"Eh?"

"Who has been here the longest? Who would know of days gone by?"

"Well, I'm older than you, so what's your question?" the merchant asked.

"The line of Auck, back to Meralda . . ."

The woman began to laugh.

"Her daughter, Colson?"

"Lady Colson," the woman replied. "Died when I was a child."

"And her child sits on the throne now?"

The merchant shook her head. "Her children both died before her, and took the line with them."

Catti-brie chewed her lip, wondering where to take the conversation next. "Do you remember Lady Colson?"

The woman shrugged. "Bits. Poor girl, born of rape and kidnapped by the rapist to add to the pain."

Catti-brie wanted to reply to that misinformation, for surely Wulfgar had not raped Meralda. Far from it. He had intervened and stolen away the baby Colson to save her from the vengeance of the Lord of Auckney, for though Meralda was the lord's wife, the foolish lord was not the child's father. Nor was Wulfgar. Meralda had been in love with another man—Catti-brie did not know his name—when the Lord of Auckney had forced her to become his bride, not knowing that she was already with child.

"The Bastard Lady," the merchant woman went on, and shook her head and sighed.

"And her father?" Catti-brie was afraid of the answer, but she had to know.

"Barbarian beast, curse his name, whatever his name might be. Not one spoken in Auckney, I warn you."

Catti-brie closed her eyes and forced herself to settle down and suppress her need to set things straight here. She looked back at the woman and nodded, managing a smile before turning away.

"You buying that apple?" the woman said sharply.

Catti-brie turned back to regard the fruit, which was certainly past its prime. But she looked at the scowling merchant and reluctantly scooped it up.

"Four pieces of silver," the merchant demanded, several times the value.

But Catti-brie wasn't about to argue any longer, so she handed over the coins, then walked somberly down the street, right out of the town of Auckney. She meandered down the stony mountain passes to the sea, settling on a dark stone and staring into the cold surf.

The scene befit her mood, for this day had fast turned into a sobering reminder of the fickle nature of memory and of time iself. Wulfgar had lived his life admirably with regards to the events in Auckney. He had helped Lady Meralda to do the right thing, and had raised Colson with love and decency, and then had, at great personal and emotional expense, returned the child to her rightful mother.

And for all that, he was not remembered fondly up here in Auckney. Quite the opposite, so it would seem.

347

Catti-brie glanced back up the rock cliffs to see the distant rooftops and snaking streams of fireplace smoke drifting up into the cold autumn air. It seemed a cold smoke to her, wrought of a cold fire in a cold place, and she realized at once that she had no desire to go back there, to ever return to Auckney.

She looked back out at the dark waters and a wry smile came over her.

She cast a spell to protect herself from the brutal elements, her right arm glowing softly, bluish tendrils curling out of her sleeve. She hiked up her white and black cape, then moved into the surf and cast another spell, this time with her left arm showing the mist of arcane energy, summoning a mount.

Her waterborne steed arrived, and she packed her leather shoes away into her backpack and settled onto the dolphin's back. This was no ordinary animal, but a magical creation, fully under her control. She grasped its dorsal fin, and with a thought, sped away.

She stayed near to the shore, her magical mount weaving around the many stones, and she tired quickly, surprised by how taxing the ride proved to be. She was in no hurry, though, other than her desire to be far from Auckney, and so she camped under the shelter of a rocky overhang, nestled beside a magical fire, eating conjured food, and drying her white gown and black shawl over a nearby tree branch.

She was out the next morning, and then again the next afternoon after a long break for lunch and rest, and then called back an enchanted mount for a third run that day, albeit a short one.

Catti-brie found herself at peace, alone with her thoughts and near to nature, near to Mielikki. By the third day, she noted the turn to the north, around the westernmost spur of the mountains, and at midday on the sixth day out of Auckney, Catti-brie stepped out of the water to feel cold dirt under her bare feet instead of wet, hard stone.

The wind thrummed in her ears, and she knew she was home.

She summoned a new mount, a spectral unicorn, and rode east along the north bank of the Shaengarne River, rushing across the leagues. Just beating the snows in the onset of the winter of 1482, Catti-brie came to the town of Bremen, on the southern banks of Maer Dualdon. The wind blew much colder now, and in a colder land than Auckney, but when Catti-brie mingled around the townsfolk of this western village in Ten-Towns, she didn't feel that way.

Quite the opposite.

She had come home, to a place she knew, and though the faces had changed with the passage of so many decades, Icewind Dale had not, and Ten-Towns had not. She took great comfort in that familiarity, going from town to town as the tendays and months drifted past. With her magical abilities, she came to be seen by the community as an asset, and she soon had friends in every tavern in every town.

She needed to build trust and a network to garner information, and none were better at knowing the comings and goings than those selling food and drink.

◯◯

The Year of the Tasked Weasel (1483 DR)
Icewind Dale

"A most unusual halfling," Catti-brie whispered, glancing down from the grass atop a ridge to the lakeshore, her eyes filling with tears.

That was how he had been described to her, by one of the many friends she had made since arriving in Icewind Dale. She wasn't a resident of any of the towns, though she had split most of her time between Bryn Shander, the dwarven complex beneath Kelvin's Cairn, and this place, Lonelywood.

In Bryn Shander, a tenday earlier, she had heard of this strange character who had come in on a caravan from Luskan, all full of dandy and decoration. A little investigating had led her here, to the outskirts of Lonelywood, looking down on the lake, looking down upon Regis.

And surely she recognized her dear old friend. He wore facial hair now, and his curly brown hair was much longer than she had known, but it was unmistakably Regis, both in appearance and demeanor.

He had survived the decades and had made it home to Icewind Dale.

What a great relief flooded over Catti-brie at that moment. For the months she had been around Ten-Towns, she had waited anxiously for this moment. In truth, she had been surprised to find out that Regis and Bruenor had not arrived in the dale before her, and that reality had only reminded her of the many dangers involved in getting here, in even surviving for twenty-one years in the dangerous Realms. The world was wild and dark; her own trials had only confirmed that.

With her friends not to be found, coupled with the news she had gleaned of Drizzt, who had not been seen around Ten-Towns in more than a decade,

349

and who, it was said, had come running to Icewind Dale in flight from a great demon, and the woman had been near to despair. Catti-brie had seen the memorial to a drow named Tiago outside of Bryn Shander's western gate, on the spot where Tiago had reportedly destroyed the balor in a great battle that had taken down part of Bryn Shander's wall and her gate. But that battle had been fifteen years and more removed, and there had been no word of Drizzt.

None.

With no sign of Drizzt and being the first of the three who had stepped out of Iruladoon to arrive, there was no small amount of doubt and fear growing in the woman over the last few months, and so her heart truly warmed now at this sight.

For here he was, Regis, reclining on the banks of Maer Dualdon, a fishing line tied to his toe. How many times had Catti-brie witnessed this scene in the years before the Spellplague?

She wanted to rush down and wrap him in a great hug, but she held herself back. She had come too far to rush headlong to Regis, at least until she had learned more about how he had come here, and what he had brought with him, inadvertently or otherwise.

For in the back of Catti-brie's mind lay her own troubles. She knew that Lady Avelyere had not given up the hunt for her. Even though nearly two years had passed since she had fled the Ivy Mansion, a magical ride that seemed to have put Avelyere off the trail, Catti-brie did not underestimate the lady's stubbornness. Avelyere knew that she was alive, that she had faked her death in Shade Enclave, and that she had traveled to the far west. Perhaps Avelyere even knew of Catti-brie's ultimate destination, Icewind Dale. Catti-brie could not be sure, since she couldn't be sure of how much she had actually divulged to Avelyere when under the hypnotic dweomers of the powerful diviner. It could well be that Lady Avelyere and her allies were somewhere within Icewind Dale, perhaps even in one of the towns, lying in wait.

If that was so and Catti-brie was caught, then what a wretched friend she would be, to both Regis and Drizzt, to have Regis dragged away beside her.

So she took her joy in seeing him from afar.

She moved back into the forest, not far from his house, and there constructed a shrine to Mielikki, a private garden sheltered from the coming winter, and that she meant to tend throughout the next season, until the night of the spring equinox.

The woman nodded at her choice. She would watch over Regis closely, but in secret.

"Boisterous bunch," Darby Snide said to Catti-brie when she moved up to the bar in his tavern in Bremen a tenday later. He was a big man, with huge hands and gigantic sideburns that rode all the way down his jawline, just short of connecting at his chin.

Catti-brie looked around, and indeed, Knuckleheader, the tavern, was full this night, and with a raucous crowd, particularly one loud group across the way by the front window. Catti-brie had heard their catcalls when she entered, moving right past them.

"Is that why you sent for me?" she asked. "Or are your larders thin for so many?"

"Could use some food, Miss Curtie, if you've the spell to conjure any," Darby admitted, and Catti-brie nodded. She had spent her first tendays in Icewind Dale right here in Bremen and had taken a room in this very inn, bartering for room and board in trade for her magical dweomers. She conjured food, healed the minor wounds of patrons, even cured a few diseases, all compliments of the Knuckleheader, and in exchange, Darby had treated her quite well.

Indeed, Catti-brie, under the name once more of Delly Curtie, had similar arrangements with a tavern in Bryn Shander, and with Stokely's dwarves under the mountain, and lesser relationships with innkeepers in all of the towns.

"They look like a Luskar crew," Catti-brie remarked.

"Ship Rethnor, say the whispers," Darby agreed.

Catti-brie nodded. "So why are you calling for me? Are you expecting a fight and hoping to sell out some healing spells?"

A surprised Darby turned fast on her, to see her wide grin, and he let out a burst of hearty laughter.

"No, lassie," he replied. "I thought you might like to know that they've been asking about a friend of yours."

Catti-brie's grin disappeared. "A friend?"

"The little halfling friend you've been looking for, and found, so say the whispers, in Lonelywood."

Catti-brie stared at him incredulously, then realized that she shouldn't be surprised her search for Regis would take her to Lonelywood. "They know of him?" she asked.

Darby shrugged. "I didn't tell them, surely, but the little one's easy to point out, with his dress and manners, from what I been hearing. My guess is that they'll find him soon enough. Might be friends of his."

Catti-brie studied the group of ruffians and found that she could not come to that conclusion.

"Be aware, Regis," came a voice out of nowhere, and the halfling, reclining on the bank of the lake, opened wide a sleepy eye. He almost jumped up, but the mention of his real name gave him pause, as did the tone of the whisper, and a strange familiarity with the voice itself.

"I am here, beside you," came another whisper. "Four from Ship Rethnor are in the woods, seeking you."

"Catti?" the halfling whispered back, suddenly catching on. Regis couldn't draw breath, and couldn't begin to sort out the words—for what did they even matter to him in that glorious moment! This was Catti-brie, he knew it! She had survived the years; their crazy plan to meet up on Kelvin's Cairn—one that had seemed incredible to Regis now that he had actually managed to return to Icewind Dale—might actually come to pass.

But here she was, after twenty-one years, standing beside him . . . invisibly?

"I will tell you when they near," she replied, bringing Regis back to the matter at hand. "Feign your nap and draw them in."

Regis shifted just a bit, moving his hand near to the crossbow handle in front of his right hip, and better angling himself for a quick leap and turn. That thought had him glancing down nervously at his one bare foot, though, and at the fishing line tied around his toe.

He felt a hand on that foot, then, and nearly jumped in surprise, as his invisible friend carefully removed the line.

"They are at the tree line," Catti-brie quietly informed him, "coming forward cautiously."

"Good to 'see' you," Regis quietly greeted, wearing a sarcastic smile, for of course, he could not see the woman at all.

Catti-brie began a soft chant, and Regis felt warmth flowing through him. He put a hand to his rapier hilt as she began a second spell, and now felt his grip intensify, as if she had loaned him the physical strength of her goddess.

She was magically preparing him for battle, he understood, covering him with wards and magical energy. He wore a grin, but it didn't last.

"A bow!" Catti-brie cried suddenly.

Up leaped the halfling, spinning around and drawing his hand crossbow as he went. As the invisible woman had informed him, four attackers came at him, three men brandishing swords and a woman, standing back with her bow leveled his way.

He heard Catti-brie chanting the words of another spell; he lifted his hand to fire, but saw the arrow speeding his way. It hit something, some magical shield perhaps, and flashed and deflected, but not harmlessly, diving down and driving hard into Regis's thigh. He yelped and fired wildly, and none of the three men charging at him slowed.

The wounded halfling stubbornly fought to hold his balance and drew his blades, grimacing through the pain as the arrow quivered, stuck fast into his leg. But not deeply, he realized, and he could put weight on that foot—and surely he'd need to.

In charged the three ruffians, barely five strides away. Regis sent his thoughts into his prism ring as he tried to figure the best angle for his warp step, seeking a position so that he could strike at two opponents quickly.

But then Catti-brie appeared between him and his enemies, her newest magical dweomer, offensive in nature, eliminating the enchantment of invisibility. She lifted her hands up before her and brought forth a fan of flames to intercept the charge.

The three attackers skidded to a stop, one diving into a roll on the beach sand, all three batting furiously at the biting fires.

"The archer!" Regis started to yell, but as the flames dissipated and he looked past Catti-brie and the attackers, he saw the distant woman lying flat on the ground, face down.

Catti-brie fell into spellcasting again, and Regis rushed past her, his rapier driving aside the sword of the man in the center. Regis rolled his blade over that sword and quick-stepped forward as he thrust, his rapier striking hard and true, the halfling's added strength driving the tip home.

Hardly watching as that man fell backward, Regis half turned to his right. Now he did use his ring, stepping forward past the charging man, too fast for the ruffian to even register the step.

The halfling's dagger went deep into that one's back, and he fell straight down, his legs folding under him.

Regis swung around, to see the man he had stuck with the rapier coming right back in, but at Catti-brie and not him. Regis flicked his wrist, throwing a small snake out at the pirate, and he yelled out, demanding the man's attention.

That proved enough to break the attacker's momentum, and by the time the ruffian realized what was transpiring, the magical snake had slithered up around his neck.

Regis winced, as always, at the sight of that leering, rotting, ghostly face, grinning back at him over the man's shoulder, pulling tight the snake garrote.

Over went the swordsman, down to the ground, his sword flying free. He thrashed around, but could not get his fingers under the choking garrote. In desperation, he took a different tact, grabbing up his blade and stabbing hard over his shoulder, as if sensing the spectral presence. To his relief, and to Regis's surprise, the ghostly creature exploded into a burst of insubstantial fog as the blade struck it in the face, flying away to nothingness, and the snake, too, died, letting go its deadly grip.

The pirate took in a big gulp of air and moved to rise, but Regis was there, stabbing down with his rapier into one shoulder, then the other, and as the pirate fell back, a second snake landed upon him and rushed up around his throat. He thrashed and tried to stab once more, but the halfling stomped on his hand and stabbed him again in the shoulder, stealing his strength.

The pirate gasped, trying desperately to draw in air. With his free hand, he clawed at the choking serpent, and tried pitifully to punch back over his shoulder, but to no avail.

His eyes bulged and Regis winced and started to turn away. But the halfling found he could not avert his gaze, and he watched, mesmerized, as the pirate's eyes rolled back and the man lay still.

Regis couldn't stomach this—it was too personal, too merciless, for him. He jabbed his rapier down again, hard, but for the ghost and not the pirate.

Another burst of fog and the specter was gone, and the second snake lay dead, and for a moment, Regis thought the pirate lay dead as well. But then the man groaned a little bit and shifted, barely drawing breath.

Confident that the wounded man would bother them no more, Regis leaped away, charging the third of the group, who had come up from the sand by then, to close in on Catti-brie.

The woman stood facing him, and her calm demeanor tipped Regis off to the truth of the encounter. For the ruffian had half-risen, one foot planted beneath him, one knee still on the ground, but there he stayed, perfectly still, frozen in place, held by some magical dweomer. Smoke wafted from his clothing still, for he had been hit fully with the burning hands of Catti-brie, and indeed, one flame returned to life, flickering on his left shoulder as he stood there.

"Your leg," Catti-brie said with alarm, and she bent toward the arrow.

Regis walked right past her as she moved to help him, though, staring at the ruffian. He patted out the flame and studied the pirate, for he recognized this one as the man he had put at rapier-tip on the Upstream Span in Luskan. He moved his rapier for the man's throat once more, thinking to finish him off.

"Regis, no!" Catti-brie scolded. "He will not threaten us for a long while, I assure you."

Regis looked around. None of the four seemed in any condition to threaten anyone any longer. One lay on the ground, the life nearly choked out of him and lines of blood around his shoulders and arms. A second squirmed around on the ground back the other way, barely moving and moving not at all from his waist down. Back by the trees, the woman archer lay very still, face down in the dirt.

Catti-brie began to cast a spell.

"What happened to her?" Regis asked, nodding his chin toward the woman, and he grunted and sucked in his breath as Catti-brie bent low and tugged the arrow from his leg, the moment of burning pain fast replaced by the soothing warmth of magical healing.

Catti-brie rose up beside him, supporting him in the uncomfortable moments until her spell took full effect.

He looked into her blue eyes once more, and it seemed to him as if the years just melted away to nothingness, as if he and his dear friend had never been apart. He pulled her into his arms and crushed her in a hug.

"My gratitude, my friend," he whispered into her ear.

"I have not forgotten how you tried to help me when I was wounded by the Spellplague," Catti-brie whispered back. "So many things, I have not forgotten!"

"Nor I!" Regis assured her, and he half broke the embrace and began to lead her off toward the woman lying by the trees.

"My aim proved better than I expected," Regis said when they arrived and he found a small quarrel sticking from the side of the woman's neck. He bent low to retrieve the hand crossbow bolt, and half-turned the sleeping woman to her side. This one, too, Regis recognized from his encounter on Luskan's bridge.

"Or my luck," the halfling added, and he could only shake his head. For he hadn't even been aiming at the archer when he fired off his hand crossbow, and what a fine bit of luck this had been indeed.

"Ah, Regis, ever the fortunate one!" Catti-brie said.

"Lucky to have friends such as Catti-brie, I agree," he replied.

The drow watched from the shadows of the trees, not sure what to make of the scene before him. Where had this ally of the halfling come from, Braelin Janquay wondered? "Spellplague?" he silently mouthed as he considered the conversation between the two. He had been sent to Icewind Dale to watch over this curious halfling, who, it seemed to him now, had become more curious the more he watched.

Braelin shook his head helplessly—after witnessing the display before him, the drow was fairly certain that little up here was as it seemed.

"Regis," he whispered, mouthing the name the woman had called the little one—who had traveled under the moniker of Spider Topolino back in Luskan.

That name, Regis, seemed to ring a distant bell, but Braelin couldn't place it. The halfling's reply, however, the naming of the woman as Catti-brie, certainly held significance even to this young drow, who had only recently entered into the ranks of Bregan D'aerthe.

Braelin Janquay nodded, thinking that Jarlaxle would be quite pleased with him when he delivered this surprising information. Hopefully, Jarlaxle would also approve of Braelin's intervention in the fight, for it was a bolt from his hand crossbow, not some lucky shot by the embattled halfling, that had felled the pirate archer.

CHAPTER 28

HOME AGAIN, HOME AGAIN

The Year of the Tasked Weasel (1483 DR)
Icewind Dale

THE FACIAL HAIR IS QUITE BECOMING," CATTI-BRIE SAID TO REGIS AS THEY sat in his small house by the lake.

Regis couldn't contain his smile, beaming wide and framed by his neatly trimmed mustache and the small goatee. He could hardly believe that he was looking at her again, at his dear friend Catti-brie, his companion through his previous life and in the days of his "death."

"But I look the same, yes?" he asked.

"Different decorations, but you are surely Regis, yes," Catti-brie teased, tugging at his long locks.

"I recognized you as soon as I heard your voice," he replied. "And seeing you now . . . it puts me right back to the slopes of Kelvin's Cairn when we were both much younger." As he spoke, he found that he was quite glad that they had come back to look like their previous incarnations. How strange it would have been to see Catti-brie in the body of another woman. But no, this was her, with her auburn hair, long and thick, and those unmistakable blue eyes.

She paced before him to put another log on the fire. "Winter fast approaches," she remarked.

"The gown," Regis said suddenly, and Catti-brie turned to regard him curiously.

"The gown you wear," he explained. "Isn't that the same one you wore in Iruladoon? How could that . . . ?"

"Similar," she admitted, twirling around and showing off the layered white dress. "I commissioned it from a dressmaker in Shade Enclave with that one from the forest in mind."

"Shade Enclave?" Regis asked. "The heart of the Empire of Netheril?" Catti-brie nodded.

"It would seem that we both have tales to tell!" Regis said with a laugh.

Catti-brie smiled in reply and gave a little twirl, holding the gown out wide at one hip. "When we were in Iruladoon, I was dressed by the goddess, was I not?"

"It is reasonable," Regis agreed, "and beautiful."

"Ever charming," Catti-brie replied, and she did blush a bit, Regis noted. "You have done well, it would seem. The gems of your rapier, the design of your hand crossbow, the hat you wear—there is a tale to tell for each, I expect."

"Winter descends. I will have time to tell you many stories, and listen to yours, of course. And yes, my life was . . . exciting." And will be again, he thought, but did not say.

"Your dagger, though," Catti-brie said haltingly. She had witnessed its dark magic, after all.

"It is an item, a tool and nothing more," Regis assured her.

Catti-brie looked at him doubtfully, warily.

"It is not Khazid'hea," he assured her. "It has no sentience. It is a tool."

"A gruesome one, it would seem."

"And my fine rapier pokes holes in hearts, and your spells burn the flesh from enemies."

The woman smiled and seemed satisfied with that. Regis could understand her hesitance, of course, for he still hadn't quite dismissed his own consternations regarding the dagger. Every time he used the garroting snakes and saw that cruel, undead specter, he found himself keenly reminded of the dirtiness of his actions, necessary or not.

He thought of the lich Ebonsoul then, and wondered if he should tell Catti-brie that perhaps he was being pursued by a powerful enemy, but he quickly dismissed the notion. It had been years since his departure from Delthuntle, and while it was possible that Ebonsoul continued to search for him, it seemed unlikely that the lich would ever actually find him. The trail was long dead, or so he hoped.

A commotion outside caught their attention, and they noted some men going past the house, the four Rethnor thugs in tow, and in chains. None had died, and Catti-brie had healed them all—even the one Regis had stabbed in the back was walking again.

"Will they hang the thieves?" he asked.

"They will put them to work, likely," Catti-brie replied. "Hands are always needed up here, you remember."

Regis nodded. In Luskan, back in the days of old, these thieves would have been brought to Prisoner's Carnival, publicly tortured and, quite likely, heinously executed. At the very least, they would have spent years in a dungeon cell, and with their hands severed. But up here in Ten-Towns, serious crimes were most often punished by hard labor.

Regis smiled at the thought—in so many ways, this frontier region on the edge of the wilds seemed so much more civilized than the supposedly great cities of Faerûn. The hardships of pressing danger created a cleaner relationship between the folk here, where coin mattered less than assistance, gold less than food, and a helping hand more than a magistrate's whip.

It was good to be home.

Bruenor leaned on the wagon, gazing anxiously to the mountains just north of his position, at the low clouds that covered their tops. It was the last caravan of the year destined for Icewind Dale, now sitting idle on the road just outside of Luskan. The dwarf had signed on as a guard, but the lead driver had offered him no coin.

"Not sure we're even to get through," the driver had explained.

Now, looking at the gray clouds obscuring the mountain tops, those words echoed keenly in Bruenor's mind. He knew what those clouds meant. He felt the bite in the air. Elient, the ninth month, had given way to Marpenoth, and while that tenth month was also named "Leaffall" in much of the Realms, in Icewind Dale, the leaves of the few trees were surely long fallen and long dead, and soon to be, if not already, buried under the first snows of winter.

"A rider!" he heard, drawing him back to the present scene. He moved out from the wagon and looked up the northern road to witness the approach of the scout the caravan's lead driver had sent ahead.

The man rode to the lead wagon and quietly conferred with a small group up there. One removed his hat and slapped it in anger against the wagon, and Bruenor knew then that he had missed his chance.

The lead driver climbed up on the wagon and called for all to gather near. Bruenor went along, but he already knew what was coming, for he understood the ways of Icewind Dale as well as any man alive, understood the season and recognized those clouds.

The window of time had been small for this last caravan. The window had closed.

"Break them down!" the lead driver ordered.

Amidst the groans and complaints, the workers went about their tasks, re-ordering the goods for the return to the stocks in Luskan, sorting the wagons of each High Captain affiliate and such. Through the din, Bruenor made his way to the lead driver, who was still conversing with the returned scout.

"Ain't no way through?" the dwarf asked.

"Snow's already waist deep to an ogre, and falling fast," said the scout.

"The pass is closed," the lead driver agreed.

"I got to get me to Ten-Towns," said Bruenor.

The two men just looked at him and shrugged.

"You might find a wizard in Luskan to send you," said the scout. "No mount, except one that's flying, will carry you through."

The dwarf did well to hide his frustration—it wasn't the fault of these two, after all, and the lead driver had been quite generous in allowing Bruenor to sign on after he had fully complemented the caravan guard.

But what was Bruenor to do? He had no coin, and wizards certainly would not come cheap.

"I got nowhere to go," he muttered.

"Most'll put up at One-Eyed Jax," said the scout. "What's your captain affiliation?"

"Me what?"

"What Ship are you with?"

"He's not of Luskan," the lead driver explained.

The scout nodded. "Well, if you've the coin, I'd suggest One-Eyed Jax. Only safe inn in Luskan for one who's not of Luskan. And you might find an affiliation. Ship Kurth's the strongest of the lot, but the most demanding, and they might not let you go so easily in the spring."

Bruenor waved his hand wildly, silencing the man. He had no intention of gaining any affiliation with one of the High Captains of Luskan, and indeed, after viewing the city on his quick pass through there, had no intention of going back into the place. He looked to the east instead, to the scattered cottages and farmhouses, some inhabited but many in ruins.

"One might put you up," the lead driver said, following his gaze and reading his thoughts.

The dwarf hardly heard him, lost in thought. He knew that the pass would be closed through the rest of the year and into early 1484. Winter came early north of the Spine of the World, and when it set its grip, there was no way to press through.

The dwarf considered abandoning his present road. Mirabar wasn't so far—he could likely get there before the snows settled deep down here south of the mountains. He mused that he could reveal himself to the leaders of that city, and perhaps they would offer him magical assistance into Icewind Dale.

He shook his head. He wasn't ready to reveal himself. He knew his place now, as a Companion of the Hall and not as the king of Mithral Hall, and he wasn't about to complicate, perhaps even compromise, the mission he had embarked upon when he had left Iruladoon by bringing such notice to himself.

But the spring equinox was less than six months away, and the passes were closed. They would remain so through the rest of the year, of course, and into the next. Travel in Icewind Dale in the first month of Hammer was always impossible, and so too for the first half of Alturiak at least, sometimes even into the third month, Ches. No caravans would head that way at least until the end of the fourth month, long past Bruenor's appointed rendezvous.

But the snows would lessen in Alturiak, Bruenor thought, nodding. It was a treacherous time to be out and about in the dale, of course, with mud pits deeper than a hill giant, and water half-frozen or full-frozen—you wouldn't know until you tried to venture across. And while the trail might seem clear on a bright morning, late winter storms often blew through with little warning, and sometimes dropped several feet of snow.

The dwarf shook his head and spat on the ground, then stomped off for the farmhouses to see if he could find lodging for the winter.

Regis pushed through the door with an armload of kindling, dropping the wood by the hearth and rushing back to secure the door against the blowing snow. Winter had come on in typical fury, and just getting to his woodshed and back had exhausted the halfling.

He turned back for the hearth, tossing his cloak aside, and nearly jumped out of his boots when he noticed the tall figure standing in the doorway to the kitchen.

"I've started a fine broth for you," Catti-brie explained. "To warm your bones."

"When did you return? How did you return?" Regis exclaimed in response. The woman had left him just a few days before the storm on her way to Brynn Shander.

"The goddess protects me," Catti-brie said with a wink.

"Good, then you go get the wood from now on," Regis replied.

"I can cast a spell to keep the cold from your bones," Catti-brie promised.

"Too late."

The woman matched Regis's wide smile, but hers could not hold.

"What word?" Regis asked, for she had gone out scouting.

"No word," she replied. "Drizzt has not been seen, and his name is spoken without affection."

"That demon incident," Regis remarked, for Catti-brie had told him the tale of the battle at Brynn Shander's western gate. Apparently Drizzt and some companions had passed through the town and headed out to the east, not to be seen again. Soon after, a great demon had arrived at Bryn Shander, seeking Drizzt, had attacked the town, and only the heroics of another drow, Tiago by name, and his band of warriors and wizards and a few half-drow, half-spider creatures, had saved the day. The story was jumbled, for the incidents had occurred many years before, when Regis was just a toddler in Eiverbreen's lean-to. Ten-Towns was a place where people came and went, and where more died than were born, and so few even remembered the fight at Bryn Shander's gate, even with the plaque set out on the spot where the great demon had been destroyed.

As far as Catti-brie and Regis could guess, it had to have been Bregan D'aerthe following the monster to Bryn Shander, and in that line of thought, Regis wondered if he had done right in not revealing himself to Jarlaxle back in Luskan. Perhaps he and Catti-brie, and Bruenor if the dwarf ever arrived, would travel back that way and find Jarlaxle, hoping to learn the whereabouts of Drizzt.

"Well then, what do we do? Was it all for naught?" As he asked the question, Regis was already formulating his own answer. If Drizzt wasn't to be found, then he would bid Catti-brie to return with him to Aglarond, to Donnola Pericolo, where she could help Morada Topolino battle the lich, if there remained a lich to battle.

And no, he told himself then, resolutely so, it had not been all for naught. Far from it. He, Spider Topolino, would forge a second life whatever fate brought before him, a life shaped in the lessons of the first.

"Hold faith," Catti-brie told him. "Mielikki told us when to meet, and that day fast approaches."

"Bruenor has not arrived, but winter has," Regis reminded. "Your Da may well be dead again, gone to Dwarfhome and his rewards."

The woman nodded, nothing in her posture or expression denying a word of what he said.

"We do the best we can, in the hope that our work will aid Mielikki and our friend," she replied.

"If Drizzt is even still alive," Regis mumbled, but he also nodded his agreement. He would climb Kelvin's Cairn beside her on the night of the equinox. He feared that they two would be up there alone, however, and from that realization, Regis came to wonder if perhaps Lady Lolth had already taken Drizzt. Was their mission to become a rescue, then? Were they, just the two of them, expected to go to the fabled Demonweb Pits to retrieve their captured friend of old?

Regis swallowed hard, thinking that a lich didn't seem so formidable after all.

"Hold faith," Catti-brie said again, and she moved to gather the pot of broth.

Regis nodded, but he could see the fear clearly stamped upon her pretty face. Drizzt was nowhere, by any accounts either of them had heard—and Catti-brie had been gathering such accounts for more than a year here in Icewind Dale. The drow had not been seen in these reaches for nearly two decades, if the stories about the battle of Brynn Shander's eastern gate were to be believed.

And indeed, Drizzt had gone out of Ten-Towns in that long past year, to the east, not the west, onto the wild tundra.

He was almost assuredly dead, Regis knew, and so did Catti-brie, he realized.

And Bruenor?

"You went to Stokely on your return from Bryn Shander?" the halfling asked suddenly.

Catti-brie turned and nodded to him, then shook her head slowly, her expression grim.

Regis understood the implications. If Bruenor had returned to Icewind Dale, he would surely have gone there, to the place he had long called his home, to be with others of Clan Battlehammer.

Bruenor was not in Icewind Dale—not alive, at least.

"There was no promise," Catti-brie said suddenly.

"What do you mean?"

"Mielikki turned the prism of reality just a bit to offer a chance, yet her design was not a prophecy, but a hope."

Regis swallowed hard. "Twenty-one years is a long time," he admitted. "I barely escaped death on several occasions, and my road remained long in doubt."

Catti-brie nodded.

"Perhaps our friend . . . our friends, were not as fortunate," the halfling said.

Catti-brie held up her hands and gave a little shrug, and Regis noted moisture rimming her deep blue eyes.

He moved quickly across the floor and wrapped Catti-brie in a tight hug, needing her support as much as he was offering his own.

The Year of the Awakened Sleepers (1484 DR)
Outside Luskan

"Ye're sure to be dead, then, and so I'll miss ye," the farmer woman said to the dwarf who had lived in her barn and worked for her and her husband through the winter. "And just when I was getting fond of ye, Mister Bonnego Battleaxe, off ye go running, and to Icewind Dale, of all the foul places! Ah, but what a fool ye are!"

Bruenor could hardly contain his grin through the woman's speech. This family had been quite good to him, swapping a bed in their barn's hayloft for his extra set of hands to help them get their farm through the wintry months.

"Winter's breaking early, so say the scouts," he replied. "I telled ye when I joined ye that me time here'd be short."

"The dale'll kill ye this time o' year."

Bruenor couldn't rightly disagree with the woman. He knew that he'd find snow and mud, deep for both, scattered around the tundra north of the Spine of the World. He knew that the wolves and the yetis and the goblinkin would be out in force, hunting for some food after their thin winter pickings. Icewind Dale woke up in the third month of each year, and more folk perished in that month than any other.

"No one's going up there," the woman scolded. "No caravan would leave for another month, at the least! Yet here ye are, so sick o' the sight of me and my family that ye'd rather run off to die than look at us anymore!"

Bruenor laughed out loud at that one, and he moved across the barn to offer his hostess a great hug—and he noticed only then that she carried something over her shoulder. He pulled up short, looking curiously.

"From my husband," she explained, and she pulled two items over her shoulder and tossed them at Bruenor's feet. "It'll give ye a chance, at least."

Bruenor stared at the curious gifts, a pair of flat disks, they seemed, made of bent wood forming a circumference and with straps of flat leather set in a weave inside the ring.

"Snow shoes," the farmer woman explained. "Ye tie 'em on and they'll help ye get across . . ."

Bruenor silenced her with another great hug. She didn't need to explain any further, for the first two words had revealed the purpose all too well. Indeed, he had seen such shoes in his first existence in Icewind Dale.

"Ye been good to this old dwarf," he whispered as he crushed the woman close.

"Old? I got a son at least yer age, ye fool!"

Bruenor just laughed and squeezed her tighter.

He set off that very morning after a hearty breakfast at the table in the main house, and the farmers stuffed his pack full of bread and eggs and a load of smoked meat.

His spirits were high as he began that journey, nearing the end of the second month of the Year of the Awakened Sleepers, but Bruenor knew well the dangers ahead, and indeed, it was hard for him to think of this trek as anything less than a suicide mission. If a late-season snowstorm didn't bury him, or the mud didn't swallow him, then surely he'd put his axe to work long before he ever saw the smoke of Ten-Towns.

But he had to try.

His oath, his word, his loyalty—everything that had made him Bruenor Battlehammer, everything that had made him a Companion of the Hall, everything that had made him twice king of Mithral Hall—meant that he had to try.

"Five days," Regis said to Catti-brie as he entered the small house on the lake and quickly closed the door against a driving rain and sleet storm pelting the whole of Icewind Dale. It was the fourteenth of Ches, the third month, five days short of the spring equinox, the most holy day of Mielikki.

Catti-brie nodded. "My birthday," she said. "Or re-birthday, I call it."

Regis managed a smile at that, but it didn't hold.

"No word?" Catti-brie asked.

"Not in Lonelywood, nor among the Silverstream dwarves under the mountain." All through the last few tendays, Regis and Catti-brie had taken turns going out from the small house and from Lonelywood to gather whispers about any newcomers venturing into the towns. But there had been no whispers to be found, just the quiet of Icewind Dale's hard winter.

That same morning, across the lake of Redwaters in the town of Bremen, the door to the Knuckleheader banged open and a half-frozen, mud-covered, wild-eyed dwarf verily fell into the common room.

Innkeeper Darby Snide was the first to the poor soul, helping him to a sitting position.

"What are you about, then?" Darby asked of the surprising visitor.

The dwarf looked at him blankly, began laughing crazily, and fell over unconscious.

"Look at his axe!" said one of the Bremen citizens, who had come into the Knuckleheader for his morning meal.

Darby noted the weapon, stained with blood and with fur the men of Icewind Dale knew all too well stuck into several of the blade's many notches. The dwarf's shield, too, showed bloodstains, and the blood found around the side of the dwarf's armor was his own, they realized as they settled him down on a cot and tried to make him comfortable, lifting his mail shirt to reveal the jagged wound of a yeti claw.

Another patron fetched some water and Darby started to clean the wound, and to the surprise of all, the dwarf sat up and shook his hairy head.

"Bah!" he snorted. "But I need to be goin'! Can I beg of ye some food?"

"Going?" Darby echoed incredulously. "You're near dead, fool! Lay back!" He pushed the dwarf's shoulder gently, forcing him to lie down.

"He's to need healing," noted a woman from the side. "Is Delly about Bremen, then?"

Others shrugged and looked around, having no answers. "Ain't seen her," said one.

"Go and ask," Darby bade them. "See if any have seen Delly Curtie, for this one could use a bit of her warmth, to be sure."

Somewhere nearby and yet far away, the dazed Bruenor heard the name, "Delly Curtie," and it registered in the back of his mind, where it flitted around for a few moments.

The dwarf's eyes popped open wide, and he pushed back against Darby's restraint. "Who'd ye say?" he demanded of the innkeeper.

"Lie back!" Darby insisted.

"Who?" Bruenor shot right back at him.

"Who?" Darby asked right back, looking confused.

"Delly Curtie, ye said!"

"Aye," said Darby.

"A witch, but a good one," said the woman.

"Tell me!" Bruenor insisted. "What's she look like?"

Darby, the woman, and some other patrons exchanged curious looks. Darby turned back to Bruenor and began describing to him this woman they knew as Delly Curtie—Delly Curtie, the name of Wulfgar's wife in a previous life, and a name the dwarf realized Catti-brie might well use as an alias. If he was Bonnego Battleaxe, then she could well be Delly Curtie.

And as Darby described the auburn-haired witch in the white gown and the black shawl, Bruenor's smile widened with every word, and he nodded knowingly.

She had made it! His daughter had survived the decades and had made the journey back to Ten-Towns. Catti-brie was alive and well, so they said, and he would soon hold her once more.

"You know her, then?" Darby asked, for Bruenor's expression revealed it all quite clearly.

"What's the day?" Bruenor asked. "Fifteenth o' Ches?"

"Fourteenth," the woman behind Darby corrected.

Bruenor grabbed Darby's arm and squeezed it tight. "Ye get me fed and give me a bit o' rest, friend, and I'll pay ye when I can."

"You know her?" Darby asked.

Bruenor nodded.

"A friend?" Darby asked, and the dwarf nodded again.

"More than ye could e'er know," Bruenor said, his tone wistful, a tear streaming from his eye. He lay back then and let himself fall into the embrace of hopeful dreams.

CHAPTER 29

BRUENOR'S CLIMB

The Year of the Awakened Sleepers (1484 DR)
Icewind Dale

THE SUN RODE LOW IN THE EASTERN SKY, THE FIRST RAYS OF DAYLIGHT reaching across Icewind Dale to tickle the icy ridges of the peaks of Kelvin's Cairn. Regis paused at his cottage door, admiring those crystalline outlines.

"Marking Bruenor's Climb with a light of hope," Catti-brie remarked when she came up beside him.

The halfling nodded, hoping her observation was prophetic. The pair solemnly started out from the small cottage near the lake. Bolstered by Catti-brie's protection spells, armed with potions Regis had brewed, and their step lightened by the much better weather that had settled over Ten-Towns in the past couple of days, the duo made good time in their westward trek.

They spoke little, however, for each settled within personal fears on this most important of nights, the spring equinox of 1484. For Catti-brie, this, her birthday, was the promise, the possible fruition of the hopes Mielikki had offered in the magical forest of Iruladoon. She was a priestess of Mielikki, indeed, Chosen of the goddess, and so she went forth with her expectations high, but with her eyes opened wide.

She knew the possibilities, all of them, and from all that she had seen, along with her understanding of Mielikki's offering of a chance and nothing more, those many potential outcomes appeared far more dire than promising.

But she had to go.

For Regis, this was the intersection, the great crossroads of his second life. Here he would repay the debt to Mielikki, and here he would know again, so he hoped, the greatest friends with whom he had ever shared a road.

But now there were others, he knew, and alternate roads that beckoned. The Grinning Ponies traveled the Trade Way, and Donnola led Morada Topolino far to the east, and either organization would welcome him back with open arms. He had not forgotten his oldest friends, of course, but Regis had hedged his bets, or at least, circumstance had given him the opportunity to do so.

The fall of darkness beat the duo to the base of Kelvin's Cairn. There they paused and looked up the familiar trails from a life lived long ago. Catti-brie had climbed the mountain the previous summer, just to ensure that Bruenor's Climb was still accessible, but she had only gone up once, and only briefly, and never to the top.

She hadn't been able to bring herself to do that, reserving the final ascent for this very night.

She reached over and took Regis by the hand, giving it a little squeeze.

"So we go," the woman said.

"To see if our hopes are realized," Regis replied. "And if not . . ."

Catti-brie squeezed his hand tighter and looked down at him, her plaintive expression stealing the words from him. Now that Regis had known love, he understood so much better now what Catti-brie had shared with Drizzt. As frightened as he was, he knew, this dear woman beside him had so much more to lose. Regis squeezed her hand back, and led the way up the side of the mountain, to that special place called Bruenor's Climb, the lower, northern peak, a bare rock that seemed lifted into the bosom of the nighttime sky, nestled among the stars themselves.

◆○◆

Eagerness flooded through Bruenor when the torchlight came into view, and he moved toward it with all the speed he could muster, hoping, expecting, to see Catti-brie, and perhaps even Drizzt and Regis beside her. Who else would be out on the side of Kelvin's Cairn in the dark of night this early in the season, after all?

His hopes were dashed when he spotted the group, and he slowed his step and moved in more stealthily, unsure of the scene, and of this unlikely trio in the clearing before him.

"He's a ranger, then, and with no small skill," he heard in a Dwarvish voice, and a female one at that. He spotted the speaker. He didn't recognize her, and she didn't look like a Battlehammer.

370

Particularly not given the company she kept, Bruenor thought as the second of the group, a skinny and twisted, ugly little creature, perhaps human, perhaps something more nefarious, replied, "But where would he go?"

"To the Battlehammer dwarves," said the third, a sturdy human man in plain-looking robes.

"We'll go by there and see," said the dwarf.

At the thought that these three were not enemies of the Battlehammers, Bruenor started forward, but he fell back immediately when the ugly little man—or tiefling, actually, Bruenor then realized—added, "Entreri said we were to leave directly, and before the dawn. To the south and the east and out of the dale."

Entreri? The name rang discordantly in Bruenor's thoughts, a name he had not heard in many decades, and one he had never wanted to hear again. He shook his head, convinced he had misheard the tiefling, but the human replied, "Entreri's wrong, then. Drizzt wouldn't leave a friend in such a state, nor will I."

"Aye," the female dwarf agreed.

Bruenor faded back a couple of quiet steps, shaking his head in confusion. "Drizzt?" he mouthed under his breath. "Entreri?"

He looked back at the firelight, unsure of his next move. Should he go to these three and learn what he might?

But Catti-brie was around Icewind Dale, he had learned from his time in Bremen at the Knuckleheader. She would be up there, on Bruenor's Climb, waiting for him.

Bruenor sneaked away, back to trails he knew so well, for little had changed in this place he had so long called home. With the strangers out of sight, he broke into a trot, climbing tirelessly, his heart beating fast, and more from anticipation than exertion.

He came to a patch of snow along the trail, shining in the moonlight. He dropped to one knee to examine a light boot print and the padded paw prints of a huge cat. Bruenor knew those well.

His joy didn't last, though, as he noted the wetness beside the small snow patch. He dipped his fingers and brought them up before his eyes and nose.

Blood.

Lots of blood, lining the trail.

Bruenor scrambled up so fast that he slipped and fell face down into the muck. He was up in a heartbeat, wiping his eyes as he ran, and barely had he begun again when he skidded to a stop, frozen in place by the long, low roar of a distant cat, a panther's roar, Guenhwyvar's call.

A mournful roar, he thought, as if a cry evincing great loss.

Regis grasped Catti-brie's forearm tightly as they beheld the sight: Drizzt, limping badly, leaning against Guenhwyvar, and surely were it not for the panther, the drow would have fallen to the ground.

Clearly dazed and battered, blood dripping from his head, one leg only gingerly touching down as he shambled toward the peak of Bruenor's Climb, the drow went along silently.

"Go, go!" Regis told Catti-brie, and when he looked at her, her face a mask of horror, the halfling shoved her along, and called more loudly "Go!"

Catti-brie scrambled forward and began to sing, the same melody Regis had heard those days in the forest of Iruladoon, calling to her goddess, singing the song of Mielikki.

Drizzt seemed to hear it, and even looked over at the approaching woman, though it seemed to Regis as if his battered friend had moved past the point of sight.

Or perhaps Drizzt did notice her, the halfling corrected himself, and he scrambled to catch up, for at that moment of recognition, all strength seemed to flee the drow and he simply collapsed.

Catti-brie caught him and she screamed, "No!" with such desperation that Regis cursed the gods.

All of this . . . and they had been a moment too late?

Down the trail, Bruenor Battlehammer heard that desperate, agonized scream, accompanied by the plaintive cry of Guenhwyvar. He tried to speed up, but stumbled and fell to his face, the impact making all of his recent wounds hurt him all the more.

He threw that aside, though, whispering, "Me girl! Me girl!" and he scrambled and clawed and ran on.

"No!" Catti-brie cried, hugging Drizzt close. "Don't you leave me! Don't you dare!"

"Heal him!" Regis implored her, stumbling forward.

But she shook her head, for she could not, she understood. The wounds were too severe, he was already falling far, far away. She hadn't the time, she hadn't the strength.

"Catti, try!" Regis yelled.

How could they say good-bye when they hadn't even said hello?

Guenhwyvar cried out, long and low, a mournful song, and when Regis neared and viewed the ghastly wound upon Drizzt's head, and the limp tilt of his body, he shared the cat's dismay. He slowed to a stop, still strides away, afraid to move closer, afraid to accept the reality before him.

Catti-brie looked to him, shaking her head.

A blue tendril of misty magic curled out of the woman's sleeves then, wrapping around her and around Drizzt, like the embrace of Mielikki herself. Catti-brie looked at it curiously, then shrugged at Regis, for it had come unbidden.

"What—?" Regis asked, or started to ask, for he was interrupted by a cry.

"Drizzt!" came a shout from back behind Regis, and he swung around and Catti-brie looked up, for they surely recognized that voice.

"Ye durned elf!" Bruenor shouted, charging up from the trail. He stumbled along and skidded to a stop, eyes wide at the scene before him, jaw falling open as any forthcoming calls had been surely stolen by the shock of the moment.

"Bruenor?" came a reply from the other way, and Regis spun around yet again, his heart leaping at the sound of the voice.

At the sound of Drizzt's voice.

Bruenor collected the halfling as he hustled by, the two crashing into Drizzt, Catti-brie, and Guenhwyvar upon the bare rock atop Bruenor's Climb, where the stars reached down to touch again the Companions of the Hall.

"You saved him!" a sobbing Regis said to Catti-brie.

She could only shake her head, confused. She had not cast a spell, nay, but she had merely been a conduit in that moment.

In that moment where Mielikki had taken back the rogue drow to her side.

The victorious drow, who had turned from the darkness.

Here then, in these friends huddled close, was his reward.

EPILOGUE

The Year of the Awakened Sleepers (1484 DR)
Shade Enclave

Brilliant," Lord Parise Ulfbinder remarked, staring into the scrying pool, looking through Lady Avelyere's divination magic to the unfolding scene atop the solitary mountain in Icewind Dale. "If we had any doubts regarding the divine inspiration of our dear little Ruqiah, they are surely dispelled."

"Catti-brie," Lady Avelyere corrected, and she gave a wistful, confirming nod, for there could be no doubt any longer. The two of them had spent most of the day studying the mountain, and to their great surprise, they had found Drizzt Do'Urden much earlier on, witnessing his confrontation with the curious elf woman wherein he had been so wounded.

"So many pieces moving around the puzzle board," Parise remarked, shaking his head. "And yet, in the end, they all fit so well together, did they not? Perhaps there is value in having a goddess at your side after all!"

Lady Avelyere turned to regard the man, who seemed almost joyous, his motions near frivolity, by this point. Despite all of the troubles of the time, the great changes wrought by the end of the Spellplague, the drifting of Abeir away from Toril, indeed the realization of the prophecies of "Cherlrigo's Darkness," Lord Parise Ulfbinder had remained in a grand and elevated mood for some time now.

"Have you become so bored with life that you take joy in the chaos, any chaos, and even that which threatens the foundations of our existence?" she dared to ask.

Parise considered her strange question for a short while, then gave a great laugh. "We are witnessing the play of the gods," he replied.

"Goddesses, apparently," she corrected, and the man laughed again.

"This is beyond the boundaries of mere mortal comfort and safety," Parise explained, and he grabbed his dear friend's hands and brought them up to his lips to kiss them. "This speaks of eternity. With all that Ruqiah, this woman Catti-brie, told to you, are you not interested in watching the play of her tale?"

Lady Avelyere turned back to the scrying pool and considered the question for a long, long while. She watched the companions gathered together, all hugs and pats as they sat beside the wounded drow, their eyes lifted heavenward to the beautiful night sky.

"Do you think the battle will commence presently?" she asked, somewhat absently.

"I do believe that perhaps this drow, Drizzt, has already waged it," Parise replied. "His fight with the elf girl—"

"You think her the champion of the Spider Queen?"

Parise shook his head and simply shrugged. "A path to Lady Lolth, perhaps. Surely, from all that we have learned, she and the others Drizzt left on the lower mountain trails definitively represented a darker road by far. Perhaps that was his trial, the battle between the goddesses."

"One might expect more of such a battle," Lady Avelyere replied dryly.

"Carnage?" Parise sarcastically replied. "Explosions of ground-shaking magic?" He laughed yet again. "Would not the more meaningful battle be one for the soul, quiet and internal?"

"You had thought to witness the struggle of gods. You don't seem disappointed."

"From all that I have learned of the Spider Queen, I suspect that this is hardly finished," the laughing lord said. "Perhaps Drizzt won the quiet battle within, but where might that lead, given the vengeance of a demon queen?"

"So Mielikki has armored him with the flesh of friends of old."

"Armored him? Or made him more vulnerable?"

With that intriguing thought in mind, the two turned back to the scrying pool, and a moment later, Parise pointed out another form, large and hulking, moving along the mountain trail for the bare rock where the others rested.

Lady Avelyere nodded. Her eyes narrowed in anticipation of a coming fight.

"Ah, me girl!" Bruenor cried, hugging and kissing Catti-brie, framing her beautiful face with his ruddy and dirty hands.

"I am dead, then," Drizzt whispered, patting Bruenor's sturdy shoulder then shifting his arm to grab at Regis and bring him in close.

"If only it were that simple, elf!" said Bruenor.

"Not dead," Regis said. "Surely not dead!"

"There is so much to tell," Catti-brie explained. "So many stories . . ."

"The forest," Drizzt surprised them all by saying. "On the banks of Lac Dinneshire . . . Mielikki's wood. Eighteen years gone . . ."

"So many stories," Catti-brie said again, her voice stolen, her breath stolen, when Drizzt tugged her in close and kissed her deeply and passionately.

"Tales to tell," Regis agreed. "And more to write."

"Aye," said Bruenor, "and many yet to write. I come back to ye, elf, to walk yer road aside ye. But don't ye doubt, I've a road to walk o' me own, and it'll be good to have yer blades lifted for Mithral Hall once more!"

That announcement brought some curious glances from Catti-brie and Regis, but Drizzt was already nodding, and smiling widely.

Guenhwyvar stood up then, quickly, her fur ruffling, issuing a low growl as she stared at a figure on the trailhead.

Time mattered not to the ghostly form, drifting as a fog on the wintry winds.

Ebonsoul settled around four old graves set to the side of a tent marketplace on the eastern side of a great bridge.

These souls had touched the thief, the lich sensed, and from these spirits Ebonsoul would better discern his road ahead. The little clues had carried the lich far, across the Sea of Fallen Stars, through the Bloodstone Lands, and to the road outside of Suzail.

A long and meandering journey, but so be it.

Time mattered not to the lich.

It would find the halfling and retrieve its coveted dagger.

It would find the thief, the graverobber, and properly punish him.

" 'Ere now, speak and be recognized!" Bruenor called as the shadowy, hulking form came into view along the trail just beyond the bare rock of Bruenor's Climb. The dwarf hopped to stand before Regis and Catti-brie. Behind them sat Drizzt, hardly recovered enough for battle. He had his hands on his blades, but could barely lift them.

The lone form, huge and hulking, continued its steady approach.

Bruenor banged his axe against his shield, ready for a fight, and Guenhwyvar, standing beside him, growled a warning once more.

"A fine greeting," said the approaching man, and he stepped into view, into the moonlight. Closer to seven feet in height than six, wearing the silvery coat of a winter wolf, the wolf's head bouncing about his massive chest, and with a great and familiar hammer resting easily over his shoulder, the newcomer smiled widely.

Guenhwyvar bounded forward.

"Me boy," whispered Bruenor, and his axe fell to the stone with a clang, and he nearly followed it down.

"Wulfgar," Regis breathed.

"But ye went into the pond," Bruenor said.

Wulfgar shook his head as he reached down to ruffle the panther's thick fur, Guenhwyvar rubbing against him with enough force to shift him back a step.

"Tempus will wait, for what is a man's lifetime in the counting of a god?" the barbarian replied. "My friends needed me, and what a sorry warrior I would be to ignore that call."

"The Companions of the Hall," said Drizzt, his voice breaking with every syllable, his dark cheeks streaked with tears of joy and renewed hope.

"Let Lady Lolth come!" they all would have said together, had they known that she was indeed.

Faerûn

Icewind Dale
Spine of the World
Citadel Adbar
Mithral Hall
Luruar
Silverymoon
Shade Enclave
Luskan
Port Llast
High Forest
Lost Peaks
Netheril
Neverwinter
Evereska
Waterdeep
Thu Pe
Daggerford
Najara
Cormyr
Marsember
Suzail
Elturgard
Westgate
Baldur's Gate
Moonshae Isles
Dragon Coast
Candlekeep
Nathlan
Sea of Swords
Amn
Erlkazar
Velen
Muranndin
Tethyr
Lake of Steam
Calimshan
Calimport
Calim Desert
N
W E
S
Chult
Shining Sea
Hazur
Lapal
Thindol

0 50 100 200 500 1000
miles